THE MARSHALL EFFECT

JOSEPH ANTHONY

ISBN 978-1-954345-78-2 (paperback)
ISBN 978-1-954345-79-9 (digital)

Rushmore Press LLC
1 800 460 9188
www.rushmorepress.com

Printed in the United States of America

DEDICATION

To Susan, who makes it all worthwhile.

BOOKS BY JOSEPH ANTHONY

Guilty but Innocent

The Last Etude

An Ordinary Man

Tales from the Blue

The Marshall Effect

ONE

The prison gates clanged shut behind him and Peter stood there in the near empty street, blinking in the weak sunshine. It was a fairly long walk to the nearest bus-stop but even if one stopped right outside the prison gates, just where would he go? Certainly not back home because that was gone. His in-laws blamed him for the death of their only daughter and had made it clear to him in the letter he had received some months back that he was not welcome in their lives. His old friends and colleagues? Forget that noise. As far as they were concerned he was dead, dead and gone just like Jean. His old college? Hah, what a laugh, You could be a drunk, a drug addict, a pedophile, an adulterer and the committer of almost any sin known to man and not get dismissed unless, of course, you got caught. Then everyone threw their hands up in horror, denied all knowledge of the person and their misdeeds and took painstaking efforts to distance themselves from even the merest mention of that person's name. Admit that he or she had been a faculty member? Perish the thought.

He was alone in London, one of the largest cities in the world and no-one wanted to know him and, for that matter, he really didn't want anyone to know him. With good behavior, he had been released after three years but he still had to regularly report to his parole officer. How could anyone hold down a half-way decent job when he had to report in every week? What crap. He dug into his back pocket and pulled out his battered wallet. Glancing through it, he could see that there was precious little in it which, when combined with the small amount of money given to released prisoners, was the sum total of all the money he had in the world. The trial as well as the law suits and legal fees involved in making restitution for the damage he had caused to other cars on that manic episode following Jean's death had drained him dry. His beloved MGB, what was left of it, and his house, mortgage and all, were gone, as were everything from the house, including his clothes. He was truly out there alone, with little money and nowhere to go. He wondered whether to apply for Social Security but the thought of standing in line for hours, then answering lots of personal questions and having to explain how he had ended up in prison had little appeal. No, he would try to manage on his own before he would even consider that.

Hefting his shabby duffle bag, he started off down the street. Eventually he found himself in a Northern suburb of London and found a small house that took in boarders. He had sufficient cash to pay the rent for a couple of months and enough left over that he could at least eat at the cheap cafes scattered here and there throughout that part of London. He had to find a job but who would want to hire an ex-con who also happened to be an ex-professor at one of the world's most prestigious universities? Besides, who for that matter would even believe that the shabbily-dressed man standing before them was a professor with an International reputation?

As he walked around the near-empty streets, he found a pub with a tattered sign in the window advertising for a part-time barman. A few words with the landlord and he was hired at minimum wage. It wasn't much but at least he had an income and he would be paid in cash. No need to pay the tax man, at least not until they caught up with him or someone snitched, neither event being very likely.

Life went on. Peter survived on a steady diet of bacon sandwiches or fish and chips, supplemented by the occasional free beer at the pub. He exercised each and every day within the confines of his small room and he kept his sexual urges under control with the odd woman picked up at the pub, usually on a Friday or Saturday night after too many drinks had liberated their libidos. They wanted a quick shag with the tall, quiet, good-looking man behind the bar with no questions asked and no expectations of commitment. Sometimes he went to their homes while a few, usually the married ones or those with nosy neighbors would come back to his dingy room. The other barmen left him alone and even the landlord avoided contact until the end of the week when he slipped Peter some money for that week's work. It was an existence, nothing more. He could pay the rent, eat and use the Laundromat but that was it…there was nothing to spare. The pub regulars tried to talk to him but their beer-laden breath was wasted on him and Peter simply nodded when they spoke to him and served them their drinks, occasionally accepting the offer of "Have one yourself while you're at it." When trade was slack, he would lean back against the mirrored wall behind the bar and allow his thoughts to roam. All too often, his mind returned to that dreadful night when Jean died and then, inexorably, it would flit to prison and his time inside. Occasionally he would smile when he thought of his former cell-mate Monk and his tales of the exploits of his military chums, the so-called Clergy, going into action doing their policing work in the Middle East, Northern Ireland or wherever else people like that were needed.

"Hey Peter, what are you smiling about?" called Sid, a wizened regular who spent hours nursing a beer at the bar. "Share the joke?"

"No, it's nothing…just a memory."

"Oh? What's that then?"

"It's nothing."

"Hey, no need to snap my head off, I was just asking."

Peter nodded and then moved down the bar to serve another customer. He was conscious of Sid's stare and then caught the appraising glance of a bleached blonde sitting alone at a small table, a glass of wine in front of her. When their eyes met, she nodded and pushed her tongue into her cheek, the common invitation to have sex. Peter smiled and nodded back, invitation received and accepted. He had seen her in here before tonight and wondered whether they had had sex previously; he didn't remember. Everything was a blur these days and had been for weeks. He wondered whether he was losing his mind, then decided that it was irrelevant. If she wanted him, it was okay, It had been a while since he had shared a bed with someone, so why not? As he walked out from behind the bar to collect empty glasses, he slid past her table and muttered, "I'm off at eleven, okay?"

"I'll wait, ducks, I'll wait," was the breathy reply. "I'm sure it'll be worth it."

Peter simply nodded and gathered up more glasses. If she wanted him, okay…but whether it was "worth it", how would he know? It was all so mechanical now…a few kisses, some fervent groping, a rolled-on condom, supplied by the woman, and then the frantic coupling. Sometimes it was only took a few minutes, other times it was drawn out. What made the difference?, Peter wondered. He really didn't remember any of them. Resuming his place behind the bar, Peter shrugged and sank back into his reveries…was this to be his life from now on? He shrugged again…it could be worse and it was better than being back in prison, that's for sure.

"Eh, luv, that were grand last night, were'nt it?"

Peter immediately jerked into consciousness at the sound of the woman's voice. Who was she? It came back to him, the bleached blonde in the bar last night. As soon as he had emerged from the side door of the pub after they closed the place down, she grabbed his arm and almost dragged him off to her small flat, a few streets away. He didn't remember much of the previous evening. The regulars had bought him more drinks than usual…Friday nights were when they got paid and they spent it with great haste and determination. Whatever had happened between them had obviously made the woman happy…what *was* her name? Peter decided it didn't matter much either way. He reached for a cigarette from the bedside cabinet, noting with distaste the overflowing ashtray, the slightly rancid smell of stale tobacco and the two glasses also on the table, one liberally smeared with lipstick. Where the hell was he?

"Hey, put that out Peter, you've got work to do…me" and the woman slapped her flabby stomach. Peter looked at her with revulsion. Smeared make-up, pendulous breasts, coarse skin, brittle bleached hair streaked with grey…what the hell was he doing here?

The day had started badly but it got worse. When he went to the pub just before the morning opening time, the pub landlord held out a small brown envelope, "Sorry Peter, I've got to let you go."

Peter just looked at him. There was nothing to say, another door had closed. The landlord, uncomfortable with the silence and half-expecting trouble from the big man standing there, hurried on, "Sorry lad, the tax man, and head office for that matter, have started to ask questions. They don't like me paying you cash and not reporting it. It's likely going to cause trouble, and trouble's something I don't need. Okay?"

Peter simply nodded. What was there to say?

"Besides," added the landlord. "The regulars don't like the fact that you never talk them. "Always dreaming" they said, never paying them no mind even when they buy you a drink. Sorry lad, it won't do." Holding out a hand, he added, "No hard feelings then?"

Peter shook his head and slipped the proffered envelope into his pocket. Quickly shaking the other man's hand, he turned on his heel and left. Time to move on and find something else. His money would soon run out and then he would be out on the street, so he'd best start looking now.

Going back to his room, he threw his few clothes into the duffle bag and closed the door behind him. Another chapter closed.

It was starting to get late and evening drew near. Peter wandered the streets aimlessly, almost out of money and he had nowhere to sleep that night, again. Then he saw another pub. Through the open doors, he could see a big man behind the bar and a few customers scattered round the inside. Deciding, he walked in. Clutching his hold-all, he walked up to the bar. The barman looked up and in a thick Glaswegian accent, asked, "What'll it be then?"

"Nothing for the moment. You need any help here?"

"Yeah, that we do. Hold on a moment, let me get the guvnor. He said he'd try to get me some help. The last guy left in a bit of a hurry, didn't he? Wait here…have a drink on the house, and I'll get 'im. Won't be long."

The barman disappeared through a door beside the bar, and said to the man sitting there, immersed in paperwork, "Hey guvnor, got someone out there who could help out."

"What's he like, this someone?"

"Oh. He's big…looks like he can take care of himself, that's what."

"Just walked in, did he?"

"Yeah. Anyway, you want to talk to him?"

"Why not? What do you think of him, Jamie?"

"As I said, he looks as though he can take care of himself. Be better than that long streak of piss we had here before. He doesn't look like he's scared of much, that's what."

The landlord grunted. As Jamie had said, the last guy didn't last long and getting hurt and then taking a runner had caused some problems. Finding help, even in these days of high unemployment, was difficult especially in a rough pub in a run-down area. The regulars were serious drinkers and, when tanked up, they let out their anger and frustration on anyone close to them, usually the barmen but often on anyone standing there. Jamie was big enough to be left alone but anyone else, like the last guy, was fair game and barmen didn't last long. It was Monday night and the local soccer team had lost again that Saturday. The regulars would be spoiling for trouble and Jamie likely would need help with stocking the bar and keeping the customers out of fights.

"Okay, I'll talk to him. Where's he at now?"

"At the bar, having a beer."

"He look like a boozer? Last thing I need is a drunk behind the bar."

"Nah, not this one. I gave him a beer to keep him busy until you decided to talk to him, that's all."

The landlord nodded and got to his feet. If this guy looked alright to Jamie, then perhaps he'd do. Besides, they were short-handed behind the bar so what choice did he have?"

The landlord talked to Peter and agreed with Jamie. The man looked solid enough and was clean. No cuts, tattoos or bruises were visible although he wondered about him. Peter Marshall, the name given to him by the newly hired barman and general help, was not the usual type that wandered in looking for work. He couldn't put his finger on it but he knew there was something different about the man. As he later said to the police, "He was different, weren't he? Can't put my finger on it but, you know, he was different. Quiet sort, though…didn't say much to anyone…at least not to me, he didn't."

"What do I have to do?" asked Peter.

"Keep the beer barrels tapped, restock the shelves, help out behind the bar when Jamie's busy, clean up when we close… that sort of thing. Okay?" The landlord was careful not to mention having to help out with the odd punch-up…sensible really since the last man got hurt when he caught a fist thrown at someone else, and that was only last Saturday.

"Fine with me," nodded Peter.

"When do you want to start?"

"How about tonight…right now?"

"Okay. Jamie'll show you the ropes." He turned away and came back, "Hey, you're not in trouble with the Law, are you? You know, are you wanted for something?"

Peter shook his head, "Not this week, I'm not." He smiled slightly.

"Okay – just checking. Had to ask, you know." And the landlord walked away, satisfied with having done his civic duty and pleased to have found someone big enough to work behind the bar without being at serious risk of getting hurt or running for cover at the first sign of trouble.

As the landlord retreated to his office behind the bar, Jamie nodded at his retreating back and muttered, "Tosser!" Turning to Peter, he said, "It's quiet here for the moment, so why don't I show you around, you know, the cellar and stuff? Then we can have a pint…it won't get busy for an hour or two, if then, being as it's Monday and all…most of the regulars are probably flat broke already."

After they got everything stored away and the shelves stocked with bottles of beer and lager, Jamie poured two glasses of beer and handed one to Peter. "This one's on the house but don't let the Guvnor see you helping yourself too much or he'll fire you, you know what I mean? He doesn't like the help drinking up his profits."

Peter nodded and sipped at his beer. Looking at him and the way Peter stared almost longingly at the barely edible wrapped sandwiches under the glass cover on the bar, Jamie made a sudden decision. "Hey, fancy some fish and chips? The place next door does a halfway decent job, so why not get us some?"

Peter looked at him and hesitated. Jamie, seeing the look on his face, dug into his pocket and pulled a few one pound coins. Handing them over, he said, "This one's on me – sort of welcome aboard… okay?"

Peter nodded and left to get their food, and his first hot meal in a couple of days.

Laster that night, when they were closing down, and Peter had started to walk off clutching his battered bag, Jamie impulsively called after him, "Hey, Pete, where are you going?"

"Oh…er…off, you know how it is."

"So, nowhere in particular, that right?"

"Yeah."

"So, if you've nowhere better to go and aren't too fussy, you can always kip down with me. It's not much – in fact, it's lousy but just round the corner. Couch do you?"

"Yeah.…yeah, thanks." And Peter moved in.

The fly paddled sluggishly out of the pool of spilled beer on the bar counter. It shook itself, staggered and then slowly tried to fly before crashing down again. Peter, watching it through half closed eyes, smiled briefly and thinking, *Even the flies get drunk in this place.* The hum of conversation rose and fell as regularly as waves coming ashore with a rising tide but, unlike the seashore, the air inside the pub got heavier and staler by the minute. The miasma was progressively thickened by the smell of spilled drinks and numerous cigarettes as the evening wore on.

Despite regularly checking that no customers were waiting to be served, Peter could feel his shoulders slumping and his eyelids closing as he fought off sleep…Wednesday, quietest night of the week. It was an old and shabby pub in a seedy and run-down part of town, frequented by rough Irish navvies, day-laborers, unemployed workers and the odd drifter in need of warm beer and cold comfort.

"Stop, Tom, you'll kill him!"

The woman's shriek cleaved the thick atmosphere and Peter's eyes jerked open instantly. He spotted the short stout woman hanging onto Big Tom's arm, desperately trying to stop him from getting at the other man. As Tom move forward, the other man, a stranger to the pub, backed away, holding his hands up placatingly and saying, "It was only a joke. I didn't mean any harm."

"That's not what it sounded like to me," growled big Tom and kept moving forwards, his massive fist bunched up ready to hit the other man. His wife, small as she was and significantly overweight, moved with surprising speed between the two men and said, "Leave it Tom, leave it. It's not worth the trouble. He's just a loud-mouthed drunk – leave him alone, 'cos nothing good can come of hitting him." Turning to the other man, she said, "If I was you, I'd best get out of here while you're still in one piece."

The man shrugged and tried desperately to smile, before he grabbed his glass and drained it quickly. Carefully sitting it back down on the bar-top, he shuffled towards the door, possibly thankful that he been spared yet another beating from somebody who was a lot stronger and nastier than he could ever be. For a moment he hesitated, possibly trying to think of something scathing to say, but decided to just keep going before trouble caught up with him.

The suddenly quietened bar came back to life as Big Tom slowly turned away with a muffled curse. He drained the last of his beer and slammed the glass down on the counter.

"Hey Pete-boy," he called, "Give me another one here" and, after looking at his wife questioningly, added "and I'll take another one for the missus, okay?"

Peter poured the drinks and leaned back against the racks of bottles behind the bar. He caught the eye of Jamie, his Glaswegian co-worker behind the bar, and they nodded at each other, both thinking *Thank God, it's only Wednesday. If it were Friday, there would have been a punch-up, broken bottles, blood spilled, furniture tossed and the police called.* As the adrenaline level slowly dropped, Peter thought gratefully that at least this time there was no trouble. Each and every time the police came to the pub, he knew that he was closer to possible arrest and getting sent back to prison. He had to get out of here but where to go and with what were questions he couldn't answer.

The past had been bad, the present was lousy, and the future looked bleak. Was this how the rest of his life had to be?

Jamie looked at his friend from the other end of the bar, if that really covered his relationship with Peter. He did not understand the other man but he knew that Peter was different. The quiet manner belied the broad muscular frame and the ever present haunted look in his eyes. Peter's build and tightly coiled inner tension hinted at an inner capacity for violence but he seemed to go to great lengths to avoid any conflict. Curiously, Peter was well-spoken and radiated intelligence, two traits that did not fit with his occupation, his shabby appearance or, indeed, his physique. Not for the first time, Jamie wondered again what secrets were locked within Peter's mind. Whatever they were, Peter never mentioned them and when anyone asked him a personal question, Peter simply ignored it or gently deflected the conversation.

Jamie remembered meeting Peter for the first time. It was just after opening time a few weeks back. He had walked in, clutching a batted hold-all in one hand and asked if they needed help. Jamie could see the man was not there for a drink, but he asked anyway. In fact, the man didn't look as though he had enough cash to buy even a half-pint. He also spotted the unnatural pallor of the other man, a dead give-away that he had been inside and only recently released. One look told him that him that Peter could look after himself and that, in itself, would be useful come the weekend when the pub patrons got to spend their weekly earnings on beer and then got drunk and belligerent with each other and everyone around them. Another big fellow behind the bar would be useful since the last guy had left after a broken nose had persuaded him to look for another occupation.

As time passed and the two men had established a convenient living arrangement, Peter was still a stranger to Jamie, and a slightly disturbing one at that, but they were friends of a sort and reasonably comfortable with each other. Soon they would be closing up the pub for the night and another dreary day would end. He could see Peter's head sinking towards his chest as he stood there leaning back against the shelves of liquor bottles. The crossed arms and closing eyes were the now familiar signs to Jamie that the other man was off again into his own world. A world peopled by demons and strange pains if the anguish showing on his face was anything to go by, that and the odd cries he sometimes heard late at night when Peter had descended into a restless sleep. Although uncurious by nature, Jamie still wondered about his workmate and living companion.

Peter rarely responded to the frequent advances made by the single, and sometimes married, women who visited the bar on a regular basis. He obviously was not gay. On several occasions Jamie had watched him courteously reject, apparently without taking offense, the occasional advances from the infrequent homosexual that came into the bar, presumably on the look-out for some rough trade. Every so often, Peter would go off with a young woman after the pub closed and he had, on rare instances, brought one back to the apartment…these usually being the married ones or women who did not want nosy neighbors knowing too much about their lives. One look at the woman's face the next morning told Jamie that whatever else Peter might be, he was neither gay nor kinky. So, Jamie concluded, sex was something that Peter indulged in on those rare occasions when hormones or the need to feel another person's body required attention other than from his firm right hand.

Fights were commonplace in the pub but generally they were resolved quickly by those involved on their own without the need for either of the barmen to get involved. Although both men were big and strong, Jamie was the more intimidating with his rough-hewn face and thick body. He was a formidable sight when advancing upon a couple of drunks arguing bitterly over something of minor importance. Usually, when Jamie arrived on the scene, whatever the problem was got resolved instantly and the men would smile at each other and carry on as though nothing had happened. His size and rough manner generally served Jamie well in his adopted role of peacekeeper within the pub. However, Jamie was well aware that Peter, quiet as he was, could certainly take care of himself.

The evening was winding down and the regulars were starting to make their way home. Glancing across the room, Jamie watched a noisy drunk start to get belligerent towards a young couple sitting at a table having drinks and quietly enjoying each other's company. The drunken laborer decided that he liked the young woman and was not going to take "no" for an answer.

"Hey, you there," he said, leaning heavily across the table and leering at the young woman. When she ignored him and turned her chair more towards her companion, the man raised his voice and snarled, "Hey you…I was talking to you. What's your name?"

Pointedly ignoring him, she leaned towards her companion and whispered something.

"Here, what did you say to that poofter you're with? Don't look like much of a man to me. Tell you what, ditch him and I'll show you what a real man's like, how about that then?'

"Look," said the young man, struggling to his feet.

"Ah shut your hole, you poofter," and a single powerful blow knocked him back into his chair sending both him and the chair crashing to the floor, along with the glasses on the table in front of them.

Peter, in his customary stance of leaning back against the serried ranks of bottles, closed his eyes and let his mind drift, the rise and fall of conversation in the pub slowly but surely starting to lull him to sleep. He missed prison, much as a man with a severe migraine registers a cessation of pain. Primitive plumbing, biting cold and dampness in winter, hot steamy days in summer, starchy food, the pervasive smell of human waste, rampant body odor and mind-numbing boredom – his life for three years but that very monotony and enforced conformism had a subtle but seductive appeal.

He looked out the window and saw the erratically-driven car swerve into the other. Smashing glass, grinding and twisting metal, and a body suddenly crashing through the windscreen, blood flying. Covered in sweat, Peter jerked awake instantly, vestiges of prison life and his cellmate Monk's training clicking into action.

An appraising glance across the room told him all he needed to know. He could see the big drunk leaning over the table and starting to grab the young woman sitting there and cowering away from him. Another quick glance at the young man struggling to get to his feet amidst broken glass and try to stop the drunk's advances on his girlfriend told Peter what was happening, and what was likely to happen next. Instinctively he moved around the bar and headed over towards the rapidly developing trouble.

As the massive and very drunk laborer grabbed the young woman's arm and tried to drag her to her feet, he suddenly felt a vice-like grip on his arm. Spinning around in a rage, he faced a calm but still ashen Peter who smiled slightly and said. "You best get out of here, mate, and I mean now." The drunk, breathing beer fumes all over Peter, simply laughed. He was bolstered by booze, stood at least three inches taller than Peter and probably outweighed him by 75 or 100 pounds. "I'm not your mate and who the fuck do you think you are, telling me what to do? I'll go when I say, not before"

"I said it's time for you to go," said Peter.

"And you're going to make me?" said the other man., "Don't make me laugh…you tosser. Get lost."

"I don't think so," said Peter quietly.

"Oh piss-off," shouted the man, and swung a huge arm topped by an enormous fist at Peter's head. There was a blur of movement, so fast that even Jamie, moving quickly across the room to help Peter out, could not say for sure what had happened when asked about it later.

Peter, glancing down at the comatose laborer, shrugged and then nodded at the girl and her boyfriend who had just regained his feet.

"Thanks for taking care of him,' said the young man. "There's no way I could have done anything to stop him. He was…"

"Yes, thank you," added his girlfriend. "That swine was starting to hurt me when you…er…sorted him out. I'm scared to think what might have happened if you hadn't stepped in."

Peter shrugged, saying "No problem" but steadily edged towards the door. As before, vestiges of an earlier life dictated that he get away before the screws, those brutal prison guards, came to get him.

"Hey wait," said the man. "Let me at least buy you a drink.

"S'alright," said Peter and vanished out the door, leaving the couple, Jamie and most of the bar patrons looking at the empty doorway.

Turning to Jamie, the girl asked, "Where'd he go? Why'd he go off like that? All we wanted to do is thank him."

Jamie shrugged and spread his hands in a "search me" gesture before walking over to the door to see where his mate had gone.

As he later told the police, "One minute the guy was standing there, taking a swing at Peter and the next, he was out cold on the floor."

"What exactly happened?" asked the senior responding police officer.

"Well, this guy knocked over the girl's boyfriend, chair and all, and then started to grab the girl, trying to pull her up. Then Peter took over. As I say, one minute this guy is grabbing the girl, the next he's out cold. I have no idea what he did but, I'll tell you one thing, it was bloody fast whatever it was. As I said, one minute this one's full of piss and vinegar, the next he's out cold. Bit like something in one of those Kung-Fu movies and it was fast, that's what."

"Really?" said the local copper. "So, where's this Kung-Fu mate of yours who laid out sleeping beauty here?" he asked, one boot lightly prodding the unconscious and bleeding drunk stretched out on the floor.

"He's gone."

"Gone, as in left the premises?"

"Yeah."

"Where'd he go and why'd he do that? This…" said with another prod of his right foot, "…this one isn't going to file a complaint and besides, the young couple just gave me a full statement. From what she tells me, he's a bit of a hero. Your mate is completely in the clear, so why'd he take off like that?"

"Beats me," said Jamie, "but he took off almost immediately after laying this one out."

"Hmm," commented the police officer. "I wonder what that's all about. Is he in trouble with the Law, or something?"

"Not to my knowledge, he isn't," averred Jamie.

"Huh! Well, I best get down all the particulars just in case Rip Van Winkle here gets a bee in his bonnet to make trouble over what happened. So, what's your mate's name and where does he live?" Turning to his partner, he added, "Best get an ambulance here, just in case this one's actually hurt. Can't have that, can we and do nothing about it, even if he did deserve it."

After getting the address of the apartment, the policeman snapped his note book closed. "Tell your friend that I'll be round in the morning…also, tell him that I'm not happy that he took off like that. It gives me the impression of a guilty conscience or that he's hiding something, you know what I mean?"

"Yeah, yeah, I'll tell him," muttered Jamie, wondering why Peter had left so quickly, and without a word to him. Daft thing to do after the police had been called and he had punched someone's lights out. What was he hiding? Usually nothing scared him but this? This was different and just how had he taken down such a big bloke, someone far larger than he was? Drunk or not, the man was formidable but Peter hadn't hesitated for an instant. He and Peter had sorted out several bar fights and punch-ups but nothing like this. Wham, bam and that was it, and Peter didn't even break a sweat. Just like in the movies but this time it was real, not like the smoke and mirrors stuff on TV or in the movies.

Instinctively he had said nothing to the police, a habit honed over a lifetime of brushes with law enforcement, and he guessed that was what Peter would have wanted. Shrugging, he started to sweep up the broken glasses, thinking, 'Odd bit of excitement for a Wednesday - can't remember anything like this in ages. Still and all, why did Peter take off like that? We've sorted out many fights without him doing a runner. If he's awake when I get home I'll ask him about it or we'll talk in the morning. I'd best warn him that the fuzz might be round to question him.'

TWO

Peter hurried away from the pub, listening to the faint cries of surprise from the people in the pub. Had he over-reacted to that drunk? Perhaps but then again, perhaps not. The man had already grabbed the girl and that sort of nasty drunk would not take kindly to a polite rejection. No, he'd had no choice but to intervene but would the police take the attitude that he'd used unnecessary force? He was no longer on parole but even working in a pub could possibly cause problems for him as an ex-con who had been imprisoned for reckless driving. What if the guy had been seriously injured? Would the drunken laborer or the Crown Prosecutorial Service bring charges, and would the police have to act on them? No, best to get the hell away. Even if nothing came of this latest punch-up, the word would get out and all the local bully-boys and hard-cases would come crowding into the pub just to see how they matched up against the giant killer behind the bar. Sooner or later, someone would get seriously injured and an ex-con like him would be back inside. No, he had to get away from there as fast as possible.

As he strode down the street, his pace accelerating with every step, Peter decided that he needed to get on the road and out of London. Exactly where he would go was open to question but go he must. Letting himself into the apartment he shared with Jamie, Peter grabbed his shabby duffle bag and threw his meager supply of clothes inside. A quick glance around the apartment to check that he had left nothing behind produced a wry smile and the muttered comment, "Not much here to mark your stay, is there old son?" He opened his wallet and noted that he still had a few quid to his name. Leaving the key on the kitchen table, Peter hefted the distressingly light bag and left the place, closing the door quietly behind him and shutting off another phase in his life.

Reaching the end of the road, he lifted his thumb in the universal request for a lift from passing motorists and settled in for an indeterminate wait until some kind soul stopped to take him on board and off to parts unknown. With luck he wouldn't have to wait too long.

After the police had left, Jamie closed down the pub for the night. As he cleared the glasses from tables and swept up the broken mess around the now upright table, he thought once again about Peter.

"Why'd you leave, old son?" he asked the empty room. "You did the right thing and that girl was really grateful you stopped that piece of shit from doing anything nasty to her. Even the police thought so too, so why did you leave like that? In the morning no-one would remember what had happened or think any more about it, so what scared you off?" He was silent for a moment and then continued his monologue, "I saw your face and something set you off, and nothing that loud-mouthed drunk said or did caused you to react like that. What was it? Before you sorted that bloke out, you looked panic-stricken and it had nothing to do with a drunk and that couple. Well, I hope you'll tell me about it when I get home…sort of clear the air, as they say."

Getting back to the apartment, the first thing Jamie saw was the door key on the kitchen table and he immediately felt the emptiness of their few rooms. Whatever else Peter might be, he was always a presence and now, clearly, he was gone but where? Once again, Jamie wondered what demons were chasing Peter. They had lived together for several months but Jamie still had little idea of what, as the Americans might say, made Peter tick. They were friends of a sort and worked well together. Whereas Jamie chattered on endlessly about his past and present, Peter always listened with interest but never said a thing about himself. "Christ man, you really are a mysterious one, ain't you?" said Jamie, looking down at the key. "So, what's it really all about then?"

Standing on the sidewalk beside one of the main thoroughfares heading out of London, Peter patiently held up his thumb. The swish of passing traffic started to lull him to sleep, that and the rapidly dissipating adrenaline in his body. Years of practice enabled him to slide into a quasi-vegetative state that let him keep his eyes open while standing but still have sensitive antennae tuned to anything unusual about him. Not quite asleep and certainly not fully awake, his mind first revisited the chaos in the pub and then slowly but surely slipped back in time. Banishing memories, Peter jerked himself awake and lit a cigarette, settling himself for a patient wait until someone decided to stop and give him a lift.

After a last heavy drag on the cigarette, he tossed it aside and went back to his thoughts.

"Hey…I thought you wanted a lift?"

Startled, Peter's head jerked up and he looked around, spotting a large semi belching fumes a dozen or so yards up the road from him, the driver of which was beckoning him.

As he climbed into the cab, he said, "Thanks for stopping," and as he tried to settle himself, the driver said in a mock gruff tone, "Gawd, mate, you're too slow to catch a cold," before letting out the clutch and pulling into traffic again.

Soon after, they were approaching the Expressway heading toward Northern England.

"Where you headed then?" asked the driver with a sideways glance at his passenger.

"Anywhere, nowhere," was the laconic response.

"Well, I'm headed up north…Newcastle way, that suit you?"

"Splendid," said Peter, and stared out the windshield as the truck started to merge onto the motorway, headed north and well away from London.

Splendid? thought the driver. *Now that's a strange word from a hitch-hiker, especially one dressed the way he is.* "Hey, you're not in trouble with the Law, are you?"

"Nah, but why'd you ask?"

"Just wondering…not that it's anything to do with me."

"No, nothing like that," Peter assured him. "It's just time for me to make a move and try my luck somewhere new. I've had it with here…you know, London…what with all the Arabs, Indians, Pakis and even the Russians taking the place over. It's just not like England anymore." He was silent for a moment, and the added, "Does it make any difference?"

"Does what make a difference?"

"That I could be in trouble with the Law?"

"Not really, no…I was just asking. As I said, nothing to do with me if you are. By the way, my name's Nobby," and he thrust a hand across at Peter, who shook it and responded,

"Nobby? I suppose your last name's Clarke."

"No, actually it's Murphy. At school they liked to call kids named Murphy "Spud" and Clarkes were called "Nobby". Since they already had three kids called Murphy when I got there and not being Irish, I got passed on being called Spud. There weren't any Clarkes, so I got called Nobby."

"I suppose that makes sense. Anyway I'm Peter, Peter Marshall… and I'm headed north."

Nobby smiled, "I can see why you're headed out of London. You're right, mate, about all them foreigners. It was bad enough when we had all those West Indians and then the Africans, the Nigerians, Kenyans and that lot came in but now? Now it's hard to find a white face anywhere these days, not that I'm prejudiced, you know," he added quickly. Glancing again at Peter's impassive face, he continued, "I just think England should be for the English although all these wogs and the like claim to be British, every single one of them…and that gives them the right to come over here and take all our jobs. And them that don't work, get right on the dole and live on taxpayer money. It ain't right, is it? Bloody politicians…only too happy to spend our money, ain't they?"

Looking for a reaction from Peter, he was slightly disappointed to catch only a non-committal shrug from his passenger. *Well, so much for politics with this one,* and he returned his attention to the road, lapsing into silence for a few minutes. After a dozen or so miles, he tried again to chat to his passenger, starting to talk about the latest soccer matches and the league championship prospects of his favorite team, Newcastle United. "What a shambles they can be and nothing like they was in the old days. One minute they are world-beaters and the next, they lose stupidly – makes no sense, does it?"

Again Peter shrugged and then joined in on the conversation about the Premier League, hesitantly at first and then with greater animation and interest. At least soccer was a safe subject for both of them, and one that would ease the passage of time and miles.

"Hey, want a fag?" asked Nobby.

"Thanks."

"Got a whole bunch of them back there," he said, with a jerk of his thumb to the trailer. "Hauling them back from France, aren't I? They always give me a few extra cartons by way of a tip." Passing over the pack to Peter, he added, "Light one for me, okay?"

Peter struck a match to Nobby's cigarette first and then to his own and took a deep drag on it, before immediately starting to cough. Nobby laughed, "They're a bit strong until you get used to them. Actually, I used to think they tasted like shit but now, seeing as they're free, I've grown to like them. Dirt cheap over there but here, posh people seem to like them and they're more expensive here than Players and Dunhill. Bloody government and its taxes. I don't buy for a minute the argument that they have to raise taxes on ciggies because it's good for your health to stop smoking. Nah, they just want to grab everything they can – bloody politicians. Greedy bastards, all of them, and rob you blind every chance they get, don't they?"

Miles passed, and Peter asked, "Been driving long?"

"Most of my life. Beats working and I'm almost my own master. See a different part of the country pretty much every day and often get over to the Continent too."

"What about your home life? Doesn't your wife mind?"

"Oh she minds alright. Minded so much that she ran off with a bank manager or some such, didn't she? Said she wanted someone who had a steady job and was home every night. Poor bugger, never knew what hit him after they got married. Thing about driving is that you get a lot of dough under the counter – you know what I mean? – so she had lots of cash to spend. Now she has to watch every penny and he's a right tight arse too, having to pay income tax on everything he gets."

Nobby gave a humorless laugh, and continued, "Ah, she's hurting now that she can't buy whatever rubbish she wants and have me to pay for it. Almost makes your heart bleed, don't it?"

"I suppose," shrugged Peter. "Did she try to get…er…get back together with you?"

"Did at first…you know, when she first went off with him, but I wasn't having any of it. If I wasn't good enough for her when we were married, why would things suddenly change now that she was on her own? Going off and screwing that bloke was stupid. Serves the silly bitch right, and that tosser she's married too. What a git!"

After a couple of minutes, Nobby added, "So, what do you do for a living? Apart from thumbing lifts?"

"At the moment, nothing much – in fact nothing at all, to tell the truth. Worked as a barman and now…well, I'm one of the great unemployed, as they say."

"Yeah? I suppose you're like all those wogs and get unemployment and that?"

"Not yet, I don't but I suppose I will one day. But don't forget, I'm vital to the country."

"You are? How so?"

"Let's face it, without me those unemployment figures would not look so impressive and then the politicians and the newspapers wouldn't be able to moan and groan about the economy and how badly the country's doing. So, by staying out of a job, lots of civil servants keep busy writing down lots of numbers and filling in forms, and that keeps them in jobs. More civil servants means higher taxes and so the people at the top can take more for themselves. So, without people like me, you wouldn't see how lucky you are to have a job and be able to pay taxes. As I said, I'm essential to the country and the economy. We need more people like me."

"You're barmy but, trouble is, you could just be right. Anyway, there's a truck-stop a few miles ahead. We'll stop there and get something to eat. After that, I'll kip down in the back so that I keep my driving hours below the limit. You can doss down here in the cab, it's plenty big enough. That all right with you?"

"Yeah, thanks. I won't be a bother to you?"

"Nah, mate. I'll get some tea, a bacon sandwich or two and then crash for a couple of hours. Have to, really. They're pretty strict these days about how many hours we drive and I can't afford to pay a fine or lose my license. It just ain't worth it. Mind you, the trucking firms turn a blind eye to how long we drive as long as we get stuff delivered on time. Ah, here it comes – best bacon sandwiches this side of the Tyne."

After several hours asleep, Peter stirred and after a momentary disorientation as to where he was, he heard muffled sounds coming from behind the cab. Seconds later, Nobby's head appeared through the connecting window, cheerily saying, "That's better. Now, let's have some breakfast and get on our way."

An hour or so later, after both men had used the shower facilities reserved for truck drivers, and nicely warmed by the food they had eaten, they were off again. Time passed, as did the miles, although there were the usual inexplicable delays when the traffic slowed to a crawl for several miles and then took off again. Cars, vans and small trucks whizzed past them, many weaving in and out of traffic trying to gain a few yards on the next person and make up for time lost when they had had to crawl for a few miles. Looking down on the traffic from the high cab of the semi, Peter likened what he was seeing to an aerial view of multi-colored ants crawling over a fallen grey tree trunk. He chuckled quietly.

"What's so funny?"

"Oh I was just thinking how all these people are driving like crazy and going nowhere fast. I mean, why bother? Seems a bit pointless to me."

"Maybe to you, being unemployed, but these geezers, they're probably off to work, trying to hold down a job so they can pay their taxes and keep the likes of you happily on the dole," snapped Nobby.

"I wasn't trying to be clever or snarky. What I meant was that driving fast and risking a collision just to get to work a few minutes sooner doesn't make sense to me. Why not relax, take it a bit easier? After all, speeding won't get you there that much sooner but staying at the speed limit at least keeps your stress level down and lowers the risk of a coronary too. Besides, it saves on petrol."

"Says you!" said Nobby and then slammed his brakes on. "Did you see that fucking idiot? He deliberately swerved in front of me. These damn motorcyclists, they love to do that along this stretch of road. They're a fucking menace. And that arsehole right in front of us is one of the worst…I see him almost every time I come this way, the little shit."

The motorcyclist was so close to the front of the truck that Peter could easily make out the words "King Rocker" laid out in studs across the back of his black leather jacket. As the motorcyclist slowed down, a second and then a third motorcycle joined him. Within a few seconds, the truck was surrounded by several motorcycles, all slowing down and forcing Nobby to do likewise. King Rocker turned in his saddle, looked back at Nobby and, with a smirk, held up two fingers in the classic and insulting V-sign.

"These fucking yobs! Every so often they like to pick on trucks. They know we usually have to meet deadlines and they think it's funny to hold us up. Nothing better to do, have they?"

As the motorcycles tried to slow Nobby still more, he glanced at Peter and said, "I'm going to try to get round them. So, hold on as I put me foot down." Blasting his horn, Nobby pushed the accelerator pedal to the floor and pulled the wheel over, surging around the encircling motorcycles. As he did so, one motorcycle did not move out of the way fast enough or care enough to let him get past, and one wheel of the truck clipped the bike's rear wheel, causing the motorcycle to spin out of control and dump the rider unceremoniously on the tarmac. The other motorbikes all slowed down and, as Nobby could see in his wing mirror, the rider had clambered to his feet and was waving his fist at the retreating truck.

Continuing down the expressway, Nobby muttered, "Well that got rid of them for the moment, silly buggers. At least we weren't going fast enough for anyone to get hurt. Hey, there's a truck stop up the road and we'll get some lunch, okay?" He hesitated for a moment or two, and then added, "Look, I'm going to have to drop you off there since I'm getting close to head office and I can't be seen having anyone with me in the cab – against company rules and that. You understand, yes?"

Peter nodded, "No problem. I'll soon catch another ride and I appreciate you getting me this far – thanks."

"You'll be okay then?" asked Nobby. Seeing Peter's affirmative nod, he continued, "Look, I'll pay for lunch and then be on my way once we've eaten. Okay? Sorry about leaving you."

"Don't worry about it and lunch sounds great." Peter hesitated, and then said, "Hey, I do have money – I can pay for my own food."

"Ah, forget it. The spare fags those Froggies gave me will give me lots of ready when I flog them, so don't think about it."

A short time, later, Nobby pulled off the highway and went down a side road, saying, "This place, looks like a dump but serves the best grub around here. Suit you?"

"Looks fine to me, "said Peter. Glancing around, he added, "At least we're away from traffic fumes. How'd you find it?"

"Oh, one of my mates told me about it and I stop here on every trip. You get the odd travelling salesman, some of the locals and quite a few bikers, you know like those shits that we passed a few miles back, but otherwise it's pretty quiet."

A few minutes later, Peter and Nobby were tucking into the traditional truck driver's lunch of sausages, eggs, chips, large wads of bread and butter, washed down with several mugs of hot, sweet, milky tea. As they lingered over the last of their tea and cigarettes, Nobby got up and said, "Look, I'll hit the loo and then be on my way." He held out his hand, "Enjoyed meeting you. You take care and lots of luck with getting a lift further north."

After Nobby left, Peter finished his meal, slowly stubbed out his cigarette, yawned and stretched. Grabbing his bag, he got to his feet and ambled towards the door. Blinking in the bright sunlight outside, he was about to head towards the road when he saw Nobby surrounded by several of the bikers they had passed earlier, King Rocker to the fore and towering over the diminutive driver.

As Peter walked towards them, he could hear King Rocker shouting loudly at Nobby, "What the fuck did you think you were doing, you stupid git. You carved us up on the road back there and tipped my mate Ozzie on his arse…could have killed him, couldn't you?"

"Now wait a minute…" Nobby started to protest.

"Wait nothing, sunshine. You tried to kill us back there and damn near succeeded with Ozzie, and you didn't try to stop to see what had happened to him. What's your game then?"

"Tried to kill you? You've got to be joking…don't make me laugh."

King Rocker moved closer, looming over Nobby and his voice getting louder, "Oh no, mate, we're not going to make you laugh. We're gonna teach you not to mess wiv us – that'll be a lesson you won't forget, that's what."

He lifted his fist as two of his mates moved to either side of Nobby, ready to grab him. Just then, King Rocker felt his swinging arm grabbed tightly, stopping it suddenly, and a quiet voice behind him said, "Not this time, old son."

Wrenching his arm out of the grip on it, King Rocker spun round and found himself facing a tall, broad-shouldered but shabbily-dressed man, who said, "Don't look for trouble my son, you might find it."

"And who the fuck are you?" snarled King Rocker. "Push off before we give you what this git's going to get."

The man smiled at him gently, adding, "I don't think so. So, why don't you just get on your way and we'll forget all about this."

"Like fuck we will," shouted King Rocker and swung at Peter, who merely said, "I did warn you." before swaying to one side and blocking the thrusting fist. Almost instantly thereafter, a scything movement by his right hand broke King Rocker's nose and a follow-through of his elbow nearly broke the other man's jaw. As the stunned King Rocker dropped to his knees, one of his pals, standing next to Nobby, jumped forward, shouting "Here, what the…" before collapsing as a stunningly fast-moving fist caught his diaphragm.

The man on the other side of Nobby started towards Peter before he too was felled by a fast kick beside his knee followed by a sharp cut from Peter's straightened hand to his carotid artery. One of the men standing next to King Rocker jumped forward to join in, only to be laid out by another lightning-fast blow from Peter. The last man standing, fumbling desperately for a switchblade from his jacket pocket, took one look at his mates and literally threw the knife on the ground at Peter's feet before taking off running.

Nobby also looked at the scattered bodies and the pitifully groaning King Rocker before remarking laconically, "Well, you did warn him, didn't you?" Glancing at the placid Peter, he added, "Blimey mate, I hate to think what you're like when you really get pissed off."

As he stepped around the supine bodies, Nobby said, "I think we'd best get out of here before someone calls the Law." As he walked quickly to his rig, he called back to Peter, "Hey, climb it and let's get going. Those frigging closed circuit cameras that are everywhere probably caught that on screen and I don't need the company to hear about it."

Accelerating back onto the expressway, Nobby glanced at Peter before saying, "Where'd you learn to do that? You some kind of martial arts expert or something?" Seeing Peter's non-committal shrug, he added, "It's no matter but I'll tell you one thing, you saved me from a nasty thumping back there and no mistake."

The miles ticked by and Nobby broke the silence once again, "Look, I told you the old lady took off, didn't I? Well, how about you kip down in the spare room tonight. I'll have to unload part of this," with a jerk of his thumb towards the rig behind the cab, "in the morning and the rest goes on up to Scotland when I'm finished. So, if it's alright with you, I'll put you on the road in the morning before I head over to the depot."

"Thank you," said Peter quietly.

"No, thank you," retorted Nobby. "Anyways, that's settled. We'll pop round to that Indian place up the road from the house for some carry-out once we get in. Remind me to get some beer too. Nothing better than a couple of beers with curry, is there? I like to think it deadens the throat so even if the food tastes like shit, the beer helps. I wonder if Dahlia's home."

"Dahlia?"

"Yeah, my daughter."

"Dahlia? That's an unusual name."

"Got it from her grandmother. My ma-in-law was called Rose and because she likes flowers, she named her kids that way. My wife just carried on the tradition."

"What about the boys?"

"Fortunately she didn't have any but my wife was called Lily and her sisters were called Hyacinth, Poppy, Myrtle and Rosemary."

"No Chrysanthemum or Hydrangea?

"Nah…but if she'd had more, I'm sure she'd have called them something like that."

"Great," said Peter. "What was her husband's name? Something exotic?"

"No, he was called Cedric. Poor sod, fancy being saddled with a name like that. I'll bet that caused him some problems at school growing up…what a name, Cedric, and with a last name like Farnsworth, he never stood a chance, did he? No wonder he died young."

Peter lit up another cigarette for them both. Handing one to Nobby, he added, "You're right, these aren't too bad once you get used to them."

"And the price is right, too," laughed Nobby. "Anyway, Dahlia's a great kid, smart, too – actually she's no longer a kid. Went to College but she's living at home for the moment – can't find a job. So, she takes care of the house and things, good thing with me being on the road so much. As I say, a good kid."

"Never married?"

"Nah. Just as well given the tossers living around us. Dead loss, most of them. Those that's got any get up and go would do just that, take off down to London."

"Why didn't Dahlia do the same?"

"No interest…Newcastle's big enough for her although the lack of jobs ain't fun. She does do some part-time work though…brings in enough for clothes and make-up, that sort of thing. She manages well enough and can get down to the pub to see her mates and even go on the odd trip abroad with them. I hate to think of what they get up when they're abroad but it's nowt to do with me, besides I can't say anything since she's a grown woman, you know what I mean?"

"I suppose so," said Peter, enjoying Nobby's chatter.

Eventually they pulled up outside a non-descript terraced house, "Here we are," said Nobby. "Home, sweet home. Get your gear and let's go in."

Opening the door, Nobby shouted, "Dahlia, you home?"

"Yes, Da, I'm here," and a very attractive young woman came clattering down the stairs to greet them.

Seeing Peter standing there, she looked at her father and asked, "So, who's this?"

"He's Peter. Picked up down London way…gave him a lift and then he helped me out with sommat, so here he is. The spare room ready?"

"Of course," Dahlia said. Then looking at Peter, she added, "If I'd known we were having company, I'd have got something in…for dinner, you know."

"Don't fret, lass," said Nobby. "We'll go round and get some Indian, some beer too. Anything good on the telly tonight?"

"Don't know yet…not that it makes much difference with you," laughed Dahlia. Turning to Peter, she added with a smile, "Once dad gets his belly full of curry and puts away a few beers, he's out like a light. Mind you, he does need his rest, being as he's on the road so much, so I just help him upstairs and into bed, and let him sleep it off. He snores a bit but nobody's perfect, as they say."

"Hey, I might not be perfect," snapped Nobby. "But I'm close to it and not so much lip from you, my girl."

They all laughed.

Later, over steaming dishes of curry, rice and various other dishes supplied by the Indian take-out down the road, Dahlia gently quizzed Nobby about his trip. Eventually she asked, "So, what's this "sommat" that Peter helped you with? What sort of thing was it?"

Needing little prompting, Nobby related the incident. "I tell you lass, one minute there's this biker gang right in my face and the next, they're all laid out on the ground. It was like one of those Kung-Fu things you see all the time on the telly. Bloody marvelous it were, bloody marvelous."

Dahlia looked sideways at Peter but, seeing the closed-down look on his face, decided not to pursue it. He didn't look the type to mix it up with a bunch of yobs but that didn't mean a whole lot since she'd had no experience with sort of thing. Although she looked at

Peter appraisingly, she simply said to him, "Thanks. Good thing you were there, weren't it?"

Peter just nodded, what was there to say?

After dinner, they all sat in the living room to watch television and allow their food to digest, Dahlia stretched out on the sofa with Nobby and Peter in the two armchairs. Nobby's eyes slowly closed and Peter and Dahlia gently chatted, not bothering too much with the programming on television, just enjoying each other's company and letting Nobby doze.

Eventually Nobby's relaxed breathing turned to gentle snores which became more raucous as time passed. Nodding at her comatose father, Dahlia murmured, "Time to get him upstairs…mind giving me a hand?" and the pair of them gently maneuvered Nobby up to his bedroom and then into bed.

Once he was settled, Dahlia turned to Peter and said, "Oh well, time to turn in, okay?"

Peter said goodnight and went into the spare room. He quickly undressed and slid into bed…pajamas were a thing of the past and he snuggled under the sheets. Realizing that he hadn't turned off the light, he climbed out of bed and snapped off the switch by the door. Just as he turned back to the bed, the door opened silently behind him. Turning, he could see Dahlia framed in the doorway, wearing a near-transparent nightie and nothing else. Her pale but shapely body was back-lit by the dim light on the hallway, and Peter could see the smile on her face.

"I didn't thank you properly for helping my dad," she breathed. "He's getting too old for punch-ups and he could have been hurt but for you, so…" and within seconds she had wrapped herself around Peter, kissing him passionately.

As they both fell onto the bed, Dahlia reached down and felt Peter rapidly getting hard. "Ah, that's good," she giggled, and pulled off her nightie. Kissing him again and running her hands, then her mouth and finally her tongue over Peter's body, enjoying his firm body and rock-hard muscles, she commented, "My, my, you do keep fit, don't you." Then she added, "This is the way we thank people up here." Within seconds, they were making love, the bed creaking and both of them murmuring sighs of passion. All too quickly, in both of their opinions, it was over and they cuddled under the bedcovers.

"Aye, that were grand," said Dahlia in a broad but fake Northern accent as she cradled Peter's now flaccid genitals in a warm hand. She paused and asked, "You enjoy it, did you?"

Peter laughed quietly, "You do ask the oddest questions. Is that something else they do up North?"

"No, not really," answered Dahlia. "It's just…ah, just that you don't say much, do you?" As Peter stayed silent, she added, "I'm used to men talking a lot, especially during and after sex. Somehow they think that dirty talk makes for more passion…I don't know if it does or not, but most of them do it, don't they?"

"I don't know," said Peter.

"Not that I've had that much experience with men," Dahlia added hastily. "It's just those that I've known seem to want to…you know, talk dirty."

"Don't women do that?"

"Some do, at least that's what some of my friends tell me but not many."

She lapsed into silence and then, leaning up one elbow, she stared down at Peter. Eventually she said, "You're different, aren't you?"

"Different how?" asked Peter.

"Oh, I don't know. You don't say much and you talk differently from the blokes around here. You… I don't know… you talk like one of the professors I had at College…sort of educated and sophisticated. You are pretty good looking and have a good body…even with those old clothes, you look pretty good. You just don't look like your average hitch-hiker. So, tell me, who are you? How'd you come to meet up with my dad?"

"It just happened."

"No, I don't buy that. All the years dad's been driving, it's been very rare for him to pick up a hitchhiker and he's never brought anyone home before. That just doesn't happen. And what about that fight of yours? How is it that you just happened to be there and sorted out that bunch of bikers for dad? That was no coincidence, or was it?"

Peter hesitated. The post-coital euphoria was rapidly dissipating. He didn't want to be brusque with Dahlia. She wasn't like the women he had screwed in London, the wham-bam birds as he termed them. No, she was very sweet and didn't deserve to be brushed off. He was aware that their love-making had been mutually beneficial but, still and all, it was a heart-felt gesture of gratitude on her part. He smiled to himself and he fought down the impulse to open up…no wonder the Russians and East Germans of old used women to soften men up and drop their defenses. It was so easy to confide in one's bedmate, especially if the sex had been good…and he had no doubt that the women employed by the Communist bloc spymasters were expert in that area. Eventually he said, "I don't know how it all happened. It just sort of did." He hesitated a moment or two, trying to find the right words. "Your dad saw me and gave me a lift. Then after he dropped me off at the rest stop and was ready to get back on the road, that gang turned up. I walked over and surprised them."

"And?" persisted Dahlia.

"Oh, I don't know. They weren't expecting me and it just sort of happened."

"I'm sure it did," muttered Dahlia sarcastically. Then, as she felt Peter slowly coming back to life, she slid down his body and took him into her mouth. As he hardened, she withdrew and slithered up his body, pressing her firm breasts against him. Looking down at him, she laughed, "Okay, now's not the time to talk, is it? So, big boy, let's see what you've got, shall we?" As she straddled him and slid Peter inside herself, she sighed, "Aah, that feels good, ah yes… yes…yes," and she climaxed quickly. Waiting for Peter to catch up, she leaned forward and gently rubbed her breasts against his face and lips, enjoying Peter's urgent thrusts. Finally, with a groan, Peter let go and they collapsed into a tangle of arms and legs, soon falling asleep in mutual satisfaction.

Several hours later, as dawn's feeble light crept through the curtains, Dahlia stirred awake. She leaned over and kissed Peter. "Time's awasting," she said. "I've got to be out of here before dad wakes up. Okay? He wouldn't like it for me to be in here with you. So, sorry, I've got to go." Kissing him again, she quickly pulled on her nightie and then leaned over to kiss Peter for the last time. "It was grand last night…thank you."

"No Dahlia, thank *you*," said Peter, and his sincerity was so evident that Dahlia felt good about herself for several days.

As she went back to her room and minimally disturbed bed, she wondered again about Peter. 'He's really something else, that man,' she thought. 'What is it about him…and what about that chain of events with dad? How'd that come about?' Shaking her head, Dahlia quickly checked that her bedroom appeared neat and tidy, and then went to shower and rinse off the smell of sex that permeated her body. As the warm water sprayed over her, she thought again about Peter and was surprised to find her nipples hardening as she remembered the night. "Ay, lass, it's been too long since you've had a man," she softly said to herself, and she giggled. "And what a man he was, wasn't he?"

THREE

After Dahlia had left him, Peter slowly came wide awake. He stretched and looked around the small room. At first he wondered whether last night's passion had been real or wholly imagined but knew that it was no dream when he looked at the rumpled sheets and the various wet patches that dotted them. He could hear the faint sounds of a shower running and the noise of Nobby rattling around in the kitchen, presumably making tea. He climbed out of bed, reflecting that this was the first time he had slept in a real bed for longer than he cared to think and then he started his regular morning routine of sit-ups, push-ups and Tae Kwan Do exercises. As he worked out, tightening and relaxing his muscles, he thought briefly about Dahlia. He wondered what he would do next and, for that matter, what to do about Dahlia. 'She's special, that one,' he thought. 'But it won't go anywhere, more's the pity…she deserves better than me, that's for sure.'

A quick shower and shave was called for and then sorting out something was that was reasonably clean to put on, ready to face the world. Nobby had already said that he would have to make his own way from now on and Peter was grateful for the other man's kindness. Sorting out the bikers had been nothing but he wondered about the drunk he had beaten up a couple of days back…was it really that long ago? He thought briefly about Jamie and then shuffled into the bathroom. As he turned on the shower and waited for the water to start running hot, he idly scratched his scrotum and then smiled at the old joke that the reason women rubbed their eyes in the morning was because they didn't have balls to scratch the way men did.

Shaved, refreshed from the shower and wearing cleaner clothes, he made his way downstairs. Nobby, hearing him come into the kitchen, looked up from the morning paper and said, "Tea's in the pot and there's some toast, butter and jam over there on the counter if you want some." Almost as an afterthought, he added, "Sleep well, did you?"

"Yes, thanks, I did."

"Good. I doubt that Dahlia's up yet or, if she is, she takes forever doing her hair and make-up, that sort of thing. Well, we'll have to make a move soon. I'm due at the depot and then off up to Scotland. Another long drive but at least I'll have the weekend off once I get back, unless of course there's a load to bring back for London or some such. They like to keep me busy, that lot. Of course I don't complain too much as it does bring in a good income."

Peter nodded idly. So he would be off on his own again in an hour or so. It didn't bother him to be alone but he knew that he would miss the talkative Nobby and definitely miss the lovely and passionate Dahlia. One day, he vowed to himself, *I'll try to repay them or, failing that, return the favor to someone else in need.*

He poured some tea, added milk and sugar. Sitting down, he buttered some toast and then applied that sticky concoction known as strawberry jam to the thick slices of bread. He smiled; strawberry jam, more sugar and artificial flavoring than actual fruit, tasted good but probably was ruinous to one's health. After swilling some tea and taking a large bite of toast, he picked up the part of the newspaper that Nobby had discarded and scanned the headlines. Same old bad economic news, ridiculous political antics and a brief synopsis of the midweek soccer scores. Nothing much had changed and Peter reflected that the French had it right when they said, *Plus change, plus le même* (everything changes, everything is the same). Nothing really does change and after spending time in prison, Peter realized that everything seemed so pointless. For a moment he envied those prisoners who had found God and had their faith to sustain them. He just felt empty and useless, a waste of the air he breathed and the space he occupied on earth. He sighed and drank more tea, catching the curious glance that Nobby shot at him before resuming his perusal of the newspaper.

Eventually, Nobby folded up the paper and said, "Well, best be going then…the day's a wasting. You set?"

Peter nodded and got to his feet. He rinsed off both sets of plates and cups in the sink and placed then neatly in the draining rack. "Fine, I'm ready…and thank you."

Nobby shrugged. "It wasn't much but it'll hold you for a bit. Okay, let's get on the road. I'll tell Dahlia goodbye for you when I talk to her later. She seemed to enjoy talking to you and it was nice for her to have another man around besides her dad. Ready to make a move?"

A few miles from the house, Nobby pulled over and stopped. "Here's where I leave you. The motorway is just around that corner and up a ways…should have no trouble getting a ride there. At least it's not raining and reasonably warm too." He held out a hand to Peter, "Here, take this…a few quid to tide you over, in case of need, you know."

Although Peter tried to push the money back, he looked very grateful at the offer and Nobby quickly added, "Hey, ain't nothing. Take care of yourself, okay? Good luck mate. You know where I am if you need me."

As he watched Peter climb out of the cabin and walk towards the motorway, Nobby wondered about his passenger. *He's different, that one,* he reflected. The unusual pallor, the ever present guarded expression on his face, the quiet moaning when he dozed and his constant watchfulness all indicated that Peter had been "inside" but he was unlike any ex-con Nobby had ever known, and he known a number in his life. Peter was obviously fit, took care of his appearance despite his shabby clothes and was obviously intelligent and well-spoken but what was he doing with all that martial arts stuff he used on those bikers? Where did that come from? That wasn't the norm for your average hitchhiker. As he later said to that police officer making inquiries, Nobby decided that Peter Marshall, if that really was his name, was a walking contradiction. He even went so far as to say, "It's funny how the Lord brings people into our lives. Peter was there when I really needed him, and then he was gone. I sometimes wonder whether I imagined it all but then I see those frigging bikers on the road, and it all comes back to me. Funnily enough, those yobs give me a wide berth now, so I know it really did happen. So, make of it what you will but I know that God put him there for a reason."

Peter, turned to wave goodbye to Nobby as he drove past, and then started to pace himself as he walked towards the motorway and, hopefully, a lift to somewhere better than where he had been in the past. Where he had been…that was a laugh. Anywhere was better than that and those recurrent nightmares.

That particular day had started out fairly normally. Thursdays were his research days and he could sleep in because he had no pressing academic duties. All his lectures were prepared for the following week and he could concentrate on his research and that nagging problem he had slaved over for weeks, if not months. He had showered and shaved although that painful nick on his chin from the new razor irritated him, and deposited a few drops of blood on the clean shirt he had just put on. He could hear his wife Jean pottering around in the kitchen making breakfast and the seductive aroma of frying bacon wafted upstairs to greet him as he approached the kitchen.

"Sleep well, dear?" asked Jean.

"Yes, yes I did…at least I think so."

"I think you did…you snored loud enough to wake the dead, so I'm sure you did. Anyway, have some breakfast. Eggs and bacon suit you?"

"Thank you…" and as Peter cannoned into Jean's swollen stomach, he added, "Just when is that dratted baby coming? I assumed it must be a girl because she's so late…just like all women… but you say it's a boy. I tell you, I'll have to have words with him about punctuality."

"Sure you will," laughed Jean. "Don't forget, all first babies tend to be late, so don't get your nickers in a twist over it. Besides, it's me who has to carry him, so stop your moaning. All you did was impregnate me and you had a great time doing so if my memory serves me."

"Yeah, yeah. Anyway, some bacon and eggs should be a great start to the day…thank you for preparing them."

"It's my pleasure, my love, my pleasure. Now, sit yourself down and I'll give you some. Might as well enjoy it because very soon, you'll be taking care of me and the little one…by the way, have you made up your mind over what we'll call him. The good thing is that you won't adopt that dreadful American habit of calling him Peter Junior…ghastly thought to have two Peters under the same roof."

Peter smiled and then concentrated on eating. Breakfast helped to dissipate the feeling of impending doom, a feeling that a second cup of coffee and his third cigarette did little to dispel. Eventually he stubbed out the cigarette, went upstairs to brush his teeth and then pulled on his sports coat. At least on Thursdays he did not have to wear a suit. Even in the present enlightened age, professors at premier institutions were expected to dress properly and his college, Royal Imperial College, University of Cambridge, was no exception.

Kissing Jean goodbye, Peter went into the attached garage and climbed into his aged but still functional MGB. As he did so, he reflected that it was a good thing they had the small SUV so Jean and the baby would be able to get around. The starter whirred and the engine hiccupped once before settling back into stony silence. He tried again and cursed loudly, calling out to Jean, "This damn thing may have to go to the knacker's yard. It's either too old or too damned temperamental these days."

"Yes dear," called Jean and resumed washing the dishes. Almost every day Peter had trouble with that car but he insisted on keeping it because, he maintained, it was a vintage vehicle and quite valuable. She smiled to herself, "Those boys and their toys", she muttered.

Eventually Peter tracked the problem to a loose wire and then he was off, ready to push back the frontiers of science as he liked to say. Inevitably, because it was a damp and gloomy morning, traffic was bad and it took longer than usual to get to the Faculty parking lot. Faculty and students who lived in the college or in town made do with the ubiquitous bicycle to get around but because Peter and Jean lived out of town, he had to drive in each day…and the heavy traffic that morning only exacerbated his irritation.

As he walked past the porter's lodge, he heard his name called and the porter held out a small bundle of letters and journals. "Your post has arrived, Dr. Marshall."

"Thank you, Frank," said Peter, as he glanced down at the bundle. "Let's hope that I got some good news today."

"I hope so too, sir," said Frank and darted back into his lodge, ready to greet the next don who walked past.

Nodding absently to his research assistant, Peter went into his office and tossed the package on his desk. He would go through it after he grabbed a cup of coffee and relaxed with yet another cigarette before getting down to work.

Andrew Newman, Peter's technician, watched Peter go through his Thursday morning ritual and smiled. After the nicotine and caffeine worked their magic, Dr. Peter Marshall would come into the laboratory and discuss their research work, becoming almost human again.

Just then he heard an angry shout, "What the hell is this? What complete and utter balderdash...I don't believe it...those morons... what were they thinking?"

Andrew waited a few moments and went to the office door. Poking his head in, he asked, "Anything wrong boss-man?"

"Yes there bloody well is," snapped Peter, irritated that Andrew simply raised an eyebrow. "And you get that stupid expression off your face too!"

Andrew, by now accustomed to his boss's frequent temper tantrums when things didn't go right, waited until Peter calmed down. Eventually, in a few terse sentences Peter told him that his latest paper had been summarily rejected by the leading scientific journal in their field. "Not only that," he added. "Those clowns even suggested, oh ever so politely I might add, that our data are wrong and that I don't know what I'm talking about." He held up the offending letter and shook it at Andrew, snarling, "Doesn't correspond to basic principles of radiochemistry...the underlying theory appears to lack a credible scientific basis. You hear that? Basic principles...credible scientific basis...what do those clowns know? Those reviewers wouldn't know a basic principle or credible science if it bit them on the arse. Utter nonsense...but that's what happens when you advance a new theory that just might turn all those hackneyed principles on their head. What utter crap."

Peter folded the letter and put it into his jacket pocket. Shooting a glance at Andrew, he added, "I'm going to get a drink at the Ploughman's Arms. If anyone looks for me, tell them you don't know where I am and if you even think about disturbing me, it had better be for an emergency…a life-threatening one at that."

As he strode down the road to the pub frequented by the College faculty, Peter muttered to himself, uttering dark imprecations about the journal editor and the reviewers. "Bloody fools" he concluded as he walked into the pub. Getting a pint of the bitter beer so liked by British drinkers, he sat down at a small table and fished the journal letter out of his pocket. He took a hefty swig of beer, lit up a cigarette and slowly read through the letter, and then re-read it. Sitting back and draining the glass, he stared unfocussed into the middle distance. After a minute or two, he got to his feet and went to the bar to order a second beer, oblivious to the fact that he was consuming a significant amount of alcohol on a near-empty stomach.

Resuming his seat, and drinking nearly half the beer, he stared off into space again, reviewing the rejected paper in his mind and the research data that the paper was based on. Slowly he pieced everything together, first mentally reviewing the data, then his explanation of the findings and finally his controversial theory. He muttered to himself, "No, surely it can't be that simple." He drained his glass and shuffled back to the bar for a refill. Sitting down again, he took another hefty swig of beer and went through everything again, and once more after that.

"Well, I'll be! What was I thinking…could I have really been that blind and stupid?"

"Probably old boy…in fact quite likely with you," drawled George Martin, his old friend and greatest rival at Royal Imperial College…in fact his greatest rival in the field of radiochemistry. "So, why all the breast beating? Having a bad day are we?"

"Oh, I was wrong about something, that's all…and yes, I'll have a drink now that you're offering."

"That's all…you were wrong about something? The great Peter Marshall admits to making a mistake? Will wonders never cease?" George smiled at his friend before continuing, "So, what'll you have?"

"Make mine a double scotch in celebration," said Peter.

"You'll have a pint of bitter, that's what," rejoined George. Then he added, "Just what are you, or rather we, celebrating?"

"Get the beer and I might, just might, tell you."

When George got back to the table, Peter grabbed the beer and drank deeply before belching rather noisily and breathing beer fumes all over his friend and colleague.

Flapping a hand in front of his face to dissipate the fumes, George stared hard at Peter before saying, "If you don't mind me asking… just how many of these have you had?" as he held up his glass.

"Oh, one or two," said Peter airily. "Nothing I can't handle."

"I'm not so sure about that," muttered George. Sipping on his beer, he asked, "So, what are we celebrating…some great scientific break-through?"

"Something like that, and, no, I'm not telling you. This is the stuff that will get me the Nobel Prize, just you wait and see."

"Well, at least you can give me an inkling, a mere hint, of your prize-winning discovery." Watching Peter drain his glass, he urged, "Come on, what gives?"

"My man," said Peter grandly but slightly slurred, "It's to do with transmutation of the elements…and unlocking almost unlimited power. I tell you, I've been looking at this all wrong…it's earth-shattering."

"What on earth…" stuttered George just as the pub doors swung open and in rushed Andrew Newman. Seeing the two friends and arch rivals sitting there, he darted over to their table and said, "Dr. Marshall, the hospital just rang. Apparently your wife slipped and fell, and the baby has started…I mean, she's just gone into labor."

"What?" slurred Peter. "What did you say?"

"There's been an accident at home and your wife had to be rushed to the hospital. They called and said she has gone into labor."

"Oh…" and Peter staggered to his feet. "I'd best get over there."

George and Andrew exchanged glances and Andrew said, "Look, I'll drive you over there. My car's just down the road. Hang on a moment here and I'll go get it."

"No, my car's here…I'll go over there myself."

"Dr. Marshall," persisted Andrew, "It might be best if I drove you…I think you've had a bit to drink and, uh…well it might be best."

"No," slurred Peter. "I'm fine…I'll be alright. I only had a couple of beers, nothing at all really."

Again George Martin and Andrew exchanged looks. They knew how stubborn Peter could be and trying to stop him would only cause a confrontation.

With a shrug, Andrew moved to one side and watched with horror as his boss and mentor weaved his way to the door. "Oh Lord," he muttered. "Please get him there safely."

Peter sat in the Maternity Ward waiting room, smoking too many cigarettes and feeling the combined effects of too much beer and insufficient food. Occasionally he would get up and pace the room, just like generations of fathers-to-be before him and probably all those who would come after him. As the wait continued, punctuated by the occasional rote reassurance of one or other staff nurse, Peter became increasingly restless. Deciding, he climbed to his feet and made his way out of the hospital and into the pub next door. "A couple of drinks'll help," he muttered to himself.

When he got back, decidedly the worse for wear, a nurse was waiting impatiently for him. "Dr. Marshall?"

"Yeah, thass me," slurred Peter.

Wrinkling her nose in disgust at the alcohol fumes emanating from the now very drunk Peter, she continued, "I'm sorry but some complications have developed."

"Complications…what sort of complications?" asked the befuddled Peter. "What's going on?"

Ignoring his question, the nurse continued, "We've called the senior Ob/Gyn specialist and he's with your wife now. We'll call you as soon as we know something."

"Oh, I see. Thass all right…I think I'll go and have a drink… be back shortly."

"Haven't you had enough already?" snapped the nurse but Peter was already on his way out the door.

When a very drunk Peter eventually got back to the waiting room, a tall distinguished-looking silver-haired man was standing there with a concerned look on his face, sadness combined with disapproval at Peter's state.

"Dr. Marshall?"

"Yeth, that's me," slurred Peter. "Who are you? Whadda you want?

"I'm Dr. Mills, the attending Ob/Gyn. in this hospital. I'm… er…well, I'm saddened to say that …we've lost your wife."

Peter just stood there, looking confused. What had this man just said? Had something happened to Jean? They had lost Jean? What was going on?

"She was very brave but complications set in. It is very rare but we tried everything and…" and the doctor watched in horror as Peter spun on his heel and rushed from the room, cannoning off the door frame. "Wait," he called. "Just wait a minute…listen to me." But Peter was already gone, the door swinging closed behind his retreating back.

Barely able to stand after putting down several whiskies, Peter staggered out of the pub. He went into the liquor store next door and bought a bottle of whiskey to take home. He couldn't, or wouldn't, take in what he had heard but decided to drink the night away. Was it possible that his Jean, that lovely and loving wife, the center of his universe, could be gone? What about the baby? What had happened? What gone so wrong? It was all so unfair.

He staggered to his car, climbed in and drove off erratically down the road trying to concentrate on driving. But the car had taken on a life of its own. It slammed into first one and then another parked car, before careening across the road and smashing into yet another parked car. Peter wrenched at the wheel but his small car bounced off another car the other side of the road before roaring through the intersection and into the oncoming traffic.

A dark shape fell across the hood of the car, lights flashed, sirens sounded, noise and broken glass everywhere, screams and shouts. What was happening? The car door was wrenched open and hands roughly grabbed him, pulling him out onto the road.

"Ah Christ," said a strange voice. "Yet another bloody drunk. You can smell him a mile away. Would you look at all those wrecked cars? This one's for the high jump and rightly so. Let's get him into the squad car and back to the station. He deserves everything that's coming to him…thank God no-one was killed…mind you, he tried hard enough, didn't he."

"Peter Marshall," intoned the judge. "You have pleaded guilty to driving under the influence of alcohol. Counsel has made a good case for mitigating circumstances and your guilty plea tells me that you clearly admit to your crimes rather than making futile protests as to your innocence. However, whereas I sympathize with the loss of your wife and child, there is no excuse for your blatant disregard of the law or for the safety of other road users. Your blood alcohol level was markedly above the legal limit and you were in no fit state to operate a vehicle. Further, your reckless behavior injured other wholly innocent road users and you caused many thousands of pounds of damage to other vehicles. Thankfully, and only by the grace of God, no-one was killed or severely injured." The judge stopped and looked balefully at the well-dressed man standing in the dock.

"Peter Marshall, your behavior, regardless of the causative circumstances, was wholly unbecoming that of a man of your education and intelligence. Therefore, I hereby sentence you to prison for a period of five years. You should be grateful that no-one was killed otherwise my sentence would have much harsher. I hope that this period of incarceration will be a lesson for you and that you will never again drink and drive. In order to prevent the repetition of such an occurrence, I hereby suspend your driving license for a period of seven years."

After the intake and the unceremonious pitching of Peter into his cell, his cell mate looked up from his bunk and nodded at him, "How long you in for?"

"Five years.…I, uh, was convicted for…"

"Look, let me give you a word of advice. No-one talks about why they're in here, only how long they're here for…what happened outside don't matter, not at all, unless of course you're in for child abuse or murder. If it's murder, then they'll leave you alone but if it's child abuse, well then, your life inside will be hell."

"No, nothing like that," Peter assured him.

"Good." The man paused and then added, "I'm Monk."

"I'm Peter, Peter Marshall but you said your name's Monk? That's it? No first name?"

"Nah, just Monk." Silence for a few moments. "You don't look like the type who usually comes here but I'll tell you what, with that fancy accent, you could be in trouble. What were you, a teacher?"

"University professor…Cambridge, you know."

"Oh, that's bad."

"Bad? Why bad?"

"You'll be a target faster than you can shake a stick. People here don't like fancy accents and most of them didn't finish high school. They don't like teachers in here."

"Really? What sort of target?"

"You don't want to know."

"Oh, I think I can take care of myself."

"No you bloody can't, not against them that are here. Even the screws are scared of some of them and those guys don't scare easily."

"Aren't you scared?"

"Me? Nah – I'm ex-SAS. They leave me well alone…at least now they do now after I put several them into the infirmary after trying it on with me. Very messy, it was."

"Oh, I see."

"Hey, Peter, don't look so worried. I tell you what, we're going to be here together for a long time and I don't want to have to listen to you crying yourself to sleep every night after they get you. Things are bad enough without that. Anyway, I'll teach you some things so you can take care of yourself…just in case I'm not around when they come after you, and they will."

"You'll teach me? You will? Why are you, uh, being so kind?"

"Let's just say that you'll owe me." Seeing the worried look on Pete's face, he added, "No, nothing like that. When you get out, you being a professor and all, you may be able to help someone else. You know, what goes round comes round, as they say. Fair enough?"

"I don't know what to say," stuttered Peter.

"Then don't. Say, you look pretty fit…play any contact sports?"

"Rugby in high school and at University, and I work out every week. Also play some squash, at least I used to."

"That's good. At least you ain't no pansy. Right, no time like the present…let's get started." And just like that, Peter started his training.

Over the months, Monk taught Peter everything he knew until Peter became almost as lethal as his mentor. The one brave soul who tried to corner Peter in the showers learned a painful lesson and Peter was left alone after that. Even the guards gave him a wide berth although Peter never gave them cause to be worried about him.

One day, after a particularly brutal work-out, Peter looked over at Monk and asked, "How'd you get into all this stuff?"

"You mean because I'm on the small side and not exactly heavy?"

"Yeah, I suppose so."

"Well, as kid I was short and skinny and was always getting bullied at school. So my dad, who used to be a professional fighter, taught me to box and it went from there. I was always in trouble at school and then I really got into trouble. The judge said I could go to prison or into the army, so I joined up."

"You did?"

"Yeah. First I was a paratrooper, being fit and active, and not too heavy. Then the SAS came calling and my training really began. I thought the paras were tough but they weren't nothing compared to those guys. Tell you what though, someone had a sense of humor once I got accepted."

"How so?"

"After you get trained, you get slotted into a team and my team had me, Monk, a guy called Priest, another guy called Bishop…and we also had Vickers and Abbott…and our sergeant was called Pope, would you believe? So we got called the Clergy. Mad buggers all of us but we worked well together. Whenever some heavy stuff was needed, they used to send the Clergy in, you know, to give them a taste of religion, as they say."

"How'd you end up here?"

"Stupid really. Some wanker was beating up his girlfriend and his mates were egging him on. I stepped in and sorted them out but I hit one guy harder than I should have. He died and here I am. Okay, enough of that ancient history, let's get back to work…you're a bit too slow in reacting at times. Also, never forget that it's them or you. Forget about giving someone a fighting chance. Lay them out and do it fast, understand? Never forget that you don't have any friends, not here, not anywhere…everyone's out to get you…you know, dog eat dog, so keep your lips zipped and your hands ready, okay?"

After his release, Peter wandered for a while. Leaving Monk had been hard. He was a man who wanted nothing from him except the one time he asked Peter to help him write a letter to his wife. "It's my missus, see? I'm in here for twenty years and she needs to find someone else. No point in her wasting her life waiting for me, you know what I mean? So, help me write that letter to her, you being educated and all. It's the right thing to do but I can't find the words, alright?"

"Surely that decision is for her to make."

"Yes it is but I've got to give her the opportunity to make it. Ain't fair to expect her to wait around for 15 to 20 years. I'll be an old man when I get out and she won't be much younger. No, got to give her permission to make a new life. You gonna help me?"

Peter missed Monk and his rough humor but gentle manner until he was provoked. He knew that life in prison could have been hell without Monk and he almost started to believe that there was a God after all when he thought about what could have been without his cellmate. As he wandered the streets trying to find somewhere to sleep, he almost missed prison.

The constant noise, the smells, the terrible food and the vicious inmates…all that combined with the incredible monotony and need to obey the shouted orders of the guards. At first, the prison social workers tried to get him to do anything that even vaguely related to his life outside.

"Come on, Marshall, you were a professor, an educated man. Try to write something…get that brain working again before it shuts down. You were a brilliant scientist, so don't let it go to waste."

Peter sat and wrote,

> The cat sat on the mat
> The dog barked
> The cow mooed
> And the sheep baa'ed

"What do you call this, Marshall? You trying to be funny or something? Write something proper and don't waste my time."

So he wrote,

> Jack and Jill ascended the elevation
> Up they went, hand in hand
> To fill a bucket of hydrogenated oxygen
> Jack upended himself and split his cranium
> And Jill tumbled thereafter

> Georgie Porgie was consuming foodstuffs
> He osculated the females and made them lachrymose
> When the male children came out to recreate
> Georgie Porgie decamped with haste.

"Alright Marshall, I get the picture. This is all very clever but you obviously don't want help and you don't seem to be willing to do anything. Message received, fair enough. I'll leave you alone. Just serve your time and go back to whatever awaits you out there."

Peter smiled to himself…whatever awaits you out there? What a joke. His life stopped dead when those heavy prison doors slammed closed behind him. Friends, colleagues and even his in-laws soon stopped visiting or even writing. The Peter Marshall they once knew was gone, and that man was unlikely to ever return. Time, tide and science wait for no man…so why should he be an exception?

FOUR

Peter walked down the street, headed towards the motorway that Nobby had mentioned. A hundred yards or so ahead he could see a car beside the road and a young woman crouching beside the vehicle and struggling with a lug wrench, trying to undo the wheel nuts. As he approached, the woman looked up, "I say, can you help me?"

Peter walked over, "What's wrong?"

"I've got a flat tire and I can't get these nuts loose…I want to put on the spare and get to a garage but I can't manage it. They're just too tight. Can you help, please?"

"That's the trouble with car wheels. When they are fitted, they tighten those nuts with power tools and it is almost impossible to get them off again," said Peter.

"I know, I know," said the woman. "Trouble is, the battery on my mobile's flat and dad can't help. I just got him out of the hospital and he's as weak as a kitten. Oh damn it all…damn, damn, damn."

"I'll try to help…don't worry."

Peter put down his bag and placed the lug wrench over a nut and stood on it. With lots of creaking, the wrench slowly turned and the nut was loosened. Eventually he got all five nuts loose enough to turn easily. Jacking the car up and replacing the wheel was a matter of minutes. Placing the wheel with a flat tire in the trunk, Peter wiped his hands on a rag in the trunk and started to walk off.

"Hey wait," called the woman. "Thank you very much…I don't know what we'd have done without you. It could have been hours before anyone came by and helped."

Peter shrugged, "It's nothing…glad to be able to help."

"Help? You've been a lifesaver. I've got to get dad home and into bed. Look, I don't know where you're headed but can we give you a lift somewhere? After that, I'll get dad home and then get that tire fixed. As I say, I can't thank you enough. Anyway, I'll drive you where you need to go. Besides, it's starting to rain, so hop in and you won't get wet, alright?"

Peter smiled at the woman's breathless outburst. "Thanks, I'd appreciate a lift."

As they got settled in the car and the woman finished fussing over her father, a pale, care-worn looking man bundled up on the rear seat, she eventually started the car and drove off towards the motorway.

"So, where are you headed, Mr. Kind Stranger?"

"Anywhere, nowhere."

"Really? Is that what you do, you know, help damsels in distress and then walk away? Not that I'm exactly a damsel, but you know what I mean," smiled the woman, looking at him curiously.

"Not too often but I do what I can," replied Peter.

"So, where are you headed? You don't look like your average hitchhiker…hey, you're not a serial rapist or a murderer on the loose are you?" asked the woman, half-jokingly but her voice tinged with concern.

"Not this week, I'm not," smiled Peter. "No, I just …I'm just off down South. Nowhere in particular, that's what."

"Down South? London? Why there?"

"It's as good a place as any, so…" and Peter lapsed into silence. As they drove, the woman chattered to him, telling Peter that they had a small bed-and-breakfast that she and her father ran. "It's a bit out of the way, you know, off the beaten track but we get a steady stream of guests and we do alright. In fact, we get a lot of repeats. People seem to like it there and we manage quite well." Apparently, she had left her home and job in London to help out after her mother had died and now, with her father being so ill and requiring hospitalization, her old life was truly over. "Not what I had planned, not at all, after graduating from the University and landing a good position in the Big Smoke" she said, using the slang description of London common in Northern England. As Peter sat looking straight ahead through the windshield, she added, "So what is it that you do, you know when you're not helping change flat tires and thumbing lifts to nowhere in particular?"

"Nothing."

"Nothing? What do you mean, nothing?"

"I don't do anything…as I say, nothing."

"Really? Not what I'd have expected from someone who talks like you do," she responded, making a clear allusion to his educated accent. "By the way, I'm Christie Hawkins. My friends and family all call me Chris. And you are?"

"Peter, Peter Marshall and my friends all call me Peter."

"Not Pete or Petey?"

"Nope, just Peter."

"So, Just Peter, how come you just happen to be in Northern England and were walking along that deserted street ready and willing to help change a tire?"

"A long story."

"I'm sure it is. Want to talk about it?"

"Not really, no."

"Okay. So where do you want me to drop you?"

"Don't drop him anywhere," came a voice from the back of the car. Chris' father had obviously woken up and had been listening to the exchange in the front of the vehicle. "If he's not got anywhere to go, why not bring him back with us. He can help out until I get back on my feet. A big guy like him can do all sorts of things around the place and you need help, so ask him to stop over with us."

"Okay, dad, okay," said Chris. "Looks like my father has decided for you. You okay with that?"

Peter hesitated for a few moments and then glanced back over his shoulder at the bundled figure in the back of the car. "If it's okay with you, Mr. Hawkins, then I should be delighted to stop over and help out…I should like that."

Chris, noting Peter's use of "should" rather than the more common but less grammatically correct "would", smiled and said, "So it's settled then, the boss has spoken. Well, Mr. Peter I Don't Do Anything and I'm Going Nowhere Marshall, it seems you're on board. Welcome, we're glad to have you."

Peter simply smiled. Fate, or was it God?, seemed to work in mysterious ways. One door closed, actually several doors had closed, but a new one had just opened. As he glanced over at Chris, he realized that she was younger than he first thought, being fooled by the severe glasses, functional haircut and minimal make-up. Not as beautiful as his Jean but definitely very attractive all the same, and a major cut above the women he had been associating with since his release from prison. Release from prison? There it was again, the 500 lb. gorilla in the corner of the room. What would Mr. and Ms. Hawkins say when it eventually came out that he had been inside? Would they be upset, even outraged and want to throw him out? Mentally he shrugged again. Nothing he could do about any of that and, as he had learned in prison, no point in worrying about the "what ifs or might bes", the present is what mattered now Still, he had trouble resisting the urge to think about what might be in the future.

As she drove, she and Peter chatted idly with the occasional interjection from the back seat. By mutual, but unspoken, agreement, neither of them talked about personal matters and Peter, for the first time in a very long time, found himself relaxing. He had forgotten the pleasure of conversing with an intelligent articulate person, and a woman at that. 'Ouch,' he thought. 'That's such a sexiest remark. An intelligent person is intelligent, regardless of gender…and with Chris being attractive to boot, then that's a bonus.'

Eventually they pulled off the busy motorway and drove through a couple of small towns and then a few villages, meandering through narrow country lanes bordered by stone walls and made beautiful with their canopies of overhanging tree branches. Occasionally the sun would peek out and the odd grazing horse or cow would raise its head to stare at them as they passed. Reading his thoughts, Chris said, "Bucolic, isn't it? Although London is bright, exciting and full of culture, it's all artificial, nothing is real. But there is something almost magical about the English countryside. Every time I drive through here, I feel blessed. Anyway, we're just about home."

The entrance to the driveway to the house was guarded by two large oak trees that leaned in towards each other, branches touching as though sharing secrets. The pebbled driveway wound its way between flower beds that bordered bright green and well-manicured lawns dotted with trees and the occasional large bush. The house itself was clearly old and constructed of stone with a slate roof and had lots of leaded-glass windows; it looked well-maintained and the large oak doors with their stained glass panels presented an inviting appearance. To one side of the entrance was a discreet sign bearing the legend,

Oak Tree Manor

A Guest House

'No wonder they have repeat customers,' thought Peter. 'This place is lovely. I can see why it wasn't too difficult for Chris to leave London and come back here. But, I'll bet, helping her father wasn't the only reason she returned. Somehow I feel that there's a broken heart or at least a failed marriage involved. Despite her brightness, I sense an underlying hurt there and a hidden but still evident distrust of men. I wonder who he was and why he was stupid enough to let her go. Whoa, now that was an interesting thought. Where did that come from?'

After they all climbed out of the car, Chris turned to Peter and said, "Let me quickly show you your room so you can unpack your things." The last words accompanied by a small smile and a nod at Peter's single hold-all. "Then I'll get dad settled in bed and perhaps we can meet up in the kitchen which is just down that corridor on the right. See you in a few minutes, okay?"

It was a medium size room on the third floor with a small bathroom attached, obviously a recent addition but nicely appointed with a shower, sink and a cabinet for his shaving gear, etc. The bedroom was papered with a neutral, vaguely modern wallpaper and the full-size bed had a firm comfortable mattress, as Peter confirmed when he plopped down to test it. Besides the bed, there was a chest of drawers and a wardrobe with a full-length mirror. As Peter stood in the middle of the room and slowly turned through 360 degrees to view it, he muttered, "So this is my new home, is it? Even if it's only temporary, it's very nice and a whole lot better than anywhere I've been in the last few years. Thank you, whoever you are that arranged this." For a moment he hesitated and said aloud, "I don't understand any of this but I thank you." A small shiver went through him. As a scientist, Peter had little inclination towards a religious bent but he felt that somehow something was guiding his steps but what? Was it fickle fate, a supreme being, what? His glance flicked over the cross hanging over the bed, the first one he had seen in a long while. He stood and stared at it for a long moment and then shook his head. Could all this be real or would he wake up, back in his jail cell again, listening to the moans and cries that saturated the night air. No, he decided, this is real but why? Why him and why now? There was no way anyone could have predicted the events of the last few days.

With a half-smile-half-grimace, he walked to the door and stepped out onto the landing. He walked slowly down the stairs, enjoying the slight give of the old oak steps and the polished feel of the bannisters. For a moment he speculated about the dozens, possibly hundreds, of people that had walked down these very stairs over the lifetime of the old place. What secrets were buried here, what joys and sorrows had the ancient walls seen and heard, he wondered. He laughed and said quietly to himself, "Hell, man, you've been in this house less than an hour and you're already caught up in the place. Come on, get real – you're a short-term employee here, so don't get any ideas and start investing too much in it. It could all be over in a flash, so get over it, right?"

He found the kitchen easily enough and could see that it was equipped with up-to-date appliances and great work surfaces for food preparation. A large butcher-block table was situated in the middle of the large room with old wood chairs set around it. Obviously this was a meeting place for the owners, staff and the odd guest that wanted to sit and chat. The atmosphere was distinctly comfortable with vestigial smells of fruit, spices and baking lingering in the air. In a word, it felt like home, the home he had never really had after he had turned 10 years of age. That was so long ago and he firmly shut down that childhood memory, a memory almost as painful as the loss of Jean and prison.

Sighing, he searched the cabinets and found a kettle. Filling it with water, he placed it on one large cooker to heat it for tea. He could see a fairly large hatch set in one wall and surmised, correctly, that it gave access onto the dining room where the guests would get breakfast and any other meals that were served here. While waiting for the kettle to boil, he searched some more and located a teapot and, in another cupboard, a canister of loose tea. Again those damn childhood memories came back and he stood still for a moment, wondering what was happening to him.

Just then, Chris bustled in, saying, "I see you found the tea things then? A cup of tea is something that'd be really welcome after this morning…thank you for taking care of things."

Peter shrugged. It was nothing and he felt useless just standing there waiting for Chris to return.

"Dad's settled then," said Chris. "He'll sleep for a couple of hours and then want something to eat, knowing him." She paused and asked, "Do you cook at all?"

"Not much…no real need." Seeing the disappointed look on Chris' face, he added, "But I can read a recipe so I'm sure that with a good cookbook, I can manage. I can follow written instructions rather well…after all, I used to be…" and then he stopped. Now was not the time to talk about his past, if ever.

"You used to be what, Peter?"

"Nothing…it's not important. Anyway, I can make tea and I'm not too bad with coffee either. What do you take in yours?" He hesitated, "What about your dad? Will he want some?"

"No, not for a while. We'll take care of him later when he wakes up. Of course then he'll want his usual full meal…and probably get sick on it from lying in bed after eating too much. Typical."

Peter smiled at the affectionate note of exasperation in her voice. Daughters and wives were all the same…always secretly glad to be able to take care of a parent, spouse or sibling but unable to resist voicing the odd complaint, however mild.

As they sat drinking their tea, Chris stretched and then reached for a notepad and pen. "I've got to start making a list of provisions… food to buy and that sort of thing." Seeing Peter's questioning look, she added, "We were closed for a few days while dad was in hospital but we've got guests coming tomorrow. So we've got to get the rooms ready…you know, beds made, rooms aired, clean linens… that sort of thing. We'll also have to get in fresh food and vegetables, not only for breakfast but some guests also want to have lunch and dinner. Not many, thank heavens, but enough to cause problems if we're not prepared for them."

As she busied herself making up a list, Chris was startled to realize that she was already including Peter in her planning…the "we" was clear evidence of that even though she had known the man for less than a few hours and he had only just got to Oak Tree Manor. What was it about Peter that made her feel so comfortable around him? He was, after all, a complete stranger and one with lots of secrets, that was for sure. In her experience, most men could not wait to spill out their life history and usually did so at length and boringly to boot. Peter, on the other hand, said nothing about himself and when he veered close to something personal, he shut down, shrugging it off with a careless "It's nothing important".

List complete, Chris got to her feet and looked down at Peter. "Will you clear the dishes while I go up and check on dad? If everything's okay, I'll check that the daily help is coming in…she'll watch over him while we go to the market…you don't mind helping me load the van up, do you?"

Peter smiled and shook his head, "Not a problem." As he got to his feet, he thought, 'Well, fancy having a female boss at my age. Chris seems embarrassed to give me orders, however pleasantly they are phrased. She doesn't realize, cannot possibly know, that I got used to being ordered about by people who were a lot less pleasant and far less educated than she is. Three years in prison does wonders in regards to taking orders!'

They waited until the daily help, Mrs. Meadows, came bustling in. Peter stood idly by as she and Chris exchanged greetings and hugs, and the pleasantly plump older woman peppered Chris with questions about her father and when the guests would be returning. Eventually they quietened down and Peter was introduced to Mrs. Meadows… "Just call me Mabel, dear" she assured him. "We're family here and nothing's too formal. My daughter Lucy also comes in, usually first thing to help serve breakfast and do some of the cleaning…that's when she's not been with that no-good boyfriend of hers all night. Can't stand him but he's good to Lucy, so I can't say anything although I don't see what she sees in him…young man like that should go and get a job instead of lounging around on the dole, him being educated and all. Goes to the Uni and sits around doing nothing…waste of an education, that."

Finally Chris and Peter were able to get away and headed towards the van parked out back followed by the sound of Mabel's assurances that she would take care of Mr. Hawkins while they were out. As they pulled around to the front of the building, Chris said, "I love Mabel to death but she does go on a bit at times. Still, she has a heart of gold and she really is more family than an employee."

"How did she come to work at Oak Tree Manor?" asked Peter.

"She lives in the village…in fact we passed their cottage on the way in this morning. She's been with my parents, when my mother was alive, for years. Her husband, now retired, used to be the local constable and I suspect he's only too happy for Mabel to come to the manor every day just so he can get some peace and quiet."

"He's a policeman?" asked Peter, a faint note of anxiety creeping into his voice…something that Chris noted but did not comment on. 'So, Peter is wary of the police, is he?' she thought. 'I wonder what that's about? He doesn't look like a criminal to me although I really have no idea what criminals usually look like. Yet another mystery.'

"He was…he's retired now and spends most of him pottering around in his garden and meeting up with his old codger friends, usually over a couple of pints at the pub. You'll meet them all soon enough. As soon as they hear that there's someone new here, they'll come beetling around just so they can say they met you. Typical village life, in case you didn't know. Since we do have a miniscule bar, they'll buy some drinks and that will help the week's takings."

As they drove, Chris pointed out the village church, a small very attractive stone building with an adjacent burial ground set a short distance back from the road. "We'd like to attend more than we do but having to serve breakfast to our guests seven days a week, we have to pass on the Sunday morning service. But we do go to the Saturday evening service…sometimes I suspect the Vicar opens the church up just so that dad and I can attend. Surprisingly, several villagers also attend, particularly when there's a good match on the telly or they want to get out and about doing something other than attend church." She paused for a moment and then asked, "Are you religious…I mean, spiritual? You know, believe in God?"

"Not really," said Peter. "I haven't seen too much evidence of His existence."

"Oh, it's there alright…just look around. Do you really believe that everything around us," Chris waved at the passing scenery, "is really all an accident? Some freak of nature or random but natural selection? All that Darwinian stuff?"

"I don't know," said Peter, his voice tinged with sadness. "I just don't know. As I say, if God really does exist, He hasn't done the best job of making His existence known to us, as Bertrand Russell used to say."

"Bertrand Russell?"

"The mathematician…he's the one that defined a number… smart fellow."

Chris glanced at Peter, wondering about him anew. Quoting Bertrand Russell and even knowing about his work…not what one might expect from your average hitchhiker. Just who is this Peter Marshall? What an enigma.

Peter also lapsed into silence. Again he had accidentally dropped something about himself and he knew that Chris had caught that one, although she was astute enough to let it go without comment. 'Does God exist?' he asked himself. At one time he would have said "No", especially after Jean had died and his world had come crashing in. But now, he wasn't quite so certain. Sharing a cell with Monk, who turned out to be his savior, was something totally unexpected. Even more surprising was Monk's spirituality. Not what one might have expected in a lethally effective killer. Then there was the meeting with Nobby and the drive up North to get away from London. He saved Nobby from a nasty thumping, a small repayment for his kindness. Then there was being on hand to help Chris change her flat tire and now becoming a member of the household at Oak Tree Manor. Were these all coincidences…being in the right place at the right time…or was it something else? He shook his head, 'What?' he asked himself, 'is going on with me? Even thinking such thoughts is alien behavior for me…so what is going on with me?'

Eventually Chris broke the silence but wondering what Peter had been thinking about. His face had been devoid of expression but she sensed it was something to do with her question about spirituality. "We'll be at the warehouse soon. By the way, will you be coming to church with us…at least with me anyway while dad's recovering?"

Peter shrugged, "Why not?" he said, thinking 'If it makes Chris happy, why not indeed?' He paused mentally…makes Chris happy? When was the last time he cared whether someone else was happy? Whoa…something strange *is* going on.

The van loaded, Peter went back inside the warehouse to use the bathroom. Emerging out into the sunlight, he saw Chris surrounded by a group of young men dressed in the leather gear of bikers. As he got closer, Peter recognized them as the same gang who had been hassling Nobby and now they were having fun with Chris, taunting her.

"Hey, looks like you've got a load of food here. What about cooking us some lunch, sweetie?" called one of them.

"Yeah," said another. "Pity to let all this food go to waste…so what about it darlin'?"

As Peter got closer he recognized King Rocker, who looked over at Peter's approach and immediately saw who it was. At that moment, his attitude changed and he called out, "Sorry, mate. We were just joking with her…didn't mean any harm, did we?" Looking at his friends, he said, "Okay lads, time to be moving," and he walked quickly to his bike and fired it up. The others, also recognizing Peter, did the same and within seconds, all of them had driven off in a cloud of exhaust fumes.

Chris looked at the retreating bikers and then at Peter. "What was all that about, Peter?"

"What d'you mean?" replied Peter.

"Oh come on, man. One minute they were giving me a hard time…not unusual for that lot…I tell you, that gang's been a menace around here for a long time…like to cause trouble for its own sake.

Anyway, they were just getting started and then you walk up and they take off like lambs."

Peter shrugged and made a dismissive gesture with his hands.

"No, Peter, no good trying to plead ignorance. That lot knew you from somewhere and they were as scared as hell of you. What's going on? What happened with them?"

"Nothing."

"Nothing? A gang of bikers get scared enough to take off as soon as they see you and you call it nothing? What aren't you telling me?"

Peter hesitated. He could see that Chris was not going to be satisfied with his usual non-response to questions. "Ah…well, I helped the last guy who gave me a lift with that same bunch. Happened the other day and they recognized me, that's all."

"That's all? Just how did you "help" this friend of yours…help him to the point that six or seven of those toughs all take off in a hurry when they see you. That must have been some help you gave him. The thing is, just what did you do?"

"Nothing much. Nobby, the guy I helped, was being…er… being harassed and I helped him out, that's all."

"Hmm," said Chris. "I sense that you helping him out didn't involve changing a flat tire but no matter…obviously you aren't going to say anything about it but it does make me wonder." She looked at Peter and furrowed her brow, "Somehow you don't look like an avenging angel but whatever you are, or whoever you are for that matter, you always seem to turn up just when help is needed and you can even scare the bejabbers out of people up to no good. It's all very strange. Well, we'd best get back…standing here isn't going to do anyone any good. Come on, get in. We'll talk about this some other time but I must tell you, you do make me wonder."

As she drove, Chris thought about what had happened or, more correctly, had not happened. A bunch of roughs took one look at Peter and drove off in a hurry. Sure he was big but not that big yet he had scared them witless, even to the point of them apologizing. What was it with this man? She wished her father was well enough for her to talk to him about Peter. Clearly her dad liked Peter and must have seen something in the man that made him want to have her bring Peter back to the manor and help out. It was all so complicated. 'Oh well, I'd best shut up and see what happens next,' she said to herself. 'If nothing else, having Peter around is definitely interesting and no matter why or how, his intervention certainly saved me from trouble with those bikers. It is all very strange – no doubt about that.'

Peter sat quietly in the passenger seat, looking at the passing countryside. 'Funny how those bikers turned up again,' he thought. 'Pity that Chris had to see that but at least I was in the right place and at the right time for her yet again. Well, thank you Monk… all those lessons, hard as they were, paid off yet again.'

The return to Oak Tree Manor was uneventful and Chris and Peter soon unloaded everything. "Tell you what, Peter," said Chris. "You go and wash up and I'll throw some lunch together for you, Mabel and me, and something for dad when he wakes up. After that we'll get started on the guest rooms, okay?"

Peter nodded, "Sounds fine…thank you. Back here in say half an hour?"

"Yes, take your time but 30 or so minutes should do it since I'm just pulling something out of the fridge and warming it up. If you've got time, take a look round the place. You might as well see what needs to be done after we've had lunch."

Peter nodded again, "Okay – will do. Anything special that I need to look out for?"

"No, nothing special. Everything's pretty straightforward. If you see Mabel, tell her lunch'll be ready shortly."

After lunch and Chris had checked in on her father, the three of them got on with readying the rooms for expected guests. Sometimes Peter worked with Chris, others he helped Mabel.

When they were finished, the two women sat down together over a late coffee and shooed Peter off into the garden for the smoke he obviously was dying to have.

"He's a good worker that man. How'd you find him Chris?" asked Mabel. "For a good-looking intelligent chap like that, it's surprising that he's willing to muck in and do anything that's needed. How'd you meet him…and what's his story for that matter? Somehow, it doesn't fit, that's what I'm thinking."

"Ah, it's a long story and, yes, I agree, Peter doesn't fit but he's here and I'm glad of the extra help, I really am."

"But what's his story…how did you meet him?"

"It's a long story," said Chris, "and all a bit strange."

After she had finished relating the story of the flat tire and then the incident at the warehouse, Mabel sat back in her chair and looked hard at Chris. "That is odd, isn't it? He looks as though he can take care of himself but to be ready to take on half a dozen young thugs is a bit more than just being able to take care of yourself. Also, did you notice how careful he was in making up the beds and cleaning? He's the first man I've known who even cared about a well-made bed let alone was prepared to do it."

"I noticed that too," said Chris. "As for his story…I've no idea. Whenever we get anywhere close to personal things, he shies away like a spooked horse. He looks honest and works hard enough, so perhaps we should just let well enough alone."

"Perhaps you're right," agreed Mabel. "I wonder what my old man would make of him."

Chris, slightly alarmed at the turn in the conversation and remembering Peter's reaction to hearing that Mabel's husband was a retired policeman, hastily said, "Let's not say anything to Nigel for the moment. Don't want to create waves until we know more about Peter. Is that okay with you?"

"Alright," agreed the mystified Mabel. "If that's what you want…" although she had her doubts whether Chris was right in not wanting anything said. 'What if Peter…what was his last name? Marshall?… what if he's an escaped prisoner? Surely they could get in trouble for harboring a fugitive, couldn't they?' went her thoughts. 'He doesn't look like a criminal but who could tell these days?' Mentally she shrugged. She'd keep her mouth shut for the moment, and possibly even warn Lucy to do the same, but still she wondered. On the other hand, Mabel had to admit she did enjoy having a good-looking man around and Chris certainly liked him. Perhaps something might get going there? At least she hoped so. It wasn't right that an attractive young woman like Chris should be buried away here in the country with no men around. All of the local men were married, at least all the eligible ones were and the rest didn't bear thinking about. Nah, say nothing and wait to see what happens was her final decision. It'll all work out one way or the other. Life was like that.

The gang of bikers sat down at a table in their favorite café, huddled over mugs of tea and wreathed in clouds of cigarette smoke, oblivious to the prominent No Smoking signs. "So," said one of them who had missed the first encounter with Peter Marshall. "Who was that bloke?"

"Which one?" responded King Rocker.

"That one back there," said the man with a vague wave in the direction of the warehouse.

"I dunno but he's bad news, that's what."

"He didn't look that scary to me," persisted the other man. "We could've taken care of him – easy."

"Yeah? Let me tell you, he could've taken us all on with one hand tied behind his back and no mistake."

"He didn't look like much to me, did he?"

"Well, let me tell you, if you'd seen him in action, you wouldn't be so cocky now, and no mistake. Funny thing is how he just turns up out of nowhere and for no reason. Weird."

"So, he's some sort of bogeyman is he?" laughed the other man. "Get real, why don't you?"

The conversation then moved onto safer ground and they started to discuss the local and National soccer teams.

FIVE

Dr. George Martin strode up the steps of the Ministry of Energy and Natural Resources in Whitehall, London. He had become successful since the tragedy that had overtaken his friend and arch-rival Peter Marshall. He was now a Fellow of Royal Imperial College, a Fellow of the Royal Society, the World's most prestigious scientific society, and had been appointed as a Deputy Scientific Advisor to the Ministry. This position was well-paid and prestigious, so George now was relatively affluent and enjoyed the respect and esteem of his colleagues - things were going well for him and he relished his success. On the odd occasion that it crossed his mind, he missed his old friend and colleague Peter and still wondered why the man had rejected every advance and overture of friendship from former friends, colleagues and family after he went to prison. They all were aware that what had happened was tragic and a major departure from Peter's normally conservative approach to life. Although he could be slightly raucous at times, he generally enjoyed a relatively quiet life and was not one to be wild or go off the rails, especially not after he and Jean had married. "No, not him at all" was the general consensus and this complete turning away from his old life was inexplicable.

'The trouble is,' he admitted to himself. 'Peter was brilliant and he obviously was on the verge of a major breakthrough in energy generation but then everything went to hell in a hand-basket as they say.' The tantalizing snippets from Peter's former technician Andrew Newman, his obscure comments and the few scribbled notes that he, George, had rescued from the table at the pub on that fateful day indicated that Peter was either on the verge of making, or had already made, a major theoretical breakthrough in the field of energy generation. 'But,' as he often asked himself. 'What precisely was he thinking?' The comment Peter had made about a Nobel Prize was no joke…that just wasn't Peter's style. He was far too literal, and modest, for that sort of facetious or boastful comment.

George had been working for two or three years trying to unravel the mystery, to no avail and now things had reached a crisis point. The Ministry had been funding, very generously, his research and the Pied-Piper had presented his bill. As the lift carried George Martin upward to the senior level floor, he felt slightly nauseous. The Right Honorable James Arthur Llewellyn-Hughes, the Permanent Under-secretary, was no fool…in fact he had a brilliant mind. If he had not been recruited by the Civil Service, he would probably have achieved the same professional and public eminence as Lord George Porter, Sir Charles Snow and several other luminaries of modern British science. Llewellyn-Hughes was a very senior civil servant, often referred to as a Whitehall Mandarin by the media and, out of earshot, by his more junior colleagues. Accordingly, he carried a big stick and wielded enormous power. If he was "sold" on a project, he could release considerable funding but, as he always warned grant supplicants, if the grantee did not deliver the promised results, then the consequences could be dire. Now Dr. George Martin was about to learn what those dire consequences could be, and he was very nervous.

George had persuaded Llewellyn-Hughes that he could advance and bring to completion Peter Marshall's theoretical work on elemental transmutation, affording almost limitless power at minimal cost. He had glossed over the fact that he was piggy-backing on someone else's work; in fact, he had not even mentioned Peter Marshall's existence and that deliberate, self-serving omission was about to come back and bite him…hard!

At the time, it had seemed all so easy. Based on a few chance remarks, scraps of notes and some gleaning of disparate data, George Martin had designed a research project. He was convinced that he could make the same breakthrough that Peter had alluded to. It was just a matter of time, good resources and dedication. After all, as he had told himself on many occasions, I'm just as good as he is.

When George had made his initial presentation to Llewellyn-Hughes, the civil servant had listened carefully and then sat back in his padded leather chair, staring hard at the Cambridge don. The large expanse of his desk separated them, a clear indication of the power and authority of one and the supplicant role of the other.

"Transmutation of the elements? Hmm…interesting. This is nothing like that foolish notion of cold fusion proposed several years back…by Fleischman and Pons, if my memory serves me?" said the Minister. "Utter bosh, wasn't it?"

"Yes," agreed George. "That was a strange concept and one without any real scientific basis. No, it's nothing like that here, not all. The science is solid." Notwithstanding his assurances to Llewellyn-Hughes, if George had been strictly honest with both himself and Llewellyn-Hughes, he would have had to admit that even he was uncertain whether his own interpretation of scientific theory actually supported his projections. 'Damn you, Peter Marshall, why were you so secretive?' he thought. 'If you had been more forthcoming, we could have worked on this together but, no, you wanted the glory all for yourself.' George's thoughts regarding Peter's apparent reluctance to share his ideas blithely ignored the fact that he, George Martin, had flat out refused to share anything with Peter in the past. In fact, he had actively worked against the other man on the odd occasion.

"I see," murmured Llewellyn-Hughes. "Now, I have perused your submission and some of my staff," said with a negligent wave of his hand, "have also read your proposal very carefully. Although we all have some doubts, we feel that there is merit in this project. Accordingly we will fund it for three to five years and we will review progress on an annual basis. That satisfy you?"

The way Llewellyn-Hughes had expressed himself, it was very clear that it was he, and he alone, that had made the funding decision. But, despite the amiable demeanor of the civil servant, George Martin was well-aware that he had to produce…partial success was not an option and here he was, after three years and a huge expenditures of time and money, with no success at all. As he walked down the corridor to Llewellyn-Hughes' office, he felt nauseous and had an incredible urge to empty his bladder and void his bowels.

After he had been ushered into Llewellyn-Hughes' office by his PA, George stood uncertainly in the doorway, waiting to be acknowledged by him as he sat reading what appeared to be his latest report. Eventually Llewellyn-Hughes looked up and waved George to the chair in front of his desk, "Sit down, Martin," he commanded. His displeasure was evident by the use of George's last name without the customary "Doctor" or "Professor" and a distinctly cold manner. As George surmised, this was going to be an unpleasant interview.

After a hard stare at George Martin and several seconds of silence, he said, "So, there has been no progress – at least none to speak of. Is that correct?"

"Yes, but…"

"No "buts" please, Martin. There has been an enormous amount of resources devoted to this…this cheap energy project of yours… and still there is nothing. What went wrong? What happened with all those promises…indeed, assurances…that you gave me?" Tapping the report on his desk, he continued, "And who, might I ask, is this Peter Marshall you mention out of the blue? This is the first I have heard of him…why only now?"

George Martin nervously cleared his throat and then launched into an account of what happened with Peter and how he had tried to take over his work.

"I see," said Llewellyn-Hughes speculatively. "It seems that we have a degree of plagiarism here?"

"Not really, no," George said hastily. "I tried to follow a…er…a tentative lead that I got from a chance remark, an aside if you will, that Peter Marshall made."

"Hmm, still sounds like plagiarism at best, theft of an idea at worst. So, where is this Peter Marshall now?"

"I don't know."

"You don't know?" asked Llewellyn-Hughes incredulously. "Just where did he go, this mystery man? Surely, if you stole his ideas, you must have some appreciation of where he is?"

"Actually no," responded an increasingly uncomfortable George Martin. The accusations of plagiarism and theft had stung but he had no option but to confess what had happened. After collecting his thoughts, he proceeded to relate the circumstances of Peter's arrest, incarceration and ultimate dropping out of society.

"Are you telling me that this brilliant scientist…I assume that he *is* brilliant from what you are saying…has just vanished? Really?" asked Llewellyn-Hughes. He stared at George Martin and then said, "So, this man made an incredible breakthrough, loses his wife in childbirth, gets drunk, wrecks lots of cars and is sent to prison. Then, after he goes to prison and serves his time, he drops out of society and no-one has heard of him since? Really?"

"Yes…he's gone but no-one knows where."

"I hope that he had has not gone over to the other side, to China, North Korea or somewhere…or, Heaven forbid, Iran?"

"No, I very much doubt it."

"Oh? Why so?" queried Llewellyn-Hughes.

"Peter was apolitical and, frankly, it would take more than money to betray his country which is what working for China, Iran and the like would be."

"I see," said Llewellyn-Hughes, who then sat back and stared first at the ceiling and then at George Martin for some minutes. Finally he said, "I surmise from what you have *not* said that this Peter Marshall is probably essential to any success you might have with *his* project, yes?"

"Well," said George hesitantly, "He could be useful, yes."

"Given the habitual understatement of you Cambridge chaps," said Llewellyn-Hughes, with the customary condescension of Oxford graduates towards those from their Oxbridge rival, Cambridge University, "I take it that this Marshall fellow is more than essential, undoubtedly vital, to any putative success." As he watched George's face redden, he could not decide whether it was due to anger or embarrassment. He waited a few beats, enjoying the other man's discomfiture, and added, "No matter. I shall set Special Branch onto finding him for you. I'm sure they will be more successful in finding him than you have been working on his idea without him. Now, toddle off back to Cambridge and we'll be in touch. I expect you'll hear from Special Branch in a day or two."

Looking down again at George's report and tapping it with a well-manicured finger nail, he added, "We'll hold off on this for the moment. You understand, yes? Also, when they find Marshall, you'll have to exert your best efforts to get him to come back into the fold and work on this." The last accompanied by another tap of a finger nail. "Oh by the way, start to trim your budget."

George Martin sat staring at Llewellyn-Hughes for a few seconds. Obviously his funding would be restricted and then, as an afterthought, he asked himself whether Llewellyn-Hughes, even as senior as he was, really had the power to arrange for Special Branch, the "political" police of the United Kingdom, to look for the missing Peter Marshall. Deciding that Llewellyn-Hughes *did* have that power, he got to his feet and bade the other man "goodbye", receiving only a dismissive wave in response. The man had spoken and the death knell for the project, *his* project, was starting to sound loud and clear. He would have to do some soul-searching on the journey back to Cambridge as he came to fully appreciate what the possible outcome could be from the morning's interview. Riding down in the elevator, he muttered, "Shit…this is bad, no – catastrophic. Much as I hate the thought of it, I hope Special Branch does find Peter. If they don't, my career could easily go up in flames…or is it down in flames? Either way, that miserable git Llewellyn-Hughes was right about Peter…he really is vital to my success. *My* success? Huh, that possibility just went out the window. And what if Peter refuses? That doesn't bear thinking about."

As he emerged from the building onto the sidewalk, looking for a taxicab, he thought, 'I always believed that it was the Lord who giveth and taketh away…now it seems that role has fallen to Llewellyn-Hughes, and he's a whole lot less forgiving than the Lord! Well, we'll see what happens next. If Peter isn't found or, worse, refuses to help, then I am in very deep trouble. Oh man, what a mess…and all because of my stupid arrogance. Talk about retribution.'

Sitting in the train on his return to Cambridge, George Martin started to worry about what would happen next. As he mulled things over, he remembered the wry comment of the eminent theoretical physicist Niels Bohr, "Prediction is very difficult, especially when it's about the future."

It had started out with such promise. The work was sound enough and there were some exciting early findings. There were indications that transmutation of the elements did occur and word had got out, as it usually does within the garrulous scientific community. George Martin's star was in the ascendant. He became a Fellow of his college, a signal honor and a clear indication that he had become one of the elite at Cambridge University. Then he was invited into the Royal Society and Dr. George Martin was now one of the leading figures in the Scientific Establishment of the United Kingdom. Nevertheless, things were not working out as George had hoped, in fact the results were almost the exact opposite of what he had hoped for and expected.

The predicted reaction sequences just did not occur and George did what most people would do in his position. He recruited more research fellows and invested more heavily in the very latest scientific equipment; after all, as he rationalized, the Ministry was paying for it and it was obviously only a matter of time before he achieved the predicted success. Through the Ministry's intervention, he now had access to the facilities at the nation's leading atomic energy research establishment and he had been able to recruit even more research fellows, graduates from the country's leading universities, the best and brightest of young minds. With each passing day, more data poured out and George thoroughly enjoyed meeting with his now large research team for morning coffee and daily discussion of the latest findings. Although the findings were sound enough, even quite exciting, his objective was as far away as ever. The bright hopes had started to dim. His research meetings went from a daily occurrence to a weekly and then to a monthly meeting. The research team worked diligently and enthusiastically but George no longer shared their enthusiasm or excitement.

Forward progress slowed and then stopped altogether. Contradictory findings started to appear. At first there were small deviations from expected behavior, reactions not occurring as fast as predicted and sometimes not even happening at all. The minor negative trends became the norm. The euphoria induced by the apparent initial successes was evaporating – solid progress was still being made but not in the direction that George wanted or predicted and the magic disappeared. As the spacing between George's laboratory visits and sit-downs with the researchers widened, the team became more embarrassed, and secretive, about their negative results. They avoided contact with Dr. Martin as much as they could and only the most senior people bothered to discuss things with George when he did appear. They all knew that science could be a hit-or-miss affair, major breakthroughs being rare occurrences. As Dr. Jarvis, the most senior researcher put it, "I should love to walk into the lab one morning, shake a test-tube and shout 'Eureka!' before writing off to the Nobel Committee in Stockholm. Sadly, it's usually more a case of 'Oh shit, what broke now?' and getting out the soldering iron to make repairs."

The peripheral findings were good and the research team justifiably took pride and pleasure in what they were achieving but they all knew that they were not anywhere near satisfying the private dreams of Dr. George Martin, whatever they might be. Morale plummeted and some even left to find other positions, no longer willing to put up with the morose behavior of their professor and team leader.

George started to walk through the labs late in the evening and often through the night. Peering at the notebooks and gathering up the odd stray notes of his team, he made copious notes on all the data, whether or not it was directly related to transmutation of elements. He studied recorder charts, diagrams and every scrap of data he could find, convinced his people were missing vital information or, worse, hiding things from him. Anything that he found interesting he took and the files in the locked drawers of his desk became voluminous.

At first the absence of notes and loose data went unnoticed but eventually George's actions started to affect the team's productivity. Most scientists tended to be untidy, if not sloppy, and it was always assumed that if something was mislaid, it would eventually turn up again. Although they wondered why George would question them closely on experimental results generated weeks if not months previously, it occurred to no-one that Dr. Martin could actually be taking their research data.

George's paranoia slowly built. When one or other scientist's hazy memory of past work differed from his own voluminous notes,

notes assembled from the very data he had secretly removed from that researcher's own files, he would accuse that person of fabricating his results, demanding to see data that he himself had removed from his or her records. When that team member had to admit that they did not know something or had simply forgotten it, George Martin would dismiss them curtly and write notes to the effect that this or that person was unreliable, evasive or was a flat-out liar in the personnel dossiers. "They are doing this on purpose just to ruin me but I'll show them, I really will. They won't get away with it."

Then came the summons to the Ministry.

Peter had settled into the routine at Oak Tree Manor and Chris was delighted that he was there. With her father still recovering, she had to rely more and more on Peter to do any and all heavy lifting and she was delighted to find that he was a very capable handyman. No longer did she have to call in an electrician or a plumber for the frequent small but annoying breakdowns that occur in any guesthouse catering to myriad visitors. Despite their best efforts at routine maintenance, accidents happened and even the most careful guests could damage fittings, and that was where someone like Peter came in. The ability to quickly and effectively undertake repairs was a very valuable commodity, and made a big difference to the profit-and-loss statements of Oak Tree Manor. Peter had also proved to be adept at serving meals, attending to the odd guest or passer-by requiring drinks from the small bar at lunch time or in the evening. He even helped out with preparing meals on the odd occasion when she, Chris, and or Mabel were caught up in other duties. The need to take care of her father consumed a lot of Chris's time and, on a daily basis, she silently thanked fate or whatever it was that brought Peter here and into their lives.

As Chris said to her father one day as he lay in bed slowly recovering his health and strength, "Dad, that Peter has proved to be a God-send. It's so strange…he's not what one might have expected."

"That he is but what were you expecting girl?"

"I don't know but it wasn't someone who can do what he does and willingly to boot."

"What's wrong with that, Chris?"

"Actually nothing – I was just wondering, that's all. He just doesn't fit the image of a hitch-hiker or someone who's on the road a lot…what used to be called a tramp in the old days. He's so…I don't know…private is a good word to describe him. He speaks well, is obviously intelligent and seems to be in excellent health – even his teeth are in great shape. It just doesn't add up, that's what."

"Chris, let me tell you something. If a man doesn't want to talk about himself, leave him alone. He'll talk when, and if, he wants. Pressing him won't do any good, and might even frighten him off." Mr. Hawkins stopped for a few moments, gathering his breath, and then said, "Chris, everyone has secrets and this Peter of yours is probably no different. Let him alone, girl, just leave him be."

Chris, startled by the "your Peter" comment, looked at her father. "Okay, I understand…at least I think I do. But you said "My Peter"…why do you say that?"

"I can see the look on your face when you talk about him…no surprise since he's a good looking fellah and I can tell you think the world of him. Just from what you and Mabel say, he's a life-saver for this place, and no mistake. So, my girl, just be careful what you say. I don't want to lose him and I'm sure that you don't either…at least not because of some female curiosity. As I say, he'll talk when he's good and ready, and not before."

"Okay, dad, okay…I hear you. Now, how are you feeling? The doctor says you are making good progress but it'll still be a while yet before you can be up and about."

"I know, I know…and that's why I tell you to back off from Peter. He's something special that man and I want to keep him here even after I'm fit and well again. That's the trouble when one gets older, it takes so damn long to get well."

With a nod of agreement, Chris leaned over and kissed her father's cheek, "Oh dad, you're so smart and, yes, I'd love Peter to stay on. Even Mabel and her daughter Lucy love him…actually I think Lucy has designs on him although I don't see any reciprocal interest from Peter."

Mr. Hawkins laughed, "See, just as I said, your Peter! Now, away with you girl and let me get some sleep…and remember what I said."

As Chris went downstairs to return to the kitchen, she thought about those comments and stopped in her tracks. Although she would follow her father's advice, she still couldn't help but wonder what secrets lay behind Peter's quiet demeanor. As her father said and she agreed, he was something special and there was something very different about him…but what? Why was he so different from the other men that she had known? What was it about him and why did he seem to be such a walking contradiction. 'Ah well,' she decided, 'I'll be patient even if I'm longing to know more about him. Maybe he'll open up at some time. At least, she sniffed, he's not letting Lucy ensnare him.' Chris laughed at herself; Lucy was a very good-looking young woman and if she found Peter attractive, something she was prey to herself, who could blame her for trying to hook up with him. At least for the time being, Peter Marshall might still be "her Peter" but for how much longer? In fact, how much longer would he stay at Oak Tree Manor? Would he just up and leave one day? After all there was nothing keeping him there and that realization stopped her short. 'Nothing keeping him here? Was that something she needed to address…but how?'

Shaking her head, she resumed her walk towards the kitchen and a welcome mid-morning coffee. With a tinge of pleasure, she realized that Peter and Mabel would be there seated at the table, happily chatting and waiting for her to join them. Maybe she and Peter would have to go the market again if they had any lunch and dinner reservations. A drive with the taciturn Peter would be yet another small pleasure to break up the day.

Early the next day, Chief Superintendent Ernest Miller had been called into the office of the head of Special Branch, a most unusual occurrence. He was handed a slim file by Commander Wilson and told, "Find this man, and fast. One of the Mandarins wants him found and made it very clear to me that this has high priority."

Miller quickly perused the file and looked up at his superior. "This is pretty thin isn't it?" he asked. "Any idea what it's all about, sir?"

"Not a clue. So, who will you put on this?"

Miller paused for a few seconds and then said, "Inspector Parsons."

"John Parsons?" asked the other man with a note of incredulity. "Isn't he getting on a bit…about to retire, I believe? I imagine he's a bit past it now?" He paused for a moment and then continued, "I know that Parsons used to be very good, one of the best actually, but now?"

"Oh, he's still very good. He might be going out to pasture soon but if anyone can find that Marshall fellow, it will be John Parsons."

"Hmm," muttered Wilson. "Well if you think he's still up to it, then…but he'd better find the fellow, and soon."

"John, old son," began Inspector John Parsons's younger and much more elegantly dressed superior as he draped himself on the visitor's chair beside Parsons's desk and stared with distaste at the overflowing ashtray.

Parsons looked up and tapped more ashes from his pipe into the ashtray, "Yes…sir?"

"The higher ups have got their nickers in a twist over something, actually over someone."

"Really?" asked Parsons, by now thoroughly disenchanted with the periodic and usually pointless flap that agitated senior Special Branch officers when one or other senior person in the Government required their involvement in some matter. What was claimed to be urgent or of highest priority usually turned out to be quite minor.

Tossing a slim file onto Parsons's desk and sending a shower of ash across the entire surface, he added, "It seems someone somewhere wants us to find this fellow…one Peter Marshall. So John, drop everything and look into it, will you?"

Although expressed as a request, Parsons knew that Chief Superintendent Miller had issued a firm order and he had to comply. As the other man walked out of Parsons's office, he added, "Keep me informed of progress, will you? Those that must be obeyed want results and fast, okay?"

Muttering to himself, Parsons pushed what he had been working on to one side and pulled the file to the front of his desk, thinking, 'This file is pretty thin for something so urgent, at least something so important to someone very senior. I wonder what gives.'

After he had read through the file and then re-read it, John Parsons sat back with a sigh. Looking up at the ceiling, he asked aloud, "So, Dr. Peter Marshall, just where are you? For that matter, who are you? Someone wants me to find you and all I know is that you're ex-Cambridge, ex-Her Majesty's Prison Service, ex-God-knows-what and now you've vanished. Where do I start to look for you and how would I recognize you even if I do find you?" He looked at the arrest and booking photograph and muttered, "What a bloody awful picture. I doubt your own mother would recognize you from this, so it isn't going to help me a whole lot. So where do I start? Your parents are dead, there are no siblings, your wife is dead…maybe your in-laws could help? Hmm…that's a possibility. Okay then, Peter Marshall, maybe I'll start there."

John Parsons sat back and pondered, 'What if they haven't a clue, what then? Peter my boy, you were released from prison and no-one has heard from you since. Where did you go? Just where the hell are you?' He tapped the file speculatively. 'You've got no money, at least none that's obvious, so going abroad or even traveling around the country wasn't an option for you. You had no visitors in prison, at least not after the first few months, so no help there. Your parole officer saw you once or twice after your release and that was that. Now that the parole period is up, he says he has no address for you…claims to be too busy with new parolees to bother with former ex-cons …lazy git! I wonder if you're living on the streets somewhere? Bit of a comedown for a Cambridge type but not unheard of…at least that's a possibility…the local Bobbies might help there. Ah well, might as well get started.'

He flipped through his Rolodex, being one of the very few police officers in the country that still used one, found the number he was looking for and then picked up the telephone.

"Andy, old boy…it's John, John Parsons. Hey, I need to pick your brains…I'm looking for someone and you may be able to help."

Chief Inspector Andrew Griffiths sat up straight in his chair. Getting a phone call from Special Branch was unusual. He hadn't spoken to his old colleague John Parsons in years and now here he was calling out of the blue. He hesitated, thinking things through and then said, "So who is it you are looking for? What'd he do?"

"Nothing…at least nothing as far as I know," replied Parsons, and then went on to outline the little that was known about Peter Marshall.

"So you think he might have gone underground, do you? Well, I suppose it's a possibility. Taller than average, well-built fellow with a posh accent…shouldn't be too hard to find him if that's where he is. I'll put one of my sergeants on it. I'll get back to you in a couple of days if we find anything. Want us to arrest him?"

"No, no need for that. Just find him if you can and we'll take it from there."

"Fine…we'll be in touch."

After hanging up, Griffith thought about the conversation and wondered what was going on. Special Branch wanted to find someone but it had to be strictly hands-off – that was unusual, to say the least. He called out for one of his sergeants to come into his office and briefly outlined what was known about Peter Marshall. "Do your best and try to find him, alright?"

"It's a bit like looking for a needle in a haystack, sir," said Detective Sergeant Mills. "Once people go underground in London, it's almost impossible to find them again. That's a wholly different part of society and they're all very secretive. Still, if he does stand out, posh accent and all, we might get lucky but I somehow doubt it."

"Well, do your best, will you?"

"What's he done, this Peter Marshall?"

"Special Branch says nothing."

"Nothing? Then why'd they want him? Isn't that unusual, sir?"

"I haven't a clue Sergeant…just do your best, okay?"

After hanging up, John Parsons looked at the file again and then muttered, "Might as well go see the in-laws. They might know something." Shrugging on his battered raincoat, he checked their address and got into his car.

The in-laws, Professor and Mrs. Fitzhugh, lived in a well-appointed detached house, situated on a smart side street in the prestigious Chelsea area of London. Looking at the exterior of their home, John Parsons surmised that these people were wealthy and that he might have to tread lightly with them.

A tall distinguished-looking man answered the doorbell and John stepped forward. "Good morning, sir, I'm Detective Inspector Parsons. I take it that you are Professor Fitzhugh?"

"I am. What's this all about? We don't often get visits from the police."

Parsons noted that there was no hesitation or reservation about the man's response. Obviously the professor had no fear or distrust of the police. No guilty conscience there.

"Well sir, I am making inquiries about your son-in-law, Peter Marshall."

"Peter? Why, what's he done?"

"Nothing as far as I know. We are just looking for him."

"I see. Well, you'd best come in, hadn't you?"

Shortly thereafter, the professor's wife joined them in the sitting room. After a quick exchange of pleasantries, Parsons asked, "What are you a professor of, sir?"

"Chemistry – at University College, London. Why do you ask?"

"Oh, no particular reason - I'm just curious. So, you know of Peter's research work, do you?"

"Yes, I do. He was a good scientist…it was through our mutual love of chemistry that I got to know him and then he and our daughter Jean hooked up, as they say. They were married within a year or two of meeting."

"I see. So, you approved of him, did you?"

"He seemed like a fine young man…" and Professor Fitzhugh left the sentence dangling. Parsons looked quickly at his wife and saw the stricken look on her face. When she saw Parsons looking at her, she straightened and said, "It was all such a tragedy, what happened. Losing our daughter was bad enough but for him to go off the rails like that…well, it was unforgivable."

Parsons nodded…what was there to say? Professor Fitzhugh looked at his wife and then at Parsons before snapping, "We told him that we wanted nothing more to do with him, not after he'd been sent to prison. Losing Jean was bad enough but to have a drunk, *a criminal*, as a son-in-law, that was too much."

"I see," said Parsons. "So, you have not seen or heard from him since he was released from prison?"

"He's out of prison now, is he? When was that? Oh no matter, the answer to your question is no, we have not heard from him and we don't want to either. Losing our daughter…"

"And it was probably all his fault," interjected the professor's wife. "He should have been there with her, not going out and getting drunk and causing all that damage to other people's property. It was disgraceful."

Professor Fitzhugh nodded in agreement and repeated, "No, we have not heard from him and we don't want to. I have no idea where he is or what he might be doing, and I can assure you, we don't care. Now, unless there is something else, I must get on with my work."

Parsons made his goodbyes and drove slowly back to his office. 'So,' he thought. 'The Fitzhughs have disavowed their son-on-law for whatever their reasons…no help there. But they mentioned prison…I wonder if anyone there, a cell-mate perhaps, could know anything? Probably not since inmates rarely spoke to the police and I've got no leverage do anything to get anyone to talk to me. I'll try anyway… one never knows.'

A day or two later, John Parsons went to Wormwood Scrubbs prison and eventually sat down with Monk, Peter's former cell-mate.

"Peter Marshall, you say?" asked Monk. "What about him?"

"Nothing about him," said Parsons.

"So why are you looking for him?"

"I can't tell you."

"You're telling me that you are making inquiries about…looking for…Peter Marshall but can't tell me why? Get real, man, why should I help you?"

"All I can tell you is that Peter's not in any trouble…we're just looking for him."

"Yeah, right. Go pull the other leg, why don't you? Detective Inspectors don't come looking for someone if they're not in any trouble. So, mate, just get lost. Even if I knew anything, which I don't, I wouldn't tell you anything. So go sling your hook. If Peter's gone missing, more power to his elbow and I hope he stays missing."

Parsons just looked at Monk. It was obvious that the man liked Peter and he wondered what their relationship had been. He made a mental note to ask the Warden about Monk. There was something there but what? It obviously came as no surprise to Monk that Peter had disappeared, in fact he seemed to approve of it. The two men had spent three years together and they must have got to know each other well during that time. So what wasn't Monk telling him? Had Peter contacted him after getting out? He'd check that with the Warden too.

As he drove back to his office, Parsons reflected that his first three leads had gone nowhere. Something might turn up from the inquiries being made around the street people in London but he doubted it. 'So, where'd he go?' he asked himself yet again. 'He's got no money and isn't drawing Social Security or unemployment benefits, so what's he living on? And where, for that matter, is he living? It's possible he went back up to Cambridge but why would he do that? There's nothing there for him and someone as well as known as him would surely have been spotted by now but I'll check again with the Cambridgeshire and the Metropolitan Police. You never know when something might turn up.'

Aloud, Parsons almost shouted, "Where the hell are you Peter Marshall? You've got to be somewhere, so why can't anyone find you?" More softly, he added, "Where did you go? And why, for that matter, does anyone want to find you so badly? That in itself is odd, very odd."

Looking at his watch, John decided to call it a day and go home although he didn't relish that either, his wife being as miserable as she usually was these days.

Ploughing his way through the congested streets of London, John Parsons thought about his life. What had gone so wrong? He and Mary had been so happy at first. He had joined the Police Force at a young age and had done well…the pair of them were happy. Money had been tight but they were in love and neither cared that they had had to put off having children. John's career had taken off and he had done well. First becoming a detective and then joining the Criminal Investigation Department and rising to Detective Sergeant. He was doing well. Mary seemed happy enough and it did not bother her that John could be out to all hours working hard on this case or that. The years passed and then it was too late to have children, both were too settled in their ways to put up with the chaos of young children in the home. At first Mary seemed to be resigned but became progressively more dissatisfied with her life. Money was a constant bone of contention between them and they became two people living in a house together but having little to do with each other. It was an existence, that was all.

John's career had shown great initial promise but when he eventually reached the rank of Inspector and then was transferred to Special Branch, everything stopped. First one case went wrong and then another. Such things could happen with any police officer but they coincided with a sudden influx of University graduates into the Police Force. Although he was intelligent and hard-working, John had not gone to a Public School, one of those curiously misnamed bastions of privilege within the British educational system, and he certainly had not attended college. Those circumstances together with a distinctly working class background had stalled his career. Now he was stuck at the rank of Inspector, not too shabby a position but nothing to write home about. Retirement was coming up and, John realized, he had nothing to look forward to. He had some savings, enough to live comfortably in retirement but with Mary? What would that be like? Perhaps he should take that Security-come-public relations job with the brewery? The extra income would be welcome and it would get him out of the house and away from his nagging, dissatisfied, permanently irritable wife.

Being a policeman tended to separate one from ordinary people, so John could not even go down to the local pub for a quiet drink. As soon as anyone saw him, he was immediately recognized as a copper, and they avoided him even if they had done nothing wrong. Why did ordinary law-abiding people have such dislike of the police? It was a curious phenomenon known the world over. As a result, police officers spent most if not all their free time with others cops and then when those very same cops moved on, got promoted or retired, then the social life of those that were left became even more circumscribed.

He arrived home and let himself in, calling out, "Hey, I'm home," and he waited for the customary response of, "Dinner'll be a while. I didn't know when you'd be home so it's not ready yet. You'll just have to wait to eat." With a shrug, John took off his raincoat, put on his slippers and shuffled into the kitchen. Might as well make some tea in the hope that Mary's attitude would improve if he took up a cup of tea to her. The perfect end to a perfect day, he smiled wryly to himself. Perhaps something would turn up the next day but, experienced as he was, John Parsons doubted it. He was far too long in the tooth to hold out much hope of anything.

SIX

Detective Inspector John Parsons sat across the desk from Dr. George Martin and silently studied the man, thinking 'What a tosser! He might be a Fellow of the Royal Society, a Fellow of Royal Imperial College, University of Cambridge and Heaven knows what else but he's furtive. When he heard that I wanted to talk to him about Peter Marshall, he got very nervous. I wonder what that's about? What's he hiding?'

Eventually, George Martin broke the silence. Nervously clearing his throat, he said, "I gather that you want to talk to me about Peter Marshall." Parsons simply nodded. He was expert at waiting out people. In his experience, most people hated silence and sooner later, usually sooner, they will start talking just to fill the gap.

"What do you want to know?"

"Well sir, I gather that he was your best friend before everything happened, is that right?"

"Yes, Inspector, that's right."

Silence.

"Again, inspector, what is it you want to know?"

"Well Dr. Martin, you say that he used to be your best friend and then he went to prison, that right?"

"Yes, there's no secret there."

Parsons nodded and thought, 'That's no secret but you are hiding something, aren't you? I wonder what? You don't seem to be too curious as to why a Detective Inspector, particularly someone from Special Branch, has come up from London to talk to you. That surely is something out of the ordinary and yet you don't ask me why I'm here. Either you are profoundly uncurious or you were expecting me. Since scientists, in my experience, tend to be notorious gossips and having inquiring minds is their stock-in-trade, then you were obviously expecting me. That raises the question of how and why you knew I was coming, especially the "why". I wonder what you know that I don't?'

"So, he was once your best friend but you haven't heard from him in years. Isn't that a bit odd?" asked Parsons.

"Not really," blustered George. "Peter was always a very private person and, well, perhaps he just wanted to keep to himself… understandable after everything that happened, isn't it?"

"You tell me, sir. After all, you did know him best, didn't you?"

This time George was silent. He nervously plucked at his trousers and wondered where this interview was going, and what this policeman knew. Llewellyn-Hughes had said that Special Branch would come calling but the man sitting opposite him was not what he was expecting. Had he expected a more polished individual, someone who spoke in a cultured accent and wore a decent suit? Certainly it wasn't this slightly shabby individual who spoke with a working class accent and who was not impressed, not in the least, with him.

Parsons stared hard at George Martin before continuing, "So, you have not heard from him, have you? Did you expect to?"

George shook his head, thinking, 'Just as well really because a sudden appearance by Peter might cause a lot of problems, especially if he found out that I had taken over his idea. That would not be good.' Aloud, he said, "Not really, no. The last time I spoke to him, shortly after he went to prison, he made it very clear that he didn't want to have any contact with anyone…anyone from the old days."

"I see…and you left it at that, did you?"

Embarrassed, George said hastily, "I was just respecting his wishes."

"Huh!" sniffed John Parsons. "Not much of a friend, are you?" and was delighted to see a wave of red travel up the other man's neck and flood his face. "Was there are any reason that you can think of, any reason at all, that would make Dr. Marshall cut himself off like that? You know, sever all connections with everybody and everything?"

"Not really, no. I didn't think about it at the time. After all I was very busy and had my work to do, you know?"

'No, I don't know,' thought Parsons. 'However, I'll bet that this work of Dr. George Martin somehow involved Peter Marshall. I don't know how but there's something there…the man is far too nervous about something but I don't know what. It'll come out eventually but somehow I don't think it has much to do with Peter's disappearance.'

"I see," said Parsons. "Well sir, you've been a great help." George Martin stared at the police officer, asking himself just how he had been a help. "Anyway," continued John. "If you do hear from him, will you please contact me at this number?" and handed over his business card. "Most people turn up sooner or later, and I expect he'll get in contact you one day. If he does, just let me know, alright?"

Dr. Martin just nodded.

As he rode the train back to London, John Parsons thought about the interview he had just had. Things weren't quite kosher but what were they? It was obvious that Dr. Martin had been expecting him but why would that be so? There was obviously something going on here and it involved both Marshall *and* Martin but what? He sighed and looked out the window at the passing countryside. As far as he could tell, whatever it was, it wasn't germane to the search for Peter Marshall, or was it? Something would break loose soon, it always did but what and when were things he'd have to wait on. A small shiver of excitement passed through him, which in itself was unusual, as was this whole case.

The next morning John Parsons found a note telling him to call Chief Inspector Griffiths. When he got through, John asked, "Hey Andy, did you find him?"

"Not yet, no but we're still looking. There is one thing though," and he paused for effect before continuing. "It seems that someone vaguely answering to the description of your man banged up some bloke in an Irish pub in Finsbury Park or some such place."

"Really? What happened?"

"It seems some drunken paddy started to hassle a young woman in a pub and one of the barmen stepped in. From the police report, it appears that it was all over in seconds and the local copper makes mention that the barman, whoever he was, did some Kung Fu magic and laid out a man much bigger than he was. I don't suppose your man has had any martial arts training, has he?"

"Not to my knowledge, no! That's not something you'd expect with your average Cambridge University professor, is it? So it's probably not the same person but I'll check into it anyway. Do you have the address of that pub? North London wasn't it?"

After providing Parsons with the address, Chief Inspector Griffiths then added, "There's also something else. A day or so after that, there was an incident at one of those roadside rest-stops off the motorway up North. The CCTV images aren't that good but it could be your man."

"Oh?" said Parsons. "What sort of incident would that be?"

"It seems that this chap suddenly appeared out of nowhere and took on a bunch of bikers known to cause trouble for truckers along that stretch of the motorway. Made short shrift of them by all accounts. So, if it is the same man, it seems he's some sort of White Knight and is given to sorting out trouble-makers. That sound like this Marshall person of yours?"

"I have no idea, to be honest, but it somehow doesn't fit, does it? On the other hand, like you, I hate coincidences, especially when these two incidents, as you call them, occur within a couple of days of each other and involve vague look-alikes. Hmm…well thanks, I'll check into it…you never know."

"Let me know what you find out, will you? You've got me interested, John, and you know how I like mysteries that get solved."

After hanging up, Parsons thought about what he'd just learned from his old friend Andy Griffiths. Where the hell had Peter Marshall, respected scientist and Cambridge Don, have acquired martial arts training? That did not fit at all and there was no mention of anything of that sort in his file. Then a stray memory struck him. Pulling out his notebook, he flipped through the pages and found the entries pertaining to Marshall's cell-mate Monk. There it was; he was ex-SAS and those blokes were trained in all manner of things and were generally expert in martial arts. He could have trained

Peter but would he? It was possible but most SAS types tended to keep very quiet about the skills they had acquired, so why would he have trained Peter Marshall?

Getting to his feet and again feeling that familiar shiver down his spine, Parsons decided he would pay another visit to Monk in prison before going to that pub. Something was definitely starting to break but what?

Sitting down opposite to Monk, John asked, "Did you …ah… give some lessons to Peter Marshall?"

"What sort of lessons are you talking about?"

"Martial arts…anything like that?"

"Me? Nah."

"Listen Monk, you are in here for the long haul but, and it is a big but, if you help me, I may be able to help you."

"How so?"

"Before I came here today, I went through your file and it seems that you might not have been fairly treated. Oh there's no question about you being guilty but 20 years was a pretty harsh sentence given the circumstances of your case. From what I gather, that judge is known to meet out stiff sentences at every opportunity. So…"

"Hey, don't promise something that you can't or won't deliver," snapped Monk.

"That's not my style," snapped Parsons back at Monk. "If I say I'll try to do something, that's exactly what I'll do. I can't promise a thing, you understand, but I shall have a quiet word with a friend in the Crown Prosecution Service. You never know what might happen."

"Okay…thanks…I believe you but why would you do that?"

"As I said, I cannot tell you why but finding Peter Marshall is important to me and anything you can tell me about him might help me find him…and that will make me very grateful."

"Hmm,' murmured Monk and he muttered semi-audibly, "This geezer's looking for Peter but he's not committed any crimes. He's asking lots of questions but nothing he's asked about, except possibly the martial arts stuff, has anything to do with any major or even minor crimes, and learning martial arts is no crime. Hell, they give lessons on them in every gym in the country, so what's the big deal?"

"You're right," agreed John Parsons, leaning in to catch Monk's mutters. "Learning martial arts isn't a big deal. However, I know all about you and the training you received in the SAS. My betting is you taught Peter some of your nasty little tricks, a lot of them I think. Did you?" And John stared hard at Monk. Silence.

Parsons continued to stare at Monk, willing him to talk. Eventually Monk nodded, "What if I did? No crime in that is there?"

"No, at least none that I know of but why would you do that? It's not something you've done before, so why with him?"

"Oh come on inspector, that guy was a target in here. Good-looking fellow, posh accent and a University professor too…give me a break. He might as well have had a bulls-eye slapped on his uniform. Poor bugger wouldn't have stood a chance the way he was when he came in. Couldn't let that happen, could I? You know what I mean?"

Parsons knew very well what Monk meant and it gave him pause for thought. He nodded and said eventually, "So, you say that he could take care of himself, could he? You trained him well?"

"Oh yes. By the time he got out, he was able to take care of himself, very well actually."

"I see. Tell me, you spent a lot of time with Peter, about three years all told, yes?"

"That's right."

"So, what was he like this Peter Marshall? Nice bloke?"

"Yeah, he was. Very smart and knew a lot, he did."

"So you talked a lot, did you?"

"Not really, no. Peter was pretty quiet, you know, private like. He wasn't secretive or unfriendly, he just didn't talk a whole lot."

"So he didn't talk about himself, or did he?"

"No, not him. On the other hand, neither did I for that matter. You learn to keep your trap shut in here."

"So you didn't talk about your army days?"

"In here? Never. You never know who might be listening…no point in looking for trouble. Anyway, as I say, Peter was pretty quiet but if you asked him something, he'd always answer, and not just about science either. I actually learned a lot from him about all sorts of things. Why'd you ask?"

"I'm just curious about him, that's all."

"What's this all about then? Detective Inspectors from Scotland Yard don't usually come to see someone like me and ask questions about ex-cons, and certainly not more than once. So, what gives? Why this big interest in him?"

Parsons sighed. Monk was quite right, senior police officers like him didn't usually waste time looking into ex-cons unless it involved a murder or a major financial or political scandal, none of which applied to Peter Marshall. On the other hand, John Parsons knew that prison walls had many, many ears and anything he said about Peter would spread through the place like wildfire and then to the outside.

"We are looking for him and it helps to know something about someone we're looking for," he said eventually.

"Why are you looking for him? Peter was no major criminal, was he?, and I don't see him being part of any great National or International conspiracy. Let's face it, Mr. Parsons, he was in here because he got drunk and banged up a whole bunch of cars. So why the interest? I agree that Peter seems to have been very unfairly treated by the judge but that's not why you're here, is it?"

John looked at the other man and sighed again. "I really can't tell you…I'm sorry but you know how it is, don't you?"

Monk sat back and stared at John Parsons for several seconds, thinking hard. This interview was turning everything he knew about Peter Marshall upside down. It made no difference to him whether Peter had been a mass-murderer, a financial scam-artist like Bernie Madoff or even a Russian spy, although he couldn't believe any of that could be true. That oblique comment from Inspector Parsons about being unable to tell him anything as well as his promise to have his case looked into by the CPS fairly shouted National Security but how could Peter be involved in anything like that?

Eventually Monk said, "Go on."

"Well, it seems that someone answering Marshall's description jumped in and sorted out some nasty drunk harassing a young woman in a North London pub. Then a couple of days later, what sounds like the same bloke took on a bunch of bikers and saved some truck driver from a nasty beating up North somewhere. Could your friend Peter Marshall be some sort of White Knight? You know, helping out when things aren't right…that sort of thing?"

"Look, Peter was a good guy, he really was. After people in here realized that he could take care of himself, he was left alone and then slowly but surely, all sorts of people would come up to him and ask for help…you know, writing letters, working out what their lawyers were saying, even helping to balance the wife's checkbook on the odd occasion although one wonders how something like that got in here. Anyway, Peter got to be pretty popular because he was always willing to help others."

Drawing a deep breath, Monk continued, "So those stories about Peter, if it was Peter, helping out others in a punch-up sound about right. After all, he did step in and help out some kid who was being set on by a couple of rough ones in here shortly before he got out. He was that sort of bloke, wasn't he? He didn't like anyone being taken advantage of, that's what. So what you're telling me comes as no surprise but him a White Knight? An avenging angel? Peter'd laugh at you if he heard that but, I don't know, he was a pretty decent bloke all round."

After leaving the prison, John Parsons thought about what he'd just learned. So Peter Marshall had had martial arts training and from someone who'd been a highly-trained killing machine. Not only that, Peter was the sort of person who would step in and help out when someone was getting into trouble through no fault of their own, or at least it seemed like that. 'Okay,' he decided. 'That's one issue sorted but was it the same person who got involved in two different fights at more or less either end of the country within a day or so? If it was him, why'd he leave London and how'd he get up there so quickly, especially as there's no record of him taking a train to anywhere? He must have got a lift from someone, but from who and to where? And if he did, where is he now?'

Driving across London, Parsons was now anxious to find that pub. The local copper's report had not mentioned what had happened after the altercation in the pub so, with any luck, Peter might still be there. "Nah," he said to himself out loud. "I'm not that lucky. Besides, if he's still in London, who was it that helped out that truck driver? Nevertheless it won't do any harm to learn a bit more about Marshall even if he did leave the place. Someone in that pub must know something, especially if he worked behind the bar. The regulars and other barmen always know everything."

John Parsons pulled up and parked his car across the road from the pub and he sat for a few moments studying the place. The Rose and Thistle was a typical working man's pub with slightly peeling paint work, large frosted windows and swinging doors. A chalk-board trestle stood beside the door, advertising typical pub foods, probably bought from a chain supermarket and sold at a huge mark-up to unsuspecting customers who were either too hungry or too drunk to care what they were eating.

Walking in, John could see a couple of men standing at the bar, some single people and two or three couples occupying a few tables scattered around the surprisingly large interior. A large, solidly built man stood behind the long mahogany bar polishing glasses and chatting to two customers. When he looked up and saw Parsons, he nodded at him and whispered something to one customer, who took a quick glance at the new arrival and then moved away from the bar to a table, taking the other customer with him. John smiled to himself. He hadn't been in the place more than five seconds before being made as a copper!

Walking up to the bar, he asked for half a pint of bitter and slid some coins over to pay for it, adding, "Have one yourself."

The barman shook his head, saying curtly, "No thanks."

Taking a small sip, John looked at the man and asked politely, "Is Peter Marshall anywhere around?"

"Who?" asked the bar man. "Never heard of him."

"Oh, I bet you have," insisted John and as the barman started to pass over his change, John reached out and grabbed the other man's wrist, tightly. Staring hard into his eyes, he added, "Look old son, I've been a copper for a long, long time and I've eaten bigger men than you for breakfast. So let me tell you, we can have a quiet chat here at the bar over a drink, the one that I just offered to you or…or we'll go down to the local nick where you'll spend several hours …it's no matter to me but you will talk." Releasing Jamie's wrist, he added, "So, what's it to be?"

Jamie shrugged and poured himself a pint of beer, taking the correct amount from the money lying on the bar. Parsons nodded at him and jerked his head at a nearby table, "Let's sit over there, nice and comfy, and that other guy can take over," indicating a second barman who had appeared behind the bar from a backroom somewhere.

After they were seated, Parsons said pleasantly enough, "Ah, this is better. So, what's your name?"

"Jamie…short for James Stewart."

"I can tell from your accent that you're from North of the Border – Glasgow is it?" When Jamie nodded in agreement, he continued, "James Stewart, is it? Well at least your Ma and Dad didn't call you Jimmy or was that what you were called growing up?"

Jamie stayed quiet, ignoring the detective's attempts at polite banter. He had been through this many times before and was not about to let his guard down. Taking another sip of his beer, an unperturbed Parsons looked at the barman, "So, Mr. Stewart…. Jamie…you say you never heard of Peter Marshall, do you? Now we both know that's not true, not in the least, so why don't you tell me about the man? Neither of us wants to waste time on this, do we?"

Resignedly, Jamie took a long pull at his drink and started to tell John Parsons how Peter had come to work at the pub those several months back.

"He stayed with you, did he?" asked John, politely ignoring Jamie's earlier denial of knowing who Peter was.

"Yeah, he did. Slept on the couch in the living room, such as it is."

"The living room or the couch?" asked John.

"Both…either…it's no matter."

"What was he like, your Peter Marshall?"

"I don't know about him being *my* Peter Marshall but he was a good bloke. Worked hard, kept the shelves stocked and the beer flowing, cleaned up at the end of the evening, helped sort out the odd fight – the usual stuff around here."

"Get lots of fights in here?" asked Parsons.

"Not too many, no. Those that come are usually on a Friday or Saturday when the regulars, those Paddy day-laborers, get paid. Most of the time it's all over before Pete or I had to get involved although the guvnor would get mad if too many glasses got broken… you know how it is."

"Is Peter still working here?"

"No, he moved on some time ago."

"Why?"

"I dunno, he just did."

"Come on Jamie, we've been doing so well up to this point and now you've just lied to me again. Tsk, tsk…we really can't have that, can we? So, why did he leave?"

"I told you, he just did!" snapped Jamie.

"Alright then, what led up to him leaving?"

Taking another long pull at his beer, Jamie told Parsons about the fight with the big drunken laborer and then how Peter had taken off suddenly without a word to anyone.

"Was there anything different about this particular fight? You know, something special that made it so different from any of the regular ones in here?"

"Funny you should say that," said Jamie. "Normally we only have to get between whoever it is, you know, grab the odd flying fist or dodge a punch, but this time, wow!"

"Wow what?" asked Parsons.

"All of a sudden Peter pulls some Kung-Fu stuff and bang, the big Paddy was out cold on the floor. Man, he was fast…never seen anything like it before. I didn't even know Peter could do that stuff…if I'd known, I'd probably have been nicer to him," and Jamie laughed.

"So, after that, Peter just left, did he?"

"Yes, just walked out…just like that. Then the coppers came and we all answered a few questions and then they sent for an ambulance to carry that bloke out…that was it. Never heard anything more about it until today."

"What happened after the police left?"

"It was nearly closing time so we finished up here, tidied up the place, washed glasses…the usual and then I went home."

"And?" persisted John.

"The place was empty…Peter had gone. He'd left some money on the table, taken his stuff and that was it."

"No note…any explanation?"

"Nothing."

"Hmmm…have you heard from him since? You know, a postcard, letter, phone call?"

"Nothing…he just vanished."

"Tell me about it," muttered John bitterly. "Okay then, what can you tell me about the man? Did he drink or anything? Get into fights? Have lots of women? You said he was a good bloke. What does that mean?"

Jamie was silent for several minutes as he thought carefully. "Fights? No. Peter never got into fights himself – he stopped them more than anything else, except of course for the last one. Drink? He had the odd pint that a customer bought for him but it was rare for him to have a drink at any other time. Funnily enough, although he worked behind the bar, I never saw him the worse for drink, ever. As for women, lots of them went after him…they liked that dark brooding look he had. He went off with one or other of them every so often but it wasn't anything regular like. They, the women that is, seemed to like what they got with him since a lot of them came back for more and those that didn't were always very friendly to Peter if and when they came in here."

"I take it he wasn't gay then?" asked Parsons.

"Peter – a poofter? Don't make me laugh. No way was he one of those," said Jamie angrily.

"Okay, okay, don't get your nickers in a twist…I had to ask." John paused and collected his thoughts before saying, "You mentioned his dark brooding look…what do you mean by that?"

"He was just quiet.…didn't say a whole lot…you know what I mean? Not one for idle chit-chat, you know. In fact he hardly said anything at all and nothing about himself. A lot of the time he seemed to be off in his own world, a strange look on his face. Funny thing is though, he was always aware of what was going on around him."

"How so?"

"One minute he seemed to be dreaming and the next, he was right there to sort out any trouble – bit uncanny really."

"I see," said John reflectively but thinking, 'Well, that's something he learned inside. I've seen that before in ex-cons and with soldiers for that matter.'

He got to his feet and started to leave and then a thought struck him. "Jamie, what about his money?"

"His money…what about it?"

"What did he do with it?" asked Parsons.

"How do you mean?"

"He was getting paid each week, so what'd he do with it - what he didn't spend?"

Jamie was silent for a few moments and then said, "Well it probably wasn't that much but he did help with the rent and we each chipped in for food, that sort of thing."

"But you tell me he didn't drink and he wasn't a big smoker… and he certainly didn't spend it on clothes or anything. So, where did it go?"

"I've no idea…never thought about it really." Jamie fell silent and then added, "I wasn't his mother or his wife so I didn't follow his every movement, you know what I mean?"

Parsons nodded but thinking, 'Now there's another mystery. Peter Marshall gets a regular pay check or rather, tax-free cash under the counter, each week. He spends some of it but where'd the rest go? I'll have to ask the pub's landlord what he paid Peter to be certain but I'm betting he squirreled it away somewhere, but where? Or he gave it away but to whom?' As he left the pub and got back into his car, Parsons reflected, 'So Dr. Marshall, you take off after a fight because the police had been called even though no complaints were filed. Your probation officer, lazy git that he is, says he hasn't heard from you but since your probation is up, he didn't need to see you. That suggests you took off because you didn't want to be questioned by the police but for no obvious reason…so, what were you scared of? Getting arrested again? Possible but unlikely given the circumstances, but it wasn't an altogether unreasonable conclusion on your part. Okay, that accounts for why you took off. Everything else fits with what

Monk and Jamie said about you except for one thing. What did you do with your money? It might not have been that much on a weekly basis but over the long haul, that might be another matter.'

Starting his engine, John Parsons drove off and merged into traffic on his way home. As he did so, he thought again about his quarry, 'You really are a mystery, aren't you Peter? Everyone likes you but no-one knows anything about you. You help pay the rent and buy food, don't drink, don't buy clothes yet the money you earn has gone somewhere, if not on yourself, where? Shit, I'm getting too old for this game.'

As he neared home, John Parsons remembered the other incident, the one off the motorway. Deciding that he would go up North to look into it, he realized that he would be gone for a couple of days and his wife would not be happy about that. Sighing, he walked into his house and called out to his wife that he was home. When he told her later of his travel plans, John knew that he could expect to suffer through an evening of complaints.

"I can't wait to retire," he muttered. "Then I'll take that brewery job, get a decent salary, have enough ready cash to keep the old woman happy and maybe we'll even get to travel a bit. You never know, it might even rekindle something between us…stranger things have happened."

When he saw his wife, he astonished both of them by gently kissing her and asking, "Hey good looking, what's for dinner,?"

Stunned, Mary Parsons stared at her husband. Did he just kiss her? Gathering her flustered thoughts, she said, "It's shepherd's pie tonight, dear…that suit you?" and was even more surprised that she had called her husband "dear". When was the last time that had happened or that she had even wanted to do so?

SEVEN

Driving on the motorway headed North, John Parsons reflected on the previous evening. He and Mary had been affectionate towards each other for the first time in months, so much so that they cuddled in bed together, a rare and much missed pleasure. Although Mary obviously did not want him to take a long driving trip up to Northern England, her parting words, "Hey, you take care of yourself, will you? Mind you come home safely!", were so unexpected that John stopped dead in his tracks and went back to kiss her goodbye again.

After the tedium of negotiating his way through the dense traffic coming out of London, he could relax and drive almost on auto-pilot. He thought aloud, "What is it with you Peter Marshall? You seem to have some sort of benign influence on everyone you come in contact with and even with those you haven't met. Look at Mary and me…I start asking questions about you and then things start turning around. Not so much with regard to finding you because you're still missing but, I don't know, something happened at home and even if this job sucks, I'm so much happier, more settled, than I've been for a while. Is it because of you or just that I'm getting older? No, it can't be because I'm getting older…I was doing that before I even heard of you. All I know is that life has suddenly turned around for me and I'm not complaining, not at all."

After a long and tedious drive, John Parsons arrived in Northern England. Pulling up outside Nobby's modest house, he sat still for a few minutes thinking about how best to approach the man. The CCTV images and a check of license plates and the haulage company that owned the truck indicated that Nobby had been the driver of the truck that the bikers had surrounded. After the young thugs had been laid out, Nobby, the truck and Peter, if it actually was Peter, had all disappeared, presumably together. John didn't want to ask straight out whether Nobby had given Peter a lift because while giving someone a ride wasn't exactly forbidden by the haulage company, it certainly wasn't encouraged. If Nobby had given Peter a lift up from London, then that would raise the eyebrows of his employers. John decided he would play it safe and say as little as possible about the possibility of Nobby picking up a hitchhiker. He would find out soon enough what had happened and there was no point in upsetting the man.

His knock on the front door was answered by a most attractive young woman who appeared to be in her early twenties. "Yes?" she asked.

"I'm Detective Inspector Parsons. I'm up here from Scotland Yard, in London you know" and held out a business card.

"You are? How nice." said the young woman with a smile. "And yes, I do know where Scotland Yard is".

John smiled back…there was obviously no concern over a police officer knocking on this front door and no guilty conscience in play either. "Yes, well, I wonder if William Murphy lives here?" he said.

"Yes he does - he's my dad. He's upstairs changing and getting cleaned up …I'll call him. Would you like a cup of tea or coffee?"

"That's very kind of you but no."

"Okay." And seconds later as he stood in the living room, John heard the young woman calling out to her father, "Dad, there's someone here to see you. Seems he's a police officer, up here from London."

"There is?" came the response. "I'll be down in a jiffy…tell him to take a seat."

Coming back into the living room, the young woman said, "I suppose you heard that, did you? Please sit down, won't you?" When John nodded and seated himself, she went on, "I'm Dahlia Murphy, his daughter but I think I told you that I'm his daughter already."

John smiled again, "You did, yes. Dahlia? That's an unusual name, how did…"

"Don't ask, it's a long story."

Just then Nobby bustled into the room. Holding out his hand, he said, "I'm William Murphy but everyone calls me Nobby…like with Dahlia's name, don't ask."

"Okay," said John. "I won't."

Nobby looked at John's business card and asked, "So, Detective Inspector Parsons, how is it that you came all the way up here to see me? Also, I see your card just says "Scotland Yard", no mention of a division or anything…that's also unusual, isn't it?"

John Parsons looked carefully at Nobby. The man was obviously no fool – he had picked up immediately on the fact that the business card didn't specify what he did.

"Not really," he said. "Not being specific helps sometimes."

"Right!" said Nobby. "So Mr. Detective Inspector, what brings you to my door?"

"Do you know a Peter Marshall?" asked John and saw startled looks on the faces of both father and daughter.

"Sort of," conceded Nobby. "What about him?"

John, noting the "sort of" comment and the odd expression that crossed Dahlia's face, decided to try a more oblique approach. "It seems that a couple of months back this Peter Marshall helped you with a gang of thugs at a rest-stop off the motorway. Is that the case?"

"Yes," said Nobby and went on to describe enthusiastically how Peter had taken on the gang of bikers. "It was bloody marvelous, I tell you. One minute they were about to give me a thumping and the next, there were bodies everywhere…just like in the movies."

"I see," said John. "He just appeared out of nowhere, did he, and took on that gang?"

Nobby stayed silent. He didn't want to admit that he had given Peter a lift up from London, something that was frowned upon if not expressly forbidden by the haulage company. No point in inviting trouble.

John read Nobby's mind and veered away from the question of a lift, asking, "And did he identify himself as Peter Marshall?"

"Yes although identify is …well, that's a bit strong, isn't it? We'd exchanged names, er…" and Nobby went silent again. So Nobby *had* given Peter a lift! The two men exchanged looks and then Nobby said, "Hey what's this all about? He was here weeks ago, so why now?"

"I'm looking for him," said John simply.

"Why?" interjected Dahlia, again with that strange look on her face, one that both John and her father picked up on. "What's he done?"

"Nothing, as far as I know," said John. "We're just looking for him, that's all."

Father and daughter exchanged looks and neither of them bought John Parsons' story. Detective Inspectors from Scotland Yard would not waste their time coming all the way up here just because they were looking for someone. The local police would normally be called in for a simple inquiry like that, so there was obviously a lot more to this search for Peter Marshall, whoever he might be. It also struck both of them as strange that someone from Scotland Yard would have even taken the trouble to find Nobby given the large numbers of trucks that traveled the motorways of England. How did they know it was Nobby that had given Peter a lift? So why was he here? After all, giving a hitchhiker a lift was hardly a crime even if it might be against company policy.

They stared at their visitor and waited for him to say more. As the silence dragged on, John eventually said, "No, he hasn't done anything wrong…we're just want to talk to him about something …you know, he could possibly help us with a big case that we're working on." As John tried to concoct a satisfactory story on the fly, he could see that he was not doing a very good job of it with the Murphy household. "No, as I say, he really hasn't done anything wrong and we're not looking for him like that. It's just that we think he might have seen something, something that could be a big help with our case against some very nasty people."

Father and daughter again exchanged looks but this time they both shrugged. Neither wholly believed what Parsons was saying but it did fit with their image of Peter Marshall.

"Okay," said Nobby eventually. "So what do you want with us?"

"Do you know where he might be? Have you seen or heard from him?"

"No, not a word," they both said, almost in unison, Nobby matter of factly and Dahlia with a touch of sadness. 'There it is again,' thought John. 'Something happened between this woman

Dahlia and Peter, not that it matters unless it helps me find Peter Marshall and that doesn't seem likely given her reaction.'

"Do you mind telling me how this all came about?" he asked Nobby, who hesitated before saying anything.

"Look," he said eventually. "None of this can get back to my company. They all know about that punch-up but…er…not how Peter came to be there. Is that alright with you?"

John nodded, "Unless it has something to with my case, there's no need for this matter to leave the room." Glancing around the room and trying to lower the tension, he spotted a carton of French cigarettes lying on a side table, "You smoke those?"

"Only when I get them for free."

John looked at him curiously and waited for an explanation.

"I make regular trips to France to pick up a load of those things and bring it back here. People seem to like them even if they cost a lot more than our cigarettes…makes no sense to me but I get paid well to do the trip, so what do I care?" Nobby said. "Anyway, the Froggies always give me a couple of cartons as a sort of tip, you know, to discourage me from nicking any. They're not bad, the ciggies that is, and once you get used to them, you kinda like them. Besides," he laughed. "The price is right."

"So where does Peter come into all this?" asked Parsons.

"I was just heading back up North after dropping some of the load in London and there he was standing by the road thumbing a lift. On the spur of the moment, I stopped and he climbed in."

"Dad almost never gives rides to hitchhikers," interjected Dahlia. "It's just not safe to do that these days, so for him to make an exception is a bit unusual…anyway he did."

With some prodding, John Parsons got the whole story out of Nobby. Sitting back, he said, "Well, I'm not going to say anything to your employers about this because all I can see is a driver helping another person out and that person then returning the favor, that favor being to take care of that biker gang. Okay?'

Both Murphy father and daughter nodded in agreement, their faces showing relief.

"I don't suppose you've heard from him," asked John again, trying to see whether they might let their guards down.

"No, nothing."

"Okay. So tell me, where did you drop him off that morning… close to the motorway, yes?" and Nobby nodded in agreement. "I don't suppose you know whether he headed North or South after he left you?"

"No. I didn't actually see him get to the motorway…I just dropped him off around the corner from it, on the high street. Those back streets are pretty narrow there and I didn't want to get stuck with the rig, you know how it is. That'd be a bit difficult to explain. Also, as we're fairly close to the depot, I didn't want anyone to see him sitting with me in the cab, you know what I mean?"

John Parsons nodded, everything made sense but he was no wiser as to Peter Marshall's whereabouts. As he was walking back to his car, a thought struck him and he retraced his steps. When Nobby appeared at the door in answer to his knock, he said, "A quick question, Mr. Murphy, if you don't mind. Where did this incident happen, you know, that fight? The report I saw was a bit vague and I don't know this area at all."

"It was down the motorway a bit, near Greydene. Those yobs seem to hang out around there."

"Thank you," said John politely. "You've been a big help. Oh, and thank your daughter too."

As he drove away, John Parsons thought about what he had just learned. The visit to the Murphy household explained how Marshall had been able to leave London and how he'd come to be there to help out Nobby. The odd look on Dahlia's face and her disappointment in not hearing from Peter suggested that something had developed between them but obviously it went no further than a single night's involvement. So, he concluded, that was yet another dead-end. He decided to find somewhere to sleep for night, get some dinner and write up his notes after he called Mary. She'd welcome a call from him, especially now.

It was possible that he might get some further information about Peter from that biker gang but he doubted it. Nevertheless, it was better than nothing so he'd start to look for them in the morning – at least they shouldn't be too hard to find. Later, as he was dropping off to sleep, he thought about Peter Marshall again.

Aloud, he said, "What is it about you, Peter? Everyone seems to like you and the ladies *really* like you, so there's something special about you. But why do you keep disappearing? You could give lessons to Harry Houdini or the Scarlet Pimpernel, couldn't you? Yet, somehow, I don't think you're deliberately trying to hide from anyone…there's no reason to do that. After all, you served your time, your probation's up, you've committed no crimes but you've still vanished. On the other hand, why did those people in Whitehall set Special Branch onto finding you? That makes no sense unless you are a Security risk but how could that be? There's something else going on here but I don't see what. My old copper's instincts tell me that there's more to this than meets the eye but I'm damned if I know what. Ah well, no matter. I'll just do my job, serve out my twenty years and get that brewery job. None of this matters in the long run." And John turned over, soon snoring peacefully.

The next morning John looked at a map and decided that he should head south towards Greydene since that was close to where the bikers used to hang out and about where Peter had taken on the gang. He looked again at the map. Greydene was a fairly large city and even had a University…a University? Hmm, would that have been a magnet for Peter? Not the same as Cambridge but a respectable enough institution. No, not likely…if Peter had dropped out of society, why would he even go to a small university like Greydene. If he was interested in going back to academics, surely he would have tried to go back to Cambridge? No, that didn't make any sense. In fact, why would he go south at all? He had left London, so why would he go back there? John doubted that the Midlands and any of its larger cities like Birmingham would hold any appeal for Peter Marshall. Likewise he doubted that Peter would have headed towards Oxford or Cambridge either if he'd turned his back on his old life. So, was there any point in he, John Parsons, going towards Greydene?

Over breakfast, John turned the matter over in his mind. There was probably no real point in going towards Greydene or even trying to find the biker gang but since both the city and the bikers were more or less on the road back to London, why not see if he could learn anything new? It could be a waste of time but since nothing else had panned out, it couldn't do any harm to make a few inquiries.

As he drove, he carefully adhered to the speed limit…as he often said, "I might be on the job but the locals don't like coppers coming up from London and speeding on their roads, so why get into a hassle?" Cruising along, enjoying the sunshine, he was startled by two motorcycles roaring up out of nowhere and screaming past him. He muttered a curse and then it struck him that those two idiots could actually be part of the gang he was looking for. He sped up and tried to get closer to the speeding bikers and when they turned off the motorway, he followed them, keeping a reasonable distance between the bikes and his car.

Eventually the bikers pulled up outside a roadside café and strutted in. The number of large motorcycles outside the place suggested that this was where the gang hung out, so John drove around the building and parked his car where he could get to it fairly easily without it being too visible from the café. No point in advertising that he was The Law until he was good and ready.

As he walked into the café, John's sinuses were immediately assailed by the clouds of tobacco smoke coming from the tables occupied by the bikers, all smoking in complete disregard of the prominent No Smoking signs scattered around the café interior. He ordered a coffee and sat down at a table near the bikers, close enough to overhear them but not so close that he appeared to be eavesdropping. Again, no point in causing trouble.

After the initial silence following his entry, the gang members started to talk again.

"I tell you, he didn't look that hard to me, did he?" said one.

"You weren't there the first time," replied King Rocker. "If you had been, you wouldn't be so cocky. Besides, why're you bringing that up again? It were a while back."

"I'm just saying that bloke didn't scare me so why'd we all take off like that…that's what I want to know."

"Look, shut up about it already. It was ages ago, so just leave it."

Another biker suddenly chimed in, "Look Ron, if you'd seen what he did, I can tell you that you'd have the same attitude as us."

"Yeah, tell me another one," sneered the loud-mouthed biker.

"Rubbish," snarled King Rocker. "You're all talk, that's what you are." Looking round, he spotted John Parsons and said, "Don't he look like one of those wankers that talk a lot but do nothing? What do you think?"

"I really don't know," said John mildly. "But I do know one thing, you chaps seem to be very wary of that fellow he's talking about," with a nod in Ron's direction. "Who is this bloke?"

King Rocker, surprised that he and his gang would be called "chaps" by this stranger, said, "I've no idea...and I don't want to know. Hey, you sound like one of those posh Londoners...what're you doing here?"

"Oh just passing through, that's all."

"Yeah right. Anyway, this bloke, well he was something else, he was."

"How so?"

King Rocker, warming to his story and taking advantage of a new audience, said, "Well there we were, just about to have some fun – you know what I mean?" Parsons just nodded, having a good idea of what "fun" involved with these thugs. "Well, as I say, one minute there's no-one around and we're about to get started and then he appears – sort of out of nowhere."

"What do you mean, out of nowhere?" asked Parsons. "Nobody just appears from out of thin air...he must have come from somewhere."

"I dunno about that. All I know is that he just appeared, that's what." persisted King Rocker. "Like some sort of ghost ...it was weird. One minute we're on our own and the next, he's there." Taking a long drag on his cigarette, he continued, "Of course he came up behind us, you know, surprised us like, and did some sort of karate and got the better of us." He paused, obviously trying to salvage some self-respect, "If we'd seen him, it would have been different but, anyway, it was all over pretty fast."

"What happened afterwards...where'd he go?" asked John.

"Fucked if I know," said King Rocker. "I didn't hang around long enough to find out."

"Yeah, sounds like you, don't it?" said Ron and was immediately cowed by the malevolent glare from the gang leader. He sensibly decided it might not be the best idea to antagonize King Rocker who could be a mean bastard if he got angry.

Parsons sat back and stared at the biker. The man was obviously scared of Peter Marshall and clearly had no idea who he was but his story rang true. After thinking for a few moments, he asked, "Who was this person…you know, the bloke he helped out?"

"Beats me. He was a truck driver …I think I've seen him once or twice on the motorway since then but I can't swear to it…you know how it is?"

Parsons nodded, "So you haven't seen this bloke since? You know, the karate expert."

"Nah," said King Rocker.

"Hey," said another biker. "That were the same bloke at that food warehouse place, weren't it?"

"Oh yeah," said King Rocker, feigning loss of memory but getting a sharp look from Ron. Seeing that Ron looked like saying something, King Rocker continued, "Sometime after that punch-up, you know where he surprised us like, we were driving around and saw some bint with a van outside that food warehouse, you know the one, off Greydene Road."

John Parsons shook his head, "Don't know the place, sorry. You said some bint?"

"Yeah, some woman driving a white van, all loaded up with food and stuff. We saw her and thought we'd have some fun like, you know how it is, don't you?"

John Parsons again ignored the comment about "fun" and said nothing. He'd let them talk and see what came up next.

"Anyway," continued King Rocker. "She weren't bad looking for an older bird, you know what I mean?"

Parsons nodded. An older bird could be any female over the age of twenty-five or thirty for these bikers but obviously she was attractive if King Rocker said something nice about her.

"So, there she was, parked over by that food warehouse over by Little Haddleston and we pulled over to talk to her, you know what I mean?"

Parsons was getting a little tired of hearing "you know what I mean?" from the other man but said nothing, just nodded.

"We was just getting started, having a bit of fun like and that same bloke came up. Just like before, he came from nowhere."

"He just appeared again?" asked John. "Just like before? Surely you must have seen him coming."

"Nah mate, he wasn't there one minute and there the next. So we took one look at him and scarpered."

"Did he say anything? For that matter, did the woman say anything?"

"Neither of them said anything but I saw the look on his face and that was enough. We took off."

"Bloody typical," interjected Ron, earning another black look from King Rocker.

"What happened then? Did you see where he went…or where the woman went?"

"Nah, nothing. We was gone, that's all."

"So," asked John,. "There's no connection between that woman and the truck driver?"

"Nah but somehow that bloke turned up with both of them, you know, the truck driver and that woman. As I say, it's weird." King Rocker stopped and stared hard at John Parsons. "What's it to you anyway? You a copper or something?"

"Yes, I am," admitted John. "It's nothing to me but I'm just interested, that's all."

The bikers exchanged looks. An older and obviously senior police officer turning up and asking questions bothered them, even if they were talking about something that happened a while back. Warily, King Rocker asked, "Hey, you're not looking to bang us up are you?"

"No. As I said, I'm just interested." He drained his coffee cup and then asked, "Tell me about that van. Did it have any markings on the side, anything?"

"Not that I noticed. It were just a van with stuff from that warehouse, nothing special."

"Okay, thank you," said Parsons. He wondered if he might be able to follow up on the woman and the van but King Rocker was very vague about when that incident had happened, so following up there would be difficult. Besides white vans were a dime a dozen so how would he locate it? He had already spoken to Nobby Murphy, the truck driver, and had got nothing helpful out of him either. As King Rocker said, Peter Marshall just seemed to turn up when he's needed and then disappear again. What was it with that guy?

Muttering, "I'm getting too old for this", John Parsons got to his feet, nodded at King Rocker and headed towards his car. Finding a missing person was always difficult but when they left no trace of where they had been or even why they had been there in the first place made it doubly difficult. As he said to himself, he was getting too old for this sort of malarkey. 'Still and all,' he thought. 'It is strange how Peter just turns up when there's about to be trouble and then disappears again. Nobby Murphy and that woman…no obvious connection between them and the two incidents occurred about twenty-five or fifty miles apart. Why here when there was no obvious connection with Northern England in Peter's past? As King Rocker had said, it really was weird.'

Driving back to London, John knew that nothing made sense. A few pieces of the puzzle had been solved but there still too many unanswered questions and he still had no idea where Peter Marshall could be. As he muttered to himself, that he knew how Peter had ended up in Northern England was one thing but how'd he get to that food warehouse and who was the woman that he helped? Again he wondered what this whole business was all about. Why had Special Branch been called in? Nothing made sense, not at first and certainly not now. For perhaps the hundredth time since he had been given the case, John Parsons muttered to himself, "I'm getting too old for this, just too frigging old!"

Time moved on and Peter Marshall was now a solid member of the Oak Tree Manor "family". Mr. Hawkins had pretty much recovered his strength and was taking a much more active part in running the guesthouse. As he said to Chris one day over coffee in the kitchen, "I cannot understand how we managed without Peter in the past. I know we did but how? There's almost nothing he can't do and he is so willing…and to think he just appeared out of the blue, just when you needed him."

"I know, dad, I know. I sometimes wonder about that too. Who put him there? I suppose I can rationalize the why but the how is what I don't or can't understand. Actually, I'm not too sure I know the "why" either, for that matter."

Her father looked at her questioningly, and Chris added, "Dad, as you know, I've never been religious, spiritual if you will, but now I'm really beginning to change my attitude. Attending church used to be something we sort of did, you know…it was expected of us and we went but now? Now the sermons seem to have a deeper meaning, more significance, than before. Things are so different now…in almost every way. Do you think it's due to Peter?"

"I don't know lass but I'll tell you one thing, your Peter has done something here but, like you, I don't know exactly what. Funny thing is though, he doesn't seem to have changed at all. He's the same person now that he was when he first turned up."

"My Peter? But you're right, dad…and, let's face it, we know very little more about him now than we did then. He's like a catalyst, isn't he?"

"What's a catalyst?" asked Mr. Hawkins.

"It's a sort of agent for chemical change. Back when I was in high school doing chemistry, we were taught that a catalyst was something that caused a reaction, a change if you will, that either would not happen on its own or only did so very slowly. Funny thing is that although a catalyst is essential for the reaction to occur, the catalyst itself remains unchanged. Bit like Peter here. Maybe that's what he is, a catalyst and a good one at that."

"Perhaps you're right but I don't think I've heard of a human catalyst before although I suppose that's what Winston Churchill did during the war for the English people. Anyway, enough of this fanciful talk, it won't get the dishes done, will it?" He started to get up and then sat down again. "Chris," he said earnestly. "Tell me again about the situation with the bikers. Did he really just walk up and they took off running? Was he that scary?"

"Frankly dad, I didn't see anything different about him. All I know is that one minute they were about to give me all sorts of trouble, the next they were off on their bikes."

"He didn't wave a gun at them or anything?"

"No, he just looked at them but it was enough and they took off."

"Huh! I wonder what that was all about. As I often say, your Peter is a man of mystery but I don't see him exerting a force field, do you?"

"A force field?" laughed Chris.

"If not that, how else did he frighten them off? These days nothing surprises me, so don't laugh too hard…you never know what's going on."

"You may be right dad," agreed Chris. "You never know, do you? Okay let's get back to work."

After the cups were cleared away, Chris turned to her father, "Hey dad, should we be paying Peter more? He does so much and we're only giving him the same as Mabel, and he does a lot more than she ever did. What do you think?"

"Well, thanks to him, we're doing much better these days so, yes, give him a raise…and Chris, don't take no for an answer. I don't want to lose him for a few pounds, okay?"

Later that day, when Chris was taking a short break, she thought about her father's comment. Peter exerting a force field? That was something only found in science fiction so, no, it wasn't possible. That left only one possibility, that those bikers had come across Peter before but when…and how? Yet another mystery surrounding the man. She shrugged and got back to work. She had received an advance booking for a visiting professor from America, a guest lecturer at Greydene University and a man who would be staying at Oak Tree Manor. The University liaison person had also asked whether they could cater a small dinner party one evening for the visiting American and a few faculty members from one of the chemistry departments at the University. After Chris and her father had discussed it, they were happy to accept the commission but knew that they would have to start planning things well in advance. Large or even small dinner parties were not the norm and they would have to get in all the provisions as well as wine, liquors and beer, and also make sure they had enough staff to take care of things. That would mean Lucy, Mabel and Peter, as well some extra people, depending on how many were likely to come that evening.

Although she was pleased with the booking, the challenges involved were already slightly daunting. "I've got to start making lists," she muttered. "When all else fails, make a list!"

Changes, large and small, were starting to loom on the horizon.

EIGHT

John Parsons sat down at the dinner table, glad to be home and hungry for what smelled like a good meal. The drive back from the North had tired him but the pleasant, almost joyful, greeting of Mary had made him feel good and made up for his disappointment over the hunt for the elusive Peter Marshall. After dinner they sat down in the living room and, for the first time in longer than either of them cared to admit, Mary asked John what he was working on.

"I've been tasked with finding someone, one Peter Marshall."

"Why, what's he done?"

"That's just it," sighed John. "He doesn't seem to have done anything but some bloody bureaucrat in Whitehall seems to have a hair up his arse, excuse my French, and demanded that Special Branch has to find him. I was given the job"

"They didn't say why?"

"No, Chief Superintendent Miller isn't one to tell the likes of a lowly inspector what the higher-ups think. He issues orders and that's that." John paused for a moment, then added, "Mind you, I suspect he doesn't know much either."

"That's odd," said Mary. "What do you know about this Peter Marshall?"

"He was some sort of scientist at Cambridge University and then went off the rails when his wife died. He got very drunk and wrecked his car and did a lot of damage to a lot of other vehicles. He injured some people too but, thank the Lord, no-one was killed. He was sent to prison for three years – bit sad really."

"I'll say," said Mary. "That sounds horrible."

"It was," agreed John. "But after he got out of prison, well, that's when things start to get interesting." After warning her not to tell anyone about anything he said, John went on to tell Mary about the martial arts that Peter had learned from Monk in prison and then how he'd sorted out a belligerent drunk in a pub. "For some reason," he added. "Peter took off when he heard the police had been called. It seems he got a lift from some truck driver up to the North of England and then somehow managed to sort out a biker gang that was going to do the truck driver over."

"So he put that training to good use, did he?" asked Mary. "Your Peter sounds like a good man. Pity about that wife of his dying and him getting so drunk and causing all that damage to those cars. It's all such a shame, isn't it? But why did he take off like that from that pub when he heard the police were coming – surely he hadn't done anything wrong? I assume those bikers didn't file charges either?"

"No, not that I can tell. I gather that the other people in the pub would have supported him and even that drunk didn't want to press charges. As for the biker gang – they just took off and that was that. Anyway, there's something else that happened with "My Peter" sometime after that punch-up with the bikers."

"There is?"

"Yes, it seems that this same Peter intervened when that same biker gang was harassing a youngish woman and he scared them off. He didn't actually need to do anything – just the sight of him sent them scurrying."

"Really? Isn't that odd?" asked Mary. "Who was the woman and how did she come to know Peter?"

"I'm not sure that she did know him. According to the bikers, he just appeared out of nowhere and they took off. They didn't know who the woman was or even how she, or Peter, got to be there in the first place. As I say, he just appeared and that was that."

"How very strange," said Mary.

"It is very odd," agreed John. "But I'll you one thing, that Peter Marshall seems to have a strange effect on people," and he went on to tell his wife about Nobby and his daughter Dahlia, without mentioning their names. A Special Branch Detective Inspector always plays his cards close to the chest, even with his wife. "I tell you, my Sweet, he has some sort of benign influence on people….I don't understand what, but he does."

Mary, conscious of the change that seemed to have occurred with her husband, smiled and said, "Your Peter Marshall sounds like some kind of avenging angel, doesn't he? I'd love to meet him."

"So would I," said John fervently. "So would I."

After getting to work, John Parsons sat down heavily at his desk. He was still tired from all the driving but Mary's welcome had made him feel good although he was still disappointed at not finding Peter Marshall. He would have to bring his chief up-to-date on progress, and that would not be pleasant. Eventually he picked up the phone and asked Chief Superintendent Miller's secretary if he could see him.

After John had given his verbal report, Miller sat back and gazed at him, "So, you had no luck in finding him?"

"No, I'm afraid not. Every time I got close to him, he seems to have gone off again. He's one elusive bugger, that one. I don't think he's doing it on purpose…actually, why would he since he doesn't even know anyone's looking for him. But he's vanished yet again. By the way, why does anyone want me to find him? He doesn't seem the sort that we, meaning Special Branch, normally take an interest in. He's not some sort of terrorist or a communist, is he? There's been no mention of him being a Muslin or anything. It doesn't make a lot of sense to me."

"Frankly John, I've no idea why anyone would want him. I received my orders and that was that. Did you find out anything about him that might even suggest why those people in Whitehall, whoever they are, would have an interest in him?"

"Nothing that I could see. He was some sort of chemist and pretty well known in his field but he's never signed The Official Secrets Act and there's no suggestion that he was privy to any defense secrets, or anything like that. He's just an ordinary University professor who got himself into a lot of trouble by getting seriously drunk because his wife had died under bad circumstances."

"As you say John, it really doesn't make a lot of sense but then again, not a whole lot does these days. Okay, I'll tell the people upstairs what's going on and after you have laid it all out in a report, keep trying to find the man, will you? He's got to be somewhere and perhaps by the time we find him, we might know what it's all about."

John nodded. He hated the thought of spending a couple of days detailing his efforts and summarizing what he had learned but he knew the Government ran on paper, and he would be in serious trouble if he didn't follows orders and give a decent report to his chief.

"So Bethany, tell me what you think," said The Right Honorable James Arthur Llewellyn-Hughes to his guest, Professor Randolph Bethany, Professor of Physical Chemistry at Christ's College, University of London and Chief Scientific Advisor at the Ministry of Energy and Natural Resources. They were having lunch at the Minister's exclusive club in London where they could talk privately and be uncommonly honest with each other. "What do you make of all this business with Martin and that chap Marshall?"

"It's complicated, Arthur, complicated."

The minister raised one eyebrow but made a slight hand gesture inviting the other man to continue. It was a sign of their familiarity and degree of comfort with each other that Bethany knew to call Llewellyn-Hughes by his preferred name.

"I put a couple of my people, Art Golding and Jim Streetly, on to it. They are both good scientists and have an intuitive grasp of things. They examined Marshall's work independently and then together before they reviewed Martin's research proposal and all his experimental data."

"And?"

"There is something there. I'll get Golding and Streetly to come in to talk to you, if you wish…I assume you want nothing in writing, is that correct?"

Llewellyn-Hughes nodded before saying, "In their opinions, individual and collective, Marshall was on to something, was he? What about Martin?"

"Martin's proposal was good, very good in fact, and most persuasive…very well written and, as I say, most convincing. But, as you say, he failed to mention that it wasn't his idea in the first place. His initial data looked good although it wasn't really germane to his central thesis, that is, almost unlimited energy from transmutation of the elements. As time went on, things seem to have gone from bad to worse and the time-honored practice of throwing money at a problem went very awry. That, I suppose, is why you asked me to have a look at all this?" Looking at his lunch host, Bethany added, "It's a pity I didn't review it in detail the first time round."

Llewellyn-Hughes nodded again; of course Bethany was right, he *should* have been asked to review the proposal when it was first submitted by Martin. Eventually he said, "Ah yes, hindsight is always 20-20, or so they say. It seems, my dear Randy, that two or three of my assistants were overly ambitious and overestimated their acumen and scientific abilities. That is something I shall have to deal with to ensure that nothing like this happens again. So, what do you suggest might be our next move?"

Professor Bethany took another sip of wine before saying, "There does seem to be some merit in this whole concept. After all, Marshall was a very sound, brilliant even, scientist and if he believed that he was onto something, then he should be treated seriously."

"I see…and what about Martin?" asked Llewellyn-Hughes.

"Oh he's sound enough, quite good really but I don't think he's in Marshall's league. He's a hard worker and very dedicated but he lacks that…uh, I don't know…he lacks that spark of creativity."

"I see," said Llewellyn-Hughes again. "What do you suggest?"

"Assuming that you do not want to waste the money invested already and there's no justification for doing so at this stage, then the answer is obvious."

"It is?" queried Llewellyn-Hughes.

"Yes…we just need to find Marshall and persuade him to get back to work. It's been a few years and he will need time to get up to speed again but I doubt that his ability has completely atrophied. Then, all being well, he could take over the project…and even have Martin working under his direction."

"You have reached the same conclusions that I have," said the Minister. "In fact, I've already put some people onto finding him. I'm told that they are very competent, so I expect I shall hear something shortly." Pausing for a few moments and studying Bethany's expression, Llewellyn-Hughes added, "Assuming that we do find him, which surely cannot be too difficult in this day and age, and also assuming that he is ready and willing to get back to work… something that might be less certain…then I venture to suggest that you and possibly those two young men you mentioned might be interested in being involved in this, yes?"

"Oh yes, indeed. In fact, I was about to ask you about that," said Bethany, and seeing the look on the face of Llewellyn-Hughes, he added, "Perhaps it might be sensible for us to get up to speed, as the Americans say, about this subject ourselves? A small stipend might help in this matter."

Llewellyn-Hughes smiled to himself, thinking, 'It always comes down to money with these academics. They spout on about scientific integrity, the good of mankind and the need for progress but it always comes back to money in the end. Oh we'll find some money to pay them…grubby little men that they are…and so predictable. Ah well, I don't have much choice, do I?, and some extra eyes might actually be valuable.' Sipping some wine, he said to his guest, "I'm sure we can find something for you…can't have you going hungry, can we? Do you agree that Martin could be a good number two for Marshall? Would those two people of yours be available to do the same, work with Marshall that is?"

Bethany nodded in agreement. He was pleased to hear that the Minister would further augment his already substantial salary and, after all, this project could actually be quite ground-breaking. If it did all work out, he would be able to garner a lot of publicity for himself as the shadow mastermind behind the project. If George Martin could do it, then so could he and he was a lot more talented and politically aware than that man. What a splendid lunch this had been, and even the food was good.

Dr. George Martin sat at his desk with his head buried in his hands. Things were getting progressively worse, both in the laboratory and at his college in general. Only the other day he heard two junior colleagues talking about him:

"You heard that things aren't going too well with Martin, are they? At least that's what I've been told."

"I heard the same thing…seems that Martin, after being the golden boy, is now a bit of a has-been in far too many eyes."

"More like a "never-was" according to the rumor mill."

"What?"

"It seems that this big project he's working on wasn't his idea, at least that's what the rumors are saying."

"Oh dear, that doesn't sound good. Any idea what this project of his is actually all about?"

"Not really…all I know is that nothing is working out and his research team is leaving left, right and center. The man's a bear to work with when things don't go right."

"That's a pity." and the two men passed out of Martin's earshot, unaware that he had even overheard them.

Eventually George decided he'd have to take matters into his own hands. He knew Peter better than any flat-footed policeman ever could. After all, they had been colleagues and friendly rivals for years. Now, what was the name of that detective who had come to see him? Perkins?, Parkins?, no, it was Parsons. He dug around in his desk until he found the man's business card. Picking up the telephone, he called Scotland Yard and asked to be put through to Detective Inspector Parsons. When John came on the line, he said brusquely, "I'd like to come down and talk to you." Silence at the other end. "If it's alright with you, I'll come down on the next train and come over to see you." Still silence from the other end. "I'd like to talk to you about Peter Marshall," he said finally.

"I see," said John. "This afternoon you say or closer to lunchtime?"

"Early afternoon…we could even go and get a late lunch. if you're free, that is."

"Okay. You know where Scotland Yard is, do you?"

George Martin got on the next train to London and was there shortly after noon. He took the underground to the station nearest Scotland Yard and then briskly walked out into the sunshine, dodging around the slower walking Londoners crowding the sidewalks. As he neared Scotland Yard, he was so immersed in his thoughts that, without looking, he stepped out into the road to get past two young women strolling along, busily texting on their cell phones. The last thing he heard was a squeal of brakes and the startled screams of the two women…then blackness. He was dead before an ambulance could be called.

Sitting in his office, John Parsons was wondering where his visitor had got to. He decided he had waited long enough for the man and started to get ready to go out for some lunch. It was already close to two o'clock and he was hungry. He was just scribbling out a note to leave with the receptionist when his sergeant poked his head around the door. John looked up, "Yes?"

"It seems some idiot walked out into the traffic and got himself killed, just around the corner," said Detective Sergeant Michael Johnson.

"So?" snapped John. "What about it?"

"Apparently he was someone called Dr. George Martin. Was he the bloke who was coming to see you?"

"Yes…so that's why he was delayed. What do the local bobbies say about it?"

"Apparently he just stepped out into the road, trying to get around two women who were texting or something. Pure accident, it was. No blame to the driver - there was no way he could have stopped in time. Stupid. You'd think that someone who's a professor would know better than to step out into the street without looking no matter how much of a hurry he's in."

John grunted. He'd have to tell Chief Superintendent Miller that yet another door had closed. Whatever George Martin knew, or didn't know, was now moot. Bloody typical. He thought for a second or two and then said suddenly, "Hey Johnson, you eaten yet?"

"Yes sir, about half an hour ago."

"No matter, Mike, come with me while I eat…I'll even buy you a pint," said John.

"Er…thank you," said Mike Johnson, astonished at the invitation and thinking, 'What's got into him that he's even offered to buy me a drink. That's a first!'

When Chief Superintendent Miller heard a few hours later that George Martin had been killed in a road traffic accident, he muttered, "Well, there's another lead dead and gone. What is it with this search for Marshall? People disappear left and right, no-one seems to know what's going on and now someone from Cambridge gets killed right on our doorstep…and someone previously close to Marshall at that. Hmm, John Parsons went up there to see the man…I'll have to ask him what this chap had said when he was interviewed. It'll all be in his report but there's no harm in asking now. I hate coincidences and this one beats the cake. What on earth is going on here? Hey ho, I'll have to tell the chief and he's not going to be happy. Knowing him, he'll think it's some sort of International murder plot…of course, he could be right…nothing would surprise me these days."

When he sat with his chief, Miller got the reaction he expected.

"Killed, you say? Run over just around the corner from here? That's a bit too convenient for my tastes. Someone makes an urgent appointment with one of our officers and beetles down here post-haste and then gets killed almost on our doorstep? This cannot be happening!"

He sat drumming his fingers on the desk and glaring at Miller. "Right!" he decided. "Miller put a couple of your people on this so-called accident and this time, you take charge. There's something not right here and I want to know what. Interview those two women and the car driver…" then seeing the look on Miller's face, he added, "You know what to do, don't you? Just keep me informed. Someone over in Whitehall is going to raise merry hell over this and I want to have some answers ready."

After Miller left his office, he slowly picked up the telephone and told his secretary to get Llewellyn-Hughes on the phone. "Might as well share the bad news now rather than wait for him to call me," he muttered.

A day or two later, Peter was bundling up old newspapers for recycling when the headline of a National daily left in his room by a guest caught his eye:

Well-known Cambridge Professor Killed in Car Accident

Dr. George Martin, Fellow of Royal Imperial College, University of Cambridge and Fellow of the Royal Society, was killed in a road traffic incident at lunchtime two days ago in London. Described as a tragic accident, our sources in Scotland Yard tell us that Dr. Martin was on his way to see a certain Detective Inspector in the Special Branch but no information has been released regarding the reason for his visit. There is no suggestion of foul play although the police are still making inquiries. *See page 5 for further details.*

The inside story continued:

There is speculation as to why a respected Cambridge Don, as senior faculty at that University are commonly known, would be visiting Scotland Yard and a Special Branch officer at that. When Dr. Martin's colleagues were approached, none of them could offer an explanation as to why he would be seeing a Special Branch officer when, as they all said, he was not involved in any secret Government research work....

Peter, after reading the article, sat staring into space. A flood of memories had come back and, like the newspaper reporter, he too wondered why his old friend and rival would visit Special Branch. He was so deep in thought that he didn't hear Chris coming into the kitchen.

Seeing him totally lost in thought, Chris said quietly, "Penny for your thoughts," and was startled by Peter's reaction. Was it a guilty look that crossed his face or fear? What was it? Pausing for a moment, she added, "What's that you're looking at?" and before Peter could react, she picked up the newspaper and scanned the headlines. Looking at him, she asked, "Did you know this man?"

"Sort of," was the flat response.

"You did?" she asked in surprise, thinking, 'How does a hitchhiker and now general handyman at Oak Tree Manor know a Cambridge University professor? I wonder what he's not telling me.'

"Oh well," said Peter. "Got to get to it…there's a dripping faucet in one of the rooms." He grabbed his tool belt and left the room without saying anything further. As Chris said to her father later, "He wasn't rude or anything…he just didn't say anything…just upped and left."

Mr. Hawkins sat back in his chair and looked fondly at his daughter. "Chris, I keep telling you, let it rest. That old saying "Let sleeping dogs lie" is good advice, and, yes, I did see that article in the paper yesterday, if you're asking. If Peter knew this fellow, then he knew him and that should be that. If he wants to tell us about it, he will but only in his own good time."

"But it's all so mysterious, dad," said Chris.

"Look, as I keep telling you, everyone has secrets and Peter's no exception. Don't upset the applecart is my motto by trying to pry things out of him."

"I know, dad, I know but…"

"No buts, Chris. Let it be. Peter's a good man and he's made a big difference here…I don't want to lose him because of female curiosity."

"Okay, dad, okay. I hear you."

After Chris had left his office, Mr. Hawkins thought about Peter. He too wondered about the man. He was too well-spoken to be the average hitchhiker or handyman. Since they had been paying him, he was now better dressed but still casual in the clothes he wore, mainly jeans and heavy-weight cotton shirts. Nevertheless, there was an indefinable gentility about the man, almost as though he was playing a role, trying to fit in as something that didn't come naturally to him. Mr. Hawkins could easily visualize Peter wearing well-cut suits or blazers, dress shirts and smart silk ties. Could he have been an Oxbridge professor in the past? Anything was possible and that would explain how he might have known this dead Martin person. But if he had been a professor, what was he doing here and why had he given up academia? It might come out eventually but he was too long in the tooth to want to press the issue. Curiosity killed the cat, as far as he was concerned, and he worried that Chris, relentless in trying to find out everything and anything about the people around her, would cause Peter to leave. That would be dreadful.

Chief Superintendent Miller slammed down the telephone. That was the fifth or sixth phone call he'd had from a newsperson asking about Dr. George Martin, and he was thoroughly irritated by the relentless questioning by reporters from every National newspaper. How the hell did he know what the man wanted? He didn't even know that Martin was coming to the Yard that day, so what could he say that wouldn't be taken out of context? Not even Parsons knew why Martin had called him, so there was no help there.

Once again he cursed the higher-ups for landing him with this problem. If he even so much as breathed a word that Martin's visit might, just might, be related to the search for Peter Marshall, then his career was over. That he didn't even know why anyone was looking for Marshall was beside the point. Once again, he wondered why it was so important to a senior someone in Whitehall to find Marshall. What the hell had he been involved in that made it so vital to find him? As he had said to his wife one evening, "Nothing makes sense and I hate to think my career hinges on something as trivial as finding a missing Cambridge University professor. I don't understand any of this."

"Oh I'm sure it will all come out in the wash, dear," his wife assured him. "It usually does."

"I hope so," he muttered. "I really hope so."

As Peter finished up changing the washer on the leaky faucet, he thought about George Martin. 'What were you doing going to see someone in Special Branch, George? That's just not you, is it? I can't believe you were working on any sort of super-secret project for the Government. I know it's been the best part of four or more years since we were in touch but, still and all, it doesn't make sense.'

He stood up and stretched, straightening his back. George Martin, radiochemistry, Cambridge University – they were all a lifetime ago and he didn't want to go back. Science and academia were nothing to him now and, truth be told, had probably contributed to Jean's death. If only he'd been there, he could at least have said goodbye. Now he had nothing. Prison had been a nightmare, leavened only by Monk, and his life after getting out hadn't been much better. He was happy to be here at Oak Tree Manor…Chris, Mr. Hawkins, Mabel and even young Lucy made life worth living but maintaining a strict silence over his previous life was beginning to wear on him. Chris, sweet, kind and affectionate Chris, was increasingly curious about him but what would her attitude be if she knew he'd been in prison? Would that negate what he'd been before everything had happened? Maybe yes, maybe no but did he want to run that risk? No, never. He felt better about himself now than he had in months if not years, so why risk it all? Thinking of Chris, he smiled again. He sensed that Chris was attracted to him but, unlike Lucy who made her interest so obvious, Chris just seemed to be biding her time but why? What did she want from him? A quick roll in the hay – that hardly seemed her style – and a long-term involvement did not seem to fit. Her marriage had not worked out and although she had not become a man-hater, she certainly made no effort to attract any man's attention.

It might have been all so trivial and meaningless but the various women that he had bedded while working behind the bar had made sure that everything was uncomplicated. They wanted him, he wanted relief and that was that. Everyone was happy, their needs met. But Chris? No, nothing seemed to fit.

Shaking his head, Peter left the guest's room, quietly closing the door behind him. It was close to lunchtime and he had to put his tools away and clean-up. Mabel would be down there, fussing over lunch and Mr. Hawkins, now back to health and strength, would be there also, happily gossiping with them about their guests, the weather, the local villagers and the appalling TV programs that were served up every day. He laughed…nothing changed and everything was so normal. It felt good to be here. Wearing a smile, he joined the others around the big kitchen table.

John Parsons put the finishing touches to his report. Satisfied, he slid it into an envelope which he placed in the Internal Mail tray. He'd hear soon enough from his chief but in the meantime, he decided, he'd better get back to trying to find Peter Marshall. He could eliminate London, Oxford and Cambridge as possible destinations for Peter and there seemed no point in his going back North. So where would he have gone? The West Country? The Midlands? Not likely, as were Scotland or Ireland as possible destinations. Although the Common Market and the European Union made travel easier, having no passport reduced the likelihood of his crossing the channel to France or Belgium, notwithstanding the lack of money. "So, "he asked himself. "Just where are you? And who was that woman you helped with those bikers? Somehow I feel that she's the key here, so how do I find her? If that was a food warehouse she had just visited when the bikers turned up, surely the warehouse people would know her because she was likely a regular customer. Regular customer? Now that's a thought. Did she work for a restaurant of some sort? Surely there can't be too many eating establishments around Greydene, even if it is a University town. Okay, that's where I'll start. Pity those bikers couldn't give me a better description. Somewhat attractive older woman, whatever that meant. Useless lot – they didn't even know the color or length of her hair, her height or even if she wore glasses."

He went down to the library within Scotland Yard to start going through the telephone and business directories for that part of the country. On his way, he collected his sergeant, telling him, "Johnson, we've got work to do," and outlined what they should be looking for.

Mike Johnson pulled a face. There was nothing he disliked more than pawing through telephone and business directories. It was tedious but essential work and there was no guarantee of success. Still, he reflected, one never knows what might turn up. Thank goodness it was Parsons and not he that would have to follow up on anything they found. Then a thought struck him, what if his Inspector decided that he had to go there too? His girlfriend would not be pleased if he had to go out of town for a few days. His girlfriend? That was a bit of a stretch and she was very demanding of his time even though, as she stoutly maintained, we're not exclusive, are we? Nothing was simple and since that Cambridge bloke had got himself killed, it was getting worse. Rumors were flying around thick and fast and he, Mike Johnson, ostensibly in the middle of it all, knew absolutely nothing, to the disgust of his friends. "Dead loss, you are," they would say when meeting up for a drink after work. "What sort of detective are you if you don't have a clue about what's going on?"

NINE

"Excuse me, sir," said Detective Sergeant Mike Johnson to Detective Inspector John Parsons. "But there seem to be a fair number of eateries in the Greydene area."

John Parsons looked up from the telephone directory for that area and grunted. His assistant was right, there *were* a lot of places to eat around and about that part of the country, everything from hotels, to pubs, to restaurants, to cafes, fast food joints and even a few coffee and tea shops. Tea shops? Did they still have such places these days given the ubiquity of Starbucks? "Mike," he said eventually. "What does Google indicate?"

"Several hundred, and that's not including the various eateries in and around the University, a couple of Teacher Training and Technical Colleges as well as schools."

"I think we can forget about the University and the various colleges and schools, at least for the moment. I imagine that those places get their food supplies delivered to them on a regular basis. On the odd occasion that they might run out of something or need to get a specialty item, they would sent someone in one of their own vehicles. Those vans or whatever would likely carry some sort of logo or emblem, or whatever it is that those places call their vehicle signs…a sort of mobile advertisement, I suppose. The same might go for the larger restaurants too."

Mike looked at his boss, "So, what do we do?"

"If we are to handle this logically, the best thing might be to separate every eating establishment into one of three categories, you know the sort of thing: Likely, Possible, Unlikely."

"Which is which?" asked his sergeant.

"Okay, "unlikely" would include the University, colleges and schools. That category also would cover the larger restaurants, hotels, burger joints and fish-and-chip shops. They would have their supplies delivered by wholesalers or their designated suppliers in the case of burger places. As for fish-and-chip shops, even those dumb bikers would have noticed the smell of fish, so we can put that sort of place on the back burner too. I'm not sure about ethnic places but I suspect that they get their supplies from specialty shops."

"That still leaves a whole lot of "likely" and "possible" places, chief," sighed Mike. "How do we know if a restaurant is big or simply a hole-in-the-wall place?"

"Difficult I grant you but if the place advertises itself online or in the telephone directory, then chances are that it's a reasonable size. That's no guarantee of course because I've come across plenty of tiny places that have large advertisements…you know, delusions of grandeur."

Mike Johnson smiled; he knew exactly what Parsons was saying, having been caught out himself trying to find a place to take his girlfriend for a meal. After thinking, he asked, "So how best do we handle this, sir?"

"Get out our laptops and literally write down each and every eating place we can find anywhere within a 25 mile radius of Greydene or that food warehouse. Then we each separate all those places into the three categories. After that, we'll compare our findings and produce one final list."

"Sir, that's going to take a while, isn't it?" complained Johnson. "Probably days, if I'm not mistaken."

"So what?" said Parsons. "We've nothing else to do and it's the best idea that we've got to go on. The people upstairs expect us to do something and as long as we can rationalize what we're doing, they'll leave us alone. Besides, you never know, we might actually get lucky. Okay lad, get to it. Oh yes, when you've got a moment, see if you can locate some large scale maps of the area – we'll probably need them." Having said that, John looked at the pages and pages of every type of eating establishment one could imagine and shuddered, thinking, 'The next time Mary wants to have dinner out," he muttered. "I'm going to tell her about this job and perhaps she'll change her mind.

In fact, the very thought of food is nauseating. Johnson's right, this will take days but what choice do we have?'

After they had been working steadily for a couple of hours, Johnson looked over at Parsons. "Sir, it has occurred to me that even if we find this woman, why should she have anything to do with Peter Marshall or even know him?"

"Logic, lad, logic," replied John.

"How so?"

"Well sergeant," said his inspector, pleased to be able to expand upon his reasoning. "Look at it this way…despite what that biker said, Peter Marshall didn't just magically appear out of nowhere like some sort of *Deus ex Machina*."

"What's that?" asked his sergeant.

"That's an old literary artifact – you know, something that miraculously comes out of nowhere and saves the day, that sort of thing."

"Really? Never heard of it," said Mike Johnson.

"Well, no matter. Anyway, I'm thinking that our man Peter was inside the building or something and then came out just in time to scare off the bikers…follow me so far?"

Sergeant Johnson nodded.

"Alright then. My scenario is that Peter was with this unknown woman, otherwise how else would he have got to that warehouse? Those bikers said there were no other cars around and I can't believe that Peter Marshall simply walked down some road in the middle of nowhere, and arrived just in time to rescue this woman from trouble. That would really stretch credibility too far. No, sergeant, I am assuming that he was with her, possibly to help load up the van and was in the bathroom or somewhere when the bikers drove up – coming out just at the right time. *Ergo*…that's Greek for therefore… he must have driven to the place with her unless she just happened to pick up a hitchhiker on the way there – which again is hardly likely. That being so, then it's not unreasonable to assume that she knows him and, if she knows him, she probably has a good idea where he's staying, otherwise how else would she have picked him up to help load the van?"

Mike Johnson stared at his boss in amazement, thinking, 'How did he work all that out? It all makes sense; no wonder he's got us looking for a restaurant or eatery up there. He's pretty smart…and there's me thinking he's getting a bit past it. Shows you what I know,' and he got back to work.

It was mid-afternoon and all the chores were done - Oak Tree Manor was ready for the guests that would trickle in towards the early evening. Lunch had been cleared away, Mabel had gone home and her father was dozing in his easy chair, so Chris decided she would take a nap and then shower before any guests arrived. Glancing out of her bedroom window, she spotted Peter trolling the lawnmower over the back gardens. In deference to the warm sunny day, he was bare-chested and wearing shorts and Chris stood transfixed, enjoying the sight of his rippling muscles as he steered the unwieldy machine around the flower beds, shrubs and trees dotting the landscape. "Oh my," she muttered. "You do have a great body, don't you? No wonder Lucy fancies you." She laughed and then admitted to herself, "Well, I suppose I do too." As she watched him, enjoying a warm but very unfamiliar feeling between her legs, she thought, 'You are so different from my ex aren't you, Peter? My ex? What a wanker! We were happily married for several years…at least *I* thought so…then he had to go off and hook up with that teenager with big tits and an empty head…had to find yourself, did you? Give me a break! Well, Larry, I wonder whether that novelty has worn off yet…if it has, then suffer you wanker, it serves you right.'

Watching Peter turn back towards the house, Chris dodged away from the window; she didn't want the man to see her staring at him…that wouldn't do at all. "How funny," she said aloud. "That's the first time I've thought about Larry in a long time. I suppose it was too painful at first, now I just don't care…I'm far better off without him." Hearing the sound of the mower moving away from the house, she stole another look out at Peter and again was struck at how well-built he was. The deathly pallor he'd had when he first arrived was rapidly disappearing and now he was slowly tanning in the warm sun. Again she muttered, "I wonder what it is about you, Peter. Everybody likes you, even that crotchety old colonel who comes in for an evening drink every so often. As for Mabel and Lucy, they love you and make no bones about it…even dad, who is very reserved, thinks the world of you. But what about me? What do I think? Oh yes, I really like you and, truth be told, I think I fancy you a bit too but what do I do about it? You really don't give me any help there, do you? What if I make a move, try to…I don't know what the modern term for a sexual advance is…but if I do that and you don't respond or take offense, what then? I've seen how you gently turn Lucy aside and I don't want that to happen to me…it would make things really awkward here, wouldn't it? Dad would never forgive if we lost you, especially if it's because I made an unwanted advance. Damn, what do I do?"

She was silent for a while and then said to herself again, "But this can't go on for much longer. Peter, I know you're a man and you've got to have needs…all men do. Actually so do women for that matter, so what do we do about it? I can't just throw myself at you, or could I? Now that's a thought. Okay, I'll sleep on it," and she turned back the covers on her bed to take a nap. Her last thoughts were, 'Something will turn up…it usually does but I hope it's soon."

Peter smiled to himself. He'd been aware that Chris was covertly studying him…no-one who'd spent time in prison was ever unaware of being watched, not matter how skillfully or unobtrusively. Not paying attention to what was happening around you could have nasty, and often painful, consequences. He thought about Chris, 'You're beautiful, aren't you girl? Oh yes, you dress down, hiding what is probably a good figure and that functional haircut and your severe glasses do nothing for you, do they? I still wonder about your ex-husband…you were obviously once married…no-one who looks like you and with your personality would stay single for long. So what sort of number did that git do on you? You're no man-hater but you are definitely wary of men, that's for sure. I certainly fancy you and, I suspect, you feel something for me but that reserve of yours gets in the way…is it because you are the boss's daughter and I'm just the hired help? Nah, that's not it because you're no snob.'

He reached the end of the broad swath he'd cut over the lawn and turned back towards the house. 'So what do we do about it? If

I make a move and she doesn't like it, then what? Will I get thrown out on my ear? That'd be a pity…in fact, that's something I'd hate. I really like it here. This is the first place I've felt comfortable in for years and I don't want to jeopardize that for a bit of nooky. Still and all, I feel that you are interested in me and the feeling's mutual. That raises the question of what should we do about it? Ah well, I'll just finish up here and have a nap and a shower. Something will turn up – it usually does but what and when?'

The Right Honorable James Arthur Llewellyn-Hughes was not a happy man, not at all. First, his staff had fallen in love with a well-written, very persuasive but slightly dubious proposal promising limitless energy at minimal cost. They were obviously taken in by the lure of a Cambridge professor. Then, after millions have been spent on research that went nowhere, it turned out that the original idea was not the applicant's at all but had come from a former colleague, and one who had managed to get himself locked up for God-knows whatever reason. After that, this person, one Dr. Peter Marshall, disappeared and had taken his ideas and knowledge with him. Not only that, no-one knows where he is or can find him. Then that idiot George Martin got himself run over, and right around the corner from Scotland Yard, which was sheer carelessness. What was he thinking? Most traffic accidents, even the fatalities, rarely got more than a brief mention on the inside pages of the newspaper. This time, however, not only did it make front page news but somehow or another it got out that he was on his way in to see Special Branch. To his intense irritation, the Press was now having a field day, speculating about all sorts of Government plots, International intrigue and the usual cant spouted by the ignorant and unaccomplished. It was all a mess and, to cap it all, questions were now being asked in Parliament. Even the Prime Minister and the Cabinet were curious about recent events and the press coverage it was receiving. Llewellyn-Hughes was now expecting a call any day from them to explain what was going on.

Deciding, he picked up the phone and called Special Branch. 'After all, if I'm uncomfortable, they can suffer too,' he thought. When he had got through, he asked, "What's happening with the hunt for this Marshall fellow?"

"We're making progress but the trouble is, every lead we get seems to evaporate."

"What?' roared Llewellyn-Hughes. "You people can sniff out well-hidden terrorist cells in every densely-populated city in this country and now you tell me that you can't find an ex-Cambridge type who's not even trying to hide from anyone? At least I don't think so, or is he?"

"My people are on it but somehow or another, the man keeps slipping away. I don't think it's a deliberate act on his part...it's just the way things seem to be working out."

"Huh," snapped Llewellyn-Hughes. "And, might I ask, just how is it that news of Martin's putative visit to one of your officers got into the press, and The National Globe at that?"

"That I don't know but we are making inquiries. There's been a leak somewhere."

"Obviously!" agreed a very irritated Llewellyn-Hughes. "This whole matter is now becoming increasingly embarrassing and I want to know what you are going to do about it."

"What *I'm* going to do about it?" was the astonished rejoinder. "How is it my problem? You asked my people to look for Marshall and gave no reason to do so, so what do you expect? Besides, if we say anything, it would mean pleading ignorance as to why a senior member of the government wants us to find someone who either can't or won't be found. If we say nothing, then the rumor mongers and conspiracy merchants will have a field day and if we just ignore it, then everyone, including Parliament, will be up in arms. So what exactly do you suggest we do?"

"Hmm, I see your point. I don't suppose there's chance of a terrorist cell being discovered or some sort of major scandal involving the Royal Family breaking out any time soon?"

"No, no chance at all. Everything's been very quiet of late and even the members of the upper crust are behaving themselves – for change."

"Pity. Well, keep me informed, will you? And," he waited a beat or two. "Make sure those people of yours get moving...we need to find Marshall. By the way, there's no suggestion of anything being amiss with Martin's getting killed, is there?"

"No sir, not at all. We interview the two women who saw it happen and the driver of that vehicle in question. The women were a couple of office girls on their way back from lunch and they were very insistent that Martin just walked out into the street, directly in front of an oncoming vehicle. As for the driver, he was a lowly clerk in an insurance company office on his way over to Lords to take in the afternoon's cricket match. He was badly shaken and he seems to be more worried about what might happen to his insurance premium than anything else. No, there's nothing there and they are all as clean as a whistle."

"Well, that's a relief. Thank heavens for small mercies."

After the Head of Special Branch hung up the telephone, he thought about the conversation he'd just had. 'Why the devil does the Ministry of Energy and Natural Resources want to find this Peter Marshall so badly? My intelligence people cannot explain it and even our contacts at Cambridge have no idea what's going on. Those Cambridge dons are usually on top of everything, the gossipy lot that they are, but this time none of them has a clue. Just what is going on?'

After pondering a bit more, he called for Chief Superintendent Miller. If the Permanent Under-secretary at the Ministry of Energy and Natural Resources was going to chew him out, then it was only right that he should do the same to Miller – after all, the man had been tasked with finding Marshall. As he waited for the more junior officer to make an appearance, he thought some more about the missing Dr. Peter Marshall. What sort of secret work had he been involved in that made it so vital he be found? There hadn't been a flap like this for decades. So what was so special about this fellow? But like Llewellyn-Hughes, he was disappointed at learning nothing from Chief Superintendent Miller.

"You can't find him? What do you mean, you can't find him? How is that possible? And, for that matter, why does anyone want to find him that badly?"

"I don't know, sir. I have no idea what makes him so valuable and as for not finding him, every time we get close, he seems to just disappear. It's very strange and my officers, who are usually very efficient in this sort of thing, are baffled."

"Well, just tell them to get unbaffled – and that is an order."

"Yes sir."

"Also, have you made any progress in finding out who leaked the fact that this Martin person was on his way in to see Parsons?"

"I'm afraid not, no. Parsons himself has no idea why the man was coming down post-haste to see him and he's way too experienced to talk about anything to anyone. Besides, he's too close to drawing his pension to risk losing it by gossiping with a reporter. Frankly, at this stage, I've no idea who leaked the story but I'll find out soon enough. We can't have this sort of thing happening."

Richard Fowler, known as Dirty Dick to friends and enemies alike, was very pleased, in fact he was delighted. His editor at The National Globe had even complimented him on his scoop and a bonus was in the offing. It was sheer good luck that he happened to be in the very same pub, The Hoop and Grapes, where Sergeant Mike Johnson and his friends were having a drink and discussing how George Martin had been run over on his way into Scotland Yard. On the other hand, Dirty Dick always maintained, as did the venerable Louis Pasteur, that fortune favors the prepared mind and his mind was always prepared for the slightest whiff of a story. Nevertheless, try as he might, he couldn't find anything about why Martin would have been going to see Special Branch. After all, he wasn't doing any secret research work, at least nothing that he could find, and apparently he didn't associate with any communists, terrorists or even Muslims. But Dirty Dick didn't get his nickname for nothing and he couldn't resist making a veiled allusion, a hint that perhaps the death of that Cambridge scientist wasn't all that it appeared to be. Even though he had tracked down the two women and the car driver and knew that it had been an accident, pure simple, it was too good an opportunity to miss and the rumors got started.

Nevertheless, Dirty Dick really did sense that something was amiss. His fine-tuned reporter's instincts made him feel that there was something else going on but he had no idea what. He was tempted to approach one or other of his contacts in Scotland Yard but decided that to do so would be risky. If Special Branch was involved, then he didn't want to run afoul of the Official Secrets Act and have his story quashed. The Government had a habit of slapping "D" notices, official prohibitions on publishing stories that they didn't want to come out and the last thing Dirty Dick wanted or needed was to have that happen. He had to tread lightly.

Perhaps he should make a habit of going into the Hoop and Grapes on a regular basis? All police officers, even those of Special Branch, liked to have a drink and if he listened often and hard enough, he'd learn more. This story wasn't going away and even if the other papers had picked up on it, at least he knew one of the players involved, and that was a major advantage. He pulled over his notepad and started jotting down notes. It was always possible that he could be drawn into a conversation at the Hoop and Grapes and experience had taught him to have some pertinent questions handy should the opportunity arise. "The prepared mind" as he always maintained.

After that day's guests had booked into Oak Tree Manor and Chris, Mr. Hawkins and Peter had eaten dinner, they sat around the kitchen table chatting as they liked to do.

"Did you tell me that Greydene University booked a room for some visiting professor from America? Is he going to stay for several days? I assume he came in yesterday or today." asked Mr. Hawkins.

"Yes, he did. Fortunately we're not too heavily booked so that we can take care of him easily enough. What might be a problem is that the University people want us to cater a private dinner for a dozen or more of them later this week. I hope we can cope. How do you feel about it, Peter?"

"Oh, I'm sure we'll manage somehow. If Mabel and Lucy come in and we all help out, we should have no problems. What'll we serve them?"

"Probably the usual, you know…roast beef, Yorkshire pudding, roast chicken, maybe some venison if I talk nicely to the butcher. I'll have to check that none of them are vegetarians or are hell-bent on having fish, otherwise it should be plain sailing. I'll talk to Mabel about what we'll have as a dessert, possibly rice pudding, apple pie, ice-cream, that sort of thing. Nothing too fancy. Good thing is that this man seems to be eating out almost every evening with one or other of them from the University although I'm sure that they might want to come back for a nightcap later if they don't go to a pub or somewhere. I gather that's what this chap likes to do, you know, have a drink before going to bed. You'll take care of the bar if they do come in later, Peter?"

"Of course, I should be delighted. Can't have Lucy coming in and flirting with our guests, can we?" he added with a smile.

Later that evening, with the guests safely in bed and all visitors gone home, Chris was going around turning off lights and checking that all the windows and doors were secured. She walked into the bar area and saw Peter bent over some papers, staring at them intently. She stopped and watched him as he picked up a pencil and started making notes on the papers spread out on the bar in from of him. Every so often he would stop, scratch his head, mutter something and then write some more. Curious, she walked up and said, "What on earth are you doing Peter? What are those papers you are looking at?"

Startled, Peter looked up. "Oh, nothing much. Just some scribblings that that American guest and a couple of those University types had made and left on the table when they left."

"But what are you writing?" and glancing over his shoulder, Chris could see that he had crossed out some things and then written in some equations. "Do you know anything about that sort of thing?"

Peter hesitated before saying, "A bit. I'm out of practice but these people seem to have got it all wrong, and I'm just making some notes for them."

Chris paused and stared at Peter. "Are you telling me that you're a scientist? That you understand all this sort of thing?"

Embarrassed at being caught out, so to speak, Peter hesitated before responding, "Well, I used to be one but that was a long time ago. Now, I'm just out of practice but something here struck me." He looked down and then added dismissively, "Oh, it's all a load of rubbish…don't mind me…I was just having fun." He gathered up all the loose pages and slipped them back into their manila folder which he laid on the bar. "Anyway, I'm off to bed…we'll be busy tomorrow and I need my beauty sleep. Good night," he said finally and went off to his room.

Chris watched his retreating back. "What was all that about?" she asked herself. "Oh Peter, what a man of mystery you are. Now it turns out that you were some sort of scientist…what else are you that we don't know anything about? For that matter, how is it that you were once a scientist and aren't one now? Surely you don't just stop being a scientist, something like a novelist who has written himself out or a politician who has retired from public life. What am I missing here and why won't you talk about it? You make me so mad at times." Then a thought struck her, and she muttered, "Peter, your interest in that Cambridge man, George Martin, who was killed recently now takes on new significance. I bet that you were there, at Cambridge yourself at one time but what are you doing here? What happened to you?"

Bemused, she gathered up the papers in their folder and made her way to bed. Perhaps she'd have a word with that American professor and show him Peter's notes…maybe he could understand them because she certainly couldn't. Like everything else about Peter, nothing made sense.

Dr. Hiram Pederson, professor of chemistry at Polk University, Utah, walked into the dining room at Oak Tree Manor. He was slightly hung-over from the previous evening but he was hungry, the smell of bacon, sausages, baked beans, frying eggs and tomatoes drawing him towards the buffet at one end of the room. As he filled his plate, he thought yet again, 'These Brits really do know how to have breakfast and set themselves up for the day. No matter what we do back home, it's never the same as here…I wonder why that is? Generally we have better produce there than here but English breakfasts are unique…as someone once said, the best way to eat in England is to have breakfast three times a day.'

Sitting down, he tucked into his food, feeling better with each mouthful but vowing never to drink so much again in the evening and thinking, 'Those damn Brits have hollow legs…how the hell can they drink so much and still keep standing?'

He drained the last of coffee and was about to pour some more when Chris appeared at his table.

"Professor Pederson?"

"Yes?" he asked and looked up. When he saw Chris standing there, he started to get to his feet but she waved him back into his seat, "Please don't get up, professor. You enjoyed your breakfast?"

"Yes, delicious… just great, thank you."

"That's good. Ah, professor, you were in the bar last evening with two or three other people, weren't you?"

"Yes. Is anything wrong…we didn't make too much noise or anything?"

"No, nothing like that." Chris hesitated and then held out the folder to him, "I believe this belongs to you. It was left on a table last evening."

"Oh good, I was wondering where that had got to…we, er, had a few too many drinks last night…you know how it is with scientists… we get talking and drinking…lose track of time, and lose other things too." Seeing the neutral expression on Chris's face, he added, "Well, thank you very much for returning this – I was afraid I had lost it or that it could have been thrown out with the trash."

Chris smiled, "Oh no, we always try to take care of guests, even when they misplace things. Anyway, I'll leave you to finish your breakfast in peace. I'm glad that we found your notes. Have a nice day, professor," and Chris walked back to the kitchen.

A little later, Chris was finishing her second cup of coffee and collecting her energy to join Peter and Mabel in cleaning the guest rooms, reviewing the day's tasks and starting to plan the dinner menu for the Greydene people the next day. The door burst open and Professor Hiram Pederson strode in, waving the manila folder at her. Before she could react and suggest to Dr. Pederson that the kitchen was off-limits to guests, he sat down at the table opposite her. Carefully placing the folder before him, he tapped it with two fingers and looked at her with a serious expression, "Just who, might I ask, made these notes on these sheets of paper?"

Hesitantly and a bit fearfully, Chris said, "It was Peter. He found the folder last night after you had gone to bed and those other people had left. He was reading it and…I hope that you aren't angry with him or anything…I'm sure he didn't mean any harm by it."

"Angry? Oh no, my dear, quite the contrary," he was about to say more and then stopped. "Did you say Peter? The man serving drinks behind the bar last evening…that man?"

"Yes, I did," responded Chris, her anxiety rising as she tried to fathom the man's attitude.

"Is he here, this Peter of yours?"

Chris hesitated, startled that someone other than her father also referred to "her Peter", and then said quietly, "Why do you ask?"

"I need to speak to him…preferably at once but as soon as possible please."

"There's nothing wrong is there? You seem so agitated, almost angry."

"No, no, no – I'm not angry, not at all, but I must speak to the man. Can you find him?"

Mystified, Chris got to her feet, saying, "Please pour yourself some coffee and I'll try to find Peter for you. I'm sure he's somewhere around…he and Mabel get started on the guest rooms while I take care of the breakfast things after everyone has finished eating and left for the day." She realized that she was getting very flustered but could not help herself. Something very strange was happening.

She was about to go and find Peter when her father walked into the kitchen. Mr. Hawkins looked at Chris and then at the American seated at the table. He nodded at the professor and raised his eyebrows in a mute question. Chris, long familiar with her father's approach to things, hastily said, "Professor Pederson wants to see Peter and I'm just off to get him."

"He does?" asked her father. "And why would he do that?" Seeing Chris about to expand on her statement, he added, "No, my dear, you go and locate Peter…Professor Pederson can tell me himself why it's so important for him to see Peter just when our workday is getting started."

After pouring himself a cup of coffee, Mr. Hawkins sat down heavily at the table. He looked questioningly at his American guest, saying nothing but making it clear to the other man that he wanted answers if he was going to be allowed to disrupt their day.

Tapping the folder on the table, Professor Pederson starting speaking, "Last evening, I was in the bar having a drink with two of my colleagues from Greydene. We were talking shop, as we usually do whenever we get together, and we were reviewing my draft manuscript." He tapped the folder again, "This one here. Anyway, we got very immersed in our discussion. Time passed and eventually we called it a night but I accidentally left this folder on the table. It was later found by Peter, the barman."

"And?" asked Mr. Hawkins.

"This barman, in a small guest house more or less in the middle of nowhere, made some notes on the manuscript, and I need to speak to him."

"He didn't deface the pages, did he? Cause any damage? If he did, I'm sure that it was an accident … Peter's not like that, not at all," said Mr. Hawkins apologetically.

Pederson hesitated and cleared his throat. He was not sure how to proceed because what he was about to say made little or no sense and the last thing he wanted was to appear to be foolish. Eventually he said, "There's an old adage in science that if you need a particular reference or a specific piece of information, you should speak to the man or woman sitting in an airplane or a train three or four rows behind you, or the fellow sitting a couple of chairs away from you in a bar, and that person will have the information you need. And that, Mr. Hawkins or is it Jim?…"

"Jim?" asked Mr. Hawkins, startled by the sudden change in direction.

"As in Jim Hawkins…you know, Treasure Island?" Seeing the look on Mr. Hawkins's face, he hurried on, "Well, that's what we have here," and he tapped the folder again. "A classic proof of that old adage."

Just then, the door to the kitchen opened and Chris walked in, closely followed by Peter.

TEN

"Dirty Dick" Fowler of The National Globe sat on a stool in *The Hoop and Grapes* and nursed a gin and tonic. He was waiting to see whether the same Special Branch officers that he had overheard would stop in for a drink. He had no reason to believe that they would appear other than his eternal optimism and his finely-tuned reporter's instincts.

Just as he was about to give up and go home, the doors swung open and several men walked, one of whom was the Special Branch officer that he had seen before. Quickly ordering another drink, Dirty Dick moved down a couple of stools so that the new entrants could gather at the bar. Pulling out his smart phone and pretending to be intently reviewing his messages, Dirty Dick listened carefully to the banter between the men standing or sitting near him.

"So, Mike, how's that search going?"

"Slowly mate, very slowly. Parsons has got me looking at every eatery near Greydene University and for food warehouses up in Derbyshire. What a bloody pain it is," said Mike Johnson. Warming to his subject, he added, "We're making lists of every bloody place that serves food within a 25 mile radius of the place…and let me tell you, there are a whole lot of them. Who'd have believed that there would be so many? Doesn't anybody up there cook at home any longer?"

"Wait up, Mike, why are you looking into food places?" asked one of his friends.

"Because that bloke Peter Marshall was seen near a commercial food warehouse and my boss has a hair up his arse that the woman he

"

was with at that warehouse would know where he's staying," snapped Mike.

"What's he done, this Peter Marshall?" asked another officer.

"Nothing, as far as I know," said Mike. "All I know is that someone upstairs wants him found but I think the order came from some ministry or other. None of it makes any sense to me but what else is new?"

"Who is this Marshall fellow?" asked another officer.

"I don't know too much about him. All I know is that he was at Cambridge and then there was all sorts of trouble and he ended up inside. After that, he just disappeared. And no, before you ask, I've no idea why anyone wants to find him."

"Did he know that George Martin bloke who got killed the other day?" asked another man.

"No idea, mate, but it wouldn't surprise me. All those scientific University types know each other. I tell you, it's frustrating to have to look for someone when you don't know what he looks like or where he could possibly be."

"Don't you have a photograph of him?" asked the first man.

"The only one I've got is his prison admission picture and I doubt his own mother would recognize him from that. Anyways, we're hunting in the dark for someone we won't recognize in a place we don't know anything about and for a reason that no-one has shared with us."

"Hah," laughed one of his friends. "Welcome to Special Branch, Mike. Nothing changes, does it?"

After that series of exchanges, the conversation moved onto other matters, notably the lamentable performance of the England team in the Cricket World Cup...useless bunch of Wallies being the general opinion of the team.

Dirty Dick downed the last of his drink and left the pub, his head spinning. As soon as he got into his car, he started dictating notes into his cassette recorder, good sense telling him that if he had used it in the pub, he would have been asking for trouble. As he drove home, he listened to his verbal notes and tried to mentally organize them. Who was this Peter Marshall that they were trying to find and why were they looking for him? What was his relationship to the deceased George Martin? What had Peter Marshall done that had landed him in prison? Why was George Martin going to see a Special Branch officer called Parsons and who was this Parsons anyway?

He knew that he'd have to do some search work that evening using Google to answer some of his questions…in fact most of them but at least he now had direction. Delighted with the success of his patience in looking for that Special Branch sergeant, or whatever he was, Dirty Dick called his wife and announced that they would eat out that evening. "Why?" she asked. "What's the occasion?"

"Oh…er…something worked out right for a change and I thought we might celebrate."

"That's nice," said Mrs. Fowler. "Are you going to tell me about it?"

"Not just yet," replied Dirty Dick. "I've got some work to do but I'll be able to soon enough. Tell you one thing though, I think there's another bonus in the offing with this one."

"That's nice…maybe we can get the new living room suite that we've been looking at?"

"I hope so," said Dirty Dick. "I certainly hope so."

Driving through the dense London traffic, Fowler tried to decide whether he wanted Italian, Chinese, Thai, Indian, Vietnamese or something else that evening. He smiled when he thought about the restaurant scene in London. At one time, English food was severely mediocre at best but in recent years, everything had changed. Now London boasted some of the best restaurants in the world but, sadly, with prices to match. Eating out was expensive and unless one had an expense account, which he did but with severe restrictions on what he could use it for, first class restaurants were not for the ordinary folk. "One day," he decided. "I'll be able to go anywhere I like and all because I overheard a chance conversation. Funny how things work out. Okay, tonight I've work to do after dinner. Now, what should my headline be…obviously something catchy, the sort of thing the editor will probably like."

Peter, standing to one side of Chris, looked at Mr. Hawkins and then at Professor Pederson's back, because the man was sitting at one end of the table, facing away from the door and looking at Mr. Hawkins at the other end of the table. He raised one eyebrow in surprise and waited to be noticed by either man.

Sensing his presence behind him, Hiram Pederson turned in his chair and stared hard at Peter. He paused and said, "You were behind the bar last evening, weren't you?" but it was more of a statement than a question. Peter simply nodded in assent, saying nothing. "Do you mind sitting down at the table – so I don't have to strain my neck looking up at you?"

After Peter had poured a cup of coffee and sat down, Pederson continued while tapping the folder on the table, "You found this in the bar after I went to bed." Again Peter nodded. Pausing but staring hard at him, the American added, "I see you made some notes for me." Peter nodded once again, still silent. Slightly irritated, Pederson snapped, "You don't say much, do you?"

"I was taught that if you have nothing to contribute to the silence, then it's best not break it," Peter eventually said with a smile, causing Chris to giggle quietly and earning an amused look from her father.

"Anyway," Pederson said eventually. "It seems you don't agree with my conclusions. Our data clearly show that the Horton-Marshall Rule doesn't apply and our mechanism is the only one that fits the findings." He looked at Peter and added, "Unless of course you don't accept the Law of Conservation of Energy?"

"Of course, I do," responded Peter. "However, and this is a major issue, we published an exception to the Horton-Marshall Rule about 18 months after our first paper…it was in Nature…perhaps you saw it? Anyway, the H-R rule only applies when there is no cascading effect and that's something you obviously have here."

As Pederson grabbed his notes and studied them carefully, Chris and her father exchanged looks. This was a wholly different Peter sitting there, discussing arcane science with a well-known scientist from America, and a guest in Oak Tree Manor at that. In their experience, Peter was always quiet and reserved, almost self-effacing but here he was arguing persuasively and emphatically with what appeared to be an expert brought over by Greydene University. Neither father nor daughter understood more than one word in five, if that, but both were aware that Peter, whoever he was, knew what he was talking about and had no hesitation in making it known – at least in this instance he didn't!

Eventually Dr. Pederson raised his eyes and fixed a speculative look at Peter, "You are right…absolutely right. Obviously I thought, mistakenly, that this," and he pointed out what looked to be a bunch of Greek symbols to Chris and her father, "was an artifact. Each time we saw it, there were slight differences so it was not unreasonable to make that assumption. If you are right, and I suspect that you might well be, then what we have is a quasi-anti Horton-Marshall effect, something that was predicted in both those earlier papers. Hmm… very interesting."

He paused and sat back thinking hard. Eventually he said, "You know, the people at Greydene will be fascinated by this and they'll probably want to discuss it further with you." Then he stopped abruptly and stared hard at Peter. "Wait a minute, you said "we published", didn't you? But if my memory serves me, Ronald Horton passed away several years ago so you must be Peter Marshall, *the* Marshall of the Horton-Marshall Rule and Cambridge University. My word, that's amazing." He paused for a moment and then added, "That, of course, raises the question of how you came to be here at Oak Tree Manor and commenting on our as-yet unpublished research work. I'd heard that you simply disappeared three or four years ago, so I repeat, what are you doing here?"

Pederson's startled comment echoed the unspoken questions that both Chris and Mr. Hawkins were asking themselves. Just how could it be that some hitch-hiker come handyman and general factotum at a small guest house in Derbyshire, miles off the beaten track, was a well-known, if not famous, scientist? What *was* he doing here? As Chris said to herself upon reflection, 'I knew that there's something different about Peter but a renowned scientist from Cambridge University? Now that's not something I would have come up with in my wildest imagination. Oh Peter, we're going to have a long conversation about this.'

While Peter and Dr. Pederson were deep into their discussion, Mabel walked into the kitchen, on her way into the storage room to collect more cleaning supplies. She blinked in surprise at seeing Peter involved in a heavy conversation with one of their guests while Mr. Hawkins just sat staring at them. It was even more surprising that Chris was simply standing there with her mouth slightly open and an astonished look on her face.

Mabel Meadows was not the most educated of people, having barely finished high school, and her articulating ability was limited. Nevertheless, she was astute and above average in intelligence. A quick survey of the room told her that something significant and very out of the ordinary was occurring. In seconds, she decided that she would beat a hasty retreat and then find out what was going on from Chris later that day. After all, they would all be getting together to start preparing the dinner for the next evening's dinner party and she and Chris would have plenty of time to talk as they chopped vegetables and seasoned and marinated the meat. As she was about to leave the room, she spotted the papers that the American guest and Peter were going over and it was obvious that whatever it was, the subject matter was very complex, full of equations and the like.

As she went back upstairs, Mabel decided she would talk to her husband about it when she went home to take care of his lunch. This situation was all too strange for her and she valued Nigel's opinion. Retired country copper he might be but he was pretty smart and had a good understanding of people, perhaps too well at times. "He'll make something of this, I know him," she muttered. "Besides, I've kept him in the dark over Peter for far too long. Keeping confidences is one thing but shouldn't I say something to Nigel about the mysterious Peter? If Chris gets upset, then so be it but she'll get over it whereas Nigel might be another matter if there really is something odd about all this."

Receiving no reply from Peter, Dr. Pederson continued, "Well, those guys at Greydene are going to love hearing about this. I can't wait to tell them. I'm sure that they'll want to talk you, maybe even ask you to give a seminar. Huh, what a stroke of luck." Chuckling, Pederson almost ran to the door in his hurry to make his way over to Greydene University, leaving Chris and her father staring after him. Out of the corner of her eye, Chris could see Peter still sitting at the table, lost in thought and she wondered what was going through his mind. She was about to say something when she caught a look from her father, who gently shook his head in mute warning that she shouldn't say anything.

Eventually Peter got to his feet and announced, "Well, I've got to get back to work…Mabel and I haven't finished all the rooms yet."

Chris was about to go after him when her father said, "Leave him be, girl. He'll explain things when he wants to and not before."

"But dad," she protested. "This was totally unexpected. Fancy him being a scientist and at Cambridge too." She reflected for a moment and then said, "I told you that there was something different about him but this is a lot more different than even I expected. As Professor Pederson said, what is he doing here? If he's as smart as that man said, why's he working as a handyman at Oak Tree Manor instead of being at Cambridge doing whatever he was doing?"

"Chris, something happened to that young man, something he's not talking about. But I'll tell you one thing, whatever it was, it must have hit him hard. No-one goes off like that and turns his back on everything he worked for on a whim. No sir, that just doesn't happen."

"Dad, this is all so mysterious. Besides what we've just heard, what was all that about with those bikers at the food warehouse? Peter scared them off by simply looking at them…that's not something a University professor usually does."

"No, it probably isn't but if I were you, I'd wait until he decides to talk to you and not before. My thinking's that Peter could easily go off again if he's pressed. Didn't you see the look on his face when that American left? We don't want to lose him, and trying to force him to talk about something painful is the best way to do that."

"Okay dad, I hear you," said Chris, and she started to clear away the coffee cups. As she did so, Chris thought about Peter and it suddenly struck her that even if he didn't want to talk about what had happened in the past, she really did need to reassure and convince him that he was wanted here…that no-one wanted him to leave.

Commander Anthony Braithwaite, Head of Special Branch, glared balefully at Chief Superintendent Miller and virtually threw the newspaper at him across his desk. "So, what have you got to say about that?"

"About what, sir?" asked Miller, unclear as to what his chief was referring.

"That!" snapped Braithwaite. "The newspaper. Didn't you read this morning's National Globe?"

"Not this morning, no. The wife's ill so I had to take the kids to school and then dropped the dog off at the vet's for her distemper shots and all that. I didn't have time to look at the newspaper; in fact I haven't even had breakfast yet."

"Look, I really don't give a damn about your domestic difficulties. Look at that headline."

With growing alarm, Miller read:

Was the Death of Cambridge Scientist linked to Disappearance of Another Cambridge Scientist?

Unconfirmed reports suggest that the recent death of Dr. George Martin, University of Cambridge, might well be connected to the disappearance of another Cambridge scientist, Dr. Peter Marshall. Marshall was a well-known chemist engaged in high level research having to do with atomic energy who has since disappeared.

Dr. Marshall, it appears, was sentenced to three years in prison under strange circumstances and then went missing after his release, and has not been seen since. However, our sources told this reporter that Detective Inspector John Parsons of Special Branch has been conducting an intensive search for the missing scientist. No reason has been given for this search but word has it that the order to locate Dr. Marshall came from a very high level in the government.

Was it just a coincidence that Dr. Martin was on his way to meet with Detective Inspector Parsons in Scotland Yard when he met with his untimely death? Surely not... it is hard to accept that such coincidences actually exist.

This newspaper will keep our readers abreast of developments as more information becomes available on this matter of National importance.

See the article on page 3 for more information on both Dr. Martin and the missing Dr. Marshall.

Eventually Miller said, "Damn. Where the devil did all this come from? Someone talked but who was it?"

"I was going to ask *you* that question," snapped Braithwaite. "Did Parsons talk to that reporter? Surely he would know better than to do something that stupid."

"Knowing John Parsons, I find it almost impossible to believe that he would do anything as foolish as talk to a reporter, especially someone like Dirty Dick Fowler, the gossip columnist par excellence of Fleet Street," said Miller. "Besides, I think Parsons is up in Derbyshire looking for Marshall, so how could he have spoken to Fowler? We can always check his cell phone records but I doubt that this story came from him."

"Well, that reporter must have spoken to someone, otherwise how could he have linked Martin and Marshall? This is something we only found about out recently ourselves and the link between those two men is tenuous, and certainly not related to Martin's death. That bloody man must have got his information from somewhere but where or, more precisely, from whom? Look into it at once, Miller, because Llewellyn-Hughes at the Ministry will be asking for an explanation very shortly."

"Llewellyn-Hughes, the Permanent Under-secretary at the Ministry of Energy and Natural Resources, that Llewellyn-Hughes? Why should he care about any of this?" asked a puzzled Chief Inspector Miller.

"Because it was he that asked me to find Marshall in the first place. That's what started all this."

"Why would the Ministry of Energy and Natural Resources be interested in finding Peter Marshall. Isn't that a bit out of their normal sphere of interest?"

"I have no idea," said Braithwaite heavily. "All I know is that when someone at that level asks for something, then we'd better have a damn good reason why we cannot take care of it for them."

"I hate to say it, sir, but this is getting to be very complicated. Frankly, I don't understand any of it."

"It's not only you that's confused, Miller," sighed Braithwaite. "Well, get on with it man, and report back to me on your progress within 24 hours."

After Mabel Meadows had served lunch up for she and Nigel, she sat looking at him across the kitchen table. Looking up and seeing the curious look of his wife's face, he asked gently, "What's bothering you, Mabel? You've been quiet for the last half hour or so, and that's unlike you."

"It's…well…it's something at Oak Tree Manor."

"Oh, and what might that be?"

"You know that I told you that they've got a new person there," she said hesitantly. "Someone working there."

"Go on," he urged.

"Well this man, Peter, is very different – not what you might expect."

"How so?"

"Chris said that she gave him a lift after he helped change a flat tire for her. Apparently he was hitchhiking and, cutting a long story short, she and her dad brought him back to the Manor and he's been there ever since. You know, working there."

"So?" said her husband. "Nothing wrong with that and didn't you say that he's a good worker?"

"Oh yes, he's great. Everyone loves him and our Lucy *really* fancies him…not that he's done anything about that."

"I don't see what the problem is…what's bothering you?"

"It's like this," said Mabel and she related what she had seen and heard to her husband.

"What a moment," he suddenly said. "Did you say his name's Peter? Is it Peter Marshall and you say he's also a scientist?"

"Yes, I think I heard that American say something about Cambridge University but I might have misheard him."

"No, I don't think you did."

"Why'd you say that, Nigel?"

"That Peter of yours is, believe it or not, a famous scientist and he used to be at Cambridge University. Not only that, it seems a lot of people want to find him."

"Find him? Why, what's he done? Oh never mind – what I want to know is how *you* know all this?" demanded Mabel.

"It was in the paper this morning," and Nigel Meadows held up a copy of The National Globe. "Do you remember that business about some University professor getting killed on his way to Scotland Yard?"

"Yes, it all sounded a bit queer to me. So, what about it then?" asked Mabel.

"The paper this morning says that your Peter knew this other man, and that there seems to be some sort of connection between them. Not only that, Special Branch is looking for this Dr. Peter Marshall of yours. They don't say why but there's some suggestion of the government being involved…it's all very mysterious."

"Did you say Peter's a doctor?"

"Yes, and quite a famous one by all accounts. Not a medical doctor you know, but some sort of scientist according to the paper."

"*Doctor* Peter Marshall, oh my," said Mabel. "I knew there was something different about him, I just knew it."

After chatting to her husband a little longer, Mabel gathered her things and set off back to Oak Tree Manor, armed with the morning's National Globe and thinking, 'What will Chris say after she sees this? Would things stay the same at the guest house? I can't see how they can but one never knows, does one?'

Dirty Dick Fowler sat in his editor's office, basking in the praise he'd just received.

"This was very good," said the editor. "You've scooped everyone and that's no mean achievement. You did very well."

Fowler nodded and waited for the editor to continue.

"Now Dick, how are you going to follow up on this? Are you getting anything else from your friends at Scotland Yard?"

"No, I doubt that will be possible any time soon. From what I gather, the "brass" are really furious about what they perceive as a leak and I don't think it's a good idea to tell them that the story is based on some lower level officers gossiping on a bar."

"No, you're right there, Dick. So, what are you thinking?"

"It's difficult but I wonder whether a trip up to Derbyshire might be in order; you know, if trying to follow D.I. Parsons might prove useful?"

"Could be, could be," mused the editor. "I tend to agree with you that you won't get anything, official or unofficial, from those secretive Special Branch people and there's no point in antagonizing them for no good reason. Yes, good idea. Go and draw some petty cash from Accounting and use the corporate credit card. It always helps to cross people's palms with silver when you want information. Keep good records of course but get going as soon as you can. My betting is that this story is about to break wide open. Did you put an intern onto digging more into Peter Marshall's story? Somehow I feel we've only scratched the surface here and I want to know more…and I'm sure our readers will too."

Returning to his desk, Dick Fowler was ecstatic. The encouragement to use an intern was great and would save him a lot of time and effort. With plenty of cash to spend, use of the corporate credit card and both time and space to work on the next instalment of his story was even better. If he was as successful as he thought he'd be, then people would stop calling him "Dirty Dick". Very soon he'd be Richard Fowler of The National Globe, a widely respected journalist who would be invited onto television chat shows to share his views on the political and any other news-worthy situation that caught the public's attention. He was feeling wonderful and couldn't wait to call his wife and tell her to pack a suitcase for him. The future looked rosy for him and he was going to make the most of it.

After the excitement of the morning, things slowly settled down at Oak Tree Manor and when Chris, Mr. Hawkins and Peter sat down to lunch, they were all rather subdued, making no mention of what had happened. Thick ham sandwiches made with locally-baked bread, a small salad and lots of hot tea satisfied their appetites while all three were busy with their own thoughts.

Every so often Chris or her father would steal a quick glance at Peter and then, as often as not, catch each other's eye but saying nothing. Peter seemed to have retreated off into some strange space, his face expressionless. 'What's he thinking?' Chris wondered. 'I can't tell whether he's pleased, annoyed or simply indifferent to that discussion with Professor Pederson. He's not mentioned a thing about it…it's almost as though it never happened.' She looked around and realized that Mabel hadn't joined them for lunch. 'Oh yes,' she recalled. 'She'd said she'd go home and fix her husband's lunch for him as she would be late home this afternoon what with all the dinner preparations.' Then Chris remembered that Mabel had come into the kitchen to get cleaning supplies when Peter and that American had been discussing science things. She had waited a few moments, got what she needed and then left again. 'I wonder what she heard.' Chris asked herself. 'More to the point, what's she likely to tell Nigel? I gather she hasn't said much to him about Peter in the past, as I'd asked her not to but this might be too good an opportunity to miss. I hope not but now things are starting to come out, it's a bit unfair expecting her not to say anything at home. Nigel's no gossip but he might say something to one of his friends, and he's got a lot of friends.'

Eventually lunch was finished and everyone got back to work: Chris cleaning up in the kitchen, her father doing the books and Peter off finishing up what he'd been doing that morning. As Chris went into the dining room to tidy things up and make sure the bar shelves were properly stocked, she made a decision. "I've got to talk to Peter," she muttered. "No, not to try to get him to talk about his past…although I'll bet that's intriguing. No, I've got to reassure him that there's no reason to feel uncomfortable here. If he wants to stay and continue as before, then that would be marvelous. On the other hand, if he feels he needs to leave, then we'll just have to give him our blessing and wish him every success. Losing him would be a major blow but we'll probably manage. We did before and no doubt we will again. Oh damn, just why did this all have to happen now that things are going so well?"

She looked up at the ceiling but mentally spoke to God, 'Dear Lord, this is all in Your plan and nothing can or will happen unless You determine it. Help me to help Peter because I think he's hurting inside…and not just because we need him here. No, help me to provide whatever support he needs for his sake and not ours. Thank You Lord.'

As Chris hesitated over what she would do next, Mabel walked in, brandishing a newspaper. "Chris," she said excitedly. "Look at this."

At about the same time that Chris was offering up silent prayers and Mabel was heading back to the Oak Tree Manor, Nigel Meadows was busily thinking. Even though he was retired, he had been a policeman for a long time and, technically, he was still an officer of the court. No-one would blame him if he said nothing about Dr. Peter Marshall being at Oak Tree Manor but he knew that if Special Branch was involved, this search for Peter Marshall was a lot more important than simply looking for some missing Cambridge professor. After years on the force, Nigel was cynical enough to dismiss the clever speculation in the newspaper but he knew that there had to be some substance to the story. But, he wondered, if I tell someone, would that put Mabel in a difficult spot with her employers? They might get annoyed with her if they thought she was gossiping about what went on there. But could he sit back and say nothing? That would be totally alien to his nature and if this Peter Marshall affair did have Security implications for the country, then it was his duty as both a citizen and a former police officer to do something about it.

He pulled his ancient briar pipe out of his pocket, loaded it with tobacco and struck a match, slowly puffing his way through half of the crumpled leaf in the bowl. Eventually he decided and went into the front room to use the telephone. Duty and conscience won out.

ELEVEN

"Have you seen this?" asked Mabel breathlessly, holding out the National Globe to Chris. Chris looked at her and silently took the paper. Quickly scanning the headlines, she sat down at the nearest table and carefully read the front page. Then without saying a word, she turned to the inside page and read the articles on George Martin and Peter Marshall.

Eventually she looked up at Mabel, asking, "Is this the morning paper?"

"Yes," said Mabel. "Nigel gave it to me when I fixed him his lunch."

Chris nodded, before saying, "Obviously you read it…did Nigel say anything about it?"

Mabel hesitated and then nodded guiltily. As Chris continued to look at her silently, she added,

"I…er…mentioned to him that I had overheard Peter talking to that American professor and one thing led to another…he showed me the morning paper."

"How did this all come up…oh, never mind, it did and that's that. What did Nigel say about all this?"

"Nothing much. He just looked surprised when he heard that Peter is the man mentioned in the newspaper."

"Did he say what…um…what he was going to do about it, although I'm not sure what…" and Chris's voice tailed off. What was it she wanted to ask? Whatever Nigel did was up to Nigel, not her. Eventually she said, "Has Peter seen this?"

Mabel shook her head, "No, I don't think so…I don't think he's had the time. Of course, if one of our guests took a copy of the paper back to their room before going out, he might've seen one that way, a copy of the paper I mean."

Chris nodded, "Well, thank you for showing me this, Mabel. It's not what I expected. What do you think about it?"

"That poor man. I wonder why Peter got sent to prison...he doesn't seem like a criminal."

"People get sent to prison for all sorts of reasons," Chris started to say and then realized how silly her comment sounded. People only get sent to prison if they've committed a crime and then were arrested, tried, convicted and sentenced. That was the law and if Peter had been sent to prison, then obviously he had committed a crime. Chris, knowing nothing about the law, wondered what sort of offense would cause him to be incarcerated for three years but assumed that it was something fairly serious otherwise he would have got off with probation or something. So, what had he done? She started to speculate and then realized that her head was spinning. The only way she could find out what had happened was to ask Peter himself or try to search the Court Records. As she had no means of doing the latter, that left asking Peter...but did she want to do that?

Getting to her feet, she made her way to her father's office, only to find him staring into space, a folded copy of The National Globe lying on his desk. Hearing her footsteps, Mr. Hawkins turned and saw the newspaper in her hand, "You've seen it then? What do you think?"

"I don't know what to think, dad."

"Put it this way then, has it changed your feelings about Peter?"

"I'm not sure what I feel now."

"Aye lass, I can understand that. You develop feelings and then something happens, and your faith in human nature gets shaken up."

"But dad, he went to prison. Peter obviously committed a crime and got punished for it...what else am I going to think?"

"Now hold on for a minute. He obviously didn't kill anyone because, if he had, he'd have received a much longer sentence. You can probably say the same if he'd committed treason. If he had stolen a lot of money or swindled someone, then they would have said so in the newspaper...the same probably holds true if he'd beaten someone up."

"So, what else could he have done that would have put him prison?" asked Chris.

"Any manner of things, even cheating on his taxes although that doesn't seem very likely as he received an income from the University, on which he'd have to pay taxes although I suppose he could have omitted to declare any outside income, which would have caused trouble. Bottom line, Chris, is that we don't know and unless he tells us, we're not going to know."

"What do we do, dad?" asked Chris plaintively.

"Nothing," was the rapid response from her father.

"Nothing? What do you mean, nothing?"

"Let me put it to you this way," and Mr. Hawkins hesitated for a moment. "You care for Peter, don't you? In fact, I think that you are very fond of him, aren't you?" Seeing her nod of assent, he continued, "Do you still trust him?" Another nod. "Well then, why do anything? The best thing is to wait and see. As the old saying goes, "In time of doubt, pursue a policy of masterly inactivity". If Peter wants to tell us what happened, he will in good time. Whatever he did was not a major crime, as they say, and he's paid his debt to society. He has proved himself to be honest and trustworthy since he first came here. So, let things be…it's best to pretend nothing happened and that we know nothing about his past. That way, nothing will change here and we'll let events take their course."

"Dad, you're probably right. You're so wise, aren't you?"

"I'm not too sure about that but I'll tell you one thing," he said with a smile.

"What's that, dad?"

"Sort your feelings out about Peter and by that I mean your emotions. I get the distinct feeling that you are more than a little fond of him, so…."

Chris grunted. Was she really that enamored of Peter? Probably, but what should she do about it?

"Okay, dad, I think you're right."

"About what, Chris?"

"Probably everything. Anyway, I've got to get back to work… the meal preparation for tomorrow isn't going to take care of itself."

Chris left the office and decided to take a quick walk through the guest house. She was sure that everything was in order but the mere act of checking on everything would make her feel better and probably settle her jumbled emotions.

She was walking past Peter's room and glanced in, only to see him standing by the window, staring out and completely motionless. The crumpled newspaper on the bed was mute testimony to the fact that he too had read the article.

Instinctively, Chris walked in and put her arms around him, pulling his back against her body. She held him for a few seconds, enjoying the feeling of his solid frame against her much softer figure and then murmured, "It'll be alright, Peter, really it will. Don't worry…we'll sort it out in due time."

She wasn't sure what exactly she meant and was startled when Peter turned in her arms and blindly kissed her forehead and then her lips. She could feel his tears on her face and tried desperately to stop herself from crying too. Then, as Peter kissed her again, she felt a tremor pass through her body. Suddenly they were kissing each other passionately and, almost of their own volition, her hands ran down his muscular arms and then his chest, and Chris felt emotions and sensations that she thought were long gone.

They both paused and pulled back from each other, their eyes meeting in surprise and confusion.

"Wow," Peter eventually muttered. "That was something else."

Chris laughed, "Yes, it was." She searched his face for a clue to what he was thinking and then she stood still, waiting for the next move.

Peter looked at her carefully, leaned forward and kissed her again, gently rather passionately before saying, "Perhaps we should take things slowly."

Chris nodded, not sure where he was going with that remark. Seeing her nod, Peter continued, "It's obvious that we have feelings about each other but…er…but given what's happened today and that newspaper story, perhaps we should tread lightly and take our time with things."

Again Chris nodded and the said, "Peter, I'm embarrassed to say that I…that I want you…women aren't supposed to say things like that but there it is. I want you."

"I want you too," Peter said. "I want you more than you realize but everything's a mess right now and I don't want to spoil things by rushing into a situation that we might both regret."

Chris stared at him, thinking that Peter was obviously right in what he said but her body was saying something else to her. She nodded and gently pulled back, with the comment, "Hurry slowly, is that what you mean?"

"Yes, yes I do. Let's give ourselves time. We know how we feel about each other and that's progress."

She smiled. He was so formal. She had felt his hardness when they were kissing and that, as they say, was something not easily faked.

"Okay…right…well, I'd best get back to work. There's lots to do in the kitchen…for tomorrow's dinner, you know," she said fatuously.

"No doubt," agreed Peter. "I'll join you downstairs in a few minutes, okay?" He smiled and then added, "I've got to calm down, if you know what I mean?"

Chris reddened slightly and then slowly turned on her heel. She knew exactly what he meant and decided to beat a hasty retreat before anything further was said or, worse, they grabbed at each other again. She had a lot of emotions to sort out as well as myriad jumbled feelings.

Dick Fowler sat in his car outside the food warehouse, studying the place. It was of medium size and probably catered to numerous small eateries in the area, the question being how far would the owners of a small establishment travel to get what they needed? Five miles, ten miles? If there were other such places nearby, then that would be a deciding factor on whether the woman was located near or far from the place. As he sat thinking, Dick's immediate thought was that it would be nice to be able to compare notes with Detective Inspector Parsons but that, he knew, was most unlikely. What was likely, however, was that the Special Branch officer would undoubtedly be following the same thought process. That being said, should he, Dick

Fowler, go into the warehouse and start asking questions? He had no official standing and lots of people disliked talking to the press, almost as much as they avoided talking to the police. It also occurred to him that if he went in and asked questions, the warehouse staff might take exception and if they knew the woman, they might tell her that people were checking up on her, notably a reporter. That sort invasion of privacy could lead to her saying nothing to anyone about what she knew…a self-defeating exercise.

As he sat reflecting, he saw a small red van pull up outside the warehouse and then watched the driver go inside. After a while, the man came out with a loaded shopping cart which he carefully placed inside the van. Deciding, Dick climbed out of his car and walked over.

"Good afternoon," he said politely.

The man stopped what he was doing and replied in kind. He looked carefully at Fowler and then asked, "Need help with something?"

"No, I was just passing and saw this place. Is it a wholesale warehouse or do they take retail customers too?" he asked.

"As far as I know it's only wholesale but you can always ask. Their stuff's pretty good and a lot fresher than what's in any supermarket."

"Really…and the prices are reasonable?"

"Yes but then most of the customers buy in bulk, and that's an automatic saving."

Fowler nodded. He paused before asking, "Do they cater only to large establishments or do smaller places come here?"

"More smaller places than the larger ones. Big restaurants and the like go into that big place in Greydene. The prices are about the same but the big warehouse has a wider selection but, mind you, it is a hassle getting there and most of us smaller places come here for convenience."

"What, lots of pubs and the like?"

"Nah, not so many. Most pubs around here are owned by the breweries and they like to supply foods themselves rather than leave it to the landlord…some sort of control thing or the need to check on what's being spent…you know how it is."

Fowler nodded and then pulled out a packet of cigarettes, taking one himself and offering the pack to the van driver, who took one and nodded his thanks. As they lit up, the van driver became more expansive.

"Once upon a time there used to be all sorts of cafes and the like around here…and a whole lot of bed-and-breakfast places. Now a lot of them have closed or they've been bought about by those big chains. As a result, there aren't too many of us independents left. In fact, I can only think of a couple now and they may be feeling the pinch too. Only last week, the wife and I got a really nice offer from some mini-hotel chain…we'll probably take it too because it's time I thought about retiring."

"Does your wife come here too?"

"Never, she hates driving and loading up the van is a bit of a struggle for her, what with her bad back and all."

"I'm sorry to hear that. So, very few women come here?"

"That's right. In fact the only regular that I know of is Chris Hawkins, over at Oak Tree Manor. I run into her every so often…she doesn't need a whole lot, so she doesn't come here that often."

"Chris Hawkins?" asked Dick.

"Yeah, pretty little thing, she is. She went to the University and moved down to London, got married and all. Then I gather the marriage broke up and when her mother died, she came back to help her dad with the place."

"Oak Tree Manor?"

"Yeah, it's a guesthouse a couple of miles away. Lovely place and does a good business. It used to be the old manor house but they bought it and did it up. Lots of people stay there because it looks Olde Worlde, you know what I mean?"

The man looked at his watch and said, "Whoops, I've got to make a move. The old woman will be wondering where I am. Anyway, nice talking to you." He trundled the shopping cart back to the warehouse and then climbed back into his van. As he drove off, he waved out of the driver side window as he passed Dick.

Although tempted, Fowler had not asked where Oak Tree Manor was located. No point in telling anyone of his interest, Dick rationalized; one never knew who might check up on him. As he got back into his car and headed towards Greydene, Dick Fowler was convinced that he had located the woman, or at least found where she worked. 'Okay,' he thought. 'I'll visit the place tomorrow…maybe even see if I can stay there. Hey, it's amazing what a chance conversation and a friendly manner can do for you in getting information.'

As he drove, Dick Fowler became more and more convinced that he might have found what he was looking for. Then he wondered whether D.I. Parsons had had the same sort of luck. Maybe yes, maybe no, not that he cared. He didn't even know whether the Special Branch man was in Derbyshire but, with luck, he had a head start on Parsons. If he could interview the woman, and possibly meet up with the mysterious Peter Marshall, then his career would get the kick-start he fondly hoped for. Tonight he'd have a good dinner, turn in early and then go and look at Oak Tree Manor. He had a good feeling about what he would find the next day and he laughed aloud. The God of Journalism and The Prepared Mind were taking care of him again.

Detective Inspector Parsons was having a bad day, in fact a very bad day. The drive up to Derbyshire with Detective Sergeant Johnson had been long and dull, Mike Johnson being a poor conversationalist with few interests outside of his job, at least nothing that he had in common with John Parsons. They had booked rooms at Greydene Hotel and checked in but John's room overlooked an inner courtyard, and was cramped and a bit noisy. Apparently Mike Johnson's wasn't much better, being located near to the elevator which seemed to ping all night long. The hotel was busy but not full; unfortunately the limited *per diem* of the Special Branch officers reduced their selection of available rooms. Not even Mike Johnson's reputed charm with the ladies had any effect on the severe receptionist, much to the irritation of John Parsons, who muttered, "Fat lot of use you are…can't even get us decent rooms."

The next morning they went down for the breakfast buffet. The latter was quite good but because of the number of hotel guests, they had to wait for the trays to be refilled as the serving staff tried to keep up. As John complained to his sergeant, "Just our luck to come up to a University town. All those students and visiting family will pack every restaurant for miles around. Not only that, every newspaper has been scarfed up by other guests…I'll have to wait until the evening news on TV to catch up on things." D. S. Johnson, after a very restless night, was likewise in a bad mood and he dreaded the thought of visiting dozens of eateries in and around Greydene.

As with most University towns, even getting around by car was proving to be a chore, as the two Special Branch detectives found as they marked off one restaurant after another in the City. Eventually, after drawing a blank at every establishment they visited, Parson said, "Let's see if we can find that food warehouse. I gather it's outside town and a bit of a drive but anything's better than crawling through all this traffic. I used to think London was bad but this place with all these vehicles and those narrow streets is miserable. Get the map and let's see where we're going."

"There seem two or three food warehouses around here, even one in Greydene itself," said Sergeant Johnson.

"I doubt that's the place. Those bikers said it was outside town and even they wouldn't confuse the countryside with the city although nothing would surprise me," said Parsons ironically. "Okay, pick a place and let's get going…and try not to get us lost."

Eventually they found what looked to be the food warehouse in question which, inevitably, was closed for lunch. "Just our luck," complained John Parsons. "All right Johnson, let's go find a pub or something and get some lunch. Mark this place on the GPS so that we can find it again. Drive around a bit…there's got to be somewhere to eat around here."

It was a bright, sunny day and even the two disgruntled police officers started to enjoy the countryside. They drove past the sign for Oak Tree Manor and Johnson slowed the car, "Should we try there, chief?"

"Nah, it looks like a bed-and-breakfast place and I doubt that they serve lunch. Besides it's so off the beaten path, I shudder to think what the food is like. Go back to that pub we passed a mile or so back."

"*The Bull and Bush*? That place?"

"Yes, whatever it was…I'm getting hungry, and thirsty…I'll even buy you a pint."

Sitting down at a worn wooden outside table in the fresh air, the two men tucked into their ploughman's lunch of French bread, hunks of cheese, pickles and beer.

"Hey, this isn't bad, is it sir? This cheese is really good, not like the stuff they serve at *The Hoop and Grapes* back home."

"Yes, sergeant, it is good cheese…probably made locally. I wonder where they get the bread from, it's pretty good too." Sitting back and enjoying the sunshine, Parsons added, "Maybe we'll get lucky now." He stopped and looked at his assistant. "You go to the *Hoop and Grapes* often?"

"Once or twice a week after work. I like to get a quick drink before going home. I usually meet up with some of the chaps from the Yard, those from our lot and other divisions, especially the CID. They're a bit wild at times…they'll talk your ear off, given half a chance."

"Really? What do you talk about mainly?"

"Football or cricket, politics, the news and what's on the TV mostly."

"You ever talk shop, you know, what you're working on?"

"Every so often if any of us are working on something interesting. Sometimes it helps to get some input from them."

"Hmm," grunted Parsons. He paused and then said, "You said that you sometimes talk shop…could anyone overhear you?" but thinking 'You lot probably gossip like old women talking over the garden fence. I shudder to think what anyone around you might hear. That used to be a problem with MI5 and MI6 types chatting loudly in the pub, what with the Russians and East Germans listening in all the time. I hope the same thing doesn't happen with our people but it wouldn't surprise me if some smart reporter listened in to their prattle.'

Checking his watch, Parsons pushed his glass over to Mike and said, "We've time for another one although you best have an orange juice or something since you're driving." As his sergeant went into the pub to get refills, John looked around and spotted a discarded newspaper on an adjacent table. Muttering about litter louds leaving refuse lying around, he picked up the paper and idly scanned the headlines. It was The National Globe and was dated the previous day but what John Parsons read shook him.

When Mike Johnson re-emerged from the pub, he held the newspaper out to him, saying, "Did you see this?"

Taking it, Mike said, "No, not really…I don't get to read the newspaper too much. I rely more on the TV news for information – too busy really." Then he looked down at the proffered paper and swore, "What's this shit?" Sitting down, he read the front page and then the inside stories. Looking up, he asked his boss, "How the hell did this reporter…" and then flipped back to check who had written the lead article, "Richard Fowler get all this information? Who the hell gave him all this? Look, he even knows who you are, sir, and also that Dr. Martin was on his way in to see you when he was run over! You don't know that reporter, do you?"

"No I bloody don't," snapped Parsons. "And even if I did, I certainly wouldn't talk to him about an ongoing case…and that raises the question of whom he spoke to. Whoever it was seems to be remarkable well-informed. Anyway, seeing this explains the phone call I had this morning from Chief Super. Miller."

"He called you this morning?"

"Yes, he virtually accused me of talking to that reporter… Fowler was it?…anyway I hadn't a clue what he was talking about and eventually convinced him that I had not spoken anyone about this case. Be that as it may, let me have another look at that paper."

Reaching out, John retrieved the newspaper and read the front page story again and then flipped through the follow-ups on Martin and Marshall on page 3. He looked speculatively across the table at Mike Johnson and said, "You know, this reporter has some information but not everything, and there's a lot of innuendo and drawing of unjustified inferences. It's almost as if he was listening into a conversation and whereas he got a lot of the story, he didn't get it all. You wouldn't know anything about that, would you?"

Seeing the slightly stricken look on Mike Johnson's face, he continued, "Did you by any chance talk to your mates in *The Hoop and Grapes* about this?" At which point, Mike turned very red. "I see" said Parsons. "So you did discuss this case with them and" trying to ease his sergeant's discomfort, "I assume that you really didn't get into too much detail."

Mike nodded and then suddenly turned reflective, thinking hard. Parsons looked at him and asked, "Something's struck you, hasn't it?"

"Funnily enough, when we were at the *Hoop and Grapes*, there was a bloke sitting at the bar a couple of seats down from us. He was busy with his smart phone or tablet, or whatever; anyway, we paid him no mind but, strange thing, he looked vaguely familiar and I thought at the time that I'd seen him in there before. I put it down to him being a regular…you know how it is?"

Parsons nodded, "Yes, I do know how it is. Look, old son, I hope you've learned a valuable lesson and will keep your trap shut in the future, especially in a public place. And Mike, don't worry, I'll not drop you in it with the Chief Superintendent. I'll sort something out but at least I could say with complete honesty to him that I had never spoken to that reporter. If I saw him right now, I wouldn't know him from Adam."

After that, the two police officers climbed into their car and headed back towards the food warehouse. Ironically, the bad mood that had afflicted them both that morning had dissipated and they actually started to chat in a friendly manner.

Arriving at the warehouse, they walked in and went up to the only employee in sight, a man wearing a clean and well-pressed long brown overall coat, covering up his regular clothes. Looking up, he asked, "Can I help you with something, gents?" He was young and enthusiastic but it was obvious even to him that his visitors were not there to buy food.

Holding out his warrant card, John Parsons introduced himself, "I'm Detective Inspector Parsons of Scotland Yard and this is my assistant, Detective Sergeant Johnson. We need to ask you a few questions."

The young man swallowed hard and looked worried. "What about?" he asked nervously. "Did I do something wrong?"

"No, not at all," Parsons assured him. He paused and then said, "We're interested in a young woman who might come here on a regular basis to buy food…do you know anyone like that?"

The young man shook his head, "I'm sorry Inspector, I've only been here a few days and really don't know any of the customers well. Truth be told, I don't recall having any female customers in here since I got hired. Maybe the manager could help? He knows pretty well everybody who comes in here."

"Okay, we'll talk to him. Is he around?"

"I'm afraid not. He had to take care of something at home and took off before lunch. He left me in charge," he added proudly.

Parsons and Johnson exchanged looks, both thinking, 'Bloody typical!' "So, said John Parsons heavily. "When will this manager of yours be in again?"

"He should be in tomorrow. Should I tell him to expect you?"

"Yes, do that, will you?"

As they drove back to Greydene, Parsons said to his sergeant, "You know, Johnson, that was typical of this bloody case. One step forward and three back"

"Should we have asked for the manager's address and tried to get in touch with him this evening?"

"We could have but my betting is that, depending on how many customers he's got, he'll need to look at his records to identify his female customers. Besides, the chances of him remembering a woman who may or may not have mentioned the biker incident that occurred a while back may be pretty slim. The other thing is whether we want to alert him that we are looking for her. Depending on his relationship with the lady, he could well warn her off and that would never do, would it?"

Johnson simply grunted. As usual John Parsons was right.

Pulling into the car park of Greydene Hotel, they were pleased to see it was not too crowded and Mike secured a spot close to the main entrance. "Okay," said Parsons. "I'm going to get a nap in and a shower. We'll meet up on the bar in a couple of hours and then get some dinner. We'll review things in the bar later. For right now, I want to clean up and think things through. Today has been one surprise after another and I need to clear my head. Okay with you?"

The last, voiced as a question, was actually an order and Mike knew better than to question his boss.

"Right you are, sir. A couple of hours it is. Actually a bit of a lie-down and a shower does sound good. At least we don't have to drive anywhere this evening." Parsons grunted. The last thing he wanted to do was go anywhere.

Later that afternoon, Parsons and Johnson sat at a table in the corner of the bar area, huddled over pints of the local ale and talking in undertones. Suddenly John saw a strange look pass over his sergeant's face. "What's up Johnson?" he asked.

"That man, the one who just walked in."

"What about him?"

"I can't swear to it but he looks a lot like that bloke who was in *The Hoop and Grapes*, the one I mentioned."

"He does?" said Parsons. "Look, go out to the front desk and check whether someone by the name of Richard Fowler from London has checked in. If it is him, then he's probably looking for that woman and Peter Marshall too, and that's something I don't like at all."

When Mike returned, he caught John's eye and nodded. After he sat down, he said, "One Richard Fowler of The National Globe booked in a couple of nights ago." "Damn,' muttered D.I. Parsons. "Just how did he know to come here? I wonder how much ahead of us he is? If he's found the woman, or worse, found Marshall, they are not going to be pleased back at the Yard."

"So, what do we do, sir?"

"I'm not sure, to be honest," was the reply.

Just then, Dirty Dick Fowler looked up and saw the two men sitting there. With his reporter's memory, he immediately recognized Mike Johnson. Fowler hesitated, picked up his drink and walked over. "Gentlemen, mind if I join you?"

Parsons looked at him steadily and was about to turn him away, when Dick Fowler said, "My name is Dick Fowler of The National Globe and I assume that you are D.I. Parsons and that you and this young man," with a nod at Mike, "are here for the same reason I am. So, why don't we sit down and have a quiet chat? I'll even buy another round, that suit you?"

TWELVE

As Chris walked into the kitchen, Mabel looked up and saw her slightly flushed face. 'Uh oh,' she thought. 'I wonder what that's all about. She went off after reading that newspaper article without saying a word. I wonder whether she spoke to Peter…I'll bet something happened between them upstairs. Whatever it was, I hope it was good because those two people deserve some happiness.'

Chris, surprised by Mabel's unaccustomed silence, said, "I suppose we'd best start thinking about tomorrow's dinner. What do you think we should serve?"

"Roast beef's always a favorite…or a brisket…and some Yorkshire pudding to go with it."

"We've got at least two or three really good-sized briskets in the freezer, so we could get them out and let them defrost overnight." She paused before adding, "Of course I can always ask the butcher if he's got some venison although making sure it's tender can be a problem if it's very fresh. We might not have enough time to marinate it properly."

The two women exchanged views about what to cook, both aware that they were studiously avoiding any mention of the newspaper article and their verbal exchanges masked their inner thoughts. Chris, ostensibly focused on the dinner menu, kept mentally returning to the embrace with Peter. The sensations she felt when she was in his arms, his hard, muscular body against her slim and pliable form, his soft lips against hers…all combined to ignite an inner warmth and she could feel herself again getting damp between her legs. Suddenly she longed to be back in his arms but this time, she wanted to be naked and open to receive his hardness inside her. She flushed with pleasure at the thought and looked guilty when Mabel suddenly asked, "Are you feeling alright Chris? You've got suddenly flushed…you're not coming down with anything are you?"

"No, I'm fine," Chris assured her, but thinking, 'Oh I'm coming down with something alright but I think it's lust. Peter, my Peter, what are we going to do?'

As often happens, Peter walked into the kitchen at that moment and Chris had a sudden urge to run and hide…what if he read her mind? Would he think her a wanton or some silly little girl that swooned at the first kiss?

Mabel looked up to greet Peter but said nothing when she saw the distracted look on his face and the guilty flush on Chris's. 'So I was right,' she thought. 'Those two did get it on, or at least started to, and about time too. It's obvious to anyone that they really care about each other and they would be perfect together, so I wonder what took them so long. All that stuff in the newspaper doesn't change who he is and if Peter went to prison, so what? He's no criminal or I'll eat my hat. Besides, no matter what he's done, he paid for it, so we should all move on. If it bothers you Chris, get over it…he's the best man you'll ever find and that little twerp Larry that you married isn't half the man Peter is, you mark my words, young lady.' Feeling her irritation growing, Mabel hastily said, "Hey Peter, finished upstairs, have you?" When he nodded, she added, "Which do you think might be best for tomorrow, beef or venison? Chris and I were wondering whether a brisket would be good."

Peter stopped and thought for a moment. Although he really wanted to think about Chris, he knew that duty called and Mabel wanted an answer. "Probably beef. A well-seasoned brisket with garlic tucked beneath the outer layer, and gravy made from the drippings, is hard to beat, especially with Yorkshire pudding and roast potatoes."

"That's what I think," said Mabel triumphantly. "Do you agree, Chris?"

"I expect you're right," said Chris. "Do you mind getting the meat from the freezer, Peter?" Turning to Mabel, she said, "So, we've got the meat dish settled and if we serve it with the Yorkshire and roast potatoes, what else should there be?"

"Peas are always a favorite or did you want something a bit different, like asparagus or something?"

"Well, as there will be so many of them, probably at least a dozen or so, we should have several different vegetables." Chris thought for a moment, then added, "We could have peas, carrots, broccoli and asparagus, all on separate serving dishes and then they can take what they want. The question is, how much of each do we prepare? Also, we've got to think about dessert. A dozen or more men will take a lot of feeding, won't they?"

As Peter laid the briskets from the freezer on the food preparation table, he caught Chris's eye and smiled slightly, and saw the slight flush travelling up Chris's face. 'So you're feeling what I am, are you, Chris?' He thought. 'Now what do we do about it? The genie is out of the lamp and he's not going back…but neither of us wants him to either.'

Mabel, silently watching Peter and Chris, almost cheered. 'I was right…something did happen between them.' She turned her eyes towards the ceiling and silently prayed, 'Lord, You do work in mysterious ways, don't You? And You have such a sense of humor…I hope that You are quietly laughing at us silly mortals. Peter and Chris were made for each other but You had to bring them together in Your own way and in Your time. I thank You Lord for them and for the happiness You will bring them.' Aloud, she said, "Okay then, now we've got the entrée settled. What about the appetizers and the dessert. Any thoughts on that?"

Before there were any comments or suggestions from Chris or Peter, Mr. Hawkins came into the kitchen, closely followed by Mabel's daughter Lucy. Looking at them all, Mr. Hawkins said, "Ah, I gather you are planning the menu for tomorrow. What are you serving?"

After he listened to Chris, he simply said, "Well the entrée sounds great but what about the soup, appetizer and salads? Also, I think some sort of dessert course or cheese and crackers would be good."

"Dad," wailed Chris. "That's what we were talking about before you came in but don't worry about it, we'll get it sorted."

Unconsciously Chris looked over at Peter and their eyes met and locked. Seeing this, Mr. Hawkins blinked and thought, 'Ah, I see they've started to interact...and in the right way. About bloody time too...I was getting worried about the pair of them. They were taking so long to get together that I was beginning to think there was something wrong with them. Well, as they say, things have a way of working themselves out. I wonder whether it was anything to do with that article in the newspaper.'

Aloud, he said, "How many are coming, do you know?"

"I think about twelve or so," said Chris.

"Well, if we're serving beef, I suppose I should get at least 10 or 12 bottles of red wine and maybe the same number of whites. The unused whites can always be served with the dessert or cheese after the meal." Turning to Peter, he asked, "Do we have enough hard stuff and drinks like sherry and port behind the bar?'

Peter, snapping out of his reverie, thought for a moment and said, "We're probably a bit low on the fortified wines...we don't get a whole lot of call for them. As for whiskey, gin and vodka, we've got lots although we might need to get more tonic water and bitter lemon."

Mr. Hawkins nodded, "Okay I'll run over to the warehouse tomorrow and pick up what we need. I'll probably need you to give me a hand carrying it all, Peter. Will you be free?"

"Of course, not a problem."

"With that many people and Mabel and me being busy in the kitchen. Who's going to serve the food?"

"That's why I came over," chimed in Lucy. "I thought that you might need a hand. Do you want me to ask my boyfriend to help out?"

"That idle layabout!" snapped Mabel. "Would good would he be...besides I doubt he even owns a shirt and tie."

"Give it a rest, mom, he can clean up very nicely when he wants. Don't worry, he'll do us all proud."

"I hope so," grunted her mother. "I certainly hope so."

Chris and then Mabel both looked at Peter, and asked almost simultaneously, "What about the bar? Is that something you'll take care of, Peter?"

"Well, I…" he started to say but was interrupted by the entrance of Dr. Hiram Pederson, Professor of Chemistry, Polk University, together with a thin bespectacled man wearing a tweed jacket and rather baggy corduroy pants, obviously someone from Greydene University.

"Of course he can't serve drinks, Mr. Hawkins. Your man here is going to be the guest of honor."

"What?" said everyone else in the kitchen.

"After I told my colleagues at Greydene who Peter actually is, they were most insistent on meeting him. In fact, Lionel here wanted to come over immediately." Turning to Peter, he added, "This is Dr. Lionel Simpson, head of radiochemistry at Greydene and he not only wanted to meet you but was most insistent that we have you join us for dinner. Isn't that so, Lionel?"

Lionel Simpson, a bit stunned to find the famous but long-missing Peter Marshall sitting in the kitchen of a guesthouse and obviously helping plan their dinner for the next day, simply nodded.

"Well say something to him, Lionel," urged Hiram. "You made enough of a fuss about coming here to meet him ahead of time!"

Hesitantly, the Greydene professor held out his hand, "I'm delighted to meet you, Dr. Marshall. I have read all your work with the greatest interest and before…and before, well you know… before everything that happened…well, your work has been groundbreaking…" and he stopped talking abruptly, thinking, 'Have I put my foot in it with this man? He could be super-sensitive about what happened to him and that newspaper article this morning cannot have helped much either. What should I say now? Maybe it wasn't such a good idea to come here today but I really did want to meet him. Besides, the provost was saying to me only the other day that we needed to recruit more faculty into the department and Peter Marshall would be ideal. Oh well, I'll keep quiet and perhaps approach him tomorrow over dinner and sound him out. Hiram didn't say anything about Marshall wanting to get back into research but I wonder whether he could be enticed to come to Greydene? Trouble is, if I try to recruit him, Hiram may also try to do the same and offer him far more money. Oh well, it's all in the lap of the gods, as they say.'

"Hmm," grunted Hiram, wondering what was on his colleague's mind. "Well, what about it, Peter, are you coming to dinner?"

Peter looked at Chris and then at her father, holding out his hands with palms upward in a mute appeal for advice. Father and daughter exchanged looks. This situation could not have been predicted and they were at a loss. It was obvious that without Peter helping with serving the food and drinks, they would be short-handed but it was possible that someone from the village could help out, or at least Lucy's boyfriend. On the other hand, the ebullient and egalitarian Professor Pederson had obviously given no thought to the position that he was putting Peter in. Dr. Peter Marshall, well-known scientist and formerly of Cambridge University, was one thing whereas Peter, employee of Oak Tree Manor, was quite another and it was apparent that the two personae were very different and wanted to stay that way.

Eventually Mr. Hawkins spoke. Clearing his throat, he said, "Well, that decision is for Peter to make but I think you are putting him in an awkward position, professor. Having dinner with you all could be interesting and even enjoyable for him and we would have no objections, would we Chris?" Seeing the latter give a nod of assent, he continued, "But his life is here at Oak Tree Manor and you are trying to push him into a situation that he may not be comfortable with. After all, until two days ago, you had no idea who he was…actually, neither did we but that's another matter. Still and all, by extending your invitation to dinner, whatever Peter decides will be awkward for him, to say the least. How can he help serve the food and drinks to a group of people who think of him as a famous scientist and want him to have dinner with them? If, on the other hand, he does dine with you, how will he feel about being forced back into a world that he consciously left several years ago for whatever reason at that time? That, sir, is placing him in the horns of a dilemma or, as you Americans say, between a rock and a hard place." With those words, Mr. Hawkins poured himself a cup of tea and sat down at the table and glared at Dr. Hiram Pederson, thinking. 'How dare this man come here and upset this household and put Peter in such a position – the nerve of the man!'

There was absolute silence in the room. Mr. Hawkins was a generally a taciturn man and rarely voiced an opinion unless pushed.

But here he was, almost reprimanding a guest and giving voice to the unexpressed opinions they all held. Astonished, Chris turned to her father, "Dad, that was most unlike you. My goodness!" Turning to Peter, she asked, "Well, what do *you* think Peter?"

Mr. Hawkins, seeing the confused and decidedly worried look on Peter's face, said emphatically, "There's another old adage, Dr. Pederson, and that is "In time of doubt, pursue a policy of masterly inactivity". So, why does Peter have to make a decision right now? Leave us in peace and we'll talk about this between ourselves. If he joins you for dinner, that will be fine but if he doesn't, then that had better be fine too! Now, we have things to do, and you and…er…Dr. Simpson, is it?…need to leave us to get on with our work."

Hiram and Lionel looked at each other. They had been dismissed and, sensible men that they were, they decided to follow the advice, if not orders, of Mr. Hawkins.

Richard (Dirty Dick) Fowler placed the drinks on the table before Parsons and Johnson and then sat down himself. "Well gentlemen," he said. "This is all very interesting, isn't it? It would appear that we are here in this fine old city of Greydene on the same mission. Before we get started, I told you that I'm Richard Fowler of The National Globe and I assume you are Detective Inspector Parsons of the Special Branch. Who might this young man be?"

Mike Johnson was about to respond when he caught the slight negative shake of John Parsons's head. John Parsons himself just looked steadily at the reporter and waited for him to continue. As the silence dragged on, Fowler eventually said, "I can see you are an expert at waiting people out, aren't you Inspector?" John smiled but said nothing.

"Okay. Let me tell you what I've found and then perhaps we could think about some degree of collaboration." Seeing D.I. Parsons raise one eyebrow, he added, "Look, we are probably here on the same mission, if you will, and it makes no sense for us all to follow each other around trying to get one up on each other. Sooner or later, probably sooner, we will find the elusive Dr. Marshall and I venture to suggest that he might be more willing to talk to me than to two Special Branch officers."

"Perhaps," admitted Parsons.

"Oh come on, John…if I may call you John?…and, again, who is this young man with you?"

"He's Detective Sergeant Mike Johnson and no, I should prefer you not to call me "John" until I know you a whole lot better."

Fowler blinked at the rebuff, saying, "I'm sorry you feel that way, I truly am."

"But not too sorry, and certainly not sorry enough to prevent you from putting a whole lot of innuendo and clever comments in that newspaper of yours," snapped John.

"Look Inspector, this is all a matter of public interest and the public have a right to know what is going on, regardless of how you feel about it. Let's face facts, shall we? It is very strange that Special Branch has been tasked with finding some scientist from Cambridge, a man who seems to have gone off the road for reasons that are not altogether clear at the moment." As John Parsons opened his mouth to comment, Fowler continued, "Rest assured, Inspector, my staff at the paper are looking into what happened with Peter Marshall and since that is a matter of public record, there is no reason why I shouldn't cover it…unless, of course, you persuade me otherwise. But leaving that aside, there is the question, more a mystery, of why another Cambridge scientist, one Dr. George Martin, scientific advisor to the Ministry of Energy and Natural Resources, would come into town to see you at Scotland Yard. It would appear that his death in a traffic accident might have been just that, an accident, but even you must admit that it was a strange coincidence that it happened minutes before he would have arrived at the Yard."

John Parsons took a small sip of his beer and looked steadily at Fowler before waving a hand to signify that he should continue.

"Alright, I am aware that I don't know everything. In fact, I'm sure that there is a lot that I don't know but let's look at what I do know. The ostensible situation is that a Special Branch detective inspector and his sergeant have been tasked to locate someone, a Dr. Peter Marshall. Who gave them that task and why are unknowns. But what I do know is that those Special Branch officers came up here to Greydene to look for some young woman who apparently has some connection with this Peter Marshall but the how and why of that connection are also unknowns. Another question that comes up is why are you two interested in some food warehouse and what is the connection with Peter Marshall?”

John Parsons was surprised at what Fowler already knew and then remembered how his sergeant had gossiped about the case in the *Hoop and Grapes* with his mates from the Yard. He cursed inwardly and then thought about what he should do. Watching him carefully, Dick Fowler took a small drink of his gin and tonic and waited while the Special Branch officer mulled things over.

Deciding, he spoke out, “Look John,” ignoring the prohibition against using Parsons’s first name, “I’ll be honest with you. I’m getting up there in years and I’ve got two sons in middle school. I know I’ve got the nickname “Dirty Dick” but, I must confess, I really don’t want to be known as that Gossip Columnist and Scandal Monger Dirty Dick Fowler any longer. Oh yes, it pays well but it’s not fair that my sons should be ashamed of what their father does. I want to gain some respectability as an honest opinion writer and this Marshall situation may help. Do you understand?”

Parsons nodded.

“Having said that, let’s reach an agreement. If you share your information with me, at least as far as you can, I’ll be careful in what I write…hell, I’ll even show it to you before it’s filed and gets into the paper. Case in point, let’s say I find this woman first, which is likely given what I learned today. Then if I write something about her, that’s her privacy blown and what would it achieve? No, I’d rather deal with this story in a professional way and report the facts, not innuendo. If there is a solid reason why someone somewhere wants to find this Peter Marshall and doesn’t involve any criminal activity, let’s cover it properly and avoid causing trouble for anyone, least of all you, this woman and Dr. Marshall. What about it?”

“If I do agree,” said John eventually. “What guarantee do I have that you’ll keep your word?”

“You don’t but if I go back on my word, then I know that I could get black-listed with every police officer in London. Frankly, I’d rather have you on my side and have an open dialogue with you based on what can be quoted, as an unnamed source of course, rather than anything else.”

John Parsons hesitated, torn between cutting the man off or at least trying to exercise some damage control. Eventually he said, "Okay, we'll be more open with you. However, you cannot, repeat cannot, attribute anything to me. That would affect me badly and could ruin Johnson's career and that I cannot allow." Out of the corner of his eye, he saw Mike relax at that comment.

"Fair enough," agreed Fowler. "As far as I can see, there's a lot of background that I can fill in and when I write it up, I'll put it in such a way that it appears to have come from open sources. By the way, why *are* you looking for this Dr. Marshall?"

"Frankly I have no idea," said Parsons. "It was an order that came from on high without explanation."

"Really?" asked an incredulous Fowler.

"Really!" stated John. "Inspectors, however senior, are often in a need-to-know position and this is a situation when I have no need to know, as they say. In fact, I'm not too sure that my chief even knows the whys and wherefores of this."

"Isn't that a bit odd?"

"Not really – happens all the time with the stuff we do."

"Okay, I'll buy that. So, can you tell me how it is that you are looking for this woman and some out-of-the-way food warehouse?"

After almost draining his pint glass and looking meaningfully at Fowler, John started to tell him and Mike Johnson about the fight in the pub, the biker incident with Nobby Murphy and the interactions at the food warehouse. After he listened carefully, Fowler got to his feet, saying, "I think we need refills…no, let's get some dinner." He looked at John Parsons shrewdly, "I'll say one thing, you must be one terrific detective to have linked all that together." Turning to Mike Johnson, he added, "You are one lucky man to have him as your mentor."

After dinner, the three men returned to the bar and sat at their corner table. Fowler opened the conversation with, "This Peter Marshall seems to be one hell of a guy, doesn't he? Talk about taking on all comers and sorting them out. I wonder how he learned to do that. I also wonder how he happened to hook up with this mystery woman but, like you, I believe what the biker said. Frankly, I'd be scared too if Marshall came out of nowhere when I was harassing someone. Damn!

"Anyway, quite by accident I think I know who this woman is and where she works." He briefly recounted how he'd chatted to the van driver outside the food warehouse and got the information from him. "It seems that she is someone called Chris Hawkins and she's the daughter of the owner of Oak Tree Manor guesthouse, out there on Bracken Road."

"Oak Tree Manor?" asked Mike. "We were just out there today but we didn't stop in. Pity that we didn't but we were looking to have lunch somewhere and thought that they probably wouldn't do that sort of thing. Ate at the *Bull and Bush* instead."

"Well, regardless," said John. "We'll have to go to the warehouse ourselves just so that I can say we were there. After that we can go on to Oak Tree Manor and see if we can find Peter Marshall after we talk to Ms. Hawkins. What will you do, Dick?"

Fowler, pleased by John Parsons using his first name, said, "I'll go out to Oak Tree Manor tomorrow, probably late morning, and try to talk to Chris Hawkins. If I get there too early and they're cleaning rooms and such, she'll not want to talk to me. As I said, you being police officers makes it easier to interview people but for lowly reporters like me, I have to be nice in order to get anyone to say anything."

After chatting a little longer, they broke up for the evening with promises to meet up for breakfast. As they rode up in the elevator together, Mike turned to Parsons and commented, "I'm surprised that you agreed to talk to that reporter, sir."

"At first I didn't want to but then I realized that it is better to demystify as far possible what's going on. He already found that woman, so why try to hide the fact that we were looking for her too? At least we now know her name and where she works…lives… whatever. Also, having a direct connection with Fowler does allow me some control over what he does and does not write in the newspaper. Let's face it, Marshall hasn't committed any crimes, at least none that we know of, so why all the secrecy? If Fowler knows what's going on, then he'll drop all the innuendo regarding Marshall and Martin. Bottom line is that we still don't know why Martin was coming to see me anyway but I'd rather that whole subject dropped out of sight. No, it's better to give a little now to avoid a whole lot of mess down the road. And, Johnson, I'd better never hear even a whisper that we talked to that reporter…not now, not ever. Understood?"

"Yes, sir."

"That means you don't talk to your mates in *The Hoop and Grapes*, to your girlfriend or anybody else. As a Special Branch officer you'd best get used to keeping your mouth about any- and everything to do with work, and that starts here and now!"

After they'd all eaten dinner and Mabel had left for home with Lucy, Mr. Hawkins looked at his daughter and Peter across the table. "Well Peter, what do you think about this dinner business? Have you made a decision?"

"Frankly I don't know what to think."

"But you must think something," urged Chris.

"To be honest, I don't like any of this," said Peter flatly. "My life is here now and that's fine by me. There's nothing out there that I really need or want, so…"

Father and daughter exchanged looks. So Peter had little inclination to move on from Oak Tree Manor, something that delighted them both but for different reasons. After a few seconds, Peter continued, "I know all this is my fault. If I hadn't been so stupid and arrogant enough to write notes on Pederson's manuscript, none of this would have happened. But I was and I did, so that's that. The question is, what happens next?" He paused, collecting his thoughts. "Joining them for dinner is not a good idea; Hiram Pederson can be as pushy as he likes, but I really don't want to do it. Frankly, that sort of coercion is something I thoroughly dislike. The same goes for serving the meal or going behind the bar…if I'm there, then there'll be all sorts of pressure to join them regardless of what I feel. Besides, there's something else."

Chris and Mr. Hawkins looked at him, curious as to where the conversation was going.

"I got the distinct impression that Lionel Simpson came out here yesterday for reasons other than simply to meet me."

"But why would he do that?" asked Chris. "What could he want with you?" She reddened for a moment, and added, "I'm sorry, that came out wrong but I think you know what I mean."

Peter nodded and smiled. "I suspect that one reason he came is that he'd like to recruit me to Greydene University...into his department."

"What's wrong with that?" asked Mr. Hawkins.

"On the face of it, nothing," replied Peter. "But if there is any mention of trying to recruit me, Pederson would switch into his "high pressure, let's make a decision" persona and do his best to drag me off to Utah or wherever he is. Frankly, I'm not sure I'm ready to even think about getting back into research let alone make that sort of decision under lots of pressure from some pushy American visiting professor. Besides, it's been a long time since I did any research and getting back into it might take longer than I would wish, if indeed I *can* get back into research and academia. So, there you have it, any possible advantages have a lot of negatives counterbalancing them."

"So, what are you going to do?" asked Chris.

"If it's alright with you both, tomorrow evening I'll take off in the van and go explore the countryside, have dinner, take in a movie and generally be unavailable all evening. I'm sorry to leave you in the lurch over the dinner but..."

"No, that's alright," Chris assured him. "We can manage and if that's the way you feel, then...er...go for it. Dad, what do you think?"

"I agree with Chris, Peter," said Mr. Hawkins. "Just go and enjoy yourself. It's about time you took some time off, even if it's only for one evening." He paused, and then added, "But I should still like you to come to the warehouse with me tomorrow morning and help get the booze for the dinner guests. That lot'll weigh quite a bit and I'd rather you do the lifting, at least until I'm back up to full strength."

"Of course he'll help you, won't you Peter?" said Chris. "After you and dad return and get some lunch here, why not take off in the afternoon and go and have fun. It's quite pretty around here, so why not go explore?"

That being said, the three of them returned to planning the following night's dinner menu and Chris added needed items to the list that her father had already compiled for liquor supplies. All three were pleased that Peter had decided the way he had. For Peter, his decision was obvious – why invite trouble when he could take off for a few hours and avoid it. If those people were disappointed, that was their problem.

Mr. Hawkins was relieved that Peter evidently wanted stay at Oak Tree Manor and that he considered it to be his surrogate home. The man was now an integral part of the guesthouse and, secretly, Mr. Hawkins believed that the longer he stayed around, the growing attraction between he and Chris would develop into something else. Mr. Hawkins was astute enough to appreciate that Peter's jottings weren't a complete accident. Subconsciously, he probably did want to get back into science but that would be his decision and one to be made when he was ready, and not before.

Chris was delighted to hear Peter's decision. Losing him would have made things a little difficult in running Oak Tree Manor in the short-term but it would not have been a disaster. Replacing him in her life, however, could well have been a disaster. Their interaction that afternoon had staggered both of them and Chris, emotionally and probably sexually awake for the first time in far too long, desperately wanted to keep those feelings alive. Everything about their meeting and subsequent events at Oak Tree Manor, including the incident with the bikers, told her that fate or more probably God had put them in each other's paths and she didn't want anything to interfere. 'Selfish or not, and newspaper articles be damned,' she thought. 'I want us to be together for at least a little while before the outside world intrudes.'

Eventually, they finished discussing the menu and after bidding each other "Goodnight", they headed off to bed in different directions. Mr. Hawkins watched as Chris slowly went upstairs and, on reaching the first landing, the regretful look directed at Peter's back as he continued to climb upwards. "Aye, lass, I know it hurts," he murmured sympathetically. "One day everything seems normal here, maybe not perfect but pretty good. You hope that you and

Peter will eventually connect and whatever hopes and dreams you each have would perhaps meld together. Then the next day, all hell breaks loose and your quiet, peaceful world is suddenly torn apart. The man you care about, and possibly dream about too, is not who you thought he was, and life becomes a whole lot more complicated. Aye, Chris, no-one said life would be easy but it could be that what's happening here is almost as much as you can bear. But let me tell you, girl, that Peter Marshall is something special and he's not going to go anywhere. Whatever happens, and I'm sure that a whole lot will be happening soon, very soon, it won't be happening without you. Have faith, that's all, have faith. It *will* be alright in the end."

Chris watched as Peter continued go upstairs and she felt for him, thinking, 'You put a good face on things about those university scientists but it must have been a wrench for you to turn down that dinner invitation, no matter what you said. At one time that was your whole life, well maybe not your whole life because you were married…now that's something we'll have to talk about if it's not too painful…but, nevertheless, to turn your back on your career and what you obviously loved must have been hard for you. I wish I could take you in my arms and comfort you. We will be together and soon, but not now, not until things get resolved and we understand what is happening to us all. Things are moving too fast. Damn…why is life so complicated at times?'

Peter, conscious of Chris's eyes on him, continued upstairs. It had been hard to say "no" to Pederson and Simpson, but it was probably the right decision. Did he really want to go back to science? He honestly did not know but he did know one thing and that was he didn't want to lose Chris. Without a word being said to Arnold Hawkins, or him saying anything to Peter, they both knew that that their interaction was turning into a quasi-father-son relationship and away from an employer-employee situation. For the first time in his life, he felt accepted, and wanted. His parents-in-law had been nice, friendly in fact, but never close. The love of his life, Jean, was gone, never to return, as was his unborn child. Now, he no longer felt alone and that was something he would not let go of, no matter what blandishments were offered. He smiled, thinking of those kisses with Chris. 'Ah Chris, I wish you were holding my hand as I'm heading upstairs to bed. You have no idea how I want to feel your body against mine. One day we'll be together. After everything that has happened in my life, it's hard to think that long-dead feelings are coming back. Maybe there is a God after all because no-one else could have planned what's happening now. Well, Chris, I'll dream of you tonight - yet again.'

THIRTEEN

After checking his battered personal telephone book, Nigel Meadows picked up the telephone and called a number. The female voice at the other end answered, "Chief Constable's office." Nigel introduced himself and asked to speak to the Chief Constable.

"May I ask what this is about, sir?" was the response and Nigel simply said, "Tell him Nigel Meadows is on the phone."

After less than a minute, the woman came back on the line and said, "I'm putting you through now, sir."

"Nigel," boomed Stanley Wilberforce, Chief Constable of Derbyshire. "My word, it has been a long time since we spoke. You are keeping well, I trust?"

"Oh indeed I am, Stan…thank you for asking."

The two men chatted for several minutes catching up on things until Wilberforce eventually said, "Well, I'm afraid I must get back to work, however pleasant this has been to chat with you. But you called me, Nigel. Is there anything in particular you want to say to me?"

"Yes, I…um…wanted to share something with you."

"Oh, what might that be?"

"There was an article in The National Globe this morning – the lead article, in fact."

"Yes, I saw it. Written by that Fowler fellow – bit of a muck raker, isn't he? What about it?"

"According to him, Special Branch is looking for a Cambridge scientist called Peter Marshall," said Nigel Meadows.

"Yes, I saw that. So?"

"Well, I know where he is."

"You do? Where is he?"

"Right here in Greydene. Actually, he's at a place a few miles outside of town, on Bracken Road."

"My word, that's interesting. And you are sure it is him?"

"Absolutely."

"Right, I see. Look, I'll get in touch with Ernie Miller. Do you remember Ernie?"

"Oh yes – he was at Hendon Police College back when we were there. I haven't spoken to him in years. How's he doing?"

"Very well indeed. He's now a Chief Superintendent and well on his way to being promoted to Commander. In fact, he's one step from being head of Special Branch."

"My word, he did do well…but I suppose you did too, Stan."

"Well Nigel, you could have done the same, couldn't you? But I gather you like the country life far better than big city policing, that so?"

"Oh, I've no regrets. I've a nice life up here and no hassles. Frankly I'm not sure that I'm cut out for all the politics and BS of fighting my way to the top."

"I expect you're right but, be that as it may, I'll give Ernie a call about this. Is it okay for him to ring you…either he or one of his men?"

"Absolutely…you have my number?"

"I'm not sure. I'll put my secretary on the line and she can take down the particulars. Anyway, it was most pleasant chatting to you, Nigel. We'll have to have lunch or dinner soon."

"That would be delightful," was Nigel's response although both men knew that it was highly unlikely that the Chief Constable of Derbyshire would seek out a lowly retired country bobby for a meal any time soon.

After Wilberforce hung up, he thought for a few minutes and then called his secretary on the intercom. "Can you find Chief Superintendent Ernest Miller of Special Branch for me? Tell him it's important and that he should call me as soon as he can. Thank you."

When Chief Superintendent Miller came on the phone, Stan Wilberforce brought him up-to-date regarding Peter Marshall.

"That's very interesting, isn't it?" said Miller. "Fancy our old friend Nigel finding him and in such an out-of-the-way place. I'll get in touch with my men up there and let them know that a retired country bobby beat them to it. What a laugh. Anyway, thanks Stan for letting me know. Let's make sure we stay in touch."

"Good," said Wilberforce. "By the way, why are you looking for this Marshall fellow?"

"Frankly I have no idea. The orders came from on high, probably from some ministry or other. Certainly no-one bothered to tell me why he's wanted. It certainly doesn't involve any crime or even national Security, so you're as wise as I am about it."

"That's so odd, isn't it? Ah well, our political masters will play their games, won't they?"

The next morning, Parsons, Johnson and Fowler all ate breakfast but Fowler sat at a separate table. They acknowledged each other with nods but maintained the polite fiction that they were barely on speaking terms. It wouldn't do to advertise the fact that they knew each other let alone were sharing information.

Parsons and Johnson eventually set off to find the food warehouse whereas Fowler left for Oak Tree Manor a couple of hours later. As he had said the previous evening, it would not be a good idea to get there too early.

John Parsons and Mike Johnson found the food warehouse without too much trouble, thanks to the car's GPS system. They were about to go inside when Mr. Hawkins and Peter pulled up outside the place. Politely, the two Special Branch men let the other two men go in first, reasoning that if they were there to stock up on food and drink, then the manager might be more disposed to talk to he and Mike after having at least done some business first.

When the manager finished tallying up the purchases for Oak Tree Manor, John moved forward and held out his warrant card, "I'm Detective Inspector Parsons from Scotland Yard…in London, you know."

The manager nodded at him and told his assistant to finish packaging up the purchases. Looking at Parsons, he said, "I know where Scotland Yard is but why are you here? It's a bit out of the way for you, isn't it?"

"We're making some inquiries here," Parsons said. When the manager raised an eyebrow, he continued, "Do you know a Chris Hawkins? I believe she works at Oak Tree Manor."

"Did you say Chris Hawkins?" interjected Mr. Hawkins.

"Yes," affirmed John, turning to the other man. "Do you know her?"

"I'd better – she's my daughter."

"Oh, I see. And you are?"

"Arnold Hawkins and I own Oak Tree Manor."

"I see. And who is this?" he added, with a nod at Peter.

"He's Peter, Peter Marshall. Peter works with us at Oak Tree Manor."

John Parsons and Mike Johnson exchanged astonished looks before John turned back to Peter, saying, "Are you *the* Peter Marshall?"

"I'm not sure about the "the" part but yes, I'm Peter Marshall," laughed Peter. "Why do you ask?"

"Well, a lot of people have been looking for you, that's why."

"Now why would that be? I've been here for some time and until yesterday, I wasn't aware that anyone cared where I was, let alone two Scotland Yard detectives." Peter paused and looked hard at John and Mike before continuing, "And just why are a lot of people, to use your words, looking for me? More to the point, why are *you* looking for me?"

With an embarrassed jerk of his head, John returned Peter's gaze and said, "That's actually a good question because I have no idea why I was told to find you but those were my instructions."

"Well, now that you've found me, what next? Are you going to arrest me, and if so, for what reason? As far as I know I have not committed any crimes."

"As far as *we* know, that's correct," said John. "You have not committed any crimes and we're certainly not here to arrest you."

"In that case," snapped Arnold Hawkins. "Just why are you here?"

"Good question, as I said. Now we've found him," with a jerk of his thumb towards Peter, "we'll report in and let them tell us what they want us to do next, or not do as the case may be."

Mr. Hawkins and Peter exchanged mystified looks. What was going on? Finally Mr. Hawkins said, "Well, Peter and I have to be getting on – we've got work to do, even if you two haven't. If you want us, we'll be at Oak Tree Manor, down the road a bit. Mind you, you'd better have a better explanation as to why you are looking for Peter rather than simply following orders. That sort of thing went out with the Nazis!"

Driving back to the guesthouse, Mr. Hawkins and Peter discussed the meeting with the two detectives. "What I don't understand," said Mr. Hawkins. "Is why they came all the way up here from London trying to find you and then, having found you, they have no idea of what to do next. That's barmy."

"I couldn't agree with you more," said Peter. "Why on earth would anyone want to find *me*? First there was that newspaper article, then the business with Hiram Pederson and what's-his-name from Greydene University, and now this. It's weird."

"It's weird, alright," agreed Mr. Hawkins. "Are you sure that you haven't done anything? Not that I'm accusing you of anything… I'm just flummoxed, that's all."

"I wish I knew," said Peter. "Nobody pays a blind bit of notice for several years and now I'm big news. Nothing's changed, I've done nothing but suddenly people are looking for me. What I can't understand is why."

"What about that George Martin fellow?"

"What about him? He is…I mean, was…a pretty good scientist and we were colleagues and friends of a sort for years at Cambridge. Actually we were rivals to a degree but that's the norm in academia."

"Why was he going to see the people at Scotland Yard?" asked Mr. Hawkins. "And Special Branch at that."

"I have no idea. We lost touch after I…er…I went inside and we've had no contact in years. No point, really."

"But there has to be a reason why people are looking for you! Let's face it, why send two Scotland Yard detectives up here to find you when the local police could have done that, and probably a lot faster. If they aren't here to arrest you, then why look for you?"

"I wish I knew," sighed Peter. Then with a laugh, he added, "All of a sudden everyone wants me. It wasn't too long ago that I was just a number in prison and while the guards and warden wanted to make sure that all of us were where we should be, no-one else cared about us. Then I got released and for a while my parole officer was concerned where I was but he was the only one. Finally, that was all over and no-one cared one iota who I was or where I was. Now, suddenly, everyone is looking for me. Frankly, I don't understand."

"You don't understand," said Mr. Hawkins. "How do you think I feel? One minute you are some hitchhiker who appeared out of nowhere and helped my daughter with a flat tire in some back street near the hospital. Then we bring you home and you start helping out at Oak Tree Manor, and very well too I might add. The next thing that happened is that Chris and you go to get some supplies at that warehouse and a bunch of bikers start to harass her. You appear and they take off like crows in a field when a farmer shoots at them. But, and here's the *but*, you didn't say a word and yet they still take off running. Then some American professor staying at the guesthouse tells us and the people at Greydene University that you are some big-wig scientist from Cambridge and they all start to make a fuss over you – a fuss that you don't want any part of. Then, there's this big article in the newspaper about the missing Dr. Peter Marshall and how he's tied in with some dead scientist, also from Cambridge University. Finally, and to crown it all, two police officers, Special Branch no less, come here and want to find you. Now they've found you, no-one knows what to do with you. So, what's it all about, Peter?"

"Damned if I know. By the way, how'd you know that they were Special Branch?"

"I'm no copper but I do know that Scotland Yard detectives don't travel around the country looking for someone unless there's been a murder and they are after a suspect. So that leads me to the logical conclusion that those two were Special Branch. However, that conclusion begs the question of why anyone would want Special Branch to come looking for you...I assume that you aren't a terrorist or anything."

"No, I am not! And neither am I a communist, a Muslim, a socialist or anything else. All I am is an ex-con who wants to be left alone and live in peace," said Peter bitterly.

"Aye lad, I can understand that," said Mr. Hawkins.

Suddenly he pulled the van over into a lay-by and stopped. Turning towards Peter he said, "Look lad, we need to talk. That newspaper article said you'd been in prison but you're no criminal, that's for sure. So, do you mind telling me what happened?"

After Peter slowly and hesitantly told Arnold Hawkins the story, the latter sat silent for a few minutes before saying, "That's a pretty awful tale, isn't it? I'm sorry that it happened to you." Peter simply nodded, what was there to say? Mr. Hawkins then continued softly, "Have you told Chris about any of this?" Seeing Peter shake his head, he added, "Look, Chris is very fond of you and I know you feel the same. Why don't you talk to her? She'll not think any the worse of you and if I know the pair of you, there shouldn't be any secrets between you, not if you are going to have any sort of relationship. Give it a try Peter, you never know what will come of it."

With that, he started the van up and drove back to Oak Tree Manor. Pulling up he said, "Well, here we are back home. Let's get that lot," with a jerk of his thumb towards the van interior, "inside the house and then you can go explore the countryside. As Chris said, it'll do you good. Also, and this only the opinion of an old man, talk to the girl, will you?"

They walked into the kitchen and brought in everything piecemeal. Then Peter picked up the cases of wine and took them into the bar and then he moved the bottles of tonic water and bitter lemon behind the bar, making several trips until everything was done. Meanwhile Mr. Hawkins sorted out the various foodstuffs that Chris had ordered. Eventually they were finished and decided to look for Chris to let her know that everything was taken care of. When they walked out into the entrance foyer, they found her talking to a sandy-haired man of medium height and an intense manner. Looking round, Chris said, "Here's my father…you can talk to him now because I've got things to do." Taking Peter's hand, she steered him back towards the kitchen, quickly putting a finger to her lips in the universal sign not to say anything. Curious as he was, Peter followed her lead and remained silent until they were safely in the kitchen when he said, "What was that all about?"

Quickly she kissed him lightly on the lips before saying, "That man is that wretched journalist who wrote all that stuff about you in the newspaper. Oh, that was a lot of "that's" wasn't it?" and then she laughed. "*That* must be catching," and laughed again. "Anyway, I assume that you don't want to talk to him, or do you?" Peter shook his head before asking, "What does he want?"

"He wants to talk you, that's what. It seems he thinks, or knows, that some police officers are looking for you although he doesn't know why. Anyway, I don't like him, intrusive person that he is, so I decided for you...I hope that's all right with you?"

"Actually your dad and I already ran into them, the two detectives that is, at the food warehouse."

"You did? What do they want?" asked Chris.

"Apparently they were told to find me, which they did."

"Why do they want to find you?"

"They said they didn't know. They did say that although they were told that they should find me and report back, they had no orders on what to do next. I got the impression that they were as much in the dark as we are," said Peter.

"You know," said Chris. "This is all very strange." She looked at Peter and said, "What is it about you that makes everyone so interested in you?"

"I wish I knew," sighed Peter. "As I said to your father on the drive back here, for years nobody gave a damn about me. I was a number, a statistic if you will, and lost to the world. Now it seems I am some sort of hot property but no-one, and I mean no-one, seems to know why."

"I expect we'll find out soon enough and then, hopefully, we'll...I mean you... will be left in peace."

"That would be nice," sighed Peter. "But somehow I sense that might be wishful thinking." He looked away for a moment and then turned back to Chris. "So, is everything ship-shape with the guest rooms, dinner for tonight, everything?"

"Yes, we've got everything under control. Look, in an hour or so, I'll get some lunch together and then you can go off and explore the countryside. As Dad and I said, it'll do you good to get away from here for a bit. Fortunately the car's got a GPS so you shouldn't get too lost. These country roads can be a real bear and every village looks pretty much like every other one around here."

They looked at each other for several long moments, both longing to take the other in their arms, and even moved slightly towards each other before Chris jerked her head impatiently. "I'd best go and see if dad's okay. I know he hates having his space invaded and that reporter is surely doing just that."

"Look, Mr. Fowlard or whatever your name is…" said Arnold Hawkins.

"Fowler, Richard Fowler," said Dirty Dick.

"Whatever! So what is it you want here?" snapped Mr. Hawkins.

"I should like to talk to Dr. Peter Marshall. I believe he is staying here, isn't he?"

"I doubt that Peter wants to talk to you after that nonsense you put in the newspaper the other day. All that innuendo and conjecture might help sell newspapers but I don't see why it's so important to pry into people's lives the way you do."

"But the public have a right to know," protested Fowler.

"The right to know what?" asked Mr. Hawkins, irritated by the reporter's unctuous manner. "That a man lost his wife, went off the rails and got sent to prison – *that* is important for the public to know? Spare me! I know that the difference between comedy and tragedy is usually only a matter of time but leave Peter Marshall alone. He paid his debt to society and he has the right…the *right*… to his privacy and to be left alone, and the public be damned. All the public wants is to be entertained and never have to think. Your sort of journalism serves up pabulum that they can relish over breakfast and tut-tut to their heart's content until the next tragedy or bit of sensationalism arrives on the scene. So, Mr. Fowler, I suggest you go back to where you came from and leave us, and I mean all of us, alone. Good day to you, sir."

With that, Mr. Hawkins pointed at the front door before stalking off in apparent high dudgeon. Chris, catching the last of her father's diatribe, smiled to herself. Whatever else her father was, he was no softie and woe-betide anyone who crossed him but she was amused by his feigned outrage. Her father cared about Peter and would do anything to protect him, of that she was sure, but all three of them, she, Peter and her father, were aware that whatever had prompted this interest in Peter was not going to go away and dismissing Richard Fowler was only delaying the inevitable. The same could be said about Peter ducking the evening's dinner party. Those people were also coming back because scientists are tenacious and would keep on probing and prodding until they had what they wanted, a bit like the police and journalists for that matter.

John Parsons and Mike Johnson were seated in their now customary corner of the lounge at Greydene Hotel and silently sipped at their coffees. Eventually Mike asked his chief, "Did you get a phone call from Chief Super. Miller, sir?"

"Yes I bloody did," snapped Parsons. "It seems that some retired bobby up here called his old friend the Chief Constable who in turn rang his old friend Ernest Miller and told him that Peter Marshall is staying at the Oak Tree Manor. Fortunately I could tell Miller that we had already found him and didn't need the help of the local coppers, retired or otherwise. He wasn't too pleased, however, when I told him that we'd seen Fowler up here and that he, Fowler, was also hot on Marshall's trail."

"So, what does he want us to do now?"

"He didn't say. I'll bet you he'll report to his boss who in turn will report to whoever it was that started all this and then, after lots of hot air and decisions are made, further instructions will trickle down to us."

"This is a bit of a waste of time, isn't it, sir?" asked Mike.

"So, what else is new, sergeant?" grunted John Parsons. "Anyway, for the time being we'll stay here and wait for further instructions. At least the weather's good and we can get out and see the countryside while that lot in London decides what's next on the agenda."

After listening to the verbal report of Detective Superintendent Miller, Commander Anthony Braithwaite, Head of Special Branch telephoned The Right Honorable James Arthur Llewellyn-Hughes, the Permanent Under-secretary at the Ministry of Energy and Natural Resources.

"Well, we've found him," announced Braithwaite.

"That's good," said Llewellyn-Hughes. "Where was he?"

After Braithwaite outlined the various steps the two detectives had taken to locate Peter Marshall, he also mentioned that the reporter Richard Fowler of The National Globe was also hot on Marshall's trail. Finally he asked, "What would you like us to do now?"

"You say he's staying in or actually is working at a guesthouse in Derbyshire, yes?"

"That's correct, yes."

"This place, it's near Greydene isn't it?"

"Yes it is and quite close too."

"Hmm, let me think about this…I'll get back to you later this afternoon. Your officers, are they still up there?"

"Yes. Should I recall them?"

"No, not for the moment…at least not until I've thought this all through. As I said, I shall get back to you later. Thank you for calling me."

After hanging up the phone, Llewellyn-Hughes thought for a few minutes and then called Professor Randolph Bethany. When Professor Bethany eventually took his call, Llewellyn-Hughes said abruptly, "Bethany, we've found him. Meet me at the club for lunch…I want to discuss this with you," and hung up the telephone, thinking 'For a change that greedy little man is going to have to earn his lucrative stipend.'

Sitting back in his chair, Llewellyn-Hughes thought about the reporter, Richard Fowler, whom he had been told was actively looking for Marshall. If Miller's men had found him, then it was likely only a matter of time before Fowler also found him and who knows what Marshall might say in an interview. As he pondered, it occurred to Llewellyn-Hughes that no-one had said how Peter Marshall had got to this guesthouse or indeed what he was really doing there. It was odd that he had managed to leave London without money and no means of transportation and yet end up in a remote guesthouse in Derbyshire. Why he went there and what he was doing were imponderables. There were also the odd circumstances of George Martin's death and what he was doing going to see Special Branch officers when he got run over. The more pressing question, however, was what should be done with Dr. Marshall now that they had found him.

The man had been out of things for several years, so would he consider going back into research, or could he even do so if he wanted? He had spent time in prison and that always left a mark. Would Marshall be bitter over what had happened and flatly refuse to have anything to do with anyone? That was quite possible based on his hiding out at that country guesthouse in Derbyshire. Was the man sane and in charge of his faculties? Would he be able to bring himself up-to-date in a reasonable period of time or was science a dim and distant memory? What inducements could be offered to bring him back into the fold, so to speak? Was going back to Cambridge even a possibility? If not Cambridge, what about somewhere else?

As he thought things through, Llewellyn-Hughes withdrew a slim notebook from an inside pocket, took a gold pen out of another pocket and started to jot down some notes for his lunchtime meeting. Soliciting Bethany's advice was likely to be less effective than presenting him with a series of options before steering him in the direction he wanted. "We must do what we can to salvage that huge, if unwise, investment in Martin. Ideally, Marshall might be persuaded to go back to Cambridge and that would solve many problems. Even if he agreed to go somewhere else, moving the equipment and staff would be expensive but anything was better than simply abandoning the project. As he snapped the notebook shut and re-pocketed his pen, Llewellyn-Hughes realized that everything depended on Peter Marshall and he had minimal information on the man.

Picking up the phone, he called one of his staff, "Fletcher, come to my office, will you?" After Stephen Fletcher appeared, Llewellyn-Hughes said, "This Martin project…the one you backed…yes, that monumental exercise in wasted revenue… well, I have been thinking. I managed to locate the originator of that whole concept, one Peter Marshall. With luck, we may be able to bring him in from the cold and have him rescue this mess. However, I suspect that it will require some finesse to do that so I need you to get as much information on Dr. Marshall as you can. Use every available resource, even go up to

Greydene or wherever he might be and talk to him. Before we can do anything about him or with him, we need to know everything about him, and I mean everything. That includes talking to his cellmate or cellmates in prison, any co-workers since he was released and even before that…when he was at Cambridge. Talk to those Special Branch officers, that reporter Fowler, everybody. This is a matter of urgency, so take care of it now and don't take too long either."

"But sir," said Fletcher hesitantly. "My wife's…"

"Fletcher, might I remind you that we are in this mess because of your heavy-handed promotion of this monumentally expensive project? I really do not care about your domestic situation, or that of your in-laws, out-laws or anyone else. Get started with getting me that information. I need hardly mention how dire the consequences could be if word gets out about this fiasco."

Suitably chastened, Stephen Fletcher went back to his office and telephoned his wife to tell her the bad news. Understandably, and predictably, Fiona Fletcher was not amused that her husband would miss their dinner party that evening and was decidedly annoyed that he was likely to be going out-of-town for several days chasing down something that he could not tell her about. "Just what is so important that you have to work all night and even have to leave London? You're a senior Civil Servant, for God's sake, why can't you send one of your minions to do this?" she furiously demanded to know.

"I cannot talk about this, my sweet, but if I don't take care of this and do it satisfactorily, I might well be looking for another position. Need I remind you that if I have to leave the Ministry, missing a dinner party or going out of town will be the least of our problems?" With that, he hung up the telephone and thought, 'Why is it that women like Fiona who have led a privileged and cosseted life all their lives, have the attitude that the world revolves around them and their wants. Well, my dear Fiona, this is the real world and reality has struck!'

Richard Fowler was having a difficult talk with his editor, Matthew Jenkins. "What can I do if the man won't talk to me?" he wailed. "I can't force him and no, I couldn't find out why anyone was looking for him in the first place. Even those Special Branch officers didn't know why they had been tasked to find him and they have no idea who gave Special Branch orders to look for him." He listened as the editor urged him to try harder and then said, "I did find out that Peter Marshall received some sort of martial arts training while in prison. Apparently his cellmate is ex-SAS and took care of him… made certain that he wouldn't get attacked, that sort of thing. I'm wondering if there's some sort of human interest story there. You know, what got him sent to prison, that sort of thing?"

Matthew Jenkins thought for a moment or two before saying, "Something tells me that you may be flogging a dead horse with regard to that search for Peter Marshall. Write something up and pose the question…also link in George Martin. I suspect that things will break loose soon enough but for the moment, see if you can talk to those Special Branch people about Marshall's time in jail and that fellow who taught him karate or whatever it was. That's sounds interesting and I want to know more, okay? Also, how on earth did that man end up at a guesthouse in Derbyshire? That makes no sense, so see what you can find there too?"

After hanging up, Dick decided he would go down to the bar in the hotel and get a pre-lunch drink. Walking into the lounge, he spotted Parsons and Johnson in their corner. He waved at them and then lifted a hand to his mouth in a drinking gesture. Getting drinks for them all, he walked over and joined his new friends at their table.

They all drank and Parsons looked at Fowler expectantly, asking, "What's happening, Dick?"

Briefly, Dick outlined the conversation with his editor and then asked John to tell him a bit more about the martial arts skills Peter possessed and asked if he had any more details of what happened in that pub in London and with the biker gang.

"Before I get into all that," said John. "I need you to do me a favor."

"And what's that?"

"I said I'd do what I could to have Monk's case looked into. It strikes me that he received a very stiff sentence when the whole situation was pretty murky. It certainly wasn't murder and I don't believe it was a premeditated attack on someone. So, will you do that for me…and for Monk? I'll get in touch with my friend at the Crown Prosecution Service but some pressure from the press would help."

"Not a problem. In fact, that might give me a hook for my story. When I get back to London, I'll go and have a word with the man myself. Good idea. You never know, we might even get some justice here. Where did you say he was?"

FOURTEEN

Richard Fowler sat across the visitor's table from Monk in Wormwood Scrubbs Prison and looked at him curiously. "Did you just say what I thought you said?"

Monk looked back at him and nodded, "Yeah, you're the second person who's come here asking me about Peter Marshall in the last couple of days. And it wasn't too long ago that that police detective also came to see me. What's going on?"

"Frankly, I wish I knew but I will tell you what *I* do know," said Fowler. "But before I get started on that, who was it that came to see you yesterday?"

"Some bloke from the Ministry of Energy and Natural Resources – he said his name was Stephen Fletcher or something like that."

"What exactly did he want?"

"Search me, mate. He asked me lots of questions about Peter and wrote down a bunch of notes, almost the same as you're doing now, but he wasn't a journalist, that's for sure."

"What makes you say that?" asked Dick curiously.

"Well for a start, he was better dressed than you and he had one of those toffee-nosed accents…you know, Public School and Oxford University type thing. Also, there's no way he's done any physical work of any kind in years – his hands are too soft and lily-white, you know what I mean?"

"Huh," said Fowler. "And he was from the Ministry of Energy and Natural Resources, you say?"

Monk nodded, "That's right. Anyway, what's this all about? In the space of a couple of weeks, I've had four visits, including you, from people asking me about Peter, and that's more than I've had

200

asking about me in years. So before I answer any more questions, what do you want with me?"

"Well Monk…that's right, isn't it?…I'm actually here to talk to you. Do you remember D.I. Parson? He was the detective that came to see you."

Monk nodded.

"It so happens that I met him recently, very recently, and he told me that he'd promised you that he would ask one of his friends in the CPS about your case. As part of that promise, he suggested I speak to you…you know…get your story and see if I can stir things up a bit on your behalf."

"He did?" asked an astonished Monk. "Do you mean to tell me that he's an honest copper and actually tries to do what he says he will? Will wonders never cease?"

"Yes," said Fowler. "He *is* a good guy and he does keep his word. So, what happened that got you put in here?"

"I was having a quiet drink in my local and left to go home. Outside the place, some bloke was beating the you-know-what out of some woman and his mates were just standing there, laughing their heads off and egging him on. Me, being me, stepped in and sorted them out. The man who was whaling into the woman got belligerent and grabbed up a beer bottle, smashed off the end and lunged at me with it. I had no choice but I hit him a bit too hard and he died on me."

"What happened then?"

"By the time the police got there, the other blokes had scarpered and the women, who was as thick as two planks, said she didn't see anything and wasn't even sure why I had hit the bloke. When the police asked her how she had got those two black eyes, she claimed she'd fallen over and hit her head. So, long story short, I got banged up for twenty years to life for doing the right thing…only goes to show, doesn't it?"

"Ouch," said Fowler. "I can see why Parsons wants to help. Tell me, you don't seem to be too bitter about what happened."

"Don't do any good to brood over it, does it? The only thing is, it was hard to tell my wife that she should get on with her life. As I said to her, by the time I get out of here, I'll be an old man and I won't be any good to anyone by that time. No, it's best for her to be shot of me and start a new life. Hurts to say it but it's the right thing to do, isn't it?"

"So, has she divorced you and moved on?"

"Nah, she's stubborn and loyal that one…she's going her own way no matter what I say. As far as she's concerned, things will work out and that's final."

"Based on what you're telling me, she could be right. Tell you what, I'll do what I can…and that's a promise. You don't mind if I go to see your wife, do you?"

"Not at all. When you do see her, tell her that I love her but she's got to get on with her life, okay?"

Fowler nodded and silently stared at Monk. This man was something else and he, like Parsons, had already developed a lot of respect for him… he would do his best to help. Finally he said, "Okay then, can we talk a little bit about Peter Marshall?"

Monk nodded and said, "Not sure that I can help much. Peter was one very quiet bloke – he only spoke if he had something to say but I'll tell you one thing, he was always ready to help anyone out. The number of letters he wrote for the other inmates is amazing and just before he got out, there was this kid who was being set upon… you know how it is in here…and Peter jumped in and sorted that out right fast. Peter was a good bloke and if he was your friend, he *was* your friend. I tell you, I miss him but I'm pleased he's out – he shouldn't have been here in the first place."

Fowler, thinking 'that makes two of you', busily made notes and when visiting hour was up, he shook Monk's hand warmly. "Hey, thanks for everything, you've been a big help…and don't worry, we are going to get you out of here if it's at all possible, okay?" Monk just nodded.

James Arthur Llewellyn-Hughes looked across the luncheon table at Professor Randolph Bethany and asked, "Well Randy, now that we've found Marshall, what are your thoughts?" Bethany hesitated before replying, "Arthur, it's good news that Marshall's been found…in Derbyshire you say?" When Llewellyn-Hughes nodded, he continued, "That being so, has anyone approached him about what his interests might be, that's to say, is he interested in coming back into science?"

"Not yet, no." said Llewellyn-Hughes. "He has been out of prison and roaming the country for some time and if he's shown no inclination to come in from the cold, so to speak, there may be little reason to think he might do so now."

"But we don't know that, do we?" protested Bethany. "People of his caliber rarely just walk away from science, do they? What I mean is that Marshall was a gifted scientist and probably still is because ability is ability and while it might go dormant, I doubt that it dies completely." Warming to his subject, Bethany continued, "I'm wondering whether it might be useful if I personally went up there to meet Marshall. If I could tell him that we are putting together a research team to work on his ideas, then that might be a sufficient inducement for him. Of course, this may not be the time for Marshall to lead the team but he certainly could work under my overall direction until he's comfortable enough to take over. What do you think?"

Llewellyn-Hughes almost laughed aloud; Bethany was so predictable, and greedy to boot. "Is that such a good idea, Randy? After all, you two have worked in different fields and Marshall might take exception to you trying to take over his brain child."

"That's possible of course, but I am quite well-known and I do have a certain reputation. Marshall might enjoy working with me…you know, take advantage of my reputation and build on it to advance his own career."

Ignoring Bethany's comment, Llewellyn-Hughes asked, "Tell me, Randy, do you know anyone at Greydene University?"

"Perhaps…I'm sure that I do but no-one comes immediately to mind. Greydene is, of course, quite sound but hardly one of the top tier universities in this country."

"That's what I thought. Is it possible that you may be able to get someone there interested in working in Marshall's field? A vague promise of some funding might help but I suggest that you do not tell them that you would be running the project - that would not do at all. A possible advisory role for you might be satisfactory but nothing more."

"Yes, well, of course – I'll do what I can." Bethany hesitated and then added, "I assume my usual per diem will apply?" Llewellyn-Hughes nodded in agreement.

After Bethany left, Llewellyn-Hughes sat back and slowly drank another coffee, mulling things over. 'Okay, Bethany will go up to Greydene University and find some hack or other to work with Marshall. We'll provide some funding and if things go the way we want, we can either take everything from Cambridge over to Greydene or shift Marshall back to Cambridge. The question remains as to whether Marshall will want to get back to work. However, I do wonder whether that damn newspaper reporter did any damage with his article. Nobody likes to have their private life spread out for the entire world to see and Marshall is probably no exception. Well, we'll see if Fletcher has come up with anything useful on Marshall. Now what do we do about those Special Branch people languishing up in Greydene? I don't want them to go to waste.'

A little later, Llewellyn-Hughes telephoned the head of Special Branch and summoned him. When the man arrived, he said, "Ah Braithwaite, good of you to drop by. Tell me, you have a couple of your officers up there in Derbyshire, don't you?" to which Braithwaite nodded. "These men, they are sound, are they?"

"Yes, very. Detective Inspector Parsons has been around for a long time and is very experienced. In fact, he's fast approaching retirement. The other man, Detective Sergeant Johnson, is of course much younger but I believe he's quite able."

"I see," said Llewellyn-Hughes. "This man Parsons…you said he's only an inspector but close to retirement, yes?" Again, Braithwaite nodded.

"So, he could be promoted, yes? If he made Chief Inspector, that would make a difference to his retirement pension, wouldn't it?"

"Yes, definitely."

"What I should like to propose is that you bring back that sergeant…Johnson, is it?… and have Parsons promoted. I assume that you are able to take care of that expeditiously."

"Of course. He has been a good officer – solid and capable – so a promotion would be in order. I'll start the paperwork immediately."

"Good," said Llewellyn-Hughes. "Now, what I propose is that you send Mrs. Parsons…I assume he's married and living in London?"

"Yes he is and they do live in London."

"Well then, bring Johnson back and send Mrs. Parsons up to Derbyshire to join her husband. Give them a free vacation as a quasi-reward to celebrate his promotion. We'll foot the bill and they can stay at that guesthouse place…just tell them to act as though they are looking around the area for a possible retirement home…I believe that part of the country is quite lovely. Anyway, while staying at the guesthouse, they can ingratiate themselves with Marshall *et al* and learn what they can about how they interact."

"I imagine so," said a mystified Braithwaite.

"Good, fine…well take care of that, will you?" commanded Llewellyn-Hughes.

"Of course…but if asked, what should Parsons say about why he had been looking for Marshall? I imagine somebody is going to want to know what that was all about."

"I am glad you raised that point. Parson's senior officer can tell him that he'd heard that the Chinese are working hard on a new energy generating process, one that might be akin to what Marshall was working on, and that people in Whitehall were concerned that he, Marshall, might have taken off to join their efforts. That's not an unreasonable justification for us to be looking for him and also happens to be true, at least to a point. Marshall is not a stupid man and after a stint in prison, he will be suspicious of any- and everything so a good cover story should ease things.

"If Parsons shares this information with his sergeant, I suspect he will talk to his friends about it, so it won't take long for that story to get out. That will satisfy the press as well as indicate that the Government is concerned that the Nation's energy work stays here and isn't lost to the Chinese, or anyone else for that matter."

"Of course, sir," agreed Braithwaite although he had no clear idea what Llewellyn-Hughes might be up to. Although Llewellyn-Hughes's ostensible reason in looking for Dr. Marshall made sense, there had to be something else going on. The Chinese and most other countries were working on energy generation but that sort of research had been going on for years, so why the sudden interest? That sort of scientific rivalry was hardly a matter of National Security, so why involve Special Branch? Also, it was curious that after all the secrecy surrounding the search for Marshall, he now wanted it to be public knowledge that Marshall had been working on energy generation. Braithwaite knew that the three primary motivations for action in people at that level were power, money and sex…and not necessarily in that order. But just how those three motivators were playing in this situation were beyond him.

On returning to his office, Braithwaite muttered to himself, "Well, whatever is going on will soon come out in the wash. Hard to believe that I'll have to wait to see what's in the newspapers to find out what it is…what on earth is happening to our country? It's not like the old days when we knew everything about everything and long before it ever got into the newspapers!"

Within a matter of hours, the promotion of D.I. Parsons to Detective Chief Inspector was in the works and Mary Parsons was busily packing for a mini-vacation with her husband in Derbyshire. After hearing the news, a delighted John Parsons rang Oak Tree Manor to book a room for several days for him and his wife. Then he and Mike Johnson had a last drink in the bar at Greydene Hotel before he took his sergeant to the train station to catch a train to London. After that, John waited patiently for his wife to arrive. Quite why the powers-that-be were doing this for him was a mystery but he had been on the force long enough not to question internal decisions too closely.

Lunch was over and the final chores in the guesthouse were done, leaving Mabel, Lucy and Chris time to get things arranged for the evening's dinner which they were happily discussing as they laid out cutlery, china and the myriad other items required for a semi-formal dinner. Mr. Hawkins had retreated to his office, mumbling about women's work and all the fuss they made. With a final admonition to Peter that he should get on the road, he closed his door and settled in his chair for a quiet snooze while everyone else got on with their afternoons.

Peter changed clothes, went outside and got into Chris's car. He wondered momentarily whether his driving license had been restored but decided he didn't care. If he got into trouble, then so be it…after what he'd been through, getting pulled over was a minor problem. Besides he was a good driver, albeit out of practice, so getting into trouble was unlikely.

As he drove, he started to look around and agreed with Chris and Arnold Hawkins, it *was* beautiful around Greydene. For the first time in ages, he felt at peace and started to enjoy the quiet hum of car tires over the smooth roads, the sun dappling trees and shrubs beside the road and the odd bird call he could hear through the open car windows. Life was suddenly good and he started to think about why he felt this way. It all came down to being at Oak Tree Manor and the calming presence of Arnold Hawkins as well as the warmth and affection of Chris. He thought about Chris and his mind leaped back to their sudden embrace and the stirred emotions resulting from it.

Continuing to drive but now barely taking notice of what he passed as he wended his way through country road after country road, Peter thought about the advice Arnold Hawkins had given him. Maybe it *was* time to talk to Chris about the past. Whatever he said to her would not, could not, change what had happened and if they were to be together, then it was only right and fair that she should know everything. Well perhaps not everything because she did not need know the details, salacious or otherwise, of his life between getting out of prison and arriving at Oak Tree Manor. While he would spare her of hearing about his love life, he did need to share other things with her. For a moment his mind shifted back to prison and Monk. What a life-saver that man had been and, to his dismay, Peter realized that he had not contacted him since getting out.

He pulled the car over and thought about Monk, and a wave of affection swept through him. Silently he vowed to get in touch with the man to whom he owed so much. Aloud, he muttered, "How could I have let things go with him for so long? Without Monk, my life would have been a living hell in prison…man, I owe you so much and what have I done to repay you? Nothing!" Then Peter thought about Nobby Murphy and his lovely daughter Dahlia, the latter with a great deal of pleasure. Nobby had taken him out of London and without Nobby, he would not have met Chris and her father…and if he had not met them, he would not be here in Derbyshire.

'And what,' he asked himself. 'Was it that had driven me out of London? Oh yes, that punch-up in the pub.' As he thought about it, Peter again acknowledged that it was Monk who had given him the wherewithal to take care of that situation and the later one involving Nobby. Aloud he said, "Monk, you've had such an influence on me, haven't you? I owe you so much!" Then Peter realized that there had been a pattern over the past few years. First there was prison and sharing a cell with Monk. Monk taught him how to defend himself. That ability was used to good effect in the pub and then saved a young woman from being molested by a big and brutal drunk. Then he left London by Nobby giving him a lift and when the time came, he was able to sort out that biker gang and save Nobby from what might have been a brutal beating. After that, Nobby brought him home and then dropped him off around the corner from where Chris was marooned with a flat tire. After he helped Chris change the tire, she gave him a lift and he ended up at Oak Tree Manor and his life became what it is now.

What kind fate was it that led to this train of events? It was a train of events because one thing followed the next in a nice logical sequence, a sequence that satisfied his scientific mind. For a moment he wondered whether there really was a God who had been watching over him but then that same scientific mind dismissed the notion… spirituality was alien to him. Then he thought about going to the food warehouse with Chris and how he had frightened off those young thugs who were harassing her, something that had surprised Chris and made her look at him with new eyes. Finally, he thought about how he had looked at Hiram Pederson's draft manuscript and made those notes, and how that simple act had led Pederson and the people at Greydene University want to meet him. Again, a strange pattern of events but where was that train headed? And what about that newspaper article, the one that had caused he and Chris to be together? Where did that fit in?

As he thought things through, Peter also wondered why those detectives had been looking for him. That made no sense and even they were unclear why they had been given that assignment. So, here he was, parked alongside a narrow country road and with a head full of questions and going heaven knows where. He smiled. Life has its ups and downs and everything was becoming all too weird for him. He was about to restart the car and drive on when he heard a voice to one side of him and a head appeared through the open car window.

"Are you having car trouble?"

Startled, Peter looked at the man standing there with a friendly smile on his face. The man looked familiar but Peter couldn't place him. "It's Peter, isn't it?" asked the man. "I'm Nigel Meadows, Mabel's husband. We met at Oak Tree Manor soon after you first got there."

"Oh yes, it had slipped my memory." Peter smiled at Nigel. "Sorry I was miles away for a while…thinking about things…you know how it goes. But no, there's nothing wrong with the car, I just stopped for a bit to take a look around and do some thinking."

"Sounds about right," agreed Nigel. "It's good to take a breather every so often and smell the roses…not that there are too many around here. Anyway, if the car's alright, I'll leave you be." He started to walk away and then came back. "Peter, there's a nice pub up the road. Why don't you follow me there and we'll have a pint of beer… that suit you?"

"Sounds good to me," said Peter. "My head's beginning to ache with so much thinking. I'm sure a beer will help."

"It'll do that," agreed Nigel. "As for thinking, I try to avoid to doing any of that these days…it's too depressing. Okay lad, just follow me. It's about a couple of miles from here and I promise you that the beer's good."

Dick Fowler put the finishing touches to his article on the successful search for Peter Marshall. He was about to send it electronically to the editor when he hesitated. Something did not feel right and just saying that a lost scientist had been found was hardly news-worthy since until recently, nobody even knew he had been missing, let alone cared.

Tilting his chair back, he fished out his cell phone and dialed John Parsons's number. After he got through, he said, "Hey John, it's Dick. What's happening up there?"

"Nothing much. They called Mike back to London but I'm staying on…actually at Oak Tree Manor and Mary, my wife, is on her way up here to stay with me for a few days."

"She is? What's the occasion?"

"Well, I did hear tell that I'm being promoted and this could well be a small celebration."

"You're getting promoted to D.C.I. – that's great and long overdue. Congratulations," said Fowler. "But wait a minute; you said this could well be a small celebration, didn't you? What exactly does that mean?"

"Dick, don't quote me but someone down there suggested that Mary and me spend a few days up here. You know, look around, get to know the people at Oak Tree Manor…that sort of thing," said John Parsons. "It all came out of the blue."

"That's nice but I wonder why?"

"Beats me but I'm not complaining."

"I'm sure you're not – a free vacation is always enjoyable," commented Dick. "Hmm, but it is strange, isn't it? Did they say anything about why you were looking for Marshall? Is there anything you can tell me…anything I can write about without getting you in trouble?"

"Actually yes, but don't quote me directly please…no matter what they said, I don't completely trust what anyone says to me these days. Anyway…" and John Parsons proceeded to outline to Dick Fowler what he had been told.

"Well, thanks John but that can't be the whole story."

"Why not?…although I tend to agree with you."

"Look, the Americans, the Chinese, the Japanese, the Germans, the Russians and everyone else is engaged in energy research, even the Indians, so why the sudden panic over the research work of a person who has been out of the field for several years? That makes no sense and, pennies to pounds, there's something else going on, and I wonder what? Well, let's play the game, shall we?"

"How'd you mean?" asked John.

"I'll write that up and suggest it makes complete sense but in the meantime I'm going to start digging…I don't like it when

Government sources try to mislead me and this time I smell a rat. There's a couple of other things that I'd also like to talk to you about."

"There are?" said John.

"First, and this is more of a favor than anything else. Stay in touch, will you?, and if anything interesting comes up, give me a call and I promise not to involve you."

"Okay. I make no promises but we'll stay in touch. What's the other thing?"

"I met your man Monk. Actually, he's Peter Marshall's man but you know what I mean."

"Yes?"

"He's a great bloke and I tend to agree with you, John, there does seem to be something amiss there. Twenty years to life is pretty steep for someone with no priors and gets arrested for trying to rescue someone from harm. I'm going to write that up…by the way, did you have any luck with your friend at the CPS?"

"I rang him and he's going to look into it. An article from you in the National Globe should help a great deal. I'll give him a call a few days after it gets covered in the newspaper…and thanks."

"My pleasure," said Fowler. "By the way, Monk told me that someone by the name of Fletcher went to see him - just the other day, yesterday in fact."

"Who's he, this Fletcher character?"

"That's just it. He's someone in the Ministry of Energy and Natural Resources – he holds some sort of mid-level position there. Went to Oxford I gather and has done quite well at the ministry. I've never heard of him before but he went to see Monk and was asking all sorts of questions about Peter Marshall."

"He was? I wonder why? If Marshall had been working on energy generation, then it's reasonable that the Ministry of Energy and Natural Resources would be interested but why were Special Branch involved and why did that Stephen Fletcher person go to talk to Monk in prison? What are they looking for? As you say, there's something else beneath all this but what?"

As he hung up, Dick Fowler smiled. So the politicians and civil servants were playing games again and the laconic comments of John Parsons confirmed it. 'Okay,' he thought. 'I'll put out the message they want me to but I'm going to start digging, and deeply at that. I'll bet it has something to do with that dead Martin guy from Cambridge. As soon as I've put my story to bed, I'll get started on writing about Monk…at least that should be straightforward enough. After that, I'm going to really look into this whole business of Dr. Peter Marshall.'

He started to jot down some notes to give to the interns assigned to him. They were going to be busy for the next few days and he mentally thanked his editor for assigning the extra help to him.

As she and Mabel put the prepared briskets into the oven to cook slowly, Chris thought about Peter, 'I hope you're enjoying yourself, Peter. You deserve a break and getting out of here and avoiding all those people over dinner is probably sensible but I do wonder whether you can hide forever. Obviously they want what's in your head but it's up to you what you do about it. Just don't let anyone take you away from me, okay?' Turning to Mabel, she said, "Okay, we got the table set, the meat's on, what do we do next?" Turning to Lucy, she added, "You're all set for tonight, aren't you. What about your boyfriend? He's coming, isn't he?"

"He'd better, if he knows what's good for him," said Lucy. "Besides, it'll be good for him to see what a bunch of professors are like when they let their hair down. Maybe it'll inspire him to do something with that degree of his?"

"Fat chance," muttered Mabel. "I'll believe it when I see it." More loudly, she asked, "Is you dad going to serve drinks or do we need another pair of hands?"

"No, dad said he'd be happy to help out. Knowing him, he just wants to listen in to what they're saying. I get the sense that he believes that Professor Pederson and that Simpson chap from Greydene are planning something. I'm not sure what exactly but dad is pretty smart, and if he thinks that something's going on, I'll bet it is. Oh well, what about those vegetables? Also, what did we finally decide on the salad and dessert?"

Stephen Fletcher sat in his car and cursed the traffic. He was not happy, not in the least. He was in the dog-house with his wife

Fiona because he had missed their dinner party the other evening. It was all very well for the Permanent Under-secretary, the Right Honorable James Arthur Llewellyn-Hughes, to tell him to find out what he could about Dr. Peter Marshall but how could he do that when no-one would speak to him?

A Google search revealed only that Dr. Peter Marshall had been faculty at Cambridge University and had published a number of scientific papers. Attempts to get information from either the University or College authorities were unproductive, everyone pleading privacy issues. With no official standing, Stephen Fletcher could make no headway at all.

The interview with that man Monk, the purported cell-mate of Peter Marshall, had yielded nothing because the man barely said anything let alone talked about Marshall. Marshall's ex-parents-in-law flatly refused to discuss him and shut the door on his protests. Trying to talk to that barman in the pub where Marshall had laid out the drunken Irishman and then had headed north had been equally unproductive. Jamie, or whatever his name was, had flatly denied even knowing Marshall and certainly would not talk about him. What had he said? "Peter Marshall? Never heard of him."

"But he worked with you behind the bar. And didn't he take on some big brute of a laborer who was drunk and attacking some young woman here? That chap…surely you know who I'm talking about? You must do."

"Not me, mate. I've never seen him and even if I had, which I haven't, why would I tell you anything? Who are you anyway?"

He had, however, been more successful when he spoke to George Martin's research team in Cambridge. None of them knew Dr. Marshall but virtually every comment about Dr. Martin had been more or less negative. The researchers had made comments about Martin being domineering, paranoid, secretive and a poor leader. When Fletcher tried to discuss their work with them, they were most reluctant to say anything and when they did, he was left almost complete in the dark with the arcane technical terms they all used. Stephen Fletcher finally was left wondering how it was that he had been so enthusiastic and supportive of Martin's proposal when he had first reviewed it.

When he had reported back to Llewellyn-Hughes, his lack of progress was received with great displeasure. "Are you telling me that no-one, and I mean no-one, even admits to knowing this man? So it would seem that you have learned nothing about Marshall, not just nothing of use, but nothing at all? Fletcher, you disappoint me. This Peter Marshall is not some Will-o'-the-wisp, no, he's a real person and someone must know him. Well, there's no point in wasting any more time on this, is there?" and Llewellyn-Hughes turned back to the papers on his desk, effectively dismissing Fletcher.

FIFTEEN

"I tell you, Peter," said Nigel Meadows. "There's almost nothing better than drinking a beer in the late afternoon sun and simply relaxing." Peter agreed and took another pull at his beer. Nigel continued, "So, Peter, why were those police officers looking for you?"

"Actually, I have no idea…and I don't think they knew either."

"But you haven't committed any crimes, have you? Although you did go to prison, I don't suppose you've done anything like that since."

"No…" Peter hesitated, surprised by the other man's direct approach in asking about his personal life. "Yes, I did get sent to prison but that was a while ago." He looked at Nigel speculatively and added, "But I think you already know that and what the reason was, don't you?"

Meadows nodded before drinking some beer. "I was the local bobby before retiring and as such, I made sure I knew what was going on all around here, and who everyone was. That was my job and I was good at it. Even now, when someone new comes here, I always do a little digging, just in case."

Peter nodded before asking, "So why do you think they came up here?"

"It strikes me as odd that those fellows came looking for you and then after finding you, there was nothing. No follow-up…nothing at all…so why look for you in the first place?" Peter shrugged. He was heartily sick of the incessant questions about his former life. The past was over and done with, and he wanted to let it rest.

After a few minutes of silence, Nigel suddenly said, "Hey, I thought there was some big dinner at Oak Tree Manor this evening.

Why aren't you there to help out? They've even got Lucy and that useless boy-friend of hers working there tonight, so why aren't you doing the same?"

Peter shrugged before saying, "They gave me the evening off."

"They did?" asked Nigel in surprise. "Short-handed as they are, not having you there to help with a large dinner party makes no sense." He stared shrewdly at Peter before adding, "So who, or what, are you trying to avoid this evening?"

Peter shrugged and said nothing. Nigel Meadows smiled wryly and took another pull at his pint. Eventually he said, "Mabel tells me that some American professor is staying at Oak Tree Manor and this dinner is a private party for him and some of the faculty from Greydene University are coming over. You're a scientist but it seems that you don't want to talk to them. Mabel did tell me that the American was very excited about something you said or wrote or something like that, and I'd have thought it would be normal to want to be with people like that, you know, similar interests and that sort of thing."

Peter stayed silent, watching the other man. Nigel Meadows was very perceptive and certainly no fool. That placid, benign exterior hid a very sharp mind and Peter wondered how much he could trust him. The ex-policeman was a soft-spoken man, exuding calm and trustworthiness, and Peter could well see how he and Mabel could be happy together. Mabel was kind-heartedness and motherly love personified and far from naïve, but she tended to rush about trying to finish every job in sight whereas her husband was slow and methodical but very shrewd. So, was it possible that he might give Peter some insight on the situation with Hiram Pederson and Lionel Simpson? Although Peter had to admit he wasn't sure quite what that situation might be. Before he could say anything, Nigel spoke up.

"Peter, let's assume that I'm right and you don't want to see that American and those University people this evening," and Nigel smiled at Peter. "Then one might wonder why that was. You are obviously intelligent and most intelligent people want to be around others who are the same. So it's obviously not that. Then you were a scientist, at least that's what they said in the newspaper, and most scientists automatically seek out other scientists. Therefore, it can be assumed that you aren't running from being around other scientists although," with a thoughtful glance at Peter, "that might be a factor, yes?"

Peter remained silent but paid rapt attention to the other man, who continued, "So the real question is why?"

"Why?" asked Peter.

"Yes, why…why are you avoiding those people tonight? Methinks it's not because you are worried about them. From what I gather, you are more than capable of taking care of yourself and you are not averse to taking care of others either. Likewise, having been inside, I doubt that there is anything anyone could say to you that would upset you unduly. So, there's something else and my betting is that it has to do with that American and possibly someone from Greydene University. Although I don't know much about science or university politics…actually I don't anything about either subject…I do know people and I'm willing to bet that you don't want either Pederson or someone from Greydene University, or both of them, trying to force you back into science. Could I be right?"

Peter's jaw dropped; perhaps this retired country copper had it right? Was that what he was worried about? He sat and thought, for so long in fact that eventually Nigel broke the silence with, "I see you are thinking about this, aren't you?" Peter nodded.

"Well, let's look at this situation," continued Nigel. "For a start, nobody can force you to do what you don't want to do, so no amount of persuasion or coercion could push you back into…what is the term, academia?"

Peter nodded in affirmation and Nigel continued, "So if it isn't coercion, then that means you are torn over something. Perhaps it's because on one hand you might want to get back to work doing science, on your own terms of course, but on the other hand you don't want to leave here. Am I right?"

Hesitantly, Peter agreed with him, "You could be right. You're putting into words what I've been thinking…at least about some of what I've been thinking."

"I thought that might be the case," said Nigel. "I know how pushy those Americans can be and it would be hard to resist the ebullient Professor Pederson without being rude to him, which would upset Chris and her dad and would be bad for business. I have no idea what those people at Greydene University are like but I suspect that they are no match, intellectually or otherwise, for someone like you. At least from what I've heard about you. Thus I conclude," said Nigel with a smile. "That you are caught in the horns of a dilemma."

Peter nodded once again and then said, "You are quite right. I don't want to leave here because…" and his words tailed off.

"I take it that you want to stay here, dare I suggest, because of Chris Hawkins?"

Peter looked at him in surprise but said nothing.

"Oh come on, Peter," said Nigel. "Mabel has told me how you and Chris look at each other and if there's nothing going on there, I'll eat my old helmet. Let's face it, lad, if it's not that, why else would you be that hesitant about leaving? It's not because you have fallen in love with this part of the country – that's for sure - although you might well like it here better than London or Cambridge. Besides, by just looking at your face, I can tell that I'm right…look at you man, you're actually blushing!"

"You could be right," said Peter eventually.

"So, why not wait and see what happens next? You scientists all want to think ahead and make contingency plans and that sort of thing but, as John Lennon once said, "Life is what happens while you're making other plans". Not one of the world's great thinkers was John Lennon but that time he had it right. So, sit back and relax and stop worrying about the future. Enjoy the present. Get on with courting Chris, who's a wonderful lady, and leave all the rest to sort itself out. If you are meant to go back into science and research, it will happen no matter what plans you make."

"Interesting," said Peter judiciously. "So, what advice are you giving me?"

"Advice? Me give advice to a Cambridge professor? I don't know about that. All I'm suggesting is that you get together with Chris and leave everything else to develop as it will. Also, why not get back to Oak Tree Manor this evening and face that lot. What have you got to lose? You might even enjoy yourself." With that, Nigel Meadows got to his feet, shook hands with Peter and climbed back into his car, waving as he drove off to go back home.

After Nigel had left, Peter sat staring into space for quite some time. Nigel Meadows, and presumably his wife too, were quite right, he *did* have strong feelings for Chris, as did Chris for him. That newspaper article had laid it all out and whereas Chris didn't know everything, she now knew he'd been in prison and why. More important, it didn't seem to bother her unduly…so what was he waiting for? Nigel had been right, he was hesitant about talking to Pederson, Simpson and the rest of them and he was also absolutely correct in saying that it was up to him, Peter Marshall, whether or not he returned to science. If he didn't like what they proposed, all he had to do was politely say no. "Oh balls," he said aloud. "I've had enough of this and enjoyable as it has been to drive around, I'm fed up with that too. Okay Oak Tree Manor, here I come."

John and Mary Parsons pulled up outside Oak Tree Manor. Mary looked at the place and said, "Oh John, what a lovely place and we're going to stay here? How on earth did you find it?"

"It was related to that job I was up here for and we passed it one day."

"Well, lucky for us that you did. By the way, what are all these cars doing here? I didn't think they'd be that busy?"

"I don't think they are. Most of those number plates look local and if you check the cars, you'll see most of them have Greydene University parking tags. So my betting is that there's some sort of function going on here. Anyway, let's check in and then we can go and find somewhere to eat. Johnson and I had a decent lunch at a pub just down the road the other day, so we could always go there."

"That's sounds lovely, John." She squeezed his arm and said, "I'm so excited to be here…what a lovely treat for us both, and you getting promoted too. Come on, let's see where we're going to sleep, or at least where we're going to bed tonight," said with a sharp but playful dig into his ribs, and a sly grin on her face. "You never know, big boy, you might get lucky." And she laughed happily.

Walking into the foyer, they could see a small crowd around the bar in the lounge and stray snippets of conversation drifted out. Mary listened for a moment or two before saying, "John, I know that they're talking English but they're using words I've never heard before. Who are they?"

"They must be the people from the University. Probably all scientists and they tend to talk shop, you know, lots of scientific terms and that sort of thing. Ah, here comes the manager."

Chris walked over from the bar area and welcomed the new guests. She booked them in and handed over two room keys, indicating the elevator but also asking whether they needed help with their luggage.

"No, we'll manage," said John. "But thank you anyway."

Just then Peter walked in and Chris, flushing with pleasure, exclaimed, "Peter, what are you doing here?"

John Parsons turned and caught Peter's eye, "Dr. Marshall, how nice to see you again. How are you?"

"I am well, Inspector, how are you?"

"He's about to become a Chief Inspector," said Mary happily. "They are going to promote him."

"Oh well done, Inspector...sorry, Chief Inspector," said Peter, and held out his hand in congratulation. "I am very happy for you."

John, shaking Peter's hand warmly, said, "Thank you, Dr. Marshall." He was about to say more when Hiram Pederson appeared and grabbed Peter's arm.

"My dear Peter, I'm so glad to see you. I was afraid you would miss our little gathering this evening but you're here. Do come and join us for a drink." He looked at John and Mary Parsons and added, "Why not have your friends join us too if they are staying here. I think we have room for two or three more at the table, don't we Chris?" The last comment was almost shouted at Chris.

Chris, startled by the man's ebullience, simply nodded. There was plenty of room and more than enough food for the buffet style dinner but what was this American professor thinking? It was all very well to include complete strangers in a dinner party over in America but that was hardly common over here in England, and certainly not in Derbyshire. Eventually she said, "Well, I'll set some more places at the table." Turning to John and Mary, she added, "Perhaps you'd like to wash up and join everyone in the lounge? We're not serving dinner for at least an hour, so you could have a drink at the bar."

John and Mary looked at each other and then thanked both Peter and Pederson for their kind invitation. A few minutes later, as they unpacked in their room, a puzzled Mary asked, "How on earth do you know that Dr. Marshall and who was that American who invited us to dinner?"

John hesitated and then said, "Well, I know Peter Marshall from my work but as for the other man, frankly I have no idea who he is but I didn't want to be rude and refuse his invitation."

Mary, ever practical, simply nodded and asked, "Do I need to dress for dinner?"

"No, I don't think so. Did you see the way those University types are dressed? Nearly all of them are wearing jeans and hiking boots – I'll bet not one of them even owns a suit. No, Mary, don't doll yourself up – the effort would be wasted."

In the few minutes between John and Mary Parsons going upstairs and coming down again, Professor Randolph Bethany arrived at Oak Tree Manor and asked to check in. Chris took care of him quickly, mentally praying that they had no other late arriving guests. She had a dinner to take care of and although her father was coping in the bar, any more interruptions could cause problems.

Bethany quickly went up to his room and dumped his suitcase, then hurried downstairs again and into the bar area. He had spotted John Parsons and correctly assumed that he was a police officer, the one that Llewellyn-Hughes had obliquely referred to in passing.

Holding out his hand, he advanced on John and boomed, "I am Professor Randolph Bethany and who might you be?"

John Parsons blinked at the man, thinking, "Who the hell is this person?"

At the sound of Bethany's booming voice, some of the younger University faculty turned to see who had arrived and immediately recognized him, whispering to each other, "That's Randolph Bethany. What's he doing here?" One junior faculty even commented, "I'll bet he's here because Dr. Marshall is staying here but I wonder how he knew?"

After a brief hesitation, John Parsons shook the other man's hand and said quietly, "I'm Detective Inspector Parsons from Scotland Yard but I'm here for a brief vacation with my wife, Mary" and he gently pulled her forward to meet the scientist. Bethany vaguely acknowledged Mary's presence and then headed towards the bar to get a drink. Watching his retreating back, Mary suddenly said, "You know, I've seen that man on television. He's an advisor to some ministry or other…I believe he's quite famous actually. Thing is, I'm not sure that I like him or even trust him; there's something about him that doesn't ring true."

"He's famous, is he?" commented John. "Hmm, I didn't know that but then I don't watch as much TV as you. Still and all, I wonder what he's doing here but I wouldn't be surprised if it's something to do with Dr. Marshall. My betting's that someone has asked him to persuade Peter to go back into research. If he also gets invited to dinner, things could get interesting." Squeezing Mary's hand, he said, "My word, what a fascinating start to our vacation…not what I was expecting at all."

Peter, almost trapped against the bar by Pederson and Simpson, glanced over at Arnold Hawkins behind the bar and raised an eyebrow. Mr. Hawkins, correctly interpreting the unspoken question, slowly shook his head, mouthing, "I'm coping – don't worry" and then he smiled, thinking, 'That poor bugger isn't going to get away from those two very easily.' Looking over the door, he spotted Bethany striding into the lounge followed, more hesitantly, by Mr. and Mrs. Parsons. He quickly looked over at Peter and, after a quick nod in Bethany's direction, raised an eyebrow. Peter followed his gaze and he looked back with a shrug and a small shake of his head…making it clear that he had no idea who the new arrival might be. When he saw John and Mary, he looked back at Arnold and mouthed, "Police". Mr. Hawkins nodded and wondered what on earth was happening in his quiet guesthouse.

Pederson, conscious that Peter's attention had drifted, suddenly commented, "We've lost you…I hope you're not bored, or are you?"

"Oh no," Peter assured him. "I'm sorry but I was briefly distracted looking at the newcomers and I wanted to check that everything was under control. We all muck in together here and help out when we get busy… I was just checking that I wasn't needed. If I was rude, I apologize…it wasn't intentional." Turning to Simpson, he said,

"Now Lionel, you said that you found…" and promptly launched into a rapid and insightful analysis of Simpson's latest research.

Pederson, listening to Peter, blinked hard. This man was far sharper than he had imagined. Even after an extended absence from the field, he was still very much in command of his subject. What a triumph it would be to have him at Polk University. As far as he was concerned, there was no way that Greydene University deserved to have to someone of Peter's caliber on the faculty but, he wondered, how am I going to even get the man to consider coming back into academia let alone move to America?

Randolph Bethany, standing near the bar, felt decidedly out of place. His Saville Row suit, crisp white shirt, rep tie and highly polished black shoes were as suited to this crowd as the proverbial black man at a Klu Klux Klan convention. Even that loud-mouthed American wearing a sports coat and turtle-neck sweater is more appropriately dressed! He caught the eye of the barman and asked for a beer in a vain attempt to be one of the crowd. Studiously ignoring the curious glances and tentative overtures of the Greydene University faculty, Bethany with beer in hand sidled over to where Peter, Pederson and Simpson were chatting and slowly infiltrated himself into their little group.

Lionel Simpson was entranced. In just a few sentences, Peter Marshall had pointed out the good, and some bad, issues in his work, leaving Lionel almost open-mouthed in admiration. As he listened raptly to Peter, he was thinking, 'How can I get him interested in coming to Greydene? He would make such a huge difference but if I say anything, Hiram will jump in and try to recruit Marshall at the merest mention of him coming back into research. Unfortunately there's no way I can compete against Polk University with their huge endowment, large salaries and fantastic facilities. I suppose the best thing I can do is bide my time and perhaps come back to Oak Tree Manor on my own…that way I might have a clear shot at talking to Dr. Marshall without having Pederson around to stir the pot.'

Professor Bethany, at last successful in placing himself between Peter and Lionel Simpson, jumped into the conversation, saying, "Dr. Marshall, I'm Randy Bethany," and held out his hand. Disconcertingly, Peter simply said, "That's nice," and finished what he was saying to Lionel. He looked at Bethany and then said, "These two gentlemen are Dr. Hiram Pederson from Polk University and Dr. Lionel Simpson from Greydene University. Now who did you say you were?"

Somewhat nonplused, Bethany swallowed hard and reddened. Aware that Peter had not been deliberately rude, he nevertheless made him feel a fool and Bethany wondered whether he had made a mistake in trying to horn in on this gathering. Hiram Pederson, courteous as always, stepped in to say, "Good evening. As Peter just said, I'm Hiram Pederson from Polk University in Utah…I'm visiting Greydene University as a visiting professor and Lionel Simpson here is chairman of radiochemistry at Greydene, my gracious host and the man who made my visit here possible. Now, you said you are Randy Bethany? I don't wish to be rude but I don't know you – where are you from? I assume it's not Greydene, or is it?"

"No, I'm not at Greydene University…I'm at Christ's College, University of London." He paused for a moment, "I'm also Chief Scientific Advisor at the Ministry of Energy and Natural Resources, in London, you know."

"That's interesting," said Hiram and reached out to shake Bethany's hand. "I'm delighted to meet you and, as Peter said, this is Lionel Simpson from Greydene University." Randy also shook Lionel's hand and was about to reach for Peter's hand and decided against it, simply nodding at him and trying to convey the message that he and Peter were well-acquainted and had no need of introductions.

Hiram looked carefully at the faces of the three men in their little group and surmised that Bethany, for all his bombast, was a definite interloper. Curious, he asked, "Professor Bethany, are you up here for a meeting or anything?"

"Oh no, I'm just taking a small break from my duties in London and I'd heard that Oak Tree Manor was a nice place to stay on one's way north. So here I am."

"But you're a scientist," Hiram said somewhat sarcastically, implying that Bethany's story didn't ring true. He was about to say more when Lionel jumped in with, "I think we could all do with another round. Peter, would you like a beer or a glass of wine? Hiram and I were so intent on talking to you that we neglected to even ask whether you might like one…I apologize. Hiram, how about you?" He hesitated for a beat or two before adding, "Professor Bethany, may I offer you another beer?"

"That's very kind of you," said Bethany. "But let me get them since I intruded on your conversation. Now, what are we all having?"

Peter, watching the interactions, was amused and thought, 'So Pederson and Simpson have sussed out that this Bethany character is here for some reason other than a brief stop on his drive to somewhere else – a pretty lame excuse if I've ever heard one. No-one drives so far off the beaten track to stay at a small guesthouse when there is a four star hotel in Greydene, one which would be much more his style than here. So, Bethany, why exactly are you here this evening?'

Randolph Bethany, after getting their drinks, moved back to the little group, and wondered how he could get himself invited to dinner. Judging by the sharp looks that Marshall and Pederson had given him, neither of them was impressed with his cover story and even Simpson had looked at him askance. He could hardly ask outright for an invitation without looking foolish and the astute American had probably already worked out why he, Randy Bethany, was here. If Pederson suspected that he, Bethany, was here because he also had designs on recruiting Marshall, then he was unlikely to lend a helping hand to anyone, let alone him. Wait and see, he decided… what else could he do?

After John had bought a beer for himself and a vodka-tonic for Mary, he raised his glass and lightly tapped hers, saying, "Here's to you, Mary…and you look lovely tonight."

Mary, glowing with pleasure, smiled at her husband happily and took a sip of her drink. She was about to comment on the evening when John asked abruptly, "You said that Bethany character is famous…what's he famous for?"

"He's some sort of scientific advisor to the Ministry of Energy and Natural Resources and is often on television spouting about this or that scientific matter. Always dresses to the nines and sounds so knowledgeable."

"Does he indeed?" said John reflectively but thinking, 'Advisor to the Ministry of Energy and Natural Resources, the very people who started this search for Peter Marshall – huh! There's no way he's here by accident.' After viewing the little group around Peter across the room, he looked at Mr. Hawkins and raised an eyebrow, who in turn simply shrugged after he too looked at Peter trapped against the bar by the other three men. 'So,' thought John. 'He thinks the arrival of Professor What's-his-name was no accident either...we'll have to have a chat about it a little later. I think he's got a pretty good idea of what's going on, and I should like to hear about it.'

Eventually, Chris sounded a gong and, in the ensuing silence, announced, "Dinner is ready. Because there are so many of you, we decided a buffet style meal would be the best approach. So, if you'd like to decide where everyone's going to sit, you can help yourself to food. We will be serving wine with extra bottles down the center of the table. Also, please do not worry about your used plates and cutlery; we'll clear them away between each course." She paused for breath and then said with a smile, "Please enjoy yourselves and if you need anything, do not hesitate to ask. *Bon Appetit* and we are delighted to have you all here."

With surprising alacrity, virtually everyone sat down, leaving Peter, Hiram, Lionel and Bethany standing by the bar and John and Mary standing uncertainly to one side. Hiram Pederson, gracious as ever, turned to Simpson and said, "Lionel, you're the host, why don't you sit at the head of the table and Peter and I can sit either side of you." Beckoning to John and Mary, he added, "Come on you two, you sit beside Peter." Finally he looked at Bethany and added, "Well since you're here, why don't you join us for dinner...that's if it's alright with you Lionel?"

Lionel Simpson simply shrugged; after all what choice did he have? and he really didn't want to snub someone as well-known as Bethany. Nevertheless, the evening was not turning out the way he had anticipated, or hoped. He resolved to say nothing about trying to recruit Peter and made a mental note to come out to Oak Tree Manor in a day or two to talk privately to Peter.

After catching her father's eye and making a small beckoning gesture that he join her in the kitchen, Chris nodded gently and left supervision of the buffet to Lucy and her boyfriend, Zack, who to everyone's surprise had dressed very nicely that evening. Not only that, he was proving to be very adept at taking care of everyone. As she later commented to Mabel, "You know Zack was terrific this evening. There's more to that young man than what you might believe based on appearances. I wonder whether he might be interested in a part-time job here, especially if we have more dinners like this?"

With everything under control in the dining room and kitchen, Chris and her father adjourned to his office and sat down with a glass of wine each. Silently toasting each other, Chris eventually said, "There's a funny undercurrent going on, isn't there?"

"Yes, I picked up on that too"

"That couple, John and Mary, are very nice but he's a policeman isn't he? Was he one of the people looking for Peter?" Her father nodded. "So, why are they here…surely not just for a few days' vacation? That's too much of coincidence, isn't it?" Again Mr. Hawkins nodded. "Then," she continued. "There's that big professor from London…some advisor to the Ministry of Energy and Natural Resources…there's no way that his arrival was an accident or coincidence either, no way at all. So, dad, what do you make of everything?"

"I'm not sure Chris but I did see that Dr. Simpson was fair bursting to talk to Peter and wasn't happy when that Bethany character turned up. Not only that, he kept looking sideways at Professor Pederson, almost afraid that he would say something to Peter."

"So, dad, what do *you* think?"

"I'm not sure but it wouldn't surprise me if they are pressuring Peter to come back into the fold, so to speak."

Chris was momentarily silent and then burst out, "But if Peter accepts a job in London, Cambridge or worse, Utah, he'll leave us, won't he?"

"Aye, lass, he might well do that but somehow I don't think that's going to happen. He's not going anywhere for the time being. Don't fret about it…things will work out, mark my words. Now, let's finish our wine and get back to work. Mabel, Lucy and Zack are doing a great job but we'd best be there to help in case we're needed.

By the way, I've been running an open tab for the bar – I hope that Dr. Simpson agreed to that before everyone started drinking."

"Don't worry dad, it's all under control and yes, we did agree on an open bar already." Happily she hugged her father and then led the way back into the dining room, feeling oddly reassured by her father's words.

SIXTEEN

Professor Randolph Bethany was not happy, not at all. His attempts at getting close to Peter Marshall had not succeeded and now here he was stuck next to Mary Parsons at the dinner table. On his other side was a very earnest young research student at Greydene University who proceeded to tell Bethany, in excruciating detail, about his PhD research project. Hearing about the young man's research efforts was bad enough but to be exposed to a constant spray of spittle and food particles as the man tried to simultaneously talk and eat was stretching the limits of Bethany's patience. He had tried to engage Mary in conversation but each attempt had run into a stone wall… they had nothing in common to talk about. Mary was an avid fan of several popular programs as well as a variety of long-running serials whereas Bethany could not remember the last time he had watched television for entertainment purposes only. Neither of them spent much time reading books for pleasure and their selection of magazines could not have been more different.

He could see out of the corner of his eye that Peter was happily chatting with that Simpson fellow from Greydene University and with Hiram Pederson who was sitting across the table from him. Straining his ear, Bethany could make out that they were discussing various topics, including some science, but so far there had been no mention of any recruitment plans. If he, Bethany, had been seated near them, he would have taken the initiative and opened that discussion but stuck here, several places down the table, it was impossible.

Bethany sighed and wondered how he could get Marshall on his own. The thought of having to stay here for two or three days was not something he looked forward to but he knew that he *had* to persuade

Marshall to come back into science if he, Bethany, was to stay on as an advisor to the Ministry and, possibly more importantly, get his knighthood. 'Yes,' he thought. 'Sir Randolph Bethany has a certain ring to it and I know Brenda would love to be called Lady Bethany. Perhaps I might even get to be made a peer, just like Lord George Porter, but if I'm not successful with Peter Marshall, then it's possible that nothing would happen. That would not please Brenda at all and I would have wasted all these years sucking up to Llewellyn-Hughes for no good purpose. How very irritating this all is. Not only that, I get the distinct impression that Pederson might suspect why I'm here and that barman, Arnold Hawkins was it?, who appears to own this place has been giving me very appraising looks. This is all very frustrating, and a waste of time.'

Peter was enjoying dinner. The brisket had turned out well and the soup, salad and fresh vegetables were delicious. He made a mental note to tell Chris and Mabel what a great job they had done. He looked over at the buffet table and watched as Lucy and Zack kept a careful eye on the food supplies as well as deftly cleared used dishes from the table. He was amused that Zack, the man that Mable and Nigel Meadows had always considered to be worthless, was proving to be very adept at ensuring the wine glasses were always full.

Chris finally signaled to Lucy and Zack to clear the dinner plates and remove everything from the buffet table. After the small platters were laid out, she announced that dessert was ready and moved quickly out of the way as everyone descended on the buffet table. She smiled to herself, 'No matter how much people have eaten, they are always willing and able to find room for dessert!'

As they savored the apple pie and other desserts, Peter turned to Simpson and said, "Lionel, I chatted earlier with a couple of your research students. They are pretty bright and are doing some really interesting stuff. Well done."

"I'm delighted to hear you say that, Peter," said Lionel. "Coming from you, that's quite a compliment." He was silent for a moment, thinking, 'Well, it's now or never.' Lionel lifted his wine glass and took a sip before adding, "Peter, would you consider giving us a seminar…you know, at Greydene?"

"Lionel, that's very inviting, but…"

"We'd be able to pay a small stipend…" interrupted Lionel.

"No, it's not about getting paid….it's… well I have to admit that I'm out of touch. I haven't kept up with the literature in several years, so I'm not sure that I could contribute very much."

"I understand," said Lionel reflectively and then said, "Look, perhaps not a seminar as such….would you be willing to sit down with the research students, one-on-one, and discuss their projects with them?" He paused before continuing, "I have to be honest with you, chairing a department takes up a lot of my time, what with university politics, grant writing and that sort of thing. Consequently, I cannot spend as much time with them as I should like. If someone of your caliber and experience *could* spend time with them, then it would be awfully helpful to everyone. Can I persuade you to think about it?"

Peter nodded, uncertain what he felt about the invitation. Talking to bright young minds would be enjoyable but would he be able to help them? It had been so long since he had done anything like that, he wondered whether he was still up to it. The challenge did not bother him but possibly letting the research students down would be upsetting.

Seeing Peter hesitate, Lionel said, "Look, don't give me an answer now…let me get back to you in a day or so, and we can discuss details then. Besides, I probably need to clear it with the University and the Dean although I cannot imagine that there will be any problems."

Hiram Pederson smiled to himself, thinking, 'Lionel, you surprise me. Out of the blue you opened a dialogue with Peter Marshall and he's even thinking about helping you with your research students. If I try to horn in now, it'll go down like a lead balloon…so, hats off to you Lionel – you are smarter and more devious than I had thought. That'll teach me to underestimate these Brits.'

Likewise, Randolph Bethany, straining to listen in, heard Lionel Simpson's offer to Peter Marshall and inwardly cursed. 'Damn, since Simpson has opened this subject with Marshall, I can no longer claim to have been the person who organized everything. For a wimpy little man, Simpson is pretty slick in how he handled this. I'll bet that bloody Yank isn't too pleased either.'

Eventually the dinner party died down and the Greydene people left for home, leaving Peter and the Oak Tree Manor guests milling around in the foyer after saying goodbye to everyone. As Lucy, Zack and Chris cleared the detritus from the tables, John and Mary Parsons, Hiram Pederson and Randolph Bethany all adjoined to the bar for a last drink. Mary stifled a yawn and then caught the eye of Mr. Hawkins standing behind the bar. He winked at her to let her know that he too was tired and sympathized with her. After everyone got a brandy, paid for by Bethany in an unusual gesture of generosity, they adjoined to a table. Seeing Mr. Hawkins still standing guard behind the bar, Hiram called out, "Arnie, grab a drink and come and join us. It's been a splendid evening and you deserve a break. If that lovely daughter of yours is anywhere around, perhaps she could join us too…put your drinks on my tab, if you will."

Mr. Hawkins nodded and poured two brandies and went to fetch Chris from the kitchen, telling her, "Leave those dishes until the morning, Chris. Professor Pederson has invited us to join everyone for a drink, so I've poured you a brandy."

"Dad, I hate to leave mess for the morning although pretty much everything is stacked in the dishwasher…okay, I'll come…a brandy sounds pretty inviting about now. Just let me fire up the dishwasher and I'll join you. Let me just thank Mabel, Lucy and Zack – they were grand this evening, weren't they?"

Mr. Hawkins picked up his drink from the bar, headed over to the table where everyone was sitting and before seating himself, he made sure that there was a vacant chair between him and Peter. Within a minute or two Chris came into the bar, collected her brandy snifter from the counter and headed towards the table. Mr. Hawkins, seeing her, got to his feet as did all the other men. Gently pulling back the spare chair, he said, "Chris, come sit over here…you know, be the rose between two thorns."

Chris grinned and took the chair, smiling nicely at everyone before delicately inhaling the bouquet from the brandy and saying, "Cheers everyone. I hope you all enjoyed yourselves this evening."

"Oh we did indeed," said Pederson. "That brisket was wonderful. You must tell me how you prepared it because my wife, Dolores, will want details when she hears how good it was."

"Yes, do tell us," echoed Mary. "It was delicious and so tender… how did you do it?"

"I'll try to write it down for you," said Chris. "I'm flattered that you liked it so much. You know Peter and Mabel helped prepare everything?"

"They did?" asked Pederson. Turning to Peter, he added, "You have hidden depths, don't you?"

Peter just smiled. He was tired after the long and rather probing session with Nigel Meadows followed by the dinner party when he had to be convivial with a group of people he did not know. He was anxious to talk to Chris and her father about Lionel Simpson's offer and get their input but this wasn't the right time to discuss anything that personal.

"Tell me," said Bethany to John Parsons. "I hear tell that you're a Special Branch officer…a Detective Inspector I believe."

"John's about to be promoted to Detective Chief Inspector.," said Mary proudly. "That's why we're here…it's a celebration for us." Turning to Chris and her father, she added, "It's so lovely here…I can see why John wanted us to stay with you. By the way, we'll be out and about during the day, you know, exploring the countryside but can we get dinner here? John said there was a pub down the road that had good food but I should rather be here."

Chris looked at her father and then said, "I'm sure we can manage something for you. Most guests eat out but a few do dine with us, so fitting you in shouldn't be a problem."

Bethany blinked in frustration. For the second time in the same evening, John and Mary Parsons had intervened between he and Peter Marshall, and he began to wonder whether it was deliberate. That soft-spoken woman was not the typical urban housewife and he carefully appraised both John and Mary. That they were here could hardly be a coincidence but who had sent them? If it was Llewellyn-Hughes, why hadn't he mentioned it? If not him, then who? For a moment, Bethany felt decidedly paranoid and then forced himself to listen to the conversations going on around the table.

"Yes," said John. "We really do like it in this part of the country and Mary and I were wondering whether to move up here when I retire. London is scarcely British any longer – at least half the people there come from other countries and house prices are going through the roof. I tell you, if we sold our house and came up to this area, we'd be able to buy a mansion…not that we'd want to but you know what I mean."

"I can understand that," agreed Mr. Hawkins. "Property is still pretty reasonable around here and there are a lot of good things to say about living in the country. Being close to Greydene means we have most of the advantages of city life without having to live in the city. Traffic, of course, is dreadful during the rush-hour but otherwise, it is pretty easy to get around. So, if you are serious, I can call a realtor that I know – he comes in here fairly regularly – and I'm sure he'd be able to put you into something nice."

"That would be wonderful," said Mary. Turning to her husband, "What do you think, dear? Are we Derbyshire bound?"

"Why not? Almost anything beats London these days…and thank you Arnie, any help you can give us would be most welcome."

Conversation paused for a moment and just as Bethany had collected his thoughts and was about to speak, Hiram Pederson commented, "Peter, it seems you had a chance to talk to some of Lionel's graduate students. What did you think of them? That one girl, you know the attractive blonde one, is very sharp, isn't she?"

"Daphne? Yes, she is very sharp but so were the others. I gather that only some of them are Greydene graduates with the rest coming in from abroad or other Universities. Quite an eclectic mix really. Lionel did well in taking them on."

Chris, secretly pleased that Peter had ignored the comment about the attractiveness of one female student in particular, picked up on the underlying theme of Pederson's question. 'So,' she thought. 'He's fishing to see if Peter might want to get back into research. Oh dear, if that's case, I wonder whether he'd leave here. Oh dad, I hope you're right about Peter wanting to stay here.'

Aware that yet another opportunity had been lost, Bethany finished his drink and slowly got to his feet, "Well everyone, my bed calls me. I've had a long day and I have to be on the road in the morning."

"Breakfast is from 7.30 to 9 am, Professor Bethany," said Chris. "Do please eat something before you leave here. We do serve quite a good breakfast, what with fresh eggs, locally-cured ham and bacon, local butter and cheese, and even fresh-baked bread that comes from the local bakery. I'm sure you'll enjoy it."

Virtually forced into going to bed, Bethany could only wish everyone a good night and went up to his room. As he slipped into his pajamas, he resolved to stop by Oak Tree Manor on his return journey and try again with Peter Marshall. Hopefully on his return, that damn Mary Parsons, or anyone else for that matter, won't be around to spoil his pitch.

After Bethany left, Mary and John joined suit, followed shortly thereafter by Hiram Pederson who assured Chris and her father that he'd had a marvelous time that evening. Mr. Hawkins, Chris and Peter sat back in their chairs and relaxed, perhaps for the first time that day.

"Well dad, what do you think?" asked Chris.

"About what?" he asked.

"The dinner this evening, silly."

"It went well, very well in fact. Everybody seemed to have had a grand time and the food was obviously pretty good, judging by how much everyone ate. What do you think, Peter?"

"Oh I agree. Dinner was a great success, so my compliments to the chef…or is it chefess?"

Chris nodded her head in acknowledgement of the compliments but the question of what was said to Peter still spun inside her head. She didn't want to raise the issue in front of her father but she had to know where the land lay. Without saying anything, she made up her mind to act.

"Okay then," said Chris. "It's getting late and I've got a breakfast to take care of in the morning. I'm off to bed…sleep well, both of you."

"Hey, I think it's time for me to retire too," said Peter. "It's been a long day. Goodnight Mr. Hawkins."

"Good night to you, lad…and, by the way, you've been here long enough to call me Arnie."

Having showered and brushed his teeth, Peter lay back on the bed with his fingers laced behind his head with only a towel knotted around his waist. A low wattage nightlight dimly lit the room and he tried to relax. Too many things had happened that day and his mind was churning nineteen to the dozen. He was trying to arrange his thoughts when there was a light tap on the door and Chris, wearing an attractive dressing gown, slipped into the room. She held up a pump container of body lotion and said softly, "I thought that you might like a back-rub to help you relax."

"That's very thoughtful of you Chris, and yes, I should like that…very much"

"Okay, turn over onto your stomach."

Chris squirted some lotion on his back and, kneeling on the bed beside him, she gently worked it into his neck and shoulders. "Oh that's great," breathed Peter. "And your hands are so soft and warm… thank you."

"Be quiet, big guy," said Chris. "Just relax, close your eyes and think beautiful thoughts."

Chris worked slowly, kneading his neck, then his shoulders and upper arms. Stopping every so often to apply more lotion, she worked her way down each arm in turn, feeling the tension in Peter dissolving away. She moved her hands down his back and folded the towel back to reveal the lower portion of his spine and the firm muscles of his buttocks. Gently she massaged this area and then slid her hands up along his sides, curling her fingers beneath his body to apply lotion to the sides of his chest, the middle fingers of each hand lightly caressing his nipples before retreating again.

Peter felt himself hardening and tried to relax, embarrassed by his reaction to Chris's touch and hoping that his slight movements to ease the increasingly uncomfortable pressure on his pubic area went unnoticed by Chris. As he moved, Chris hesitated for a moment and then smiled as she continued kneading his back. Finally, she shucked off her dressing gown, revealing her naked body to the unseeing Peter. Placing herself between his spread legs, Chris gently ran her breasts up his back and kissed his neck. Feeling her against his back, Peter slowly turned over and grasped her body, pulling Chris against him until their lips met in a passionate kiss. Slowly she mounted him and coaxed his penis inside her body, tightening her vaginal muscles until Peter groaned and jerked his eyes open. He pulled her more tightly against his chest and within seconds, their bodies were moving against each in the throes of near-uncontrollable passion.

Peter cried out as he let go, followed by a stifled scream from Chris as she too orgasmed. Chris collapsed on top of Peter and they lay entwined, too spent to say or do anything except breathe deeply and wait for their blood pressures to return to normal.

Eventually, Peter murmured, "At last. I wanted to make love to you from the very first time I met you but it never seemed to be the right time…"

Chris gently placed one finger over his lips, saying, "Shhh…it was always going to happen, the only question was when…so I took matters in my own hands. I hope that you…"

"Chris, my love…thank you…you are wonderful – everything that I dreamed of, and more."

After that, the floodgates opened and Chris and Peter whispered quietly about everything and nothing. They were together and life was complete for both of them. It did not take long for Peter to get aroused again and they made love slowly and languidly, relishing the feel of each other and whispering endearments as they approached orgasm.

Eventually Chris said, "I should go back to my room; it wouldn't do for dad or Mabel to find us like this."

"Wait," said Peter. "I hope that this wasn't…wasn't, you know, er…"

"A one-time thing? Don't be silly, my darling, it most certainly wasn't but I need to take care of things here before we can share a room…dad is still somewhat old-fashioned and…"

"Should I say something to him?" asked Peter.

"No, not yet. Let me do it…I think he knows or at least suspects how we feel about each other but, still and all, I do need to say something to him. Now, I need to get my beauty sleep. We're going to be busy tomorrow and you might just need to get some sleep too."

Peter laughed quietly, "I do? What makes you think that? Just because I am completely drained and devoid of all energy is beside the point."

"You're crazy," laughed Chris. She quickly kissed him again and then slipped into her dressing gown. As she opened to door to return to her room, Chris turned and said, "Tomorrow, after I speak to dad, I think the three of us should talk about what happened at dinner and later…and I don't mean what just happened. Okay?"

"That was what I was thinking about before I was so rudely but pleasurably interrupted. Yes, we do need to talk about things because, like it or not, events are rapidly overtaking us. As Nigel Meadows said to me today, quoting John Lennon, life is what happen while you are making other plans, and life is surely happening now."

"Goodnight my darling…" said Chris, and gently closed the door, thinking, 'So Peter is thinking about things but, as dad so rightly predicted, I think those plans will involve me.'

Richard Fowler sat back and read his latest story with satisfaction. He and his aides had devoted time and energy into checking everything they could learn about the Monk trial and Fowler at last could write about it. Writing usually came quite easily to him, the words flowing from his fingers through the word processor onto the computer screen but this time it has been extra-ordinarily easy. After he had talked to Monk in prison, he had interviewed Monk's wife Audrey, and had really liked her.

Audrey was a very attractive thirty-something administrative assistant in a large insurance firm and although she had to raise their two children on her own, she was coping well because she had a good job, a decent income and easily managed the monthly mortgage payments. Both her own and Monk's parents were wholly supportive and neither her son Sean nor her daughter Angie lacked for any of the essentials such as love, decent food and a roof over their heads. When Fowler asked her about Monk, tears flowed readily, "He's a good man. Served his country well but because he helped someone, the country turned its back on him. What happened to that man was an accident and although he probably deserved it, having him die was still an accident. Nobody could have known he had a brain aneurism and when Monk knocked him down and hit his head, he died…an accident."

Fowler, busy taking notes, stopped writing and looked at her keenly. "He had a brain aneurism? The victim had a brain aneurism? How do you know this?"

"It came out when they did an autopsy."

"What?" exclaimed Fowler. "You must be kidding me. Didn't Monk's lawyer say anything about that…I mean surely it was a contributory factor in the man's death?"

"The pathologist claimed that it was an undiagnosed condition and he wasn't sure whether it did or didn't contribute to his dying. Mind you, I don't think Monk's lawyer, barrister or whatever he was, was all that good. We couldn't afford a proper lawyer and the man legal aid gave us was pretty young. Although he didn't say as much, I gather that Monk was his first homicide case. As they say, there's one law for the rich and another for the rest of us."

"Do you know who that lawyer was…you know, do you have his name or anything?"

"I'm not sure. I might have it written down somewhere but after it was all over, I didn't want anything to do with him or anyone else connected to that case…it hurt too much to even think about it."

"What happened afterwards?" asked Fowler.

"I had to get on with my life…you know, go back to work otherwise we'd have had nothing to eat or be able to pay the mortgage. We've managed pretty well over the past seven or eight years without Monk but the kids really miss their father…not as much as I miss him, but they do. It isn't right for children to have to grow up without a father. Still, that's life, isn't it? One good thing though, is that I became a Christian after everything happened. I know that Jesus will help."

As Audrey talked, Richard Fowler felt the story forming in his mind. How could Monk's lawyer have not stressed the victim's brain aneurism? Did he tackle the pathologist on that point or simply let it slide? Cynic that he was, Fowler knew he would have to check into every facet of what had happened at trial but already he could feel a sense of outrage welling inside. Monk got a raw deal and his lawyer had not helped matters much either. He resolved to check the trial transcripts.

Eventually he said, "Well, I think I've got everything I need for the moment. We'll be back in touch but I'm going to do what I can for Monk."

"That would be wonderful," said Audrey. "I'll pray for you and for your success…and thank you for coming to see me and for trying to help Monk."

"Well, I'm going to do my best…and maybe your prayers *will* be answered. I'm no lawyer but what happened just doesn't seem right."

A few days later, Richard Fowler tracked down the woman, one Donna Smith, whom Monk had defended. Within a few minutes of talking to her, he realized that she was really dumb…what had someone said about her? Oh yes, thick as a brick or something equally condemnatory.

"So, Donna, what can you tell me about that evening?"

"Which one was that?"

"The evening when your boyfriend was beating on you outside the pub and that man Monk helped you, that evening."

"Oh that evening. It was so long ago and I don't remember much about it now. All I know is that Sid, that's my boyfriend Sidney Green, died after that man, was his name Monk?, hit him and he fell down and hit his head."

"What led up to the attack?"

"Sid had been drinking with his mates and Sid, when he's had a few, always gets a bit nasty."

"Nasty how?"

"He looks for fights, that sort of thing…you know how it is, don't you?" 'No,' thought Fowler. 'I don't know how it is and I don't want to know either.'

"Anyway, if there's no-one else around, he smacks me up a bit."

"Did he do that often?" asked Fowler, surprised that Donna used the present tense in talking about the man.

"Only if he's been drinking."

"Did he do that a lot? I mean drink and then slap you around?"

"Not too often…only once or twice a week. He didn't mean anything by it, it was just his way. Besides, he said the drink helped his headaches, so who could blame him?"

"Headaches? He had a lot of headaches, did he?"

"All the time. I kept telling him to go to the doctor, but he wouldn't, would he? Stubborn like that he was, said all he needed was a drink and it would go away."

"Why did you stay with him if he hit you…once or twice a week you said?"

"Oh when he weren't drinking, Sid was real good to me. Bought me things all the time and he took me and my kids in, he was good that way. Besides, he were good in bed."

Fowler noted the change in tense but didn't pursue it. He was no psychologist but this woman was clearly a co-dependent. "What about his mates? The ones who were there?"

"I dunno about that. Sid smacked me a few times and it hurt… gave me a couple of black eyes, he did…but he didn't mean it…it was just his way."

'Good grief,' thought Fowler. "Is this woman for real?' but saying, "So, you don't remember much about what happened?"

"No. When I had to go to court, the lawyer…I think he was called a prosecutor or something…told me what to say and I did."

"Didn't the other lawyer, the one defending Monk, ask you anything?"

"No, not much. When I said that I couldn't see anything because of my eyes, he just left it."

After a few more questions, a thoroughly disgusted Fowler left the house. He nearly went back to ask who Donna was living with now but decided that enough was enough. Willing victims sickened him, especially when someone else paid the price for helping them.

Richard Fowler had the essentials of the story written but was debating with himself how he should entitle it. He looked at some possibilities:

No Good Deed Goes Unpunished
Being a Good Samaritan Doesn't Work
Giving a Helping Hand Results in Disaster
Sent to Prison for Doing the Right Thing

"That's it," he said aloud. "Sent to Prison for Doing the Right Thing - catchy and tells it like it is. The article says what happened and shows up the problems with the Legal Aid system. Okay, after it gets into print, I'll ring John Parsons and get him to talk again to his friend in the CPS. Maybe we can get something done for Monk. If The National Globe helps with the legal costs, we may be able to have a new trial and possibly get Monk off. Wow – that would be fantastic if we can get his slate wiped clean."

He sent the story off to his editor and sat back, pleased with himself. He switched off his computer and then thought about how everything had developed. A weird, almost pointless search for a missing scientist who wasn't missing, a senior person in a Ministry pulling all sorts of strings to get Special Branch involved in an affair that had nothing to do with National Security, the accidental death of a Cambridge professor on his way to visit with Special Branch, his meeting with John Parsons, learning about the miscarriage of justice with Monk, the Good Samaritan who landed in jail for helping a woman who had no idea what was going on with her brain-impaired boyfriend – the list went on. It all revolved around Dr. Peter Marshall who seemingly was unaffected by everything that happened around him after he had served his time in prison.

Looking up at the ceiling, Dick Fowler muttered, "One day I'm going to get a firm handle on all of this and understand it. Just how many lives have been affected by one man who lost his wife during childbirth and then went off the rails in despair? Oh fickle fate – the games you play."

Straightening himself, he said, "Okay, time to go home…perhaps I'll take the wife out to dinner again. She deserves it. Tomorrow, I'll call John Parsons and see what's happening up there at Oak Tree Manor. I'll give him advance notice of this story and ….wait…what did he say about Peter Marshall? That he's some sort of *Deus ex Machina* – was that it? Everything does seem to stem from Dr. Peter Marshall, like he has some sort of catalytic effect on things. How strange – not like me to be that fanciful at all. Perhaps I do need to go up there and sit down with everyone. Given what's been happening, I think that I might even be able to write a book. Now that's a turn up for the books," and he laughed. "That's a great play on words, Dick my boy."

SEVENTEEN

Breakfast had been cleared away, Mabel and Peter were checking on the guest rooms, so Chris decided she would talk to her father.

"Dad," she began. "I…er…need to talk to you about something. Let's go into the kitchen and have a cup of coffee so we can talk."

Mr. Hawkins looked sharply at his daughter for a moment or two and then nodded, "Okay. A coffee would be nice – time for us to relax a bit before anything else happens around here."

Sitting across the table from her father, Chris began to speak, "Dad, it's about Peter and me. Um, we…er…well we were together last night…you know, after everyone had left or were in bed."

"Yes, Chris, I know."

"You know?" she asked, astonished and unable to prevent an embarrassed flush spreading across her face. "How could you know?"

"Look my girl, I know I'm getting on years, my back's giving me merry hell and I'm not as strong as I once was but there's nothing wrong with my hearing."

"Oh!"

"I heard you leave your room after everyone was settled and then I heard the pair of you somewhat later."

"Oh, dad," Chris exclaimed. "I'm so embarrassed."

"Don't be. I used to be young myself once and, to be honest, it's about time you two got together – I was getting worried about it… you know, thought that I'd missed something."

"No dad, you didn't miss a thing – you never do, do you?"

"Maybe so," said Arnold Hawkins. "But you never know…I've been wrong before."

"Of course you have dad…I think it was on a Thursday about three years ago, wasn't it?" laughed Chris, and promptly got up and went round the table to hug her father. "Thanks, dad…for understanding."

Just then Peter walked into the kitchen and smiled when he saw Chris hugging her father. Looking up, Chris saw him and blushed again, which made her father chuckle.

"Hey lad, come and sit down. We're just having a coffee…do you want one?"

"That would be nice…thanks," said Peter. After he was settled at the table, a steaming mug of coffee before him, Chris lightly touched his arm and said quietly, "Dad heard us last night."

"Oh," said Peter, looking stricken.

"It's alright…he understands…so we'll not talk about it anymore" said Chris but lightly squeezed his arm, whispering, "At least not until tonight anyway."

Peter coughed with embarrassment and looked away. The last twelve hours had brought surprise after surprise and he was nonplussed.

Eventually he said, "Look I should like to raise something with you both…I need some input – advice if you will."

Mr. Hawkins and Chris both turned to look at him, wondering what might be coming next.

Peter hesitated, gathering his thoughts. "At dinner last evening, Lionel Simpson asked me to give a seminar to the research students in his department and when I said that I was out-of-date…he suggested that I conduct one-on-one research guidance sessions with them."

"I'm not sure that I understand," said Arnold Hawkins. "What do you mean that you're out-of-date?"

"As you know, I spent time in prison…no point in denying it, is there? After I got out, I turned my back on my old life…frankly I didn't want science and science didn't seem to want me, so I just let everything slip."

"But knowledge doesn't just go away, does it?" asked Chris.

"Probably not the basics, no, but I haven't kept up with the literature – you know, all those journal articles that we have to read on a monthly or even weekly basis to know what's going on – so I'm out of touch."

"How badly are you out-of-touch, as you say?"

"Frankly I don't know. As I have little idea of what's been happening in my field or in any related areas for the past several years, there's no telling what I do and don't know now."

"Is that bad?" asked Mr. Hawkins innocently.

"In itself, probably not but if I am to be able to help young researchers…you know…give them guidance on what to do and how to do it as well as help them interpret their findings, then any gaps in my knowledge could be doing them a major disservice."

"How long would it take for you to catch up again?" asked Chris.

"That's a bit like asking how long a piece of string is. It all depends on what has happened…what's in the literature as they say. That, more than anything else, will determine how long it would take me to get up to speed to even understand recent research work."

"So it might be possible, then?" asked Chris.

"Yes but it would likely take an awful lot of time and effort. To be honest, I wonder if I'm still capable of that sort of commitment or if it's even worth it."

"But what about those notes you wrote on Pederson's sheets of paper? Doesn't that indicate you still have it…whatever "it" might be?" asked Arnold Hawkins, his brow furrowed.

"I think that was just a fluke…something caught my eye and I started jotting things down before I realized what I was doing." He drained his coffee mug and got to his feet, "Well, time to get to work…I don't want Mabel complaining that I'm not pulling my weight."

"But we can't just leave things hanging, can we?" argued Chris. "What do *you* want to do? What do…why did you…why even talk about it if you're just going to let it drop?"

"My life is now here, here at Oak Tree Manor, and anything that impinges on my life will also involve everyone here. I mentioned what Simpson said to me so that if he raises it with you, it won't be something that comes out of the blue."

"I can understand that, Peter, but there's something else, isn't there?" asked Chris.

"There is?" asked Peter.

"Of course there is!" snapped Arnold Hawkins. "I don't even presume to know what's going on but you can't tell me that two Special Branch officers just happened to be visiting Greydene on a whim nor do I believe that Professor Bethany stopped here overnight because he likes country guesthouses. Likewise, it's possible that Mr. and Mrs. Parsons are indeed looking to retire up here and staying at Oak Tree Manor does provide them with a useful base. But I don't believe in coincidences, at least not that many with everything circling around one man, which is you, Peter. So, when we resume this conversation, we'll start to explore things a bit more with you. I don't mean to put you on the spot but you're family now and we're here to help in any way we can, isn't that right Chris?"

The Right Honorable James Arthur Llewellyn-Hughes replaced the phone in its cradle and muttered something unintelligible under his breath. As often happens by chance, it was at that moment that Stephen Fletcher appeared in the doorway of the office, announcing his presence by saying, "Excuse me sir, I don't want to interrupt anything but I just came across this intelligence report from China."

"And what might that be, Fletcher?"

"It seems that their work on transmutation of elements has not been as successful as expected and they might be curtailing their research."

"Interesting," said Llewellyn-Hughes. "What progress have the Americans and Germans made in this area?"

"I don't know but I gather they are still working steadily."

"I see."

"What's happening with this Marshall fellow? Has any progress been made there, sir?"

"Good question, Fletcher. Now, I do not want our conversation to leave this office but I should like to share recent events with you."

"Thank you, sir," said Fletcher, pleased to be taken into Llewellyn-Hughes's confidence.

"As you may know, Dr. Marshall disappeared after he was released from prison and has since re-appeared in Derbyshire."

"In a guesthouse near Greydene, I believe," said Fletcher.

"Yes, but please don't interrupt," snapped Llewellyn-Hughes. "Anyway, the whereabouts of Marshall were established by officers of Special Branch through the efforts of their own officers and information provided by a retired police officer who happens to know both the Chief Constable up there as well as a senior officer at Scotland Yard. Cutting a long story sideways, I encouraged Professor Bethany…you know of Bethany, of course?" When Stephen Fletcher nodded, he continued, "I encouraged Bethany to stay at that particular guesthouse and perhaps engage Marshall in conversation, possibly even persuade him to return to the research field. What I had hoped was that if Bethany were to be persuasive enough, Marshall might have agreed to return to Cambridge and rescue that lamentable project initiated by Dr. George Martin. Yes, the project that seems to be going disastrously wrong and which, I believe, was strongly endorsed by you."

Stephen Fletcher flushed, thinking, 'He's never going to let me live that down, is he? How was I to know that it wasn't Martin's idea? He was so convincing and even Llewellyn-Hughes agreed that it showed promise. Well if Dr. Marshall might agree to take it over, maybe disaster can be averted and we'll all save face.' Aloud, Fletcher simply agreed with Llewellyn-Hughes and asked, "Did he agree, Marshall I mean?"

"That's an open question. Apparently Bethany was unable to get close enough to Marshall to address the issue…he blamed the wife of a Special Branch officer was also staying at that guest house."

"It was deliberate, her interference I mean?" asked Fletcher.

"Possibly," admitted Llewellyn-Hughes judiciously.

"If it wasn't, what was she doing there anyway?"

"That I don't know," said Llewellyn-Hughes. "Of greater import is the fact that someone from Greydene University got in first and Marshall has been invited to give seminars to the research students there."

"He has?" asked Fletcher in surprise. "And he agreed?"

"Again, that is something I do not know," admitted Llewellyn-Hughes.

"Sir, I'm not sure where we go from here. If Marshall does agree to give some seminars or tutorials – whatever – what happens next?"

"Ideally, he might be persuaded to join the faculty at Greydene. It would not be ideal but at least he would be getting back to work and perhaps, just perhaps, we may be able to salvage that huge investment in Dr. Martin."

"But what happens if he doesn't join the faculty…will we have to write it all off?" asked Fletcher.

"That is something we must avoid at all costs. What I am thinking is that we wait until Marshall makes up his mind regarding the seminars. I suspect he will agree to give them. That being the case, then we'll ask that Special Branch officer to make nice with Marshall and find out what his plans might be. If he's leaning towards joining the faculty, then I shall require you to go up to Greydene and offer to provide them with whatever support they need to encourage Marshall to get back to work. So, Fletcher start thinking about this and be prepared to travel up to Derbyshire," concluded Llewellyn-Hughes.

"Yes, sir," agreed Fletcher. Although he was not happy that the blame for everything going wrong was being laid at his doorstep, at least the Permanent Under-Secretary was giving him an opportunity to make things right and straighten matters out.

It was time for him to return to Utah and Dr. Hiram Pederson signed the bill for his stay at Oak Tree Manor. He had enjoyed the trip and he was very sincere in his thanks and hugs for Chris, her father, Mabel and even Peter when he appeared in the entrance lobby. As Pederson wrapped his arms around Peter, he said quietly, "My boy, should you ever think of returning to academia, there's a home for you at Polk University and I have left my contact information with Arnold Hawkins."

"Thank you," replied Peter. "I'm not sure what I think at the moment but I do appreciate the offer."

"Well, no matter. I shall be back next year and I'll tell you now, I intend to try to recruit you for Polk, mark my words!." With a final slap on the back, he warmly shook Peter's hand and turned to face his hosts for the last time, "I thank you all for a great stay and I look forward to coming back. I've taken some brochures and I'm going to encourage my friends to stay here too. Thank you all."

With that, he grabbed his roll-on bags and strode towards the door and the waiting taxi, thinking, 'If Lionel Simpson recruits Peter, more power to his elbow but I shall do my utmost to get him Stateside. We need him as much if not more than Greydene does. But, whatever happens, I shall stay in touch with everyone here… what a great visit.'

Sitting in the taxi riding to the airport, Pederson reflected on his visit and then sat up straight as a thought struck him. 'I wonder what that man Bethany was doing there? He stuck out like the proverbial turd in the punch bowl and looked decidedly unhappy when Lionel made that approach to Peter Marshall. I wonder what that was all about. Not only that, I think I'll delve into what Marshall was working on before everything went wrong for him. There has to be a connection between Marshall's work and a visitation from the Chief Scientific Advisor to the Ministry of Energy and Natural Resources. For someone in his position to stop off at Oak Tree Manor, however lovely the guesthouse might be, is hardly likely as a random act. No, there's something else going on and when I get home, I shall give Lionel a call and see what has happened. Even if I can't recruit Marshall, his being at Greydene would still be good if I can come back here on an annual or even a semi-annual basis.'

As he pulled up outside Oak Tree Manor, John looked at his wife and said, "We're home."

"Oh yes, John, so we are. It's so nice here…can we retire up here in Derbyshire? I just love it and the people are really nice…this would be perfect for us. I love the thought of moving out of London, away from all the noise and overcrowding and that traffic. What do you think?"

"It's quite an idea…and property doesn't cost anything like what it would in London. Let's ask Arnie if he could introduce us to his realtor friend. After all, we own our home in London and if we sold it and bought up here, we'd have a lot left over so we could travel and that sort of thing."

"Oh John, that would be wonderful."

"Okay then, let's do it," agreed John, and climbed out of the car.

As Mary joined him and they walked hand-in-hand into the guesthouse, she looked at him archly and asked, "Just why are we here, John? I know it's sort of a mini-vacation for us but that's not the whole story, is it?"

"No, I'm afraid not. I was told to come up here but quite why isn't altogether clear. At least not to me, it isn't."

"Didn't they tell you what you had to do while up here?"

"Not really. All they told me was to get know everyone and check back in every so often."

"That's very odd," said Mary.

"Isn't it though," agreed John. "What can I say to them about the people here? That Peter and Chris are very close and that her father approves? Mabel, Lucy and her boyfriend Zack are hard-working and did a great job with that dinner the other night. I was interested when that Lionel Simpson from Greydene University asked Peter to give some seminars and it seems he got in before that American professor could ask Peter the same sort of thing."

"Did Peter say yes to Dr. Simpson?"

"I don't know. I got the impression that making a decision on that could be causing him some difficulty but I'm not sure quite what the trouble might be."

"What about that Professor Bethany? What was he doing here? I thought he was rather boring and so full of himself. He certainly didn't want to talk to me and looked almost angry that he was seated so far away from Peter, which was a bit cheeky as he was only included at the last minute…and simply at Dr. Pederson's insistence at that."

"As usual my dear, you are right. Frankly I don't know why he was here but I'm sure it has something to do with why we are here although quite why that might be is beyond me."

As they entered the guesthouse, a man approached them and held out his hand, "Hello there. I'm Nigel Meadows – Mabel's husband."

"Oh," said John and shook his hand. Searching for something to say, he added, "Your wife, and I believe your daughter and her boyfriend, did a great job the other night…with dinner, that is," he added lamely.

"I'm glad to hear it," said Nigel. "I'm especially pleased that Zack proved to be such a help. I always thought that there was more to that boy than meets the eye."

Uncertain what to say, John and Mary started to edge past Nigel when he said, "I forgot to introduce myself…I used to be the local constable here. I retired a while back but I like to keep my hand in, so to speak. I gather that you are a Detective Inspector but about to become a Chief Inspector…is that right?"

John nodded, thinking, 'I wonder how he knew that?'

Seeing the questioning look on John's face, Nigel added, "I've kept in touch, only on an intermittent basis of course, with some of my old friends. I believe you know Ernie Miller and possibly Stan Wilberforce. Stan is doing very well …he became Chief Constable up here quite recently and I believe Ernie is about to get promoted to Commander and probably will end up as Head of Special Branch."

John was astonished. Just who was this character that appeared out of nowhere and had such high level connections? He cleared his throat and asked, "How do you know these people?" making it clear that retired country coppers generally were not acquainted with police officers at the top of their professions.

"Oh we went to Police College together," said Nigel. "I got tired of all the politics and moved back here years ago; frankly, I couldn't brown nose enough to get to the top…I didn't think it was worth it."

'I see,' said John, thinking, 'So this man has connections but why is he telling me all this? The comment about knowing my boss, Chief Superintendent Miller, had a purpose but what was it? Also, just why is there all this interest in Oak Tree Manor? It's an ordinary, if very pretty, out of the way place, so why is everyone so fascinated by it, unless it has to do with Peter Marshall being here. If it's the latter, then what's his importance to all these higher-ups? Now I'm even more confused than I was before.'

As the silence started to stretch, Nigel said, "Look, let's go and have a drink at the bar…you know, get acquainted."

Glancing at his wife, John nodded, "Okay, that might be nice." At which Mary jumped in, "Look, why don't you boys go on in and I'll take our things upstairs, John. I'll join you as soon as I've freshened up a bit…I shouldn't be too long."

"Alright love, I'll get you a G&T," said John.

A few minutes later as they sat drinking beer and waited for Mary to join them, Nigel opened the conversation with, "I know you're Special Branch, John, but what I don't know is why you're here. Not the sort of thing people like you usually get into."

"We're up here for a little break. You know, have a look around. We might even buy somewhere to retire. It's very pretty and property is downright cheap compared to London."

"John, I'm not stupid. Special Branch officers aren't usually part of a nation-wide manhunt for a missing scientist unless it is a matter of National Security or involves a major crime, which is hardly likely in the case of Dr. Peter Marshall, unless I'm much mistaken. So, I don't understand what you're doing here."

"Frankly, Nigel, neither do I. Obviously if it was something to do with National Security, I couldn't talk about it but, like you, I'm at a loss."

"I see. I don't suppose you know why that Bethany fellow was here last night either?"

"No I don't. I didn't even know who he was until Mary enlightened me," said John.

"Oak Tree Manor is hardly the place where I'd expect someone like him to stay, so he was obviously here for a reason."

"Good point but I still can't answer you. I know as much, or as little, as you," admitted John.

"The bottom line," said Nigel pensively. "is that everything seems to be revolving around Peter Marshall but why?"

"Again, a good question and I can't answer that either. But I'll tell you one thing – whatever is going on, my sense is that it has something to do with the Ministry of Energy and Natural Resources."

"Why do you say that?"

"Because there is no other plausible reason for Bethany to come here unless he was directed to do so by someone at that ministry."

"Makes sense," said Nigel judiciously.

At that point, Mary Parsons joined them and the conversation veered to subjects of more general interest. Discussion of Peter Marshall had stopped but was not forgotten.

After intense discussions between Richard Fowler and his editor, it was agreed that The National Globe would underwrite the retrial of Monk. The services of an eminent barrister were retained and Sir Ronald Arbuthnot, Queens Counsel, was briefed to appear on behalf of the plaintiff, Monk. Fortunately, thanks to a quiet word from John Parsons to his friend at the Crown Prosecution Service, it was agreed that if a plea for a mistrial were lodged, then the CPS would not oppose the motion and, hopefully, Monk would be released from prison. In exchange for this legal assistance, Monk and his wife agreed to give their stories exclusively to The National Globe, an arrangement that suited everyone.

Eventually a court appearance was scheduled. On the trial day, Sir Ronald Armstrong QC, adjusted his wig and got his feet. He bowed slightly and spoke carefully, "Your Honor, if it pleases you…"

"Sir Ronald, I am surprised to see someone of your standing present in my court today," said His Honor Judge Benjamin Nugent, presiding judge at The Northern District Circuit Court of London.

"Your Honor, it is my privilege and honor to be here in your court today, especially as this is an important case."

"It is? Well, Sir Ronald, please enlighten me."

"We have here a case in which a man who took on the role of The Good Samaritan in defending a woman being assaulted by a man, ostensibly her boyfriend and someone she was living with at that time. Unfortunately, that man, one Sidney Green, entered into a fracas with the defendant, Cuthbert Monk, commonly known as Monk. It appears that Sidney Green was rather drunk as were his friends when the incident we are addressing occurred. Mr. Green assaulted his live-in girlfriend, Donna Smith, egged on by his friends, and gave her two black eyes, the ocular damage being so severe that Ms. Smith was unable to see what actually transpired between Green and Monk. To compound the problem, the two friends of Green took off running when Monk stepped in to stop the assault on Ms. Smith by Green.

"In a statement made to the police, who arrived shortly after the unfortunate demise of Sidney Green, Mr. Monk stated that he had physically restrained Mr. Green from doing any further damage to Donna Smith. At which point, Green pulled away from Mr. Monk, snatched up an abandoned beer bottle outside the pub, broke off the base of the bottle and lunged at Mr. Monk with the broken bottle on his hand, intent on inflicting severe damage to Mr. Monk. Mr. Monk side-stepped the attack from Green and delivered a firm blow to his assailant. As a result of this blow, Mr. Green fell backward onto the ground and hit his head on the sidewalk, which caused a head injury from which he subsequently died."

Sir Ronald paused before he presented the rest of his case. The fact that Sid Green had an undiagnosed brain aneurism, discovered during the post-mortem, was brought out. Sir Ronald stressed that the aneurism was a possible contributory role in Green's death and that neither the prosecution nor the defense during the first trial even mentioned this medical condition. The chronic alcoholism of the deceased, his repeated complaints over severe head-aches and migraines together with his persistent belligerent attitude were also cited. Finally he mentioned that Donna Smith, a somewhat unreliable witness at best, was coached by the prosecution regarding what to say at Monk's trial despite her own admission that she could not comment on what had happened because of the blows she had received.

When Sir Ronald Arbuthnot had finished his presentation, His Honor Judge Benjamin Nugent gravely thanked him and turned to Alexander Lees QC, counsel for the Crown Prosecution Service, "Mr. Lees, have you anything that you wish to say to the court before Sir Ronald calls his first witness?"

"Your Honor, my learned friend Sir Ronald Arbuthnot has presented an admirable summary of the circumstances surrounding the arrest and conviction of Cuthbert Monk. He made several statements which, if substantiated, would bring into question many of the facets of the original trial of Mr. Monk. If, and I must stress the word if, it is demonstrated that certain exculpatory facts were not in evidence during the first trial and that misleading and/or unsubstantiated statements were made by at least one prosecution witness, the Crown Prosecution Service will admit to there having being a grave miscarriage of justice. That being the case, application will be made for the exoneration of Cuthbert Monk."

"Thank you, Mr. Lees. Sir Ronald, you may call your first witness," said the judge.

The first witness called by Sir Ronald was the police officer who was the first responder to the 999 police emergency call. His statement was matter-of-fact and established that the defendant Cuthbert Monk had related to him the incident that had led up to the death of Sidney Green. The policeman affirmed that a broken beer bottle lay close to the supine body of Green and that Donna Smith appeared to have such severe bruising and swelling around both her eyes that her vision appeared to be restricted. He also confirmed that Ms. Smith could only say that the defendant had intervened in Sidney Green's assault on her but could neither remember nor clearly see what had happened. The police officer also testified that Ms. Smith was only marginally acquainted with the two friends of Green who encouraged him to attack her and then took off running when Monk intervened.

The only questions asked by Mr. Lees was whether the defendant appeared to be drunk or if the defendant had demonstrated any boastfulness regarding the final outcome of his intervention with Sidney Green. The police officer answered both questions in the negative.

Then Dr. Horace Pugh, the Home Office pathologist who performed the *post mortem* examination of Sid Green, was called by Sir Ronald. Dr. Pugh, a quiet and unassuming man, testified that he had, indeed, performed the autopsy on Sidney Green and that he had determined the cause of death as blunt force trauma resulting from hitting his head on the concrete sidewalk outside the pub where the incident occurred. During questioning, Dr. Pugh admitted that he had established the presence of an aneurism within the brain of the victim and this finding was entered into his report.

Sir Ronald then drew himself up to his full height and grasping the front of his silk robes with both hands, he asked, "Dr. Pugh, did you express any opinion as to whether that brain aneurism might have contributed in any way to the death of Sidney Green?"

"Not in writing, no."

"No?" boomed Sir Ronald. "But I assume that you must have had some opinion on the matter, did you not?"

"I did, Sir Ronald," admitted Dr. Pugh. "When asked, I mentioned to the Crown Prosecutor at that time that I was in two minds whether it had been a contributory factor in Green's death but I was leaning more towards it being so."

"I see. So you told the prosecutor that you thought that Sid Green's brain was ripe for hemorrhage following blunt force trauma because of the presence of that aneurism, did you? This was a verbal comment, was it not?"

"Your Honor, I must protest that Sir Ronald is leading the witness," interjected Alexander Lees.

"I must agree with your objection, Mr. Lees. Sir Ronald, you know better than to lead witnesses...please refrain from doing so again."

"Yes, Your Honor," said a barely contrite Sir Ronald. "Dr. Pugh, were your findings released to the defense?"

"Yes, a full report was made available to the defense as soon as it became available."

"Did defense counsel discuss those findings with you...in particular, the significance of the brain aneurism?"

"No, he did not."

"Did you think to raise this matter with him...advise him so-to-speak on the significance of the brain aneurism?"

"Sir Ronald, I am a scientist and my function is to present the facts, in this case the autopsy findings. Unless counsel raises an issue with me, I avoid speculation as much as possible."

"But Dr. Pugh, you were aware, were you not, that the defense counsel was relatively young and inexperienced? Surely you were beholden to the proper serving of justice to inform him of the possible significance of Green's aneurism?"

Horace Pugh sat silent, matching Arbuthnot's accusatory stare with a placid look on his face.

"You have not answered, sir," said Sir Ronald.

"Unfortunately," said Dr. Pugh hesitantly. "The defense counsel was a very brash, arrogant and boastful man who adamantly refused to discuss any part of the autopsy findings. He gave me the distinct impression that it was an open-and-shut case to him and that he had no need to delve further into what had happened."

"I see," said Sir Ronald. "In other words, he could not be bothered. Now, Dr. Pugh, experienced pathologist that you are, would it surprise you that a leading neuro-anatomist and pathologist has stated that in his opinion Green's brain aneurism was a strong contributory factor in his death?"

"No it would not," said Dr. Pugh. "If your expert witness is who I think it is, I should have no hesitation is deferring to his opinion since he is a world-renowned expert in precisely this field."

After Sir Ronald's examination was complete, it was the turn of Alexander Lees to cross-examine the witness. Like Sir Ronald, he also raised the question of the possible contributory influence of the brain aneurism but the pathologist's opinion was unshakable.

Sir Ronald then called Professor Dennis Singleton and it was quickly established that he had a world-wide reputation as a neuro-anatomist and pathologist. With a few questions, Sir Ronald was able to elicit the opinion from Professor Singleton that Green's brain aneurism was a major contributory factor to the brain hemorrhage that killed him. In Singleton's opinion, "That aneurism could have ruptured at any day and any head trauma would have caused the fatal sequence of events. Further, the seriousness of that particular pathology was evident from the increasingly frequent severe headaches and anti-social behavior of Sidney Green."

Alexander Lees did not challenge Professor Singleton's opinion since it was not only in agreement with but amplified the pathologist's comments.

Donna Smith's testimony was a disaster from beginning to end and clearly indicated that the Crown Prosecutor had verged on malfeasance in his witness preparation. At the insistence of Sir Ronald, and the reluctant acquiescence of Mr. Lees, Donna Smith was ruled a non-credible witness and her testimony declared inadmissible.

Monk's testimony merely confirmed his comments to the responding police officer at the time of the incident and it was clear that he had no intention of inflicting serious injury to Sid Green. He clearly stated that Green's death was an accident resulting from his defense against an attack upon him, Cuthbert Monk, with a broken bottle. Questioning by Alexander Lees only provided further affirmation of Monk's Good Samaritan behavior. Monk's military experience, notably his service in the SAS, was deemed irrelevant to the trial.

It was not possible for Sir Ronald Arbuthnot to call either the defense counsel or the Crown Prosecutor as witnesses since such a course of action would be severely frowned upon as creating an undesirable legal precedent. Nevertheless, he was able to demonstrate that he was highly critical of both sides of the court in Monk's first trial.

After the three day trial ended, the judge thanked both counsel and said he would render an opinion the next day.

The next morning, Sir Ronald Arbuthnot, Alexander Lees, the two instructing solicitors, Richard Fowler, Monk and his wife Audrey all sat in the courtroom and impatiently waited for His Honor Judge Benjamin Nugent to be seated.

The judge surveyed the courtroom, lightly rapped his gavel and asked both the prosecution and defense counsel to approach the bench. He studied them both and then leaned forward, "Sir Ronald, you presented a most convincing series of arguments and I must congratulate you on your skilled presentation of the facts, and opinions, surrounding this unfortunate case. Mr. Lees, you were given a difficult task and it is clear that you had to argue an almost inarguable case. However, you did so honestly and honorably, and you did not impugn the Crown Prosecutor in the first trial or, indeed, defense counsel. Given what I have heard and the evidence of prosecutorial misconduct, defense counsel ineptitude and a very unreliable witness, I have no recourse but to overrule the findings of the first trial. I felt that I should share my opinion and findings with you before I announce them in open court, namely that I shall declare Cuthbert Monk innocent of the charges. After my decision is rendered, unless Mr. Lees wishes to lodge an appeal, I should like to suggest that you apply to the Home Secretary for the immediate release of Cuthbert Monk. Thank you both for presenting a most interesting case."

Shortly thereafter, Monk was declared innocent and was informed that application was to be made for his release by Sir Ronald Arbuthnot and that the application would be supported by Alexander Lees. When she heard the ruling, Audrey Monk burst into tears and hugged her husband tightly, and then both of them grabbed Dick Fowler and included him in the embrace.

Out of earshot of the happy defendant and his wife, Sir Ronald Arbuthnot leaned over towards the prosecutor and said quietly, "Alex, thanks for not making things difficult. I know you had a problem with justifying what happened in the first trial but that doesn't always mean people will do the right thing."

"Ron, if I'd have had my way, this whole case would never have come to trial. I cannot imagine what had been going through the heads of the CPS back then and that defense counsel should never have been admitted to the bar. Do we know in which chambers he is situated?"

"I'm not sure but when I do find out, I shall have a few words in the right quarter. People like that give the rest of us a bad name. Anyway, things worked out right in the end."

"Yes, they did," agreed Alex Lees. "It's a pity that poor bugger Monk had to waste all those years in prison but at least he has the satisfaction of being exonerated and of knowing that his wife stuck with him throughout it all. He's a lucky man."

"Indeed he is. Anyway, how about lunch at the Club – are you free?"

EIGHTEEN

Chris snuggled closer to Peter, enjoying the feel of his hard muscular body pressed up against her own soft yielding flesh. As she breathed in the faint residual smell of his aftershave and the slightly more acrid odor of perspiration, sweat that their fervent love-making had generated, she realized that perhaps for the first time in her life she relished the sheer joy of snuggling with a man she loved. She had enjoyed sex with Larry but was it love-making? Probably not because within minutes of having serviced himself and his wife, Larry would almost leap out of bed and go back to whatever urgent task he had put on hold while he and Chris coupled frantically in bed. Sadly, reflected Chris, she had married at too young an age and she was too inexperienced then to know that sex and love-making were often poles apart. Now, spending time with Peter was so different and so fulfilling that she snuggled closer to him and almost purred with happiness.

After a while, Chris asked, "What are you thinking Peter? You are so quiet. One minute I sense that you are smiling at something and then it seems a wave of sadness almost overwhelms you. Can you…do you want to talk about it? There's nothing you can say that will shock or alarm me…I just want to make you as happy with me as I am with you."

Peter was silent, looking up unseeing at the ceiling. Eventually he said, "I heard today from John Parsons that Dick Fowler…you remember him, that reporter from The National Globe…anyway Fowler and The National Globe arranged a re-trial of Monk. It seems that the case against Monk was dismissed and he has been exonerated. The upshot is that he will be released shortly."

"That sounds like good news but I have to ask, who is Monk? I don't think you've ever mentioned him before."

"Monk saved me…without him, my life in prison would have been absolute hell, that's assuming I would even have survived there."

"How did he do that? Who was he?"

"Monk was my cellmate and he taught me everything I know… everything about self-defense, if that's what you want to call it," said Peter. "He was in prison for killing someone. When you're inside, you never talk about why you were there…as far as anyone says anything, all inmates are innocent, every single one. You are all fair game for the prison guards, other inmates, everyone. The only ones left alone were murderers and the very few who could take care of themselves."

Chris slid slightly away from Peter, propped herself up on one elbow and looked down at him, "That's far from the whole story, isn't it? I can hear something in your voice…why don't you tell me about it? I know it must be painful but I love you and I want to know… everything."

Slowly Peter started telling Chris about how he had been put into a cell with Monk and told her who the man was, who he had been and how he had ended up in prison. "He trained me," said Peter. "He taught me almost everything he had learned in the SAS and he turned me into the fighter I had to be in order to survive in prison. Without him, I would have been broken, if not dead, within a couple of months."

"Oh!" and Chris was silent as she thought about what Peter had said. "Peter, tell me about what he taught you…those martial arts, if that's what they're called?"

Peter nodded and then slowly, hesitantly he told her how he had learned to be able to kill someone with just his hands, his instruction in where the trigger points and weaknesses of the human body were located, acquiring the ability to deliver blows that ranged from being able to numb someone or kill them…the skills that the trained killers of the SAS, US Army Rangers and the US Navy Seals relied upon in combat.

"Didn't it bother you to learn all that, you a University professor and a man of science?" asked Chris. "Wasn't all that something totally alien to you?"

"Alien to me? Absolutely but it was essential for my survival. I have to confess that I didn't want to do any of it at first but after I had to defend myself against three thugs in prison who took exception to my posh accent, as Monk called it, I realized why I had to be able to do what Monk had trained me to do. It wasn't a question of choice but necessity."

Then the significance of past events, like the gang of bikers outside the food warehouse, started to make some sense to Chris, who said, "I can understand your need for them in prison but you have used those skills since then, haven't you?"

"Once or twice, yes," admitted Peter.

"That gang of bikers at the food warehouse…the ones who took off running when they saw you…they'd seen you before, hadn't they?" When Peter nodded, she continued, "What happened with them?"

"It's part of a long story," said Peter.

"So, we've got all night and there's nowhere we have to go…" and Chris snuggled back against Peter. "Tell me what happened, please."

Again Peter nodded and then slowly told her what his life had been like when he was first released from prison. "Prison was horrible, a living hell. You have zero privacy, the food was dreadful, it was cold and damp in the winter and damp and smelly in the summer, the guards are often sadistic brutes and the inmates are worse. You make no decisions, none, for yourself and you do what you are told, at once and without question. Inside you are a number…a statistic if you will…and no-one cares what you were outside or what you will go back to being once released. Prison is your whole universe."

"That's ghastly," breathed Chris.

"Well, as someone once said, *If you can't do the time, don't do the crime!* I was stupid and paid for it, and I have no-one to blame but myself," the last accompanied by a stifled sob. "The real problem is that you are completely unprepared for what faces you when you get out. As with most released convicts, I had precious little money and nowhere to go…I was on my own."

Peter went on to relate how he had survived working behind the bar of various pubs until the last encounter with the drunken laborer.

"Dossing down with Jamie wasn't the greatest but it beat sleeping rough and I missed the sense of belonging, such as it was, working with him. Laying out that drunk when he was manhandling a young woman put an end to all that, and I took off."

Slowly Peter related how he had been given a lift by Nobby to the North of England and how he had spared Nobby a brutal beating by the same gang of bikers that were hassling Chris.

"So that's what that was all about, was it?" asked Chris.

Peter nodded and told her how Nobby had dropped him off around the corner from where Chris had a flat tire and, as he said with a small smile, "The rest you already know."

"Oh Peter, there's much more, isn't there?"

"What, after I left prison?"

"No silly, I mean before all this happened to you…you know your life at Cambridge…that sort of thing."

"Another time, Chris, another time. That life is long gone and probably doesn't bear talking about…it's all over now." Again there was that stifled sob.

"But it really isn't all over, is it? That American professor, and the people from Greydene University and even those police officers all looking for you…I don't believe it's all over and I don't think you believe it either."

"I just don't know Chris. Things aren't that simple…they never are." Peter turned to look at her and suddenly kissed her, hard and passionately, before saying, "The night's awasting and the feel of you against me is too good to waste. Come here…"

As Chris felt herself pulled into his welcoming arms, her last thoughts before losing herself in passion were that she would ask him about his former life another time…Peter was right, the night was awasting!

Nigel and John lifted their pint glasses and toasted each other and then Mary, who ceremoniously lifted her gin-and-tonic in silent greeting, "Cheers."

"Nigel, good idea to meet up for a drink here at The Bull and Bush – nice pub, by the way. Your suggestion came at the right time. Mary and I were getting a little tired of looking at cows, sheep and fields, and neither of us fancied going into Greydene… after living in London, we've had enough of traffic and busy streets to last a lifetime."

"Are you really thinking of moving up here?" asked Nigel.

John and Mary looked at each other and then back at Nigel, "Actually, yes. London isn't what it used to be, what with the traffic and congestion and all those foreigners living there. Obviously we're not country folk but I think we can learn, can't we John," said Mary. John nodded and took a hefty swig at his beer. With Mary happy, anything was possible and the thought of making new friends such as a retired copper like Nigel, Mabel Meadows and Arnie Hawkins, gave him a great sense of satisfaction. Perhaps this was where they should be.

The three of them were chatting over a second round of drinks when Mabel arrived to join them. Within minutes, Mary and Mabel were gossiping happily while John and Nigel swapped cop stories as police officers do all over the world. Eventually Nigel broached the subject that hovered over them like the proverbial elephant in the corner of the room, "Why did they send you up here to find Peter Marshall?"

"Frankly, Nigel, I have no idea."

"That's odd."

"Yes, it was. After we found him and reported back, I was told to watch and wait, so to speak…that's all."

"So you have no idea why?"

"No…but then that's not unusual for detective inspectors of Special Branch. We do what we're told and don't ask questions. Lots of things we do make little sense, so what else is new?"

"That I understand…not asking questions and the like…but what was so special about Dr. Marshall? And who, for that matter, set off the search for him?"

"I have no idea and, to be honest, I don't care. All I know is that he had a checkered past between leaving prison and arriving here… and I don't think I ever got the whole story either."

"Nothing bad, I hope," said Nigel.

"No, at least nothing criminal anyway. He sorted out a gang of bikers for the man who gave him a lift up North and his intervention stopped what might have been a nasty beating. Before that, he was pretty good at preventing trouble and punch-ups in the various pubs where he worked in London. In fact, the last one, when he stopped some drunk from manhandling a young woman seems to be the reason he took off up North."

"Really? I wonder why he did that if he was helping someone out," said Nigel.

"No idea. Frankly nothing makes sense to me because he is or was no threat to National Security. So I can only assume that the reason anyone wanted to find him had to do with his work at Cambridge before all hell broke loose in his life."

"Hmm," said Nigel. "So what was he working on before all this happened?"

"Search me," said John. "The only thing I know about science is that water freezes at 0 degrees Centigrade and boils at 90 degrees," the last said with a mischievous grin on his face.

"Wait a minute, water boils at 100 degrees Celsius, doesn't it?"

"See what I mean," said John and burst out laughing.

After drinking a bit more, Nigel eventually said, "Well, whatever it was must have been important to send you looking for him."

"Got me there but it'll all come out in the wash sooner or later."

Matthew Jenkins, Senior Editor at The National Globe, looked across his desk at his new star reporter, Richard Fowler, and said, "You were right about that Monk character, weren't you? The increase in circulation and the favorable publicity resulting from his release more than paid for any legal expenses and, strange to say, we actually did some good for a change."

Fowler nodded, pleased with what had been achieved. "When the dust settles, we'll get him to tell his story. Strangely enough, there was a movie recently in which the leading character, Nicolas Cage I believe, had a similar experience. Although I doubt that we'll get a movie out of Monk's story, a book might be handy."

"Go for it, Dick…but only after we publish his story first, okay?"

"Of course," agreed Dick.

"By the way, Dick, why and for that matter who started this search for Peter Marshall?"

"I'm not sure but I am working on it. Nothing makes sense about any of this but my instinct tells me that there is quite a story just waiting to be told…and I'm going to find out what it is."

"Good. By the way, have those interns been any help to you?"

"Absolutely…can I hold on to them a bit longer?"

"Certainly…if you can get another scoop like Monk's… Cuthbert Monk, what a name. No wonder he only wants to be called Monk…who would want to be known as Cuthbert?"

"Well, it could always have been shortened to Bert but Monk doesn't look like a Bert to me."

"Dick, that was dreadful…go away and get back to work."

James Arthur Llewellyn-Hughes looked across his desk at Stephen Fletcher and asked, "What is happening up in Derbyshire with Peter Marshall?"

"Apparently nothing. That American professor, Hiram Pederson has gone back to Utah or wherever he came from and Lionel Simpson asked Marshall to give some seminars at Greydene University."

"And?"

"Nothing, I'm afraid. Apparently Marshall has neither agreed nor refused and the matter has been left hanging for the moment."

"Hmm. I wonder if we can do anything to move things along? We do need to have Marshall get back to work."

"I could always go up there and have a chat with the people at Greydene University and with Marshall but…"

"I share your hesitation, Fletcher," said Llewellyn-Hughes. "Pushing them may do more harm than good. Perhaps Bethany could drop by that guesthouse or whatever it is again and chat to Marshall. He's egregious I grant you but he can be quite persuasive at times. Maybe if he talks to Marshall and stirs up his interest, he might actually want to get back into science."

"Bethany? I thought he was already into science," asked Fletcher facetiously.

"No you fool – Marshall. I am well aware of what Bethany does…it's Marshall that I am talking about here. Anyway, just be ready to travel if needs be while I talk to Bethany and try to stir the pot."

The daily chores were done and Mabel had gone home to prepare lunch for Nigel. Lucy and Zack were off in Zack's small flat above Nigel's garage. Both were excited at the prospect of Zack working at Oak Manor Inn. "Sometimes I wonder why I went to University when what I might end up doing has nothing to do with what I spent three years studying," commented Zack.

"Zack Freeman," said Lucy sternly. "You spent three years learning economics…you even got a degree, didn't you? Anyway, just because you didn't want to became an accountant or some sort of financial whizz doesn't mean that your education will be wasted."

"How so?" asked Zack.

"Look, I love you dearly but sometimes you drive me crazy."

"I do? Why?"

"Look Zack, it's obvious that Chris and Peter are in love and if I read the signs right, Peter will go off and work at the University. He and Chris will marry and she'll go with him, and have to leave the guesthouse. Mr. Hawkins is getting on a bit and he'll need help running the place, keeping the books and such. I'll help mum and you'll be able to help Mr. Hawkins…you never know, we might even get married and settle down here."

Zack stared at Lucy, thinking, 'She's got it all planned out and it sounds pretty good to me. It was fun working that dinner the other night and I really enjoyed being part of Oak Tree Manor. Hey, marrying Lucy also sound pretty good to me…I wonder if she'll say "yes" when I ask her? Her parents didn't approve of me at first but they've changed their attitude since that dinner, so they might actually be happy if Lucy and I get married. Besides, they've got to want grandchildren…actually I wouldn't mind a couple of kids myself.' Aloud he said, "Sounds like you've got everything planned out for us, Lucy."

"What's wrong with that?"

"Nothing…in fact it sounds pretty good to me."

"Okay then, let's go talk to Mr. Hawkins about you working there."

Arnold Hawkins, Chris and Peter had finished lunch and were sitting back enjoying coffee. After reviewing the day's guest bookings and deciding whether they needed to cater dinner for anyone, Mr. Hawkins said, "Well, that's the Oak Tree Manor's business settled for the day, what about your business Peter?"

"How do you mean?"

"That invitation to lecture or teach at Greydene University, that's the business I'm talking about." When Peter and Chris looked at him questioningly, he continued, "Look Peter, this isn't the life for you. You've been a God-send to us and we couldn't have managed without you but it can't continue, can it?"

"You want me to leave?" asked Peter.

"Don't talk daft, lad! Of course I don't want you to leave and Chris would never forgive me if that happened. No, you are welcome to stay as long as you like…you're family now and part of everything here. But let's face it, someone as brilliant as you…oh don't pull faces at me, you know how smart you are and pretending you aren't doesn't cut it with me. Anyway, you should get back to doing what you were…are…good at and stop hiding from life."

"It's not that easy…" said Peter and both Chris and Mr. Hawkins said almost simultaneously, "It never is."

"No lad," continued Mr. Hawkins. "If life were easy, anyone could do it." and earned quick smiles from Peter and Chris. "But seriously, that nonsense over people looking for you all over the country tells me that whatever you were doing has to be important… very important…and whether you like it or not, it's time to get back to it. Chris, do you agree with me?" and Chris nodded but wondered where her father was going with this conversation.

"Look Mr. Hawkins…Arnie…getting back into science isn't like riding a bike after several years…you know, something like that once learned is not forgotten. No, science is…"

"Oh spare me, lad," snapped Mr. Hawkins. "We know doing science at your level is hard but you did it and were very good at it judging by the fuss that Professor Pederson and Dr. Simpson made over you. I know what you're thinking…you are out-of-date and not abreast of recent research and so forth…but so what? Let me tell you, you are not the first and most certainly won't be the last person to have had to start afresh…except it won't really be a fresh start, will it? Those notes you made for Professor Pederson tells me, and you too for that matter, that whatever skills and talents you once had are still there, dormant maybe but certainly not dead and gone."

Peter was silent for a few moments, digesting what Mr. Hawkins had said. Eventually he nodded and got to his feet, saying, "I'll think about it."

Mr. Hawkins stared at him for a second or two and added, "Make sure you do, Peter. There's a lot at stake here. Oh, and by the way, I told you to call me Arnie…so do so, please.'"

Later that night, after another bout of passionate lovemaking, Chris snuggled against Peter and said quietly, "What are you afraid of, Peter?"

"I'm not afraid of anything…"

"Hush, Peter," said Chris, placing a finger on his lips. "I know you well enough and love you too deeply to be fooled by what you are saying. You may not be scared of any man and I don't think you are afraid to face challenges but there is something that's stopping you from going back to science and teaching, things that once you loved and were the very core of your being."

"I'm worried about being unable to cut the mustard – you know, failing."

"It's not that, is it? Your ability…brilliance even…didn't just go away, never to return," said Chris emphatically. "Talent such as you have doesn't just die, even you know that. No, it is something else… so what is it that is holding you back?"

Peter lay stiff in bed, staring sightlessly at the ceiling and saying nothing. As the silence stretched on, Chris hugged him tightly and waited patiently for him to talk. Eventually he said, "I am scared… not about whether I can teach or do research…it's…it's because I don't want to lose you and everything we have together."

"How would you do that, silly?" said Chris and was startled to feel Peter's body suddenly wracked with sobs and the sprinkling of tears that flowed down his cheeks. After a few seconds, she said gently, "What is it, my darling? Talk to me so that I can understand… help you if you if I can."

Wiping his eyes and allowing his shaking body to relax, Peter quietly talked about his life at Cambridge and his wife. How his work had been almost all-consuming. He told Chris that on the very day that Jean had gone into labor, he had made a major theoretical break-through and had been drinking steadily until he was called to the hospital. When he heard about her death, he had gone off the deep end and started drinking even more heavily. Although he had caused a lot of damage to other cars and injured a few people, only by the Grace of God had he avoided killing anyone. After that, prison was the only fitting punishment for someone such as he who gone so far off the rails.

"That must have been dreadful – unimaginable," said Chris quietly. "But why are you so scared now? Things like that hardly ever happen, and certainly not twice to the same person."

"You don't know that, Chris. None of us do and I cannot bear to run that risk again…it just isn't worth it. Not to me, not to you and not to your father. I just can't do it."

"Now you just listen to me, Peter Marshall," snapped Chris. "I'm not going to let you throw your life away for some noble sentiment that only you drag around like a ball-and-chain. You are going to accept that position at Greydene University, we are going to get married and have lots of children and you, my love, are going to get back to work and win that Nobel prize."

"Oh?"

"Yes, you heard me. I am not having you hold our lives hostage to fortune because of what happened in the past. No sir…it's not going to happen. So, tomorrow morning, you are going to call that Dr. Simpson and tell him you accept his invitation…and I don't want to hear anything more about it, the subject is closed!" She waited a beat or two and then added, "Now, you big silly, you get back to making love and doing what you should have been doing before all this up. And let me tell you, I shouldn't have to ask you to do what we both want."

NINETEEN

Peter Marshall looked at the eager faces of the research students and smiled. It was good to be back in academia, able to share ideas and concepts with receptive minds that were eager to learn. Chris and Arnie Hawkins *were* right, this was where he belonged. It had been difficult at first, trying to establish some degree of rapport with the post-graduates but after several sessions, he had slipped back into the role he once had had at Cambridge. Not seamlessly, not by a long shot, but slowly he was able to interact with them and provide much needed guidance on their research projects, even those working in fields outside his own particular area of expertise. At first, only Lionel Simpson had sat in on his seminars but, slowly, more and more faculty stopped by to listen to him and even joined in the to-and-fro of arcane discussions on the various research projects.

After several successful seminars, Lionel stopped Peter on his way back to Oak Tree Manor. "Peter, a word with you, if I may?" he asked. Peter stopped and looked at him questioningly.

"Peter, your seminars are definitely a hit with the post-graduates. They, and even the faculty, want more. Believe or not, some of the senior undergraduates have been sitting in…have you seen them?"

"I thought I saw some strange faces but, to be honest, I am so focused on the research students that I don't pay that much attention to anyone sitting at the back of the room."

"I thought as much," said Lionel. "Anyway, the undergrads are asking for you to give them seminars too…no, not on your research work but on more general topics…you know, how to organize research and how to think scientifically…that sort of thing."

"Really?" asked Peter. "They are that interested?"

"Yes because it has been mandated by the University Senate that all undergraduates must do a research project and the students want…actually need…help to do this. The bottom line is, can you come on board full-time and help us? We'll try to keep your teaching load to a minimum and give you plenty of time to do your own research. How about it?"

"Well, that's a turn-up for the books, isn't it? I'll think about it and get back to you when I next come in…is that okay with you?"

"Of course it is. Listen, any help you can provide is most welcome and, to be honest, even I'm astonished just how popular your seminars have become. We'll sort out salary and benefits in the meantime…we will make it worth your while to come here full-time."

"Lionel, I haven't been doing this for the money…"

"I know but we are taking up more and more of your time so it is only fair that we make proper arrangements to pay you. Fair is fair, you know."

Peter simply nodded and continued on his way. As he drove back to Oak Tree Manor, it occurred to him that if he started to earn a salary, he could afford to buy his own vehicle to get around… nothing fancy of course, and definitely not a sports car, but something serviceable so that he and Chris could go tootling about and not use the van or her ancient car as they had been.

When he got back to Oak Tree Manor, he found Chris and her father waiting for him in the kitchen with a pot of fresh-made tea, cups and saucers and a tray of cakes. Seeing the lay-out, Peter raised an eyebrow questioningly, "So, what are celebrating?"

"Sit yourself down, Peter, and help yourself to tea and cake," said Arnie Hawkins.

Mystified, Peter did as instructed and after pouring some tea and taking a piece of cake, he looked inquiringly at Mr. Hawkins.

"Chris and I have been talking, Peter," announced Mr. Hawkins.

'Uh oh,' thought Peter. 'This may not be good news….which would be a pity after the good news I had from Lionel today.' Aloud, he simply asked, "Yes?"

"I know about how close you and Chris have become and…er… how Chris sneaks into your room every night after she thinks I've fallen asleep. Oh don't look so shocked, lad, I was young once myself.

To be honest I still miss Chris's mom and the feel of a warm body beside me in bed-but that's my problem, not yours. Anyway, Chris and I were talking and we've come to a decision."

Peter nodded but the feeling of foreboding was reinforced.

"Oak Tree Manor is…was…the local manor house and, as such, there are various cottages scattered around the place, as you know. So, to cut a long story short, it has been decided, subject to your approval of course, that you and Chris move into the largest one. It's in great shape and we'll get the decorators in and tart it up but it might make a great home for the pair of you. What do you think?"

Peter swallowed hard and wiped the nascent tears from his eyes, "I don't know what to say, I really don't."

"Is it all right with you, Peter?" asked Chris anxiously, having seen the burgeoning tears. "We don't want to force anything on you but it could be for the best, and give us some privacy…please say yes."

"Of course I'm saying yes…it is wonderful of you Arnie to even think of us like this." He hesitated for a moment and then continued, "As you said, Chris and I are getting closer by the day and I hope that we can get married but I was worried about where we might live. I'm not exactly flush with funds and even renting a nice apartment was likely impossible, at least it was until today."

"Peter, dad isn't going to charge us rent, silly! So your comment about a lack of funds has no bearing on anything."

"That's not what I meant," said Peter and then went on to tell them about Lionel Simpson's offer.

"That's wonderful," cried Chris and rushed over to hug him. "Absolutely wonderful…isn't it dad?"

"Aye, it is at that. Congratulations Peter."

"If I do take it, at least I'll be able to afford a small car for us to get around in but one thing does bother me and that's what is going to happen here in Oak Tree Manor. Can you do without me?"

"Actually we can. Lucy and Zack came to see us this morning and they want to get married and both of them work here. Lucy will help her mom and Zack will do all the things you used to you and, blessing of blessings, he'll help me with the books and finances. He's got a degree in economics and really knows about finance."

"Sounds to me as though you've got it all sorted out," said Peter wryly and then burst out laughing. "It's funny how everything came together in one day. By the way, where will Lucy and Zack live? Surely his room above Nigel's garage must be a bit cramped for them."

"No problem…they'll take one of the other cottages. Both of them are anxious to decorate a home of their own."

"It sounds as though you two have everything sorted. It's just as well that Greydene University wants me…I'd have been out of job here," and Peter laughed again.

There was a sudden silence and then Mr. Hawkins looked hard at Peter, "Did you just say that you and Chris want to get married?"

"Yes…can I have your permission?"

"Wait a minute," said Chris, laughing. "Don't I get a say in all this? Who said I wanted to marry you?"

"Okay then," said Peter sternly, and got to his feet. He walked around the table and went down on one knee beside Chris, took her hand and said solemnly, "Christie Hawkins, I love you dearly and want to spend the rest of my life with you. Would you do me the honor of accepting my proposal of marriage and become my wife?"

"Well, if you put it like that," said Chris. "Of course I will."

"Hmm," muttered Mr. Hawkins. "I'd like to know what's going on around here, what with all these people suddenly deciding to get married. Must be some sort of infection going around…I've never heard the like before." Looking at Chris and Peter, he added, "I'm happy for both of you and you have my blessing, Peter…not that you needed it."

Matthew Jenkins stared at Dick Fowler in surprise. "Now, let me be sure that I actually did hear what I think I heard. You are telling me that a senior person in the Ministry of Energy and Natural Resources… one of those Mandarins in charge of our country… set off a manhunt for this Dr. Peter Marshall all over the country without actually telling anyone why he was wanted it done. Really?"

"Yes, that's what I said."

"Wait…how did you find this out? No, forget that question since you wouldn't tell me anyway – protecting your informants and all that. So, do we know who this person was?"

"I am told it was Arthur Llewellyn-Hughes, the Permanent Under-secretary who started all this. Apparently after Marshall was eventually found at a small guesthouse in Derbyshire, he even sent his lap-dog scientist, Randy Bethany, up there to persuade Marshall to get back into science."

"That blow-hard, huh! Anyway, I take it that what you're telling me is the search for Peter Marshall had nothing whatsoever to do with National Security."

"No, not that I can see and neither can anyone else. Which does raise the question of why Llewellyn-Hughes, or anyone else for that matter, brought in Special Branch?" said Dick.

"Sounds like an abuse of power to me…so where are we now on this story? And what about that Dr. Martin fellow who got himself killed on his way into Scotland Yard?"

"Everything seems to indicate that Martin getting run over was an accident, pure and simple. Unbelievable as it may seem, it really does appear to be a coincidence."

"Really? A real coincidence? How curious. Anyway, do we know why he was going to see…who was it in charge of finding Marshall?"

"Detective Inspector, now Chief Inspector, John Parsons."

"Whatever. Anyway, why was Martin going to see him?"

"I'm not sure but the story is far more involved than it would appear."

"It is?" asked Jenkins. "So enlighten me."

Clearing his throat, Dick Fowler outlined what he knew about Marshall, Martin, Cambridge and the Ministry of Energy and Natural Resources. When Fowler was finished, Jenkins sat back and stared at the ceiling, thinking hard. Eventually he spoke, "Let me see if I have this right. Peter Marshall makes some sort of discovery that has to do with generating almost limitless energy. But before he puts anything down on paper, his wife dies in childbirth and he goes off the rails, the upshot being he gets sent to jail. Let's leave out the stuff about what happened to him in jail and all that…which is a major story in itself. Anyway, it seems that this Dr. George Martin, a so-called friend and colleague of Marshall's, steals his ideas and gets some sort of grant from the Ministry to work on what Marshall started. But, and this is a major "but", Martin can't get it right and has to tell the Ministry that the project is in grave danger of collapsing, wasting a whole bunch of money. Llewellyn-Hughes panics and decides Marshall needs to be brought back and persuaded to work on his idea, saving all that grant money and doing a lot of good for the country. Is that about it?"

"Just about. Mind you there is a lot more to it, particularly what happened to Marshall in jail and afterwards - you know that stuff with his ex-cellmate Monk."

"Oh I'm sure there is but let's stick with the science bit. What is happening now?"

"That's interesting too," said Dick, who went on to talk about Oak Tree Manor and the various people who lived and worked there.

"Oh boy, this is beginning to sound more and more like a romance novel," said Jenkins. "No-one could make all this up, not even a writer of your ability, Dick."

"Hell, I have trouble believing it all myself," agreed Fowler. "But yes, it really is all true."

"So, you have found out that Marshall has just taken a faculty position at Greydene University, DCI Parsons has retired and with his wife has moved to Derbyshire. That right?"

"Yes."

"Hmm. It sounds as though the efforts involved in getting him to that University are interesting in and of themselves...you might think about writing that up as well as doing a piece on Marshall's discovery, assuming you can get him to talk about it. Do we know the circumstances surrounding Marshall's recruitment to the University?"

"That we do," said Fowler and told his editor what he had learned about Pederson, Simpson and the dinner as well as the notes that Peter had written on Pederson's manuscript.

"Fascinating," breathed Jenkins. "What about Bethany? Did he have a hand in any of this?"

"Not from what I have learned. Apparently, he tried to horn in on it all and get soundly rebuffed...serves the arrogant twit right," said Dick.

"Well, it seems you've earned your paycheck these past months, Dick. Not only that, you've got a lot of writing to do...well done, lad,

I'm delighted with what you've managed to piece together. When you have your story, actually stories, put together, let's get those people in Legal to check everything…we don't want to ruffle too many feathers in Whitehall, do we?"

After Dick Fowler returned to his desk but before he started working, he called his wife, "We're going out to dinner tonight. The editor is really pleased with me, so we're going to celebrate. How does that strike you? When you've got a minute, sort out where we're going to eat, can you? I was wondering about that new Portuguese place around the corner from us. The paper's food critic said it was pretty good."

"Peter," said Chris breathlessly over his mobile phone. "Are you coming home soon?"

"Actually, yes, I'm done for the day and I should be there in about 30 minutes. Why'd you call?"

"Oh, there's something I need you to look at."

"Is it that urgent?"

"Very much so. We're in the kitchen."

Mystified, Peter drove back to Oak Tree Manor but the parking lot of the guesthouse was empty and there was no sign of life anywhere. 'What on earth is going on?' he asked himself. 'Usually by this time we have at least a couple of guests getting checked in. Obviously a quiet day today.'

Walking into the foyer, Peter saw there was no-one about and he was even more perplexed…surely someone had booked in by now? As he approached the kitchen, he was struck by the absence of sound – normally he would have heard conversation and a certain amount of laugher inside. Taking a deep breath, he opened the door.

"Surprise!" everyone shouted loudly and there facing him were Chris and her father, Mabel and Nigel Meadows, Lucy and Zack, John and Mary Parsons and, unbelievably, Monk with an attractive lady by his side. "Happy birthday, darling," said Chris and dashed over to kiss him.

"How…how did you know it was my birthday? And Monk, what are you doing here? How on earth did you find us?" said Peter as he rushed to grab his old friend in a bear hug. "Monk, you old tosser, it's great to see you…and this must be your lovely wife."

"It is indeed, Peter." Monk gently pulled his wife forward and said, "This is Audrey, the cornerstone of my life."

Peter hesitated and then grabbed her in a tight hug, kissing her on the cheek. "Audrey, I've heard so much about you from Monk, so I'm delighted to meet you. But how on earth did you find us?"

"Simple, Peter," said Monk. "A quick phone call to Dick Fowler and here we are."

"You are staying here, aren't you?" asked Peter.

"Of course they are, Peter," announced Chris. "By the way, when you told me about Monk, you didn't say how good-looking he is and that his wife is just lovely. If it hadn't been for Monk, I don't think I'd have even known it was your birthday – shame on you!" and she laughed. "No more secrets, okay?"

"Sorry darling…I won't do it again."

"You'd better not," said Monk sternly. "I don't want to have to smack you around again. Anyway, enough of that. At least I have now met Chris although quite what someone like her is doing with an ugly bleeder like you is beyond me. As for Arnie Hawkins…what was he thinking when he gave you permission to marry his daughter? Even John Parsons…oh sorry, I mean Detective Chief Inspector Parsons…was shocked when he heard and it's hard to shock Special Branch officers." Then Monk laughed loudly and slapped Peter on the back, "Man, it's good to see you." More somberly, he added, "If it wasn't for you, John Parsons and Dick Fowler, I might still be in prison…"

"Yes," said Audrey. "Thank you all. As Shakespeare once said, *All's well that ends well* although this has been one heck of an adventure."

"Adventure?" said Monk and Peter almost in unison, and Monk added, "Well, I suppose it could be called that but it's not the term I'd use to describe it."

"Alright then," said Mr. Hawkins. "Enough of all this meeting and greeting – we've got cake to eat, champagne to drink and then dinner to eat…that's assuming Chris, Mabel, Lucy and Mary are sober enough to cook for us all…and no Peter, you can take Monk,

Zack and John, and me for that matter, off to the *Bull and Bush* for a drink while the ladies do something useful for a change." Seeing the black looks emanating from all the ladies in the room, Arnie Hawkins added quickly, "I was only joking but I was serious when I said that we should get out of your hair."

"Hey, what about me?" cried Audrey. "I can cook…so why are you leaving me out of it?"

"Sorry Audrey…I assumed that as you're a guest here, you'd want to go powder your nose or something."

"Dad," said Chris with exasperation. "I think you should shut-up now before you put your foot any deeper into your mouth… powder her nose indeed! Audrey is one of us now, and don't you forget it." Raising her glass, Chris said, "Happy Birthday Peter and may you have many more of them…but only if you share them with us all here."

Wiping the tears from his eyes, Peter raised his glass in return and said, "Thank you…thank you all for what is truly the best birthday a man could ever ask for…thank you."

"Oh put a sock in it, lad," said Arnie Hawkins with mock gruffness. "Let's get on with drinking this fizzy stuff and watch you open your presents. Then we'll go down to the *Bull and Bush* and celebrate properly…" and seeing the look on Chris's face, he added, "I mean, we'll go have some beer and do some catching up. Zack, you up for driving us all in the van, you being teetotal and such?"

"No problem, old'un, I'll take care of it," said Zack, causing everyone to laugh as Arnie Hawkins spluttered about being called old.

Eventually, the laden van arrived at the pub and Monk and Peter got out first. Monk looked around and saw serried ranks of motorcycles parked outside. With a jerk of his head, he said, "Peter, perhaps you and me should go in first? You know, suss everything out first."

Peter, following Monk's glance, said, "Guys, hold on a moment while Monk and I go see which bar is empty – we don't want to frighten the locals, a rowdy bunch like us arriving unexpected."

Monk rapidly walked inside the pub with Peter close on his heels and, as Peter expected, there was King Rocker and his crew sprawled out at every table and propping up the bar, the whole place wreathed in dense cigarette smoke. The barman looked up and caught Peter's eye, shrugging slightly as if to say "What can I do with this lot here?"

King Rocker had just drained his glass and was about to order another round for everyone when he saw Peter and the very formidable-looking Monk standing in the doorway. Startled, he stopped dead and then said loudly, "Hey, let's head on out. I've had enough of this dump…come on," and he almost ran to the door in his haste to get away. The other bikers, especially those that had encountered Peter before, took off after King Rocker. The rest, deciding that discretion was the better part of valor, also headed hastily towards the door, even if they didn't quite know why.

Arnie Hawkins, Zack, Nigel and John stood outside by the van and watched in amazement as a goodly number of leather-clad younger men rushed out of the pub and climbed onto their bikes, all taking off in a roar of powerful engines and muttered curses. When they walked into the now empty pub, they looked at each other and then at Monk and Peter quietly standing at the bar sipping on glasses of the local brew. "What the hell happened?" asked Arnie. "Why did all those bikers take off like that?" Then he looked at Peter and Monk, both with angelic looks on their faces, and remembered the incident with a bike gang that Chris had told him about. "Don't tell me," he said. "That was the same lot of bikers that was harassing Chris, wasn't it?"

Peter just looked at him and shrugged, "No idea what you're talking about Arnie. Hey, come have a beer – I'm buying now that I'm actually employed and getting an income."

"Whatever, lad, whatever. I'll have a pint of mild-and-bitter, if you please."

Nigel and John exchanged looks; they had a very good idea of what had happened but, as experienced coppers, they kept their mouths closed, trying desperately not to laugh.

Later that evening, Peter and Monk were able to get off to one side and chat unreservedly. "Joking aside, Peter, you did well finding Chris. She's a doll. How'd you meet her?"

Peter slowly related a condensed version of what had happened since his release from prison. After hearing about the various punch-ups as a barman and then the incident with Nobby, Monk laughed and said, "Well, it seems that you put my training to good use after all. Glad to hear it. Now what's going on with this University here? The way I hear it from Dick Fowler, you're some sort of genius and everyone wants to pick your brains. What gives?"

"I'm not sure about being a genius but there has been a bit of interest in my research from back in the day."

"Yeah? Tell me about it."

After Monk heard what had happened with George Martin and the desperate search for him by John Parsons, he asked, "So, has there been any follow-up from the people in Whitehall?"

"Not yet, no but I sense that they will come knocking sooner or later although whether I can tell them anything is another matter… at least not for some time yet."

"Hmm. Okay then, what about your love life and the beautiful Chris?"

"Funny you should mention that. I was thinking of asking you to be my best man. I know Chris, Mabel and Lucy have been talking about it for some time and now that Mary Parsons and hopefully Audrey too are here, they're going to have a high old time with planning the wedding. I tell you Monk, it scares the hell out of me to even think about it."

Monk laughed. "You are just going to have to man up, Peter. Once those ladies take this wedding and its planning over, you're gone, never to be seen again. It's all over for you…and yes, I will be your best man and I'm glad to do it…it's about time Chris made an honest man of you." He slapped Peter on the back and added, "Listen mate, I am so happy for you and I know that you two are going to be great together. By the way, Audrey and I will be the godparents of at least the first one, okay?"

TWENTY

Plans for the wedding were going ahead full steam. What had started out as an interesting exercise for Chris and Mabel, with input from Lucy, was now the predominant topic of discussion between Chris, Mabel, Mary, Lucy and Audrey. Arnold Hawkins, relegated to holding his head and writing checks, spent most of his time muttering about the cost of everything and asking why his daughter had found it impossible to elope. When consulted about any of the wedding details, Peter simply agreed with whatever decisions Chris *et al* had made and went back to work.

"But Peter," cried Chris. "This is your wedding too. Don't you have any opinion?"

"Not bloody likely. Do you think I'm crazy enough to get in the way of you ladies?"

"Oh Peter!" snapped Chris in exasperation. "You are simply too much." She smiled at him fondly before asking, "Who did you want to invite to the wedding?" Seeing him shrug, she added, "Now, don't give me that *I don't care* look of yours. I know that there are people who you would want to be there. I need some input here."

"Well, Monk is going to be my best man – he's already agreed to do it…in fact he's rather chuffed to do so, if you ask me. I assume that you have already included Monk and Audrey as well as John and Mary Parsons. Obviously Mabel and Nigel as well as Lucy and Zack have to be there too. Given what's happened, I wonder whether we should invite Dick Fowler and his wife. If it's alright with you, I should like Nobby Murphy and Dahlia to come too."

"Nobby Murphy? Is he the chap who gave you a lift up from London?"

"Yes…and it's because of him that I actually met you, so…"

"Of course, inviting him is a must! When you have a moment, I want you to tell me about Nobby – he sounds a real character. I assume Dahlia is his wife…is she?"

"No, his daughter."

"Really…hmm. Now you have caught my attention. What do you want to tell me about Dahlia…no, perhaps I don't want to know. That's all ancient history now, isn't it? Anyway, do you have his address? If you do, let me have it, please. Now, what about Dick Fowler….how do we get hold of him?"

"That's easy…call him at the newspaper and then send him an invite," said Peter laconically, secretly relieved that Chris was not going to pursue questioning him about Dahlia.

Chris was about to join the other ladies in the kitchen, which had become the central wedding planning room, when she stopped and asked, "What about anyone at Greydene University…and perhaps Professor Pederson? They all, at least those two, seem to be involved in everything."

"Lionel Simpson? Why not – he's a good chap and Hiram Pederson? Well, if he's likely to be over here any time soon, he's a must too."

"Well we can't plan our wedding around a visit from Pederson but I should like him to be here, if he can make it," agreed Chris. She looked fondly at Peter for a moment before saying, "You old fraud. You've been thinking about who we should invite for some time, haven't you? I should have known."

Gathering up her notes, Chris was almost out the door of the cottage when she popped her head back in, "By the way, we've got an appointment with the vicar on Friday afternoon…so don't be late leaving the University after lunch. Also, we've got to set a firm date for the wedding. Dad says he'll spring for the reception – actually he didn't have much choice after we girls all started working on him, but that's another story. The upshot is that we'll have it at Greydene Hotel, if you agree."

"Of course, of course, whatever," sighed Peter, fully aware that he had no say in the matter anyway.

After hanging up the phone on Randolph Bethany, Arthur Llewellyn-Hughes summoned Stephen Fletcher to his office. "It seems that Professor Bethany struck out with Marshall, as they say in America,. According to him, he got nowhere fast in trying to talk to Marshall or that Simpson fellow at Greydene University."

"I see," said Fletcher judiciously, although he was unclear what his leader expected him to say.

Llewellyn-Hughes stared at him for a moment before saying, "Well, you know what they always say…if you want something done and done properly, you have to do it yourself."

"Yes sir," agreed Fletcher, for want of something to say.

"What I suggest," continued Llewellyn-Hughes. "Is that you arrange for us all to go and visit Marshall and Simpson, is it?, at Greydene University. Dangle the offer of research funding, you know what to say, and make sure that both of them are available."

"You said "us all", sir. Who did you have in mind to go up there?"

"Well, obviously you and I but I want you to tell Golding and Streetly to come too."

"Golding and Streetly?" asked Fletcher.

"Of course I want those two to come with us. They are responsible in no small part for all this mess with Martin and Marshall, so they'd better be available for a trip up to Greydene. Arrange for transport, will you, Fletcher? One of the larger vehicles should do nicely, with a driver of course. Let's go up there next week…just tell my secretary when everything's arranged."

"Hey thanks, John. I really appreciate you giving me a heads-up on this," said Dick Fowler but thinking, 'At least something is now starting to break. I was afraid all that Ministry and Peter Marshall stuff was going to fizzle out but now it seems the mountain is coming to Mohammed and the big guns are going up to see Marshall…right on! Okay, just how do I get close to Peter and find out what really is going on with him. That huge search for him and all the pressure to get him back to his research must mean something but what? Why was the Ministry of Energy and Natural Resources so panicked about this Marshall Effect or whatever they want to call it? It doesn't seem logical that a senior person at one of the smaller ministries is in a panic over wasted money. That has been going for decades, so why now? What's so special in this particular case?

'I suppose the only way to find out is to go up there and ask Peter himself. After all, the worst that can happen is for him to tell me to get lost and, besides, if he can't or won't tell me anything, it's always possible that Lionel Simpson will. My betting is that as faculty in one of the lesser universities, he'd love to have some free publicity. Okay, it's time to ask for more travel money from the boss and to make arrangements to stay at Oak Tree Manor again. Being Johnny on The Spot when things start happening might be good. Sooner or later this whole strange business will become clear and I want to be the person who clarifies it.'

"Peter, how did the visitation with the people from Whitehall go today?" asked Chris. She had been on tenterhooks all day and finally curiosity and impatience got the better of her, and she called Peter on his mobile phone.

"It was all rather strange…I'll tell you about it when I get home."

"When will that be?"

"Oh I don't know…soon. Lionel and I need to discuss this because they made some unexpected suggestions and we really don't want to get into it here."

"Well I'll tell you what, why not bring him home for dinner? We're having roast beef and Yorkshire pudding and there's plenty for everyone. Besides, guess what?"

"What my dear?" asked Peter.

"Dick Fowler has turned up and has booked in for a couple of days."

"He has? Really? Now that's an odd coincidence what with the bigwigs from the Ministry of Energy and Natural Resources just happening to come visiting today," said Peter. He hesitated for a few seconds and then continued, "Nah, it's no coincidence. He knew they were coming and I'll bet John Parsons told him…that'll teach me to say anything to anyone about what's happening here."

Peter sighed and thought for a few moments. "Okay, can we invite all the usual suspects to dinner tonight?"

"Pardon?" asked Chris. "What usual suspects are you talking about?"

"That's just a figure of speech. Don't you remember in the old black-and-white movies…you know the old Humphrey Bogart ones…well anyway, every time anything happened, the local police chief would always have the usual suspects rounded up."

"Peter, you're crazy. What do old black-and-white movies have to do with anything?"

"Nothing actually…oh just forget it, it isn't important. But I am serious in thinking we should have Fowler, Parsons and obviously your dad all in the same place at the same time so that they can hear from Lionel and me what happened today. It will save having to tell each and every one of them separately…besides, you know how things get twisted with endless repetitions."

"Okay, okay," said Chris. "I'm not sure what you're talking about but if you want everyone around the same table, your wish is my command…at least it will be until we're married," she added with a laugh.

"I was afraid that might happen," said Peter and joined in laughing.

After everyone had eaten and had settled back with coffee, Dick Fowler opened the subject that had been hovering over the dinner table like a large cloud. "So, Peter and Lionel, what did the pope and his cardinals want to see you about?"

"The pope and his cardinals?" said Lionel. "Do you mean The Right Honorable Llewellyn-Hughes and his minions?"

"Yes," said Dick. "Doesn't he act like His Holiness when he's talking to you? Of course, I do wonder exactly which ring he expects you to kiss."

Arnie Hawkins sniggered quietly and muttered something to the effect that he just did not need to know the fine details.

"I suppose he does," agreed Lionel, oblivious to Mr. Hawkins. "I just hadn't thought of him like that." A comment that earned another snigger from Mr. Hawkins.

"You might as well get used to it," said John Parsons. "He's used to issuing papal decrees and expects everyone to kneel in obeisance and so forth whenever he says anything, arrogant but powerful git that he is."

"Is he really that important?" asked Chris.

"Oh come on people," snapped Arnie Hawkins. "Enough of this…let's hear what happened today…we're all dying to know."

Peter and Lionel exchanged looks and Peter nodded, "Go for it Lionel…it's more your show than mine."

"I'm not sure about that but…"

"Oh get on with it," urged Chris. "Let's hear what happened."

Lionel cleared his throat, glanced again at Peter and then around the table before starting to speak, "It seems that Peter here made a startling discovery. I won't get into the technical details but it looks as though he came up with a way to produce almost limitless energy at minimal cost. A major scientific breakthrough, as they say. Somehow or other, it was called the Marshall Effect – not the Horton-Marshall Rule or Effect but the Marshall Effect."

"Who called it that?" asked Fowler. "And, for that matter, what exactly is this "it" we're all talking about?"

"Yes," agreed Chris. "Just what are you actually talking about? Like Dick says, I'm wondering how some sort of research discovery can be named after my fiancé and none of us, especially Peter, know nothing about it?"

"That sort of thing happens…not quite all the time but quite often. I remember one of my professors at London University telling me that he had mentioned some research work of his at a meeting and everyone kept talking about this work for a couple of years after. Eventually someone asked him why he hadn't published his findings and he simply said *If everyone keeps talking about it, I won't have to publish it at all.* As I said, that sort of thing just happens in science - and in other fields too. Although people may not know the details of Peter's discovery, calling it the Marshall Effect is a shorthand way of referring to it.

"Anyway, back to today's visitation. Cutting a long story sideways, this discovery of the Marshall Effect, so-to-speak, came about before…well, before everything went to hell in a hand-basket for Peter…" Lionel stopped and looked questioningly at Peter who said, "It's alright Lionel, they all know what happened."

"Okay…good…ah, well…it appears that one of Peter's former colleagues took Peter's idea and went to the Ministry and got funding to work on it. However, he didn't say that it wasn't his idea."

"Surely he can't do that?" exclaimed a horrified Chris. "Isn't that theft or something?"

"It was unethical but ideas are just that, ideas. It is hard to claim ownership of something like that. Let me give you an example. If someone comes up with an idea for a book, a plot if you will, and someone else takes that idea and runs with it and writes a best seller, does the originator of the idea, something that he simply spouted out at a party or the like, actually own or have the right to claim credit for any success the book might have" Lionel looked at everyone and waited as they thought about his question. Then he answered the question himself, "No, not really. Because someone has a good idea but does nothing with it… you know, doesn't work on it… he or she cannot claim ownership. It is a bit more complicated when a person does a whole lot of research but doesn't write it up while a collaborator or colleague, who didn't have the original idea but did some work, actually wrote it up. In such cases, credit is shared…this happened with Crick and Watson, the discoverers of DNA. Crick had the idea and did the research work but Watson wrote it up. Anyway, we're getting off the subject.

"So, Martin got all this funding for what looked like a fantastic idea but …er…well, things didn't work out the way he had hoped. The Ministry people were getting very impatient with him and were demanding results. The upshot of all this is that Llewellyn-Hughes and his lot have pumped a lot, and I mean a *lot*, of money into a project that's gone nowhere and they are sitting there with egg on their faces. When they found out that Peter Marshall actually came up with this idea, they decided that someone should find him and persuade him to go back to work. That's how John here got involved and George Martin got run over when he was going to see John Parsons at Scotland Yard."

"That was Dr. George Martin, wasn't it?" asked Fowler.

"Yes," continued Lionel. "It was.

"Serves them right for being sneaky," snapped Chris.

"Not exactly," said Lionel. "Anyway, they, the Ministry people, want Peter to resume work on his idea and they are willing to pump even more money into the project to get it going."

"So that's why Bethany has been hovering around," mused Dick. Seeing the curious looks on everyone's faces, he added, "Professor Randy Bethany is the Chief Scientific Advisor to the Ministry and he likes to have a hand in anything that is being supported by the Ministry, especially if he can get any credit, deserved or not, for being part of it."

"Huh," muttered Arnie. "Bloody typical." John Parsons nodded in agreement.

"So, there we have it in a nutshell," said Lionel. "Our man Peter is now a hot property and the Ministry wants to give him lots of money to get back to work. That of course raises the question of where he'll go but…"

"That's easily answered," said Peter. "I'm staying here…here at Greydene and to hell with them. If they want me to work on this, I'm doing it where I want to be, not where they want me to go."

"But surely they have better equipment and things at Cambridge, don't they?" asked Chris.

"So?" said Peter. "It's me they want and part and parcel of that is the fact that I want to be here. If they don't like it, well they can lump it."

"Well there you have it," said Arnie. "I told you Peter's a genius Chris, and you didn't believe me. Now perhaps you'll pay more attention to me." Turning to his future son-in-law, he added, "So, what happens now, Peter?"

"Oh, they'll ship all sorts of equipment here from Cambridge, shower money on the University and give me lots of research assistants."

"And what do you think about all this Lionel?" asked Dick.

"I think it's great. It's a win-win situation all round although Peter is going to be very busy, what with his research, all those lectures and his seminars …but Peter says he can cope, so that's what it's going to be."

"You are really going to stay here, Peter?" asked Chris anxiously.

"Of course, I am," said Peter. "I'm not going anywhere, and don't you forget it."

Dick Fowler jumped to his feet and warmly shook Peter's hand, "This is fantastic, Peter. Congratulations." He hesitated for a moment, "Say, do you mind if I write this up now? It makes one hell of a story and explains so much. I tell you, my editor is going to be very pleased…provided, of course, you don't mind, or do you?"

"Frankly, I don't give a toss," said Peter. "Lionel and I have to get things sorted at the University and we've got to find people to help us, but it's going to be exciting, isn't it Lionel?"

"I'm not sure about the "we" and "us" part," said Lionel. "But if I can help…be involved…then we're going for it."

"There is one thing though," interjected Arnie Hawkins.

"What's that, dad?" asked Chris.

"Why is everyone so hot and bothered about this Marshall Effect, whatever it is? The Government has wasted millions and millions on all sorts of things, so why are they so concerned about yet another failure? Makes no sense to me."

"That's a great question," replied Dick Fowler. "On the face of it, it does seem a bit nonsensical. However, I think that there is a deeper reason behind all this broo-ha-ha."

"And what might that be?" asked Peter. Everyone sitting at the table turned to look at him. He smiled and added, "Look folks, it's great that everyone is gung-ho over some work that I did but at the moment, it is only a theory and nothing more. If it works out, this so-called Marshall Effect, then it could be great but there is still a big "if" involved here and no-one can make any promises. So, I repeat, why has everyone, particularly that big wheel Llewellyn-Hughes, got his nickers in a twist over what is best described as a maybe?"

"As I said, a good question," said Fowler. "But I've heard that Members of Parliament, the backbenchers, are beginning to voice complaints about the Ministry of Energy and Natural Resources. They're asking more and more frequently what use it is and whether it should be as large as it is. So unless the Ministry can show that they are doing a useful job, their power and influence will get cut and possibly even done away with. If that happens, Mr. Llewellyn-

Hughes will get the boot or demoted and his chance of getting a knighthood will vanish."

"On other words, it's all about power and influence, is it?" asked Chris.

"You've got it, Chris. That's exactly what I think it's all about," agreed Dick.

"That's terrible," exclaimed Chris. "So, no-one actually cares whether the country could become energy independent thanks to Peter. It's all about whether some toffee-nosed bureaucrat can be called Sir Something or other and not about what's good for the country?"

"You've got it in one."

Driving back to London, Arthur Llewellyn-Hughes was uncharacteristically silent. Eventually Stephen Fletcher broke the silence, commenting, "I think it went well today, didn't it?" and Golding and Streetly happily agreed. Llewellyn-Hughes simply glared at them. After a few miles, he eventually spoke, "If you call what happened up there a success, then you are all supreme optimists. I agree it wasn't a disaster but I hardly think that it was a resounding success." Seeing the blank looks of the faces of the others he added, "Dr. Marshall made it clear that he would undertake this project but only on his terms. Not only that, he has no intention of returning to Cambridge. That means we have to get all that equipment out of his and Martin's laboratories and get it moved to Greydene. That is not a problem in and of itself but someone somewhere is going to ask why a whole lot of very expensive equipment has to be moved across the country, and at Government expense. Further, we are going to have to find money to pay for recruiting more research staff, more equipment, modifying the existing and rather inadequate facilities in Greydene to accommodate Marshall's research, research that may or may not pan out, as they say. No gentlemen, it was hardly a success but at least Marshall will get back to work. If I were you, I should start praying that Marshall is successful in what he is attempting to do."

"But..." stuttered Fletcher.

"There is no "but", Fletcher," snapped Llewellyn-Hughes. "The fact that Marshall refuses to go back to Cambridge means that the story will eventually get out about Martin stealing Marshall's ideas and that we funded the wrong person, and very expensively at that." He stopped and thought for a moment or two before continuing, "Let us never forget that theory is all well and good but it doesn't always match up with reality. If Marshall's theories prove to be correct, then everything will work out but if he's wrong, then, gentlemen, we have yet another disaster on our hands." And Llewellyn-Hughes lapsed into silence, leaving his three associates even more worried.

At last the wedding day arrived and, atypically for an English summer's day, it was warm and sunny. The vicar, delighted to be able to celebrate a big wedding in his quiet little parish, delivered a simple homily and joined Peter Marshall and Christie Hawkins in marriage. The bride looked radiant in a long white dress and Arnold Hawkins, proud as Punch, escorted her down the aisle in a specially rented morning suit. Monk, attired in a well-cut suit that even surprised Audrey, performed his best-man duties with aplomb. The small son and daughter of one of Mabel's many relatives, dressed in delightful new clothes, were the flower girl and ring carrier respectively and were adorable in their serious attention to their important duties.

The small church was packed to overflowing with the invited guests and virtually everyone from the surrounding villages who wanted to see what all the fuss was about. Dick Fowler's newspaper story about Dr. Peter Marshall, nascent genius, resulted in significant press coverage of the wedding and even television crews came to record the happy event.

Chris, seeing all the reporters and television cameras outside the church as she and Arnie drove up in the hired limousine, turned to her father and asked, "Dad, what on earth is happening? Who are all these people? What are they doing here?"

"Well, a fair number have come to see the beautiful bride getting married to her handsome husband but, after what Dick Fowler put into the newspaper, you and Peter are now celebrities."

"But dad..." wailed Chris.

"Get used to it, girl. Whether you like it or not, you two are now famous. That'll teach you to marry a genius. Still, he's a sight better than…no, let's not talk about him…you and Peter are perfect together and I couldn't be happier for you both. Life's good and no mistake. Okay, Chris, we're here. Get ready for all the cameras…this is your big day."

The wedding reception was a great success with plenty of food and wine to go round. Eventually Monk climbed unsteadily to his feet and cleared his throat. "Unaccustomed as I am to public speaking…"

"We can tell," said the irrepressible Hiram Pederson who had flown over specially to attend the wedding. Monk laughed and continued, "Well, before I was so rudely interrupted, we are here today to celebrate the wedding of Chris and Peter, and what a wonderful and happy occasion it is. Chris is one of a kind. Beautiful, talented and, frankly, one of the nicest people I have ever met. Amongst the guests here today we have John and Mary Parsons, Richard Fowler and his charming wife Sheila, Mabel and Nigel Meadows, their daughter Lucy and husband-to-be Zack, my lovely wife Audrey and yours truly, not forgetting Lionel Simpson and his wife Anne. Chris has welcomed each and every one of us into her life – we are now family. Not only that, she has even been nice to our Transatlantic friend, Professor Hiram Pederson, who flew over from Utah or somewhere like that just to be here for the wedding." Turning to Hiram, Monk added, "It's all right Hiram. I think you're a good guy no matter what anyone says about you", earning laughter.

Taking a large sip of wine, Monk continued, "Arnie Hawkins… that's him in the morning suit…didn't lose a beautiful and talented daughter. No, he's gained a son. None of us are quite sure why Chris decided to marry him but marry him she did and he looks better for it already. Peter, like his bride, is beautiful and talented…nah, he's not beautiful but he does clean up well, doesn't he? Anyway, Peter is a good guy and he is someone we can respect, not only because he's a brilliant scientist but because he's a decent and honorable man. So, let us all raise our glasses and salute the bride and groom and wish them every happiness and success in their new life together. Ladies and gentlemen, I give you Dr. Peter and Mrs. Christie Marshall."

After the toasts and cheers, Monk added, "Just in case anyone asks, they are taking their honeymoon in Majorca. And no, none of us are invited. As you know, they only speak Spanish in Majorca but that won't be a problem for Chris and Peter because I don't think they'll have time or even want to talk to anyone while they're there. At least, that's what I've heard."

When Monk sat down, Peter climbed to his feet and gracefully thanked everyone for being there that day and for their good wishes and congratulations. After Peter resumed his seat, Arnie Hawkins jumped up and likewise thanked everyone for coming, offered his congratulations to the bride and groom and then embarked on a series of ribald jokes which had everyone howling. All in all, it was the most fun anyone had had at a wedding in years.

The tables were then cleared and space was created for the newlyweds and their guests to dance. As the evening wore on, Peter and Chris quietly slipped away to the honeymoon suite in Greydene Hotel while the party continued unabated without them. As John said to Dick Fowler, "there's going be a lot of hurting heads tomorrow morning."

Later that evening, after the ladies having given up for the night and Lionel and Anne had made their way home, Arnie, John, Dick, Monk, Nigel and Hiram sat in the bar area of Oak Tree Manor. Arnie, to mark the occasion, had unearthed a vintage Armagnac and the men were taking full advantage of the heady brandy. Hiram, happy to be with men of a similar age, raised his glass to Mr. Hawkins, saying, "Arnie, you did us proud. What a great wedding and reception. Thank you for doing this for Chris and Peter. They are a great couple and you sent them off as they deserved. Well done, old sport, well done."

"I'll second that," hiccupped Dick, and deeply breathed in the Armagnac fumes from his balloon glass. The other men did likewise and then quietly started to talk about Dick's newspaper coverage of Peter and his work.

"I knew he was something special," slurred Hiram, definitely the worse for wear. "After I looked at his jottings on my manuscript,

I knew I was in the presence of greatness. That boy's going to get a Nobel prize and deservedly so…just you mark my words."

"I hope so," said Arnie good-humoredly. "I'll need some of that prize money to pay for their damn wedding."

"Oh stop whining," said Monk. "It's not every day that you get a potential genius as a son-in-law. Besides, it was Chris that did everything, Chris and the other ladies. All you did was dress up in a monkey suit and write a few checks."

Dick, decidedly drunk by now, nodded in agreement before saying, "Thanks to Peter and John here, my career is pretty golden and everything worked out well, didn't it? Hey, we were even able to sort Monk out too."

"You did indeed," agreed John. "Still, I do wonder how it all came about."

"Don't ask," said Nigel. "Things have a habit of doing that, you know. And they usually do when you least expect it."

With that, the men drained their glasses, exchanged handshakes and slaps on the back and headed off to bed. Food, wine and vintage brandy had won out after all.

TWENTY-ONE

Reginald Parker, Minister for Energy and Natural Resources, walked into the Cabinet Office at No. 10 Downing Street, the Prime Minister's official residence. As he did so, Sir Laurence Richardson, The Cabinet Secretary, lightly touched his arm and murmured, "Reggie, the Prime Minister wants a quiet word with you after the Cabinet Meeting. Just hold on for a few minutes after the finish of business."

George Armstrong, Prime Minister of Great Britain and Northern Ireland, finally closed his Cabinet Meeting and wished his ministers a good day. Seeing Reginald Parker hovering near the door after the others had left, he brusquely waved him to a chair across the table from his own.

"Reggie, you are well, I trust?"

"Yes thank you, Prime Minister."

"Good – I am glad to hear it." The PM glanced at his Cabinet Secretary, nodded and made a slightly beckoning movement of his hand. At the PM's cue, Sir Laurence took a chair next to the Prime Minister and laid some notes on the table.

Armstrong glanced at them and then looked sternly at Reginald Parker. "Reggie, we are hearing some disturbing things coming out of your Ministry, very disturbing."

"Really, Prime Minister? What appears to be the problem?" asked Reggie Parker. Although he actually was an intelligent and well-educated man, Parker relied more on his good looks, personal charm and a well-heeled wife than on hard work for his success. In fact, if he were to be honest with himself, he would have to admit that he could not believe that he had been elected to Parliament let alone now held a Cabinet position. As far as he was concerned, the Permanent Under-secretary James Arthur Llewellyn-Hughes did a far better job of running the Ministry than he ever could, so he left things to him and had done so for the past two years that he had been a minister.

The PM nodded again at the Cabinet Secretary who took over the informal meeting. "Minister, we have received a report from the new Head of Special Branch, Commander Miller, that your permanent Under-Secretary Llewellyn-Hughes overstepped the mark with regard to using valuable resources in the past, something that has only just come to light."

"He did? How astonishing. What did he do?"

"It appears that he requested, actually more ordered, Special Branch to look for a missing scientist…"

"Well, I'm sure that was because it was a matter of National Security," interrupted Parker. "If a scientist goes missing, that's often a major cause for concern, isn't it?"

"In this case, no," snapped Richardson, who then went on to outline the circumstances surrounding the disappearance and later re-appearance of Peter Marshall. "Not only that, we have these newspaper articles, written by the former gossip columnist Richard Fowler, that are very critical of this Government and the whole Marshall affair. Somehow or another, that reporter knows far more about what's going on within your Ministry than you do."

"Well, I'll just have to have a few words with Llewellyn-Hughes…we can't have this sort of thing happening, can we?" said Parker unctuously.

"It's a little more serious than that," said the Prime Minister. There was a pregnant silence for a few seconds before he added, "It would appear that a good friend of your Mr. Llewellyn-Hughes is in serious trouble with the police who are, at this very moment, looking into the connection between this person and your Permanent Under-Secretary."

"In short," interjected Sir Laurence Richardson. "It might be expedient for Mr. Llewellyn-Hughes to…er…step down, as it were."

A stunned Reginald Parker looked first at the Prime Minister and then the Cabinet Secretary. He nodded and said meekly, "I shall attend to…ah…this matter immediately. Of course…you are right, it's very serious indeed…immediately." As he left No. 10 Downing Street, The Right Honorable Reginald Parker, Minister for Energy and Natural Resources wondered how long he would remain a Minister. Silently he cursed Llewellyn-Hughes and signaled for his driver to collect him from the most famous doorstep in England. This was a problem that he did not even want to think about let alone address.

"Well look at you, all suntanned and radiant, Chris," cried Arnie Hawkins, sitting in his office chair and beaming at his daughter. "It looks like you and Peter had a good time…and I won't ask what you did over there because I've got a very good idea already."

"Oh dad, it was great. Lots of sun, surf and fantastic food. It was truly wonderful."

"I'm glad to hear it, really glad. And where's Peter?"

"Oh he's off unpacking and catching up on Emails – you know, all sorts of guy things."

"Of course he is," said Arnie. "It's funny how someone will take off for a few days…actually ten days in your case…and after not caring a wink about what has been going on back home, no sooner do they return, they have to be back in the thick of things."

"Dad, you're no different. Whenever you and mom went off for a trip, you'd call every day and sometimes twice a day just to make sure the place hadn't burned down in your absence," laughed Chris. "As for Peter, I'm not worried about him. That Ministry contract will place a heavy burden on him and I know he's anxious to get back to work. The last thing he would want to have happen is for it all to fail. It wouldn't be the end of the world but it would hit him hard after what he's been through."

"Oh don't worry. My betting is that he's not only going to be very successful but he'll do even better than anyone hoped or expected. I have a feeling about him and I know the Lord's got his back."

"Dad, I've not heard you being particularly spiritual before but I like it."

"After everything that's happened, including Peter coming into our lives, what choice do I have?" said Mr. Hawkins, and chuckled. "He works in mysterious ways does God, and don't you forget it."

The pair of them sat companionably for a few minutes, quietly sipping on the obligatory cup of tea. Eventually Chris said, "So dad, how are Lucy and Zack working out? I was a bit worried about what was happening here," said Chris.

"I have news for you Chris. While you were off on your honeymoon in Majorca, Lucy took over everything you did. Not only that, Mabel and her new bosom-buddies Mary Parsons and Audrey Monk clean this place like a whirlwind every day."

"Really? That's grand."

"Not only that, it turns out that Zack is some sort of financial whizz. Our books are in better shape now than they've been for years and he's actually saving us money. There is one thing, though."

"Uh oh. What's that?" asked Chris with a worried frown.

"Well it seems that the ladies, Mabel, Mary and Audrey, with some input from Lucy too, have got the bit between their teeth about food."

"Food?"

"Well, it seems that big dinner for Professor Pederson started a trend. We've even got a small party going on tonight."

"Really?" asked Chris.

"Oh yes indeed. Not only that, those ladies all compete with each other to come up with the most innovative meals. Curiously, Audrey is a great pastry cook and Lucy loves to help her. So Mabel and Mary do the entrees while Audrey and Lucy take care of the cakes and desserts. Believe it or not, they sometimes call me in to make the soup. Now they're asking us to add a small restaurant to the building and offer select meals. You know, have some sort of high class eatery but probably not one that'll be open every day."

"Dad, what on earth has happened? I go away for less than a fortnight and everything's changed. A premiere restaurant…here?" Chris was silent for a few moments as she thought about things. "You know, dad, that's not a bad idea. It was always a pain to take care of the odd guest that wanted dinner but if we can offer high class dining, at a price of course, it could work out well. Well I'm blessed."

"I thought you might be intrigued with the notion. Zack and I will have to sort out the finances but it might be possible as long as we're careful what we are trying to do."

"You know, the idea of a restaurant is pretty good, it really is," said Chris. "With all the ladies running things, does that mean you don't need me anymore?"

"Of course we do … but…wait a minute, why do you ask… that's not like you. I've never known you to have doubts like that."

"For the record, dad, I think I'm pregnant."

"You are? That's wonderful. What does Peter think?"

"Oh he's really happy although we'll have to wait until the doctor confirms it. It's only been a couple of weeks since you know…"

"You don't have to spell it out for me, Chris. I've been down that road before," smiled Mr. Hawkins. "The good thing is that you are young, fit and healthy, and that makes all the difference when you are pregnant. With those things on your side, we can hope and pray that everything comes out right. Actually, talking about things coming right, it seems that Lucy is also expecting. Must be going round…first you and then her. I know her parents are delighted."

"Are they going to get married?"

"Maybe, maybe not. I gather marriage isn't high on their list of priorities but I know Mabel and Nigel would like it if they did even if they have to pay for the wedding."

"I'll have to go find Lucy and congratulate her. If our babies are due at about the same time, it'll be like having a sister, you know, we'll be able to help each other and possibly commiserate."

"I'm sure you will, Chris. Well, I suppose I should go check on what Lucy and Mabel are doing for dinner tonight. I know Audrey is planning some sort special dessert from New Zealand, a Pavlova cake or something like that. Whatever it is, it sounds delicious."

"How are Mabel and Nigel?" asked Chris.

"As I said, Mabel and Mary Parsons work very well together and now that Audrey Monk's with them, they're almost inseparable. As for Nigel and John Parsons – those two are thick as thieves although being ex-coppers, that's not something one should say about them."

"Oh my, it does seem as though everything is working out well. What about Monk?"

"He's got some job in Greydene that keeps him busy – not too sure what he does but he's really happy. He spends a lot of time now with Audrey and the kids, and loves it. He even gets together with Nigel and John for the odd drink. Actually, they are talking about setting up a poker group for the four of us…maybe even include Peter and Lionel."

Wow!" laughed Chris. "As I said, I'm now superfluous,"

"Not really, you never will be but things are running well. So, Chris, you can think about the baby and taking care of Peter. You say he's working hard?"

"Yes, and he will be for some time to come, a long time in fact, but I know he loves it."

"So Fletcher, what do you hear from Marshall and Simpson up at Greydene?" asked Llewellyn-Hughes.

"I gather that things are going well. They have had all their equipment up and running for some time now and Marshall is making great progress…at least that's what they tell me."

"Let's hope so. We don't want another debacle like the one we had with Martin."

"I don't think that's the case with Dr. Marshall. He's less…er… ebullient than Martin. To be honest, Martin always struck me as some sort of salesman, you know, flogging his ideas to the highest bidder, that sort of thing."

"You didn't share that reservation with me before, Fletcher."

"I only met him once or twice and then only for a few minutes. Let's not forget, he was…er.. from somewhat humble origins, you know, working class, grammar school boy made good, that sort of thing."

"And?"

"I put down my reservations to his not having the right accent… prejudice, if you will," said Fletcher, somewhat embarrassed to have even raised the subject.

"Hmm. Well Fletcher, not everyone went to Harrow and Oxford you know and that hasn't stopped a number of people from being very able, gifted in fact."

"Quite right, sir," said Fletcher, feeling suitably admonished for his snobbish attitude.

"Well, keep me informed on progress, will you?" and Llewellyn-Hughes returned to studying the documents on his desk but silently hoping that Fletcher was right about Peter Marshall. For the moment, personal and professional disaster had been averted but that situation could change overnight if the purported benefits of the Marshall Effect did not materialize.

Seconds after Fletcher left his office, the intercom buzzed and Llewellyn-Hughes's secretary announced that a Detective Chief Inspector was waiting to see him.

"Hey Peter, how are things going?" asked Lionel as he popped into Peter's laboratory.

"They're great...on fact, they're terrific."

"Terrific? What does that mean?"

"Well enlighten me, what's so terrific as you put it?"

"It works, believe it or not – IT WORKS."

"It does? Wait, you mean your theory actually works? Really? Really and truly? Honestly?" cried Lionel. "Oh man, show me."

"Lookee here, my man," and Peter flipped a switch. Suddenly a spot-light lit up. "See?"

"Okay, I see the lamp has come on but...wait...oh wow...it's not plugged in to the mains! How did you do that?"

"See that small reaction vessel and the wires running to the lamp? Well, we're generating enough power in that small vessel to power the lamp, with a whole lot more to spare."

"But that lamp bulb operates on alternating current...how'd you manage that?"

"That was easy...I just put an inverter in the circuit...that small box beside the reaction vessel converts the direct current from the reaction into alternating current and Bob's your uncle."

"Actually he's my cousin but I get your point," said Lionel with a smile. "Okay, let me look at everything for a minute and, by the way, what's in the reaction vessel?"

"Well, we're feeding protons and electrons from..." and Peter launched into an arcane discussion of the inner workings of his transmutation effects.

After listening carefully to Peter's explanation and asking some very pertinent questions, Lionel sat down on a handy stool and stared at his colleague before saying, "So it does work – amazing. I thought your theory was pretty convincing but actually seeing it in action is a whole other matter. Look, just for my own satisfaction, let's run through it all again."

Peter smiled. Lionel was right, running through both the theory and the practical demonstration were valuable exercises. Not just for now, but as preparation for future presentations to less sophisticated audiences. After listening to everything again, Lionel stood up and clapped Peter on the shoulder. "You know, forget that old saw about your average genius shaking test-tubes and shouting *Eureka* before writing off to Stockholm. Now I see that all it involves is flipping a switch and a light coming on. Sorry Peter, you'll have to do something more impressive." Seeing the closed-in look on Peter's face, Lionel laughed and hastily added, "Hey, I was only joking - this is truly a major breakthrough. Have you told anyone else about this yet?"

"Yes, I did call Chris and told her but you are really the first to see things actually working."

"Are you going to tell the Ministry people?"

"In time. First we have to run everything again, and again after that to determine reproducibility. Then I want to confirm all the flux density data and check my calculations on power output."

"The power output was good, was it?"

"Far better than I expected so I have to check that we didn't miss anything or possibly might be indulging in wishful thinking… you know, the usual checks and balances."

"Indeed, indeed. Well, I'll leave you to it but don't hesitate to ask if I can do anything to help. Look, would it help if *I* called London? I know you can't stand those pompous asses but they are funding us. If you agree, I'll give them a ring in a day or so."

"Whatever, Lionel! If you think it would help, be my guest… just leave me out of it and, please, don't invite them up at least for a while. I don't need the distraction, okay?"

"How's Peter doing these days?" asked Mr. Hawkins. "I hardly ever see him now. Mind you, I could say almost the same of you, can't I? The baby lump is getting bigger by the day and when you are here, you seem to spend most of your time gossiping with the ladies in the kitchen. Are they enjoying themselves?"

"Oh dad, they love it here. Oak Tree Manor seems to be ticking over very nicely and the restaurant is really doing well. Some of the meals they come up with are really something. I mean, fancy our being able to offer lobster thermidor, quail eggs, crab bisque and the like. People are starting to come from all over just to eat here and no-one has ever complained about the cost. We should have done this years ago, have a top class restaurant I mean."

"It's not that easy, Chris. You have to have the right people in the right place at the right time. It's only now that everything came together." Arnie was silent as he thought about what had happened over the past year or so. "You know something, it's all come about since Peter appeared on the scene. If he hadn't been there to help change that flat tire, we wouldn't have got home for hours. Then he comes back with us and you two fall in love. In the midst of all that, there was that big manhunt-type thing for Peter and through that we met John and Mary Parsons who moved up here. On top of that, Richard Fowler, ace reporter, gets involved and through him and John, Monk gets released from prison. Finally, Peter sees some sort of manuscript written by Hiram Pederson, makes some notes and gets recruited to Greydene University. I tell you girl, it's all very strange."

"Indeed, dad, it is indeed. By the way, how is Monk?"

"Oh he's great. Loves that Security job of his and Audrey is really happy they moved up here too. From what Monk tells me she's happy in her job…apparently her co-workers are much nicer than those down in London. There is less pressure on her up here and she divides her time between the insurance company and cooking with Mabel and Mary."

"Yes, I can believe that. By the way, Mabel says you all play poker regularly…how is that going?"

"John, Nigel, Monk and I get together on a fairly regular basis and play poker – just penny-ante stuff but we have fun. In fact, we've taken to inviting Zack to join in. He's surprisingly good. Hey, do you think Peter might want to play? Of course, with his mind he probably has an unfair advantage but he might enjoy a break from work and all that baby-talk of an evening."

"I'll ask him. Besides, what's wrong with baby-talk? Lucy and I enjoy planning our nurseries and it looks as though the babies will arrive within days of each other, so enough of your lip," laughed Chris. "And before you ask, Peter's working very hard and I think he's happy with progress. He had to work really hard to get up to speed, as he called it, now things are going well. Of course he's distracted a lot of the time but I don't mind since I can devote my time and efforts to take care of the house, decorate the baby's room, cook meals – that sort of thing…you know how it is, don't you?"

"Aye, yes I do. By the way, Professor Pederson is due back here any day now."

"Oh that's good. I'd love to see him again…after all, it was through him that all this business with the University got started in the first place."

"Yes it did, didn't it," said Mr. Hawkins reflectively. "Funny how it all worked out…not what any of us expected was it? By the way, did you see any of those articles written by our favorite reporter, Dick Fowler?"

"I did. They were fascinating, weren't they? Even I learned stuff about Peter that I never knew. He's brilliant, isn't he but so modest. You'd never know from talking to him. By the way, he just called me to say that his experiments seem to be working out right after all. In fact, he was quite excited about things – not like him at all."

"That's great," said her father. "Did he go into any details?"

"Not really but you know Peter – the Mr. Strong and Silent type. Anyway, I'm off to see the ladies in the kitchen…you know, some girl-talk" and Chris kissed her father's cheek. "I'll be back later."

It was not too late but both Chris and Peter admitted they were tired, Chris from the strain of the new life burgeoning in her uterus and Peter from the many hours he spent at the University. "I tell you, my darling, I had forgotten just how hard it can be to do research, look after post-grad students and try to keep up with the literature. The hours just melt away. Anyway, how are you feeling? Every time I cuddle up to you in bed that baby starts kicking…it's almost as if he can't wait to get out and take on the world."

"I don't know about that," said Chris. "But I'll tell you one thing, I wish I could just lay an egg or something. This nine month thing gets old after a while. Still, the doctor says that his activity is a good thing."

"Oh good – man, that was a hefty kick, wasn't it?" exclaimed Peter. "I wonder if he's going to turn out to be a soccer star. If he does, who do you think he'll play for?"

"You men!" said Chris. "You've got his life planned out before he's even been born. By the way, have you seen Monk recently?"

"Oh yes, we had lunch today, as a matter of fact. Not only that, I got a phone call from Nobby. He and his daughter, Dahlia, are doing really well and they are thinking of visiting us here again."

"Now you tell me," said Chris exasperated. "Monk is well, is he?"

"Oh yes, he and Audrey are really delighted that they moved out of London. By the way, Dick Fowler and Monk are going to collaborate on writing a book."

"They are? How wonderful. I really like Monk. It's hard to believe that someone with his gruff exterior can be so kind and I love his sense of humor. He's great, isn't he?"

"Hey, John, how are things going?" asked Dick Fowler.

"Pretty good," said John Parsons. "In fact, things are going great up here."

"That's good to hear. How is everyone?"

"Well, all sorts of things are happening at Oak Tree Manor and most of us have settled into a pretty comfortable routine," after which John went on to tell Dick about the new restaurant, how well the ladies were doing, the poker get-togethers and, almost belatedly, that Peter's research seemed to be going extremely satisfactorily.

"You're right; it does seem to be a happening place up there. You said Peter's work is going well…what do you mean?"

"Although I have no idea about the details, I gather that his predictions or whatever worked out and he's very excited about it all."

"That's great! I'll have to make another trip up there and talk to him. If nothing else, the world needs to know what he's done."

"I suppose but I wouldn't count on him telling you too much, at least not just now."

"Why ever not?"

"Chris is rapidly approaching term with the baby and the last thing Peter needs is another distraction. By the way, have you talked to Monk recently?"

"I do all the time," said Dick. "We spend a fair amount of time, almost on a daily basis, working on his life story. It might even be a best-seller if I can get him to open up about his service experiences. He's a funny bloke when you get to know him. He did a lot for this country and I cannot believe how he was treated. Mind you, that's not unusual for England. Even going back to Elizabethan times, veterans were treated like dog-noonies after the war was over. Things are better now but only to a degree. The same thing's been happening over the pond in America for years. The military are heroes during wartime but almost an embarrassment in peace-time. Disgraceful really."

"It's pretty much the same for the police, isn't it?" said John. "Everyone loves us when a crime's been committed on you or there's damage to your property but if you get pulled over for speeding or drunk driving, then the police are the enemy."

"I hear you. By the way, what's the food like in that restaurant?"

"It's pretty good by all accounts. In fact, some of the patrons refer to it as a gourmet oasis in a fast-food landscape."

"Really! Well I can't wait to get up there and sample it. Thanks for the heads-up."

TWENTY-TWO

After the police officer was ushered into his office, Llewellyn-Hughes looked up, signed for the man to take a seat and looked at him questioningly. Detective Chief Inspector Reynolds looked hard at the civil servant and waited for the other man to speak. Eventually, Llewellyn-Hughes said, "You came without an appointment. I presume you are here on an important matter, yes?"

Reynolds nodded and sat silently for a few seconds before saying, "You know Professor Randolph Bethany?" although it was more a statement than a question. Llewellyn-Hughes nodded, wondering where the detective was going with this interview. After another pause DCI Reynolds asked, "How well do you know Professor Bethany?"

"Quite well, actually," said Llewellyn-Hughes. "We were at Oxford together and have known each other for about thirty years, give or take."

"You are friends?"

"Well, we have lunch on a reasonably regular basis and my wife and I have dinner with Randy and his wife every two or three months, depending on how busy we are…you know, when our social obligations permit – that sort of thing. Professor Bethany is also the Chief Scientific Advisor to this ministry and has held that position for several years – quite admirably too for that matter."

"So you admit to knowing Bethany very well?"

"Chief Inspector, that is a curious turn of phrase, isn't it? Why do you ask if I "admit" to knowing someone…either I do or I don't."

"I'm just trying to establish what sort of relationship you have with Bethany."

"Again, Chief Inspector, you are using a curious turn of phrase. Would you mind telling me what this is all about? Is Professor Bethany being accused of some crime or other?"

"That remains to be seen, doesn't it, Mr. Llewellyn-Hughes? Why do *you* raise the issue of Bethany being accused of criminal activity?"

"Chief Inspector, I do not appreciate you barging into my office unannounced and then trying to play cat-and-mouse with me. If there is something averse, some sort of malfeasance that involves Professor Bethany, do me the courtesy of coming out with it directly. I am far too busy to play games with you or anyone else."

"Well, let me put it this way Mr. Llewellyn-Hughes, have you visited Professor Bethany's home?" As Llewellyn-Hughes was about to snap at him, Reynolds held up a hand and continued, "What I am asking is whether you and Bethany have spent time together alone at either your home or his…without your wives being present?"

"What on earth are you suggesting, man? Surely you are not implying that Bethany and I have some sort of inappropriate sexual relationship?"

"Not directly, no."

"Just what does that mean?" demanded Llewellyn-Hughes angrily. "I can assure you that neither Bethany nor I have any homosexual tendencies, none! Although I am aware that indulging in homosexuality is no longer a crime in this country, I can assure you that my interests are entirely heterosexual and I am insulted that you should even raise the issue."

"And Bethany?" asked Reynolds mildly.

"As far as I know Randy is "straight" if you will and I have never detected even an inkling that he has ever had any homosexual leanings in all the years I have known him."

"So you can vouch for *Randy*, as you put it?"

"Yes, I just did. Now, for the last time Chief Inspector, just what is this all about?"

"Before I get to that, Mr. Llewellyn-Hughes, let me ask if you and *Randy* Bethany ever exchange Emails or data on line? Do you have, say, private Email accounts that you share with each other but not with most other people?"

"I can't speak for Randy but I believe he does have a personal Email account as well as his University account. He may even have access to the server for the Ministry – in fact I know he does. Anyway, with regard to my personal Emails, someone in my position customarily has a private Email account separate from Government servers. That is usually necessary so that we can share greetings, family news…that sort of thing…with family and friends and be able to keep such personal and private matters away from public scrutiny."

"So you need to keep certain things from public scrutiny?"

"Again, Chief Inspector, there is an underlying insinuation to your remarks. Just what are you getting at?"

"Well sir, you admit to knowing Randolph Bethany very well and have been friends for decades, yes? Then you admit that you have a private Email account and that you and Bethany exchange private Emails on a regular basis. You also say that certain exchanges need to be kept from public scrutiny. Is that correct?"

"You are twisting my words and drawing salacious conclusions from simple statements of fact. Again I must insist that you tell me what this is all about or I shall have you escorted from this building."

"Mr. Llewellyn-Hughes, have you ever exchanged with Professor Randolph Bethany any Emails, information on Internet sites or Internet data including written matter or pictorial images that might be construed as salacious, pornographic or illegal in any way, shape or form?"

"That is an outrageous suggestion, Chief Inspector."

"But you haven't answered me, Mr. Llewellyn-Hughes," said D.C. I. Reynolds mildly.

"No, and I don't intend to give any credibility to any of your statements or accusations. I suggest that you leave now and if you wish to see me again, please contact me through my solicitor…my secretary will provide that information to you on your way out. Good day to you."

D.C. I. Reynolds nodded politely at Llewellyn-Hughes, smiled and left the room thinking, 'He's hiding something but unless he's an Oscar-worthy actor, I doubt that he's one of Bethany's sick circle of pedophile friends. Unfortunately, whether or not he's one of those sickies, Llewellyn-Hughes is going to get tarred by the same brush simply because of his long-term relationship with Bethany. Shame really but he is an arrogant git and nasty with it. I can only imagine what his reaction is going to be when the news of Bethany's arrest goes viral later today. He's hiding something about his relationship with Bethany but no matter what the truth of the situation, Mr. Llewellyn-Hughes' reputation is likely ruined and his career will go down in flames.'

Matt Jenkins lightly tapped his monitor screen and cast a look at Dick Fowler, "What's this Dick, are you now trying to be The National Globe's food critic too?"

"What do you mean?" asked Dick innocently.

"This article is what I mean. Let me quote your headline: *Gourmet Treasure in Derbyshire.* You go up there to report on this discovery by Dr. Marshall and come back with an article on fine dining at a small guesthouse. What is it with you and that place?"

"Well, the food *was* good."

"I don't doubt it but since your culinary expertise extends only to where you can get a good Vindaloo curry, your credentials regarding food are somewhat suspect. I don't know what hold Oak Tree Manor has on you but I'm beginning to wonder when you are going to write a rave review about the accommodation there too."

"But it is a nice place, boss, it really is."

"I don't doubt it but that's hardly the reason for you going up there, is it? So when are you going to tell our readers about the great discovery that Dr. Peter Marshall, late of Cambridge and now at Greydene University, has made?"

"I'm just trying to set the stage…"

"Dick, you are a great reporter but we pay you to report the news not give me all this fluff about rural Derbyshire, okay?"

"Okay, okay but it is interesting…what's going on up there, I mean."

"I'm sure it is but not now. You can put it all in that book you are writing with Monk…by the way, how is that going? I did like the series you wrote about him."

"It's going well. Hopefully we'll get it done in a couple of months."

"Good. Now my man, get back to work...your proper work, okay?"

"Yes sir," said an admonished Dick.

"Mind you," said Matt Jenkins. "You do make that place sound inviting. The wife and I will have to go up there just to see for ourselves...I suppose that was the basic idea, wasn't it?" Dick smiled and nodded. Seeing the smile, Jenkins just said, "Oh go away ...you're impossible."

It was late on a Friday afternoon and the gang of Arnie, Monk, Nigel and John were sitting in The Bull and Bush enjoying a drink. Eventually Monk said, "It looks as though things are coming out about that Ministry and all that stuff about the manhunt for Peter is coming to light, John."

"It does, doesn't it?" agreed John.

"I didn't actually meet Bethany," said Nigel. "But I did see him the last time he was up here and frankly there was something about him that I didn't like."

"Are you just saying that?" asked Monk.

"No, not really. I've been a copper for a long time and you get a sense about people after a while," said Nigel. "There was something off about him although to be honest, I couldn't say what. Now we know."

"So, Bethany's a pedophile," said John. "Which raises the question of what Llewellyn-Hughes has to do with all that? Even if he's not a sicko, I still wonder why he set me onto finding Peter. Dick Fowler told us the other day when he was here that *His Holiness* was trying to save his reputation but it was a daft thing to do...you know, get Special Branch involved."

"That was bloody stupid of him, wasn't it?" said Monk. "But, as things worked out, if John hadn't started to dig around, he might not, in fact I know he wouldn't have, found out about me and he and Fowler wouldn't have got me out of prison."

"That was a convoluted sentence, Monk," said Arnie. "But you are right, things did work out right in the end. Funny thing that."

"Aye, it was funny," agreed Nigel. "Anyway, enough of that, let's have another drink and then we go home and hear what our wives have been up to today." He paused and added, "As you say, it looks as though Llewellyn-Hughes got his come-uppance for being sneaky." Draining his glass, he added darkly, "It only goes to show, doesn't it?"

"Do you think he was one of those also?" asked Monk. "You know, a pedophile?"

"I have no idea," said Arnie. "But like Nigel, I just didn't like that Bethany fellow. There was something…I don't know…something slimy about him. Hiram Pederson couldn't stand him and Hiram is a pretty smart fellow, even if he is a Yank."

"Oh Arnie, you can't have that attitude about one of our American cousins."

"Oh yes I can," said Arnie stoutly. "I can still remember the stories from the war, you know those newspaper headlines talking about the American G.I.'s stationed in England just before Normandy. How did they go? Ah yes, *Overpaid, over-sexed, over here* – pretty dreadful it was."

"Oh come on, Arnie," sighed John. "You were just a baby back then. How would you know what they were like?"

"I heard tales, I did," muttered Arnie darkly.

"I'm sure you did and those tales grow by the day, don't they?" laughed Nigel. More somberly, he added, "I still wonder what a man as astute as Llewellyn-Hughes had been thinking when he set John Parsons to go looking for Peter. That probably was a major factor in getting him fired, because fired he was."

"Actually he didn't directly set me onto finding Peter – that order came from on high but he did start it all off. I think his real downfall came as the result of his association with Professor Bethany," said John. "It doesn't matter if you're as white and pure as driven snow, if you lie down with dogs, you'll wake up with fleas. Llewellyn-Hughes may or may not have been one of them but simply by hanging around someone like that for all those years does make one wonder what he did, or did not, know about him. It's hard to believe that Bethany had been able to hide his…ah…proclivities that well from old friends and colleagues without anyone suspecting a thing." John stopped for a moment to have another sip of his beer before continuing, "No, forget about the fiasco over finding Peter – that was stupid on the part of Llewellyn-Hughes but I doubt that it was enough to get him fired. I think it was the possible association with, and perhaps actual involvement in pedophilia that did him in. No way would a God-fearing, bible-thumping Prime Minister like George Armstrong want someone like that anywhere near his government. Guilt by association is a horrible thing but, as they always say, there's no smoke without a fire and it's up to Llewellyn-Hughes to get that sorted out, not us. Now, who's round is it?"

Sanjay Mukadee burst into the seminar room, causing everyone to stop their discussion in mid-sentence and stare at him. Peter, unaccustomed to interruptions, was about to snap at his research assistant when the young man said hurriedly in his sing-song accent, "Dr. Marshall, your father-in-law just rang. Apparently they had to drive your wife to the hospital because they think that the baby has started…I mean, she's just gone into labor."

"What?" said Peter, trying desperately to understand the man's slightly garbled statement. "Look, slow down, will you? What happened?"

"We just got a phone call…your cell phone is off…so they called the office and the office called the laboratory and I answered the telephone."

"I got that. Now, tell me, what did they say to you?"

"I don't know the details but they said that your wife had to go to the hospital. Something has happened."

"Oh…" and Peter jumped to his feet. "I'd best get over there." He looked at his students, saying, "Sorry, I've got to go. We'll resume this another time. I'll get a message to you as soon as I know what's happening, okay?"

Running out of the building, Peter climbed into his car and drove frantically but under control to the hospital, memories of the last time this had happened flooding his brain. 'Not again God, please not again' sounded over and over in his mind.

He screeched to stop outside the hospital and slotted his car into a spot reserved for Hospital Staff, thinking, 'Hell I'm a doctor…well, sort of…so I'll leave it here." He dashed in and found the Inquiry Desk, staffed by an officious-looking older lady. "Excuse me," said Peter. "I'm…"

"I'm sorry, young man," said the woman. "But you'll have to wait a moment while I finish this."

"Look, my wife's just been brought here…some sort of emergency and I want to know what's going on."

"I'm sure you do," snapped the woman. "But the world doesn't revolve around you or your wife, so you'll just have to be patient."

Peter swallowed hard and then reached over the counter and grabbed up the papers that woman was fiddling with. Holding them up, he snapped angrily, "Now you listen to me. I don't care what you are doing but when I get an emergency call, I expect you to try to help me, not tell me to be patient while you shuffle paper about."

"Now, just you wait a moment, young man…"

"No, you wait a minute. I am Dr. Marshall and when I get an urgent call summoning me to this hospital, I expect a little concern from you and at least a modicum of assistance in tracking down where my wife might be. It would take less than a minute for you to check where she is, so don't tell me to be patient while you continue to shuffle paper for no reason other than to look busy."

For a moment the woman looked outraged and then it sunk in that the man standing there had said he was a *doctor*. What if he was a staff physician? Being rude or officious with him could lose her this job or, at the very least, garner a severe reprimand. She sniffed loudly and flipped through the computer listing of hospital admissions. "Ah yes, Mrs. Christie Marshall….I see she's up in Obstetrics."

"Fine," snapped Peter. "Now where do I find Obstetrics?"

"It's on the third floor."

"Thank you. Now how do I get there?"

"The elevators are just around the corner…just press button 3 and it'll take you up there."

"Thank you, I did not know that," said Peter sarcastically and dashed off to the bank of elevators.

When he got to the maternity ward, a nurse was waiting for him. "Dr. Marshall?"

"Yes, that's me," said Peter.

"Your wife's here and the senior Ob/Gyn specialist is with your wife now. As soon as we know something, we'll let you know."

"Is anything wrong? Has something happened?" asked Peter anxiously.

"As I said, Dr. Marshall, we'll let you know as soon as we know something ourselves," snapped the nurse, satisfied to be able to put a doctor in his place for a change.

Feeling sick to his stomach, Peter collapsed in a chair and started praying, praying hard. "Lord, please don't let anything happen to Chris. I love her with all my heart and she is the very cornerstone of my life. Please, please don't let anything happen to her."

As he sat back, Peter felt a light touch on his arm. Opening his eyes, he saw Arnie Hawkins standing a few feet away. "Aye, lad, here's a coffee. I saw you praying and I didn't want to say anything until you finished."

"You didn't touch my arm?" asked Peter.

"No, it's not for me to disturb a man who's praying. Anyway, here's a coffee for you – black and no sugar, just as you like it."

Even as he took his first sip, a distinguished-looking man in surgical scrubs stood before him with an odd look on his face, "Dr. Marshall?"

"Yes?" said Peter fearfully.

"Dr. Marshall, your wife is going to be just fine."

"What happened to her?"

"It seems she tripped over something and grabbed at the kitchen counter to stop herself falling, and wrenched her back. That caused a lot of pain and she thought that the baby had started. Chris did the sensible thing and called for help and her friends brought her immediately to the hospital."

"But she's alright?" asked Peter.

"Oh yes, just in a lot of pain from her back…that's pretty common, as you probably know yourself. We were slightly worried that there may have been complications because, like a lot of slightly older women, she has endometriosis, you know, the professional woman's complaint, but suddenly everything resolved itself. She's fine. Besides, the female mafia in there with her would give me merry hell if anything went wrong."

"Female mafia? What female mafia?" asked a confused Peter.

"Those four ladies in there hovering over us…one of whom looks pretty pregnant to me, so I wonder what she's doing here with your wife. Anyway, be that as it may, they are fussing over your wife and won't even let the nurse near her."

Peter laughed in relief – he had a very good idea of just who comprised the Female Mafia. "So, what happens now?"

"We've administered a muscle relaxant and it'll knock her out for the rest of the day. We'll keep her in overnight just to make sure she's alright and then she can go home." The doctor smiled and added, "When you go home, will you take the ladies with you… please!"

Peter nodded, relieved beyond measure. "By the way," said the Ob/Gyn specialist, "You and your wife are going to have one very fine child but not today. As I said, we'll keep her overnight so she can get her strength back and I expect we'll be able to deliver your son in a fortnight or so. In the meantime, I suggest you start catching up on your sleep. Seeing how the little fellow is kicking, I imagine he's going to be one very active baby and you might need all the rest you can get."

Shaking Peter's hand, he added, "I don't expect anything to happen for at least two or so weeks but if something does develop, just give me a call. At this stage though, there's nothing for you to worry about. Just get some sleep and let nature take its course. By the way, I read that newspaper article about you in The National Globe. It sounds as though you have made a tremendous breakthrough – congratulations. We're all very proud of you here and rest assured that we're taking the best care of your wife." With a laugh, he added, "Besides, I'd be afraid to face those very fierce ladies should anything go wrong."

The fearsome four gathered around Chris and cooed over the baby. "He's beautiful!" was the universal opinion followed by such remarks as, "And look at all that hair! He's going to be a lady's man, that one, mark my words."

Eventually they all settled down and even Lucy, about to give birth any minute, was heard to say, "My daughter is going to marry him, that's if she ever gets out from inside me."

"That's alright Lucy," said Monk. "She's a woman and women are always late."

"Male chauvinist pig," muttered Audrey. "You're not too punctual yourself, are you?"

"Now, now children – behave," admonished Arnie Hawkins.

"Oh give over granddad," said Nigel. "What do you know about it?"

"Granddad?" spluttered Arnie. "Granddad? Well, I suppose I am now…okay Nigel, you can call me granddad but only for the moment. Don't forget, this granddad whipped your rear end playing poker the other night, so less of your lip."

At that moment, Peter walked into the room and stopped dead in his tracks when he saw everyone there. "Whoa, what's going on? Did someone throw a party and forget to invite me?"

"Peter, come and join us," said Monk magnanimously. "We were just wondering how an ugly bleeder like you could father a son as beautiful is this one. You sure the postman didn't come knocking? By the way, what are you calling him…not Cuthbert I hope?"

"Not likely, Monk; having you as his Godfather is bad enough without lumbering him with your name!" Peter looked at Chris and winked before saying, "We were going to call him Peter…you know, Peter Marshall junior, but…"

"Don't you dare!" said Mary, Mabel and Audrey almost in unison. "You've got to give him a proper name."

"Oh alright," sighed Peter, then he beamed, "Chris and I decided that Byron Arnold Marshall might be suitable for him."

"Byron Arnold Marshall…that does have a ring to it," said John. "I like it although giving him Arnold as a middle name is…well…"

"Don't say it," said Arnie Hawkins mock-threateningly.

"Okay granddad," sighed John. "I'll try to be nice to you…at least for today. After that…well…"

"Well that's got Little BAM settled for at least a couple of hours," said Chris as she came into the cottage living room. Leaning over, she lightly kissed the top of Peter's head and asked, "How are you, my darling?"

"A little tired but happy. How are you?"

"The same, I'm glad to say."

"By the way, did I hear you refer to my son and heir as BAM?"

"Yes dear, BAM…you know, short for Byron Arnold Marshall…BAM."

"I just don't want to know," sighed Peter. "Now, what I do want to know is what's for dinner?" and promptly ducked as Chris hurled a sofa cushion at him. "Only kidding, darling, only kidding. Actually, I did hear that there is a very interesting special on the menu at the restaurant tonight and, if you're up for it, let's go there."

Later, as they ate Wiener Schnitzel accompanied by red cabbage and sautéed thin-sliced potatoes, Peter looked at Chris and said, "You know, I never thought I could ever be this happy…thank you."

"Thank me? I think you have someone else to thank - He did everything, not me. I was just along for the ride."

Peter shrugged, "Perhaps you're right." He was quiet for a few seconds before saying, "By the way, Nature, the premier journal in science, has accepted my paper and the Times of London, The New York Times, Newsweek and Time are all lining up for interviews. Lionel is as happy as a dog with two tails at all the attention that the University is getting and I'm fighting off applicants for research positions. I tell you Chris, it has been one hell of a ride but getting here, right here and now, has made it all worthwhile." He looked up for a moment and said quietly, "Thank you, Lord, thank you."

ABOUT THE AUTHOR

Joseph Anthony is the pen-name of an Internationally-respected scientist. He lives in Boerne, Texas with his wife Susan and their two cats. This book is his first novel.